THE WIZARD OF OZ

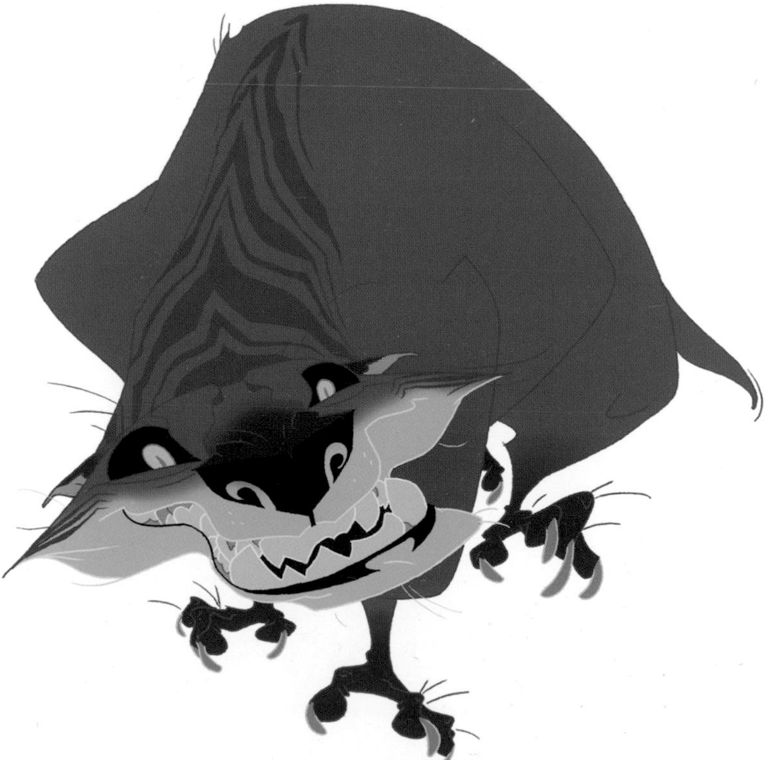

FOR ANGELA

I'D STILL GIVE NAPOLEON
ALL HIS KINGDOMS
AND ALL HIS SEA
FOR A DAY ON THE SHORE
WITH YOU

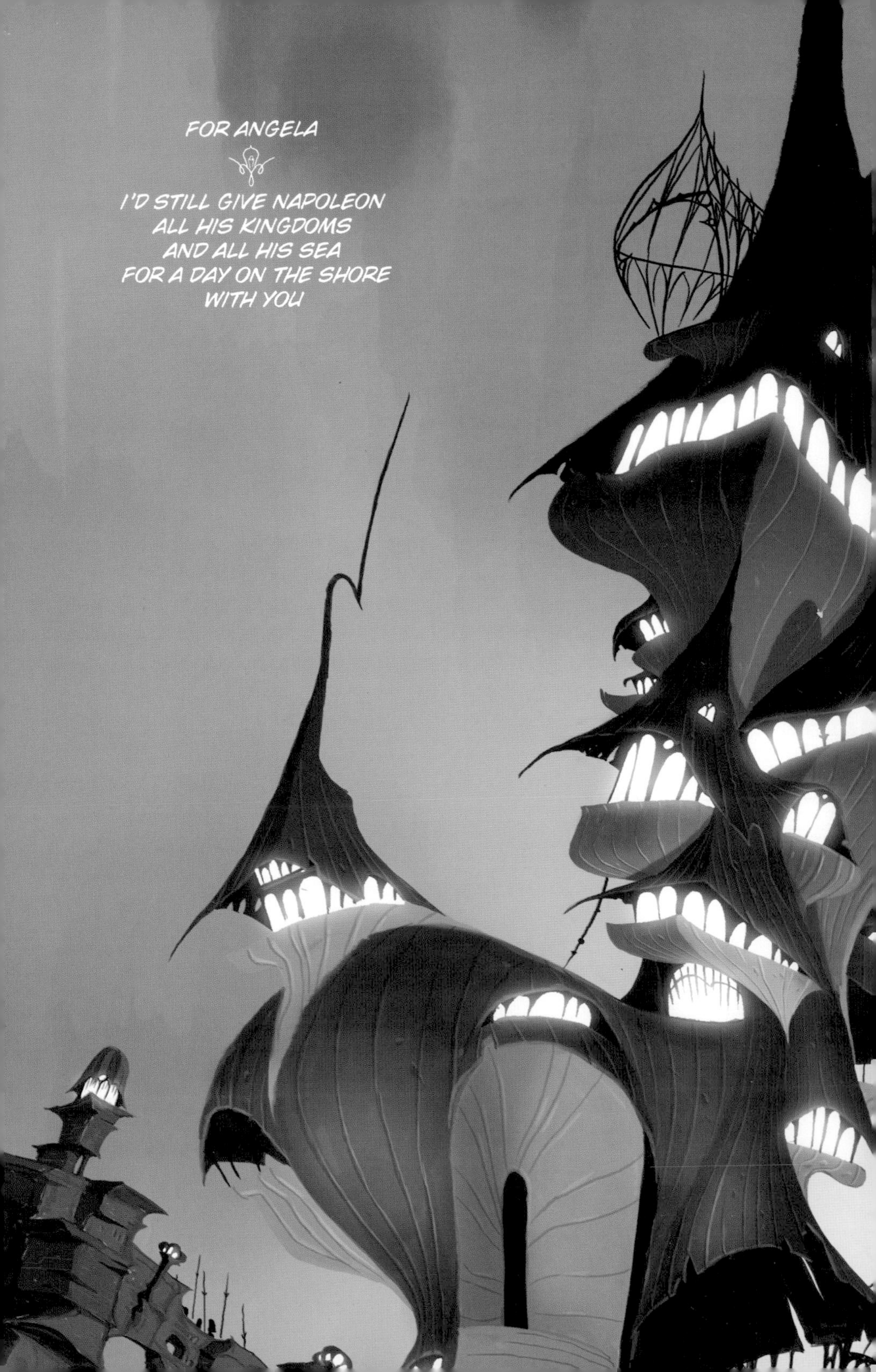

ALL-ACTION CLASSICS PRESENTS

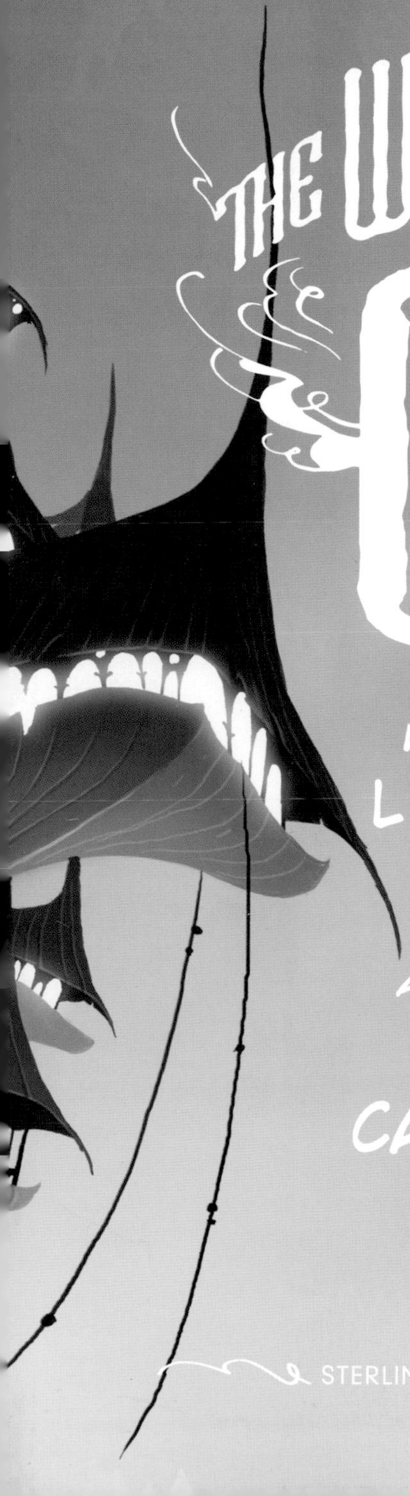

THE WIZARD OF OZ

WRITTEN BY
L. FRANK BAUM

ADAPTED BY
BEN CALDWELL

STERLING CHILDREN'S BOOKS
New York

STERLING CHILDREN'S BOOKS
New York

An Imprint of Sterling Publishing
387 Park Avenue South
New York, NY 10016

AN IMPRINT OF STERLING PUBLISHING
387 PARK AVENUE SOUTH
NEW YORK, NY 10016

ISBN 978-1-4027-3153-2

DISTRIBUTED IN CANADA BY STERLING PUBLISHING
C/O CANADIAN MANDA GROUP, 165 DUFFERIN STREET
TORONTO, ONTARIO, CANADA M6K 3H6
DISTRIBUTED IN THE UNITED KINGDOM BY GMC DISTRIBUTION SERVICES
CASTLE PLACE, 166 HIGH STREET, LEWES, EAST SUSSEX, ENGLAND BN7 1XU
DISTRIBUTED IN AUSTRALIA BY CAPRICORN LINK (AUSTRALIA) PTY. LTD.
P.O. BOX 704, WINDSOR, NSW 2756, AUSTRALIA

FOR INFORMATION ABOUT CUSTOM EDITIONS,
SPECIAL SALES, PREMIUM AND CORPORATE PURCHASES,
PLEASE CONTACT STERLING SPECIAL SALES
AT 800-805-5489 OR
SPECIALSALES@STERLINGPUBLISHING.COM

MANUFACTURED IN CHINA
LOT#:
2 4 6 8 10 9 7 5 3 1
06/12

WWW.STERLINGPUBLISHING.COM/KIDS

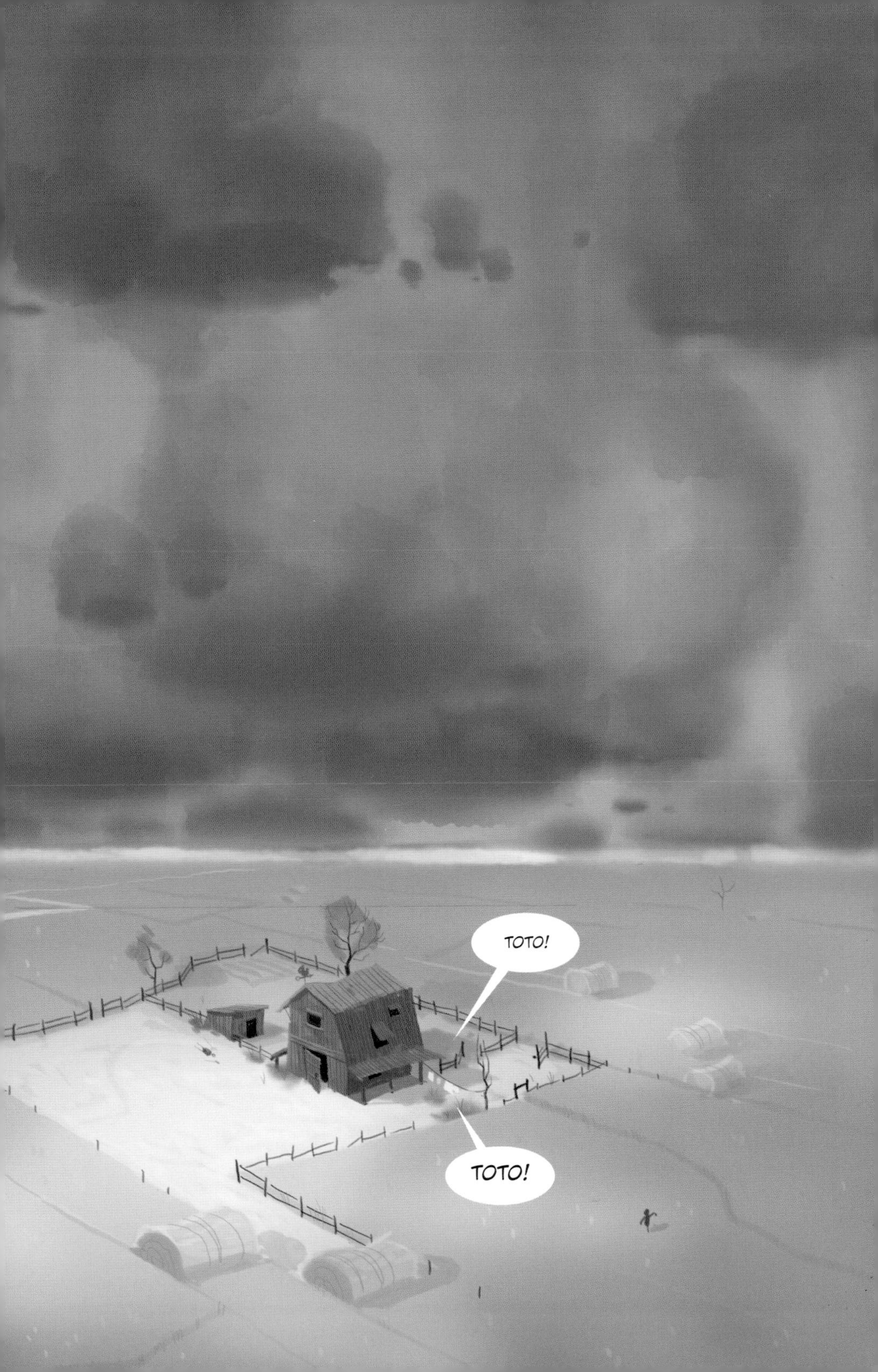
TOTO!
TOTO!

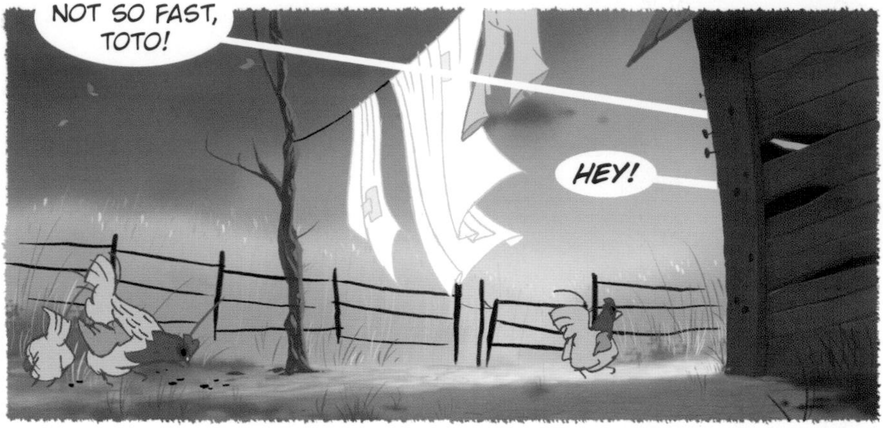
NOT SO FAST, TOTO!
HEY!

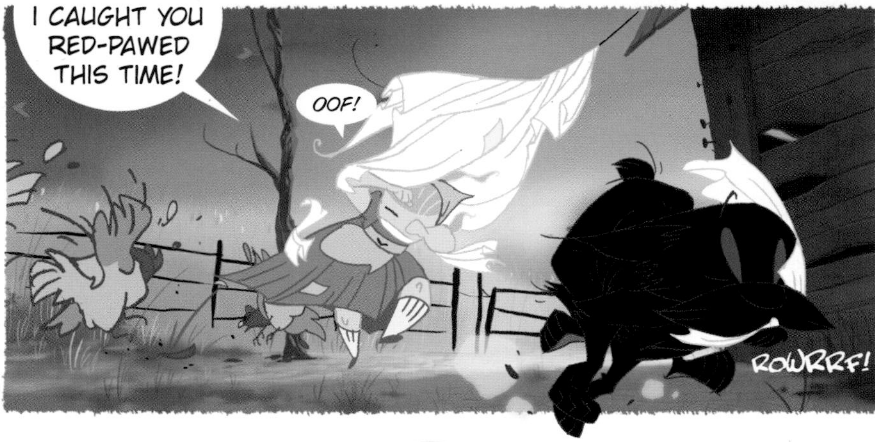
I CAUGHT YOU RED-PAWED THIS TIME!
OOF!
ROWRRF!

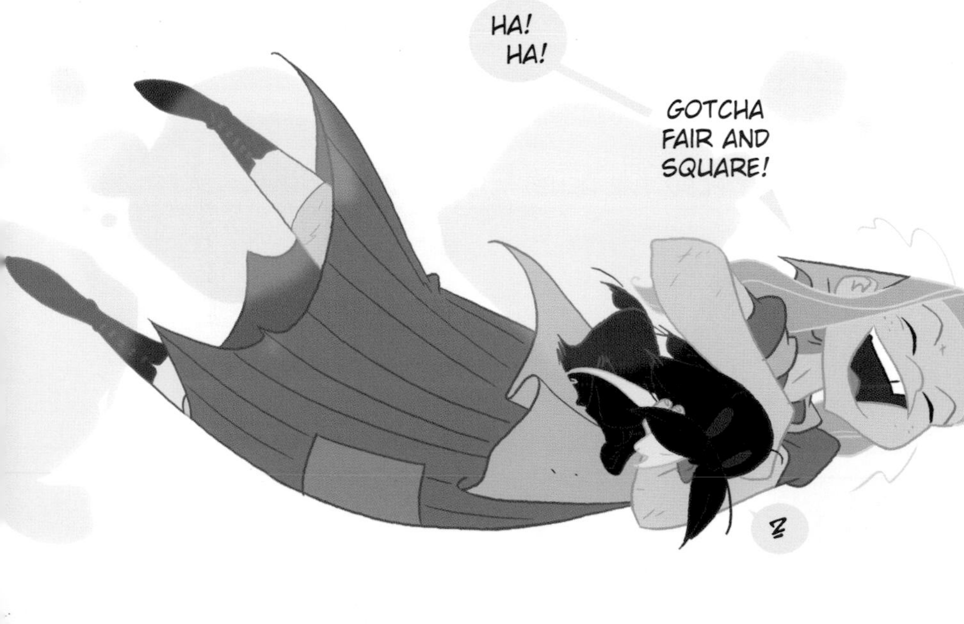
HA! HA!
GOTCHA FAIR AND SQUARE!

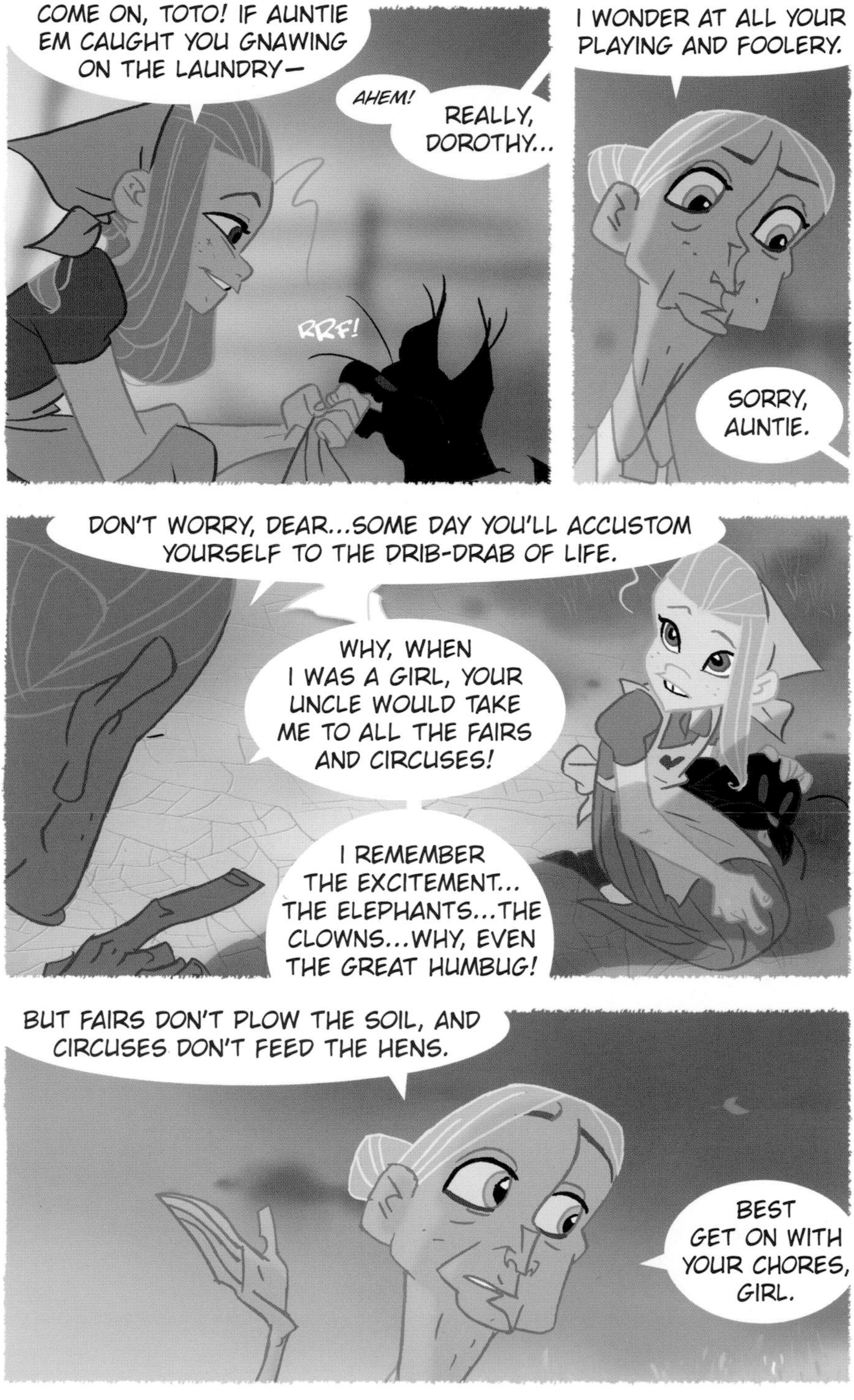
COME ON, TOTO! IF AUNTIE EM CAUGHT YOU GNAWING ON THE LAUNDRY—
RRF!
AHEM!
REALLY, DOROTHY...
I WONDER AT ALL YOUR PLAYING AND FOOLERY.
SORRY, AUNTIE.
DON'T WORRY, DEAR...SOME DAY YOU'LL ACCUSTOM YOURSELF TO THE DRIB-DRAB OF LIFE.
WHY, WHEN I WAS A GIRL, YOUR UNCLE WOULD TAKE ME TO ALL THE FAIRS AND CIRCUSES!
I REMEMBER THE EXCITEMENT... THE ELEPHANTS...THE CLOWNS...WHY, EVEN THE GREAT HUMBUG!
BUT FAIRS DON'T PLOW THE SOIL, AND CIRCUSES DON'T FEED THE HENS.
BEST GET ON WITH YOUR CHORES, GIRL.

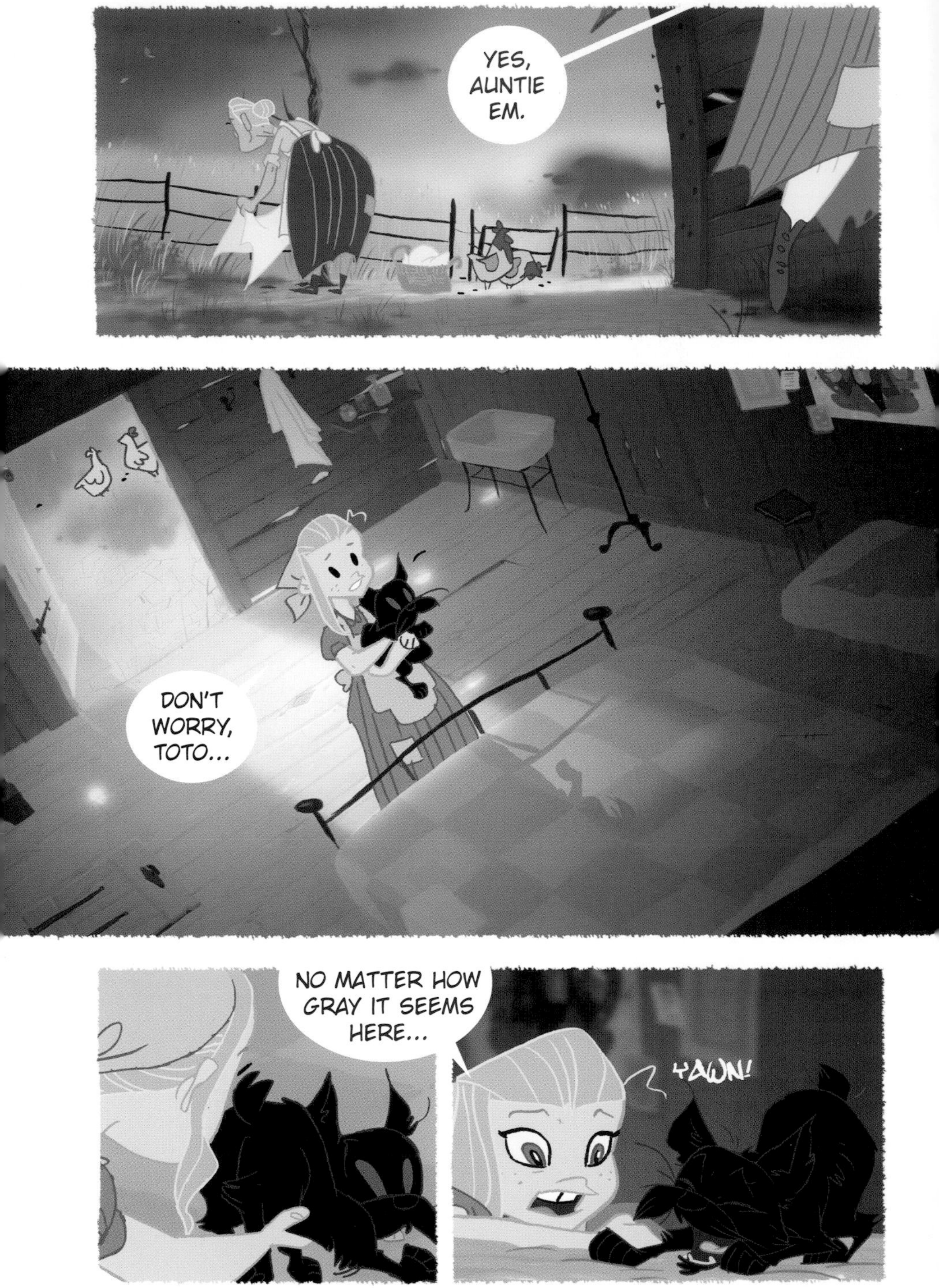
YES, AUNTIE EM.
DON'T WORRY, TOTO...
NO MATTER HOW GRAY IT SEEMS HERE...
YAWN!

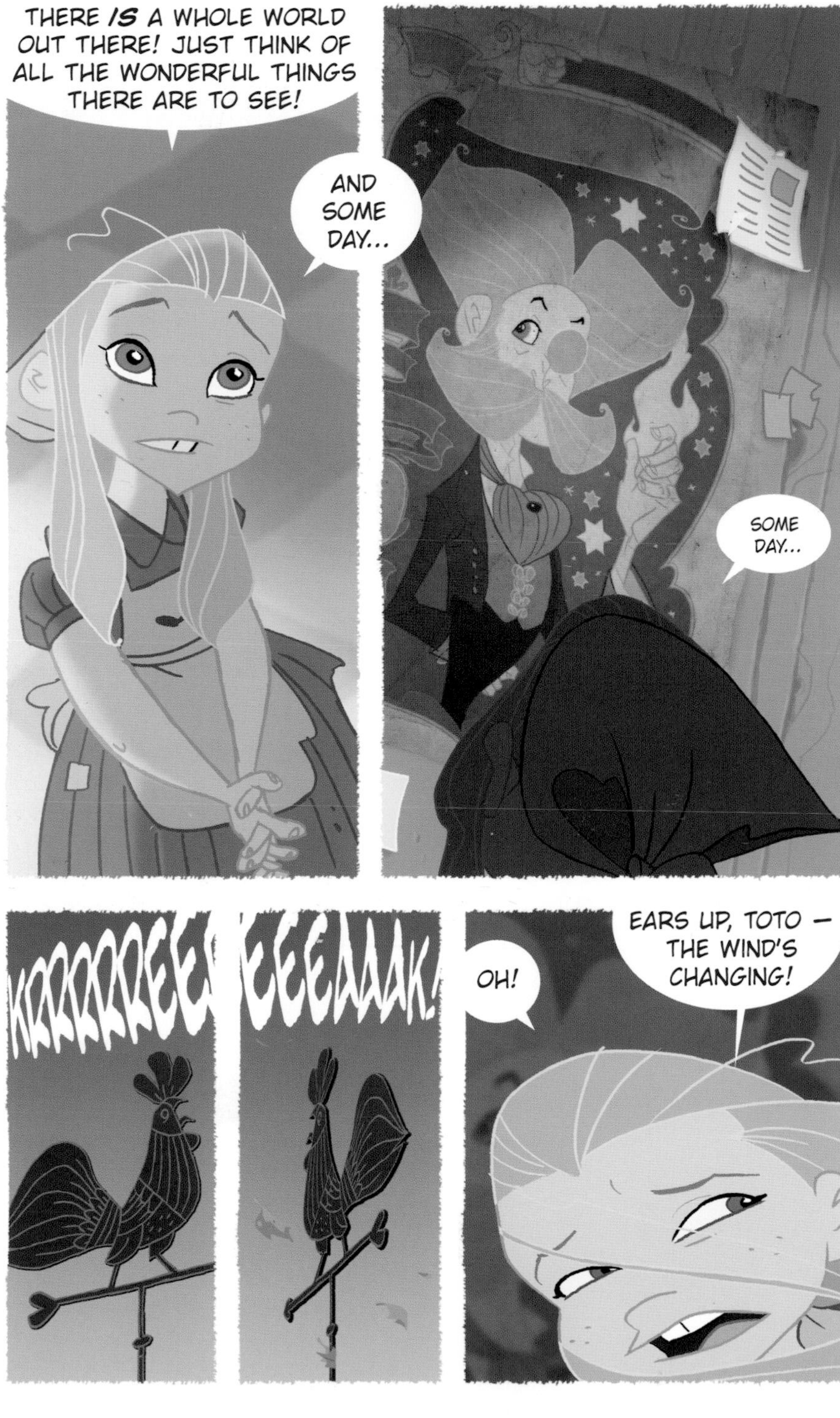
THERE *IS* A WHOLE WORLD OUT THERE! JUST THINK OF ALL THE WONDERFUL THINGS THERE ARE TO SEE!
AND SOME DAY...
SOME DAY...
KRRRRREEEEEEEAAAK!
OH!
EARS UP, TOTO — THE WIND'S CHANGING!

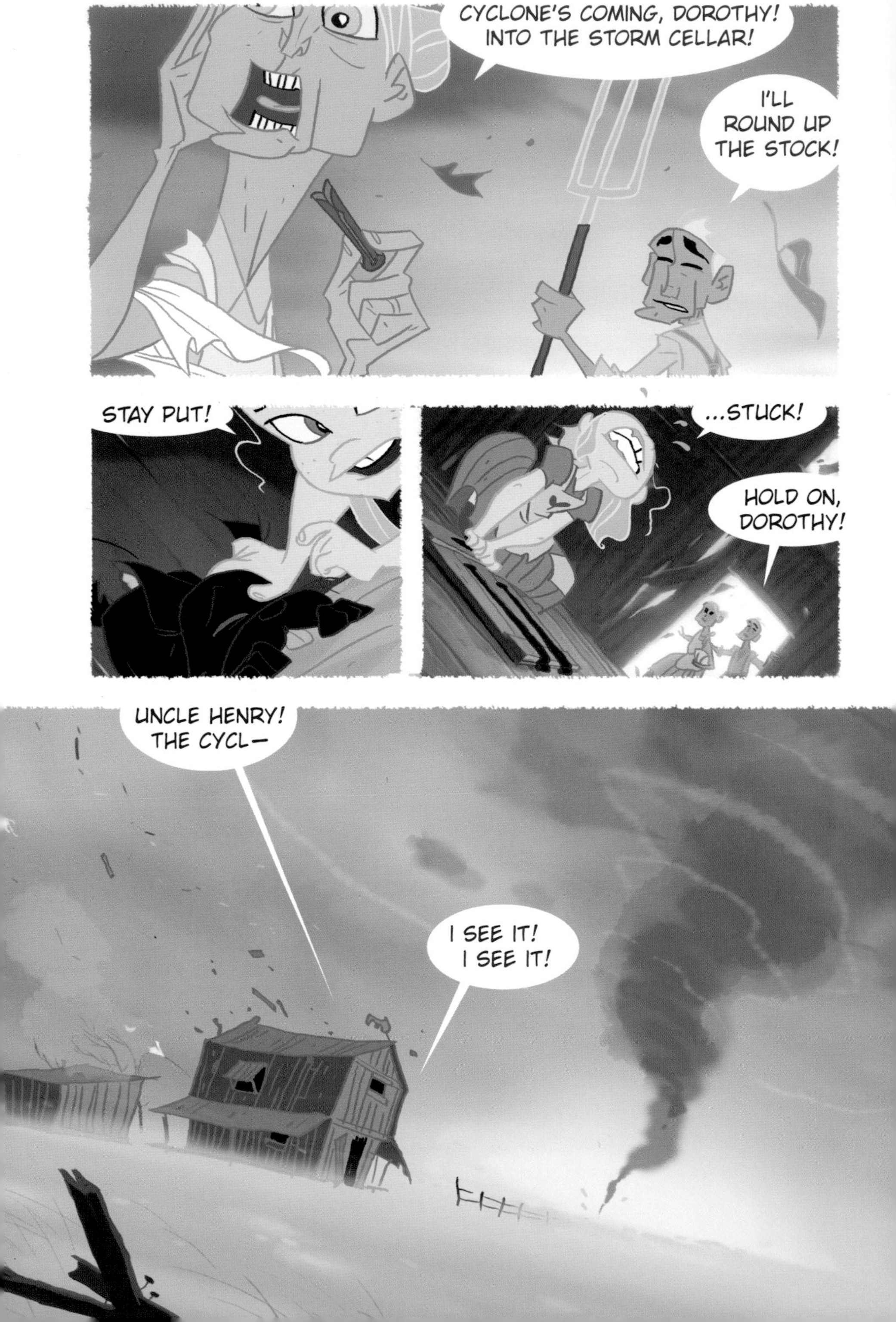
CYCLONE'S COMING, DOROTHY! INTO THE STORM CELLAR!
I'LL ROUND UP THE STOCK!
STAY PUT!
...STUCK!
HOLD ON, DOROTHY!
UNCLE HENRY! THE CYCL—
I SEE IT! I SEE IT!

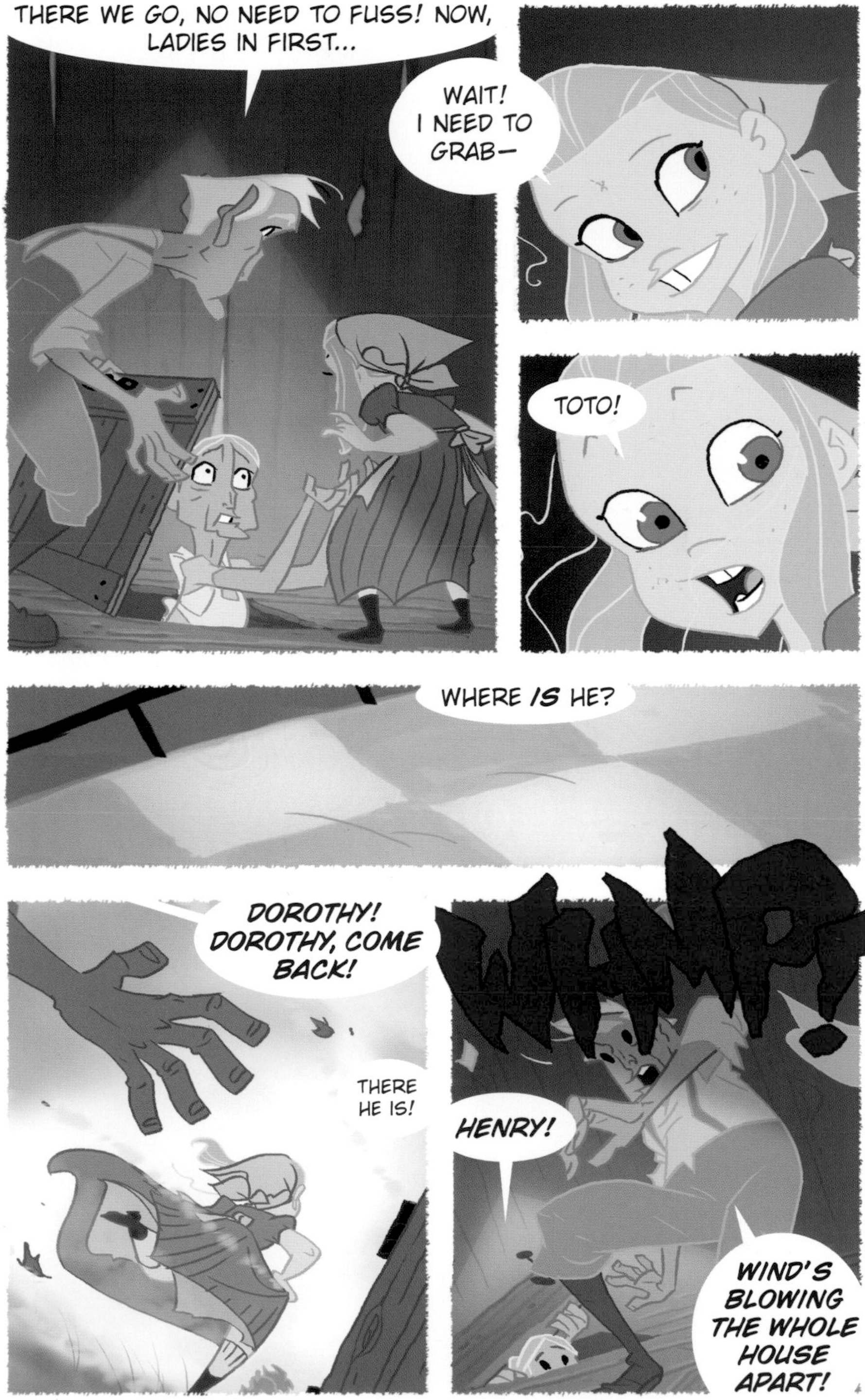
THERE WE GO, NO NEED TO FUSS! NOW, LADIES IN FIRST...
WAIT! I NEED TO GRAB—
TOTO!
WHERE *IS* HE?
DOROTHY! DOROTHY, COME BACK!
THERE HE IS!
WHUMP!
HENRY!
WIND'S BLOWING THE WHOLE HOUSE APART!

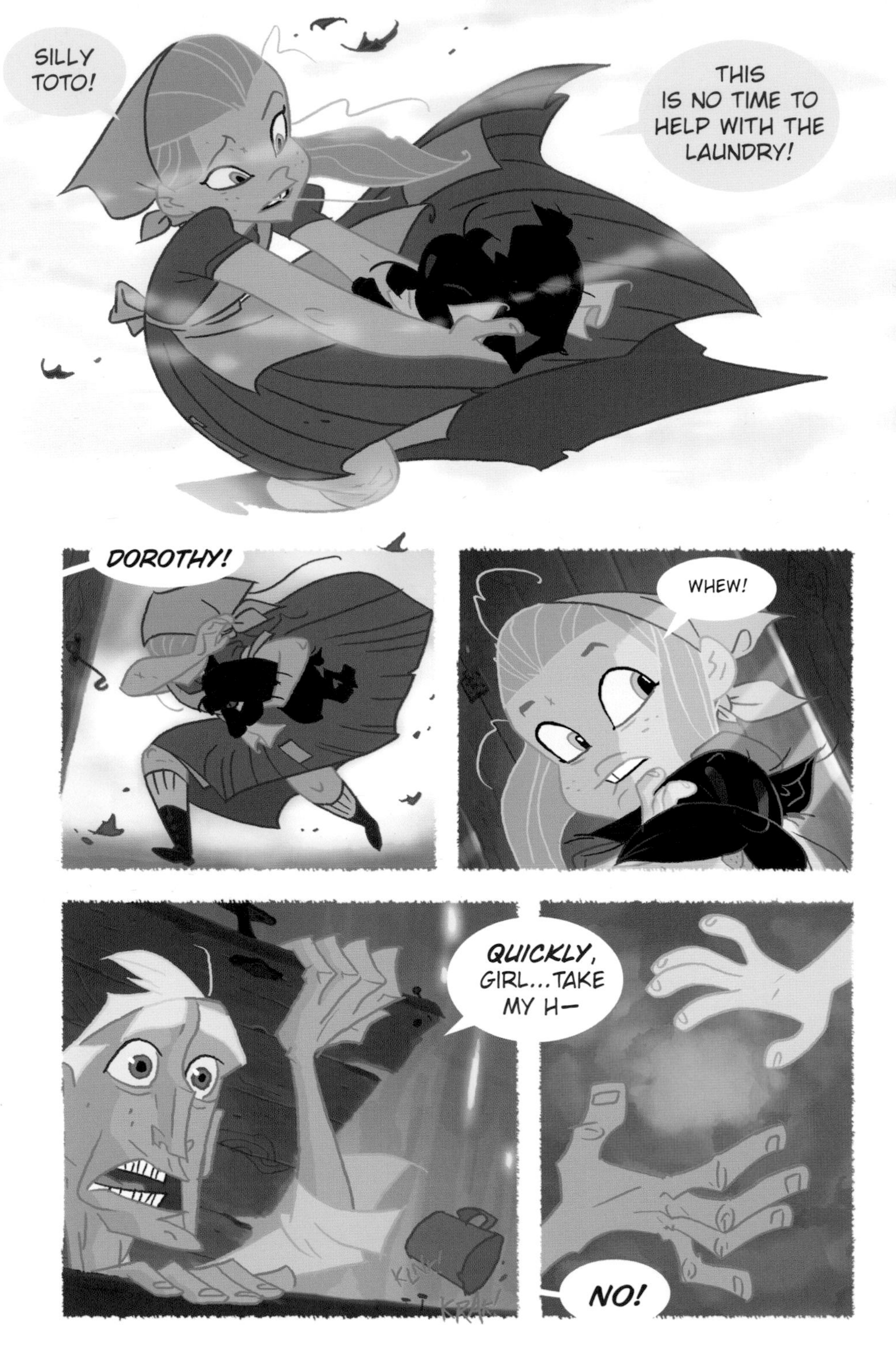
SILLY TOTO!
THIS IS NO TIME TO HELP WITH THE LAUNDRY!
DOROTHY!
WHEW!
QUICKLY, GIRL...TAKE MY H—
NO!

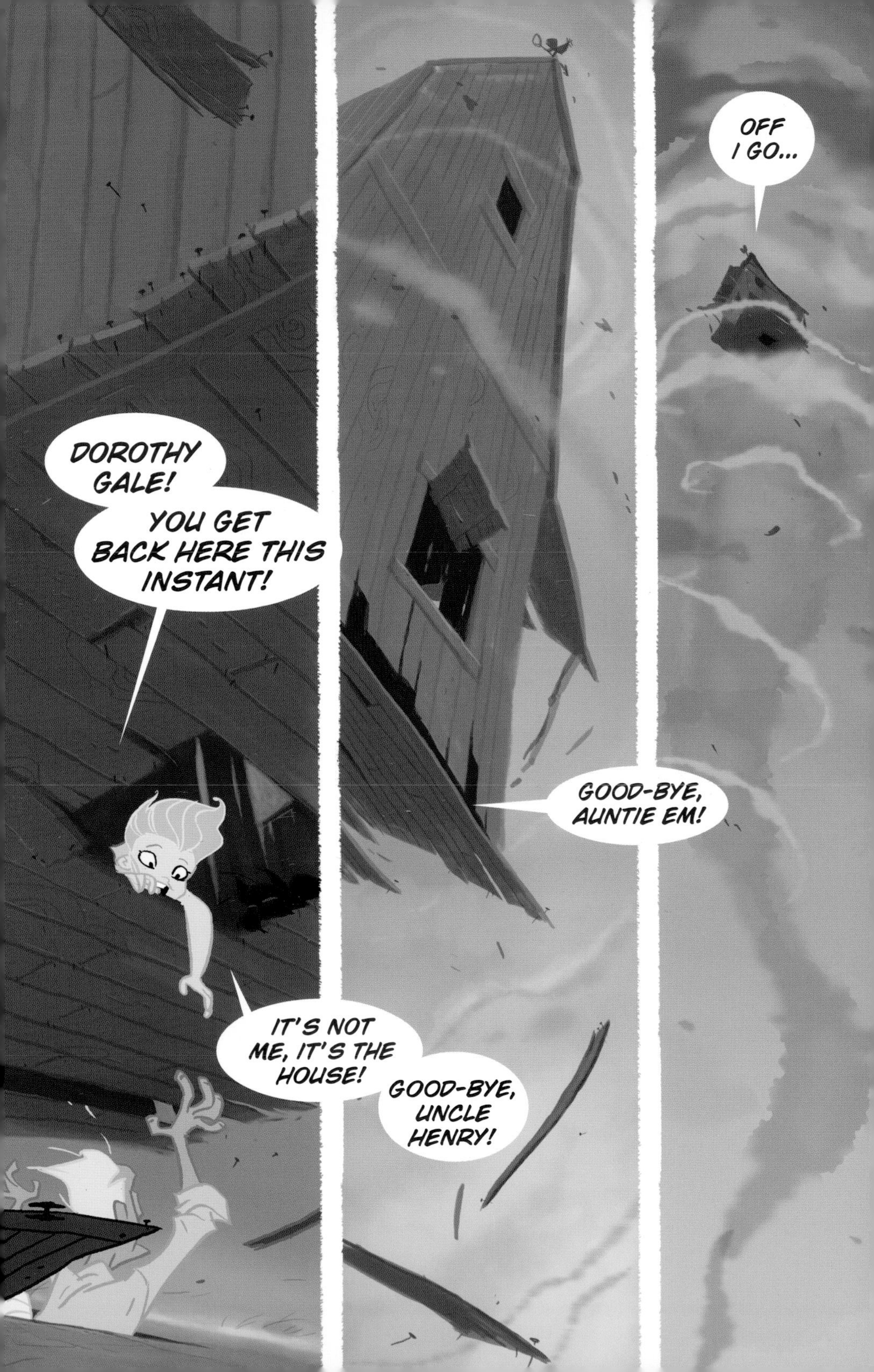
DOROTHY GALE!
YOU GET BACK HERE THIS INSTANT!
IT'S NOT ME, IT'S THE HOUSE!
GOOD-BYE, UNCLE HENRY!
GOOD-BYE, AUNTIE EM!
OFF I GO...

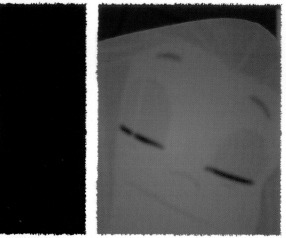

YAWN...

HUH...

I'M PRETTY SURE I REMEMBER KANSAS HAVING MORE PRAIRIE AND LESS BLUE HOUSES.

RRFZ

H— HELLO?

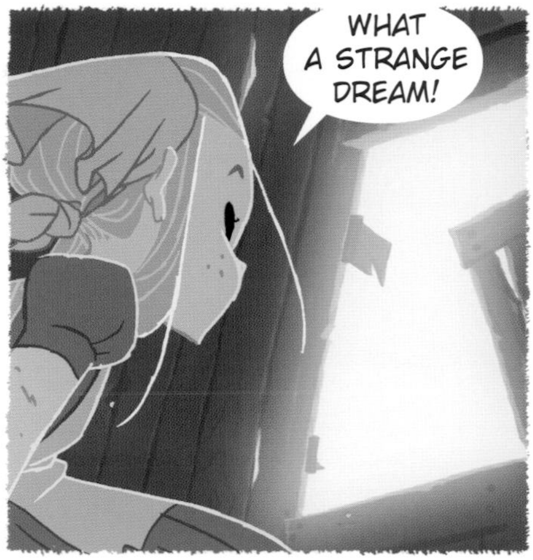
WHAT A STRANGE DREAM!

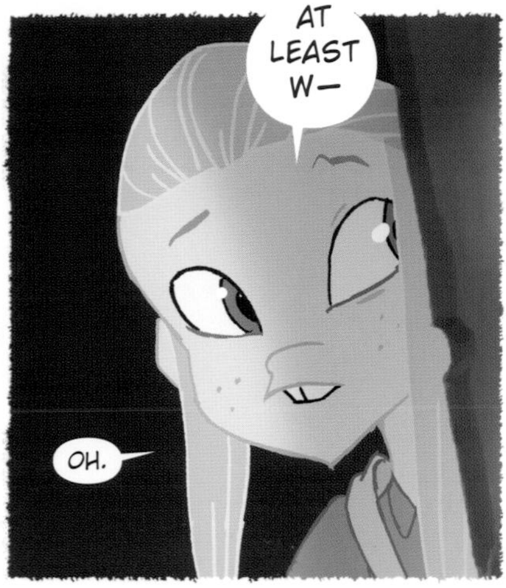
AT LEAST W—
OH.

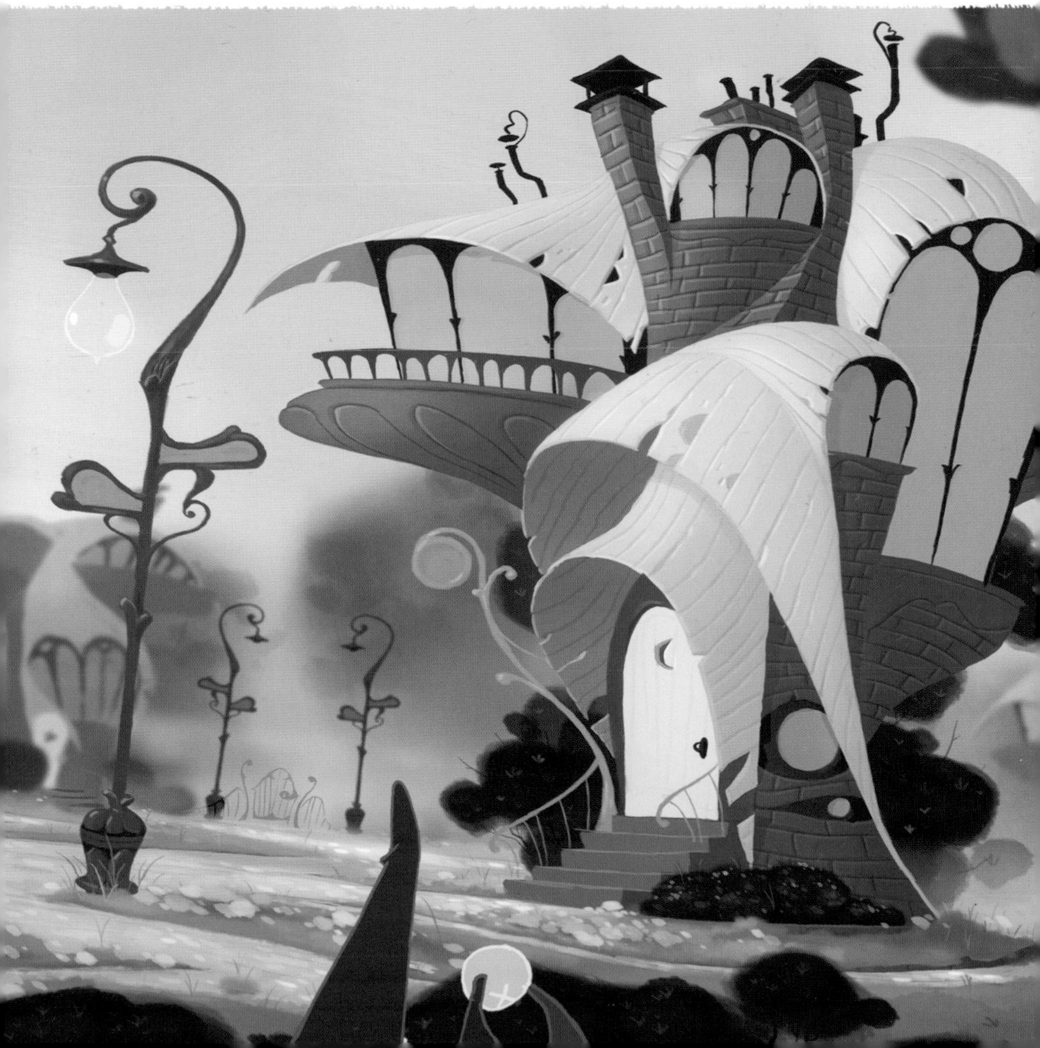

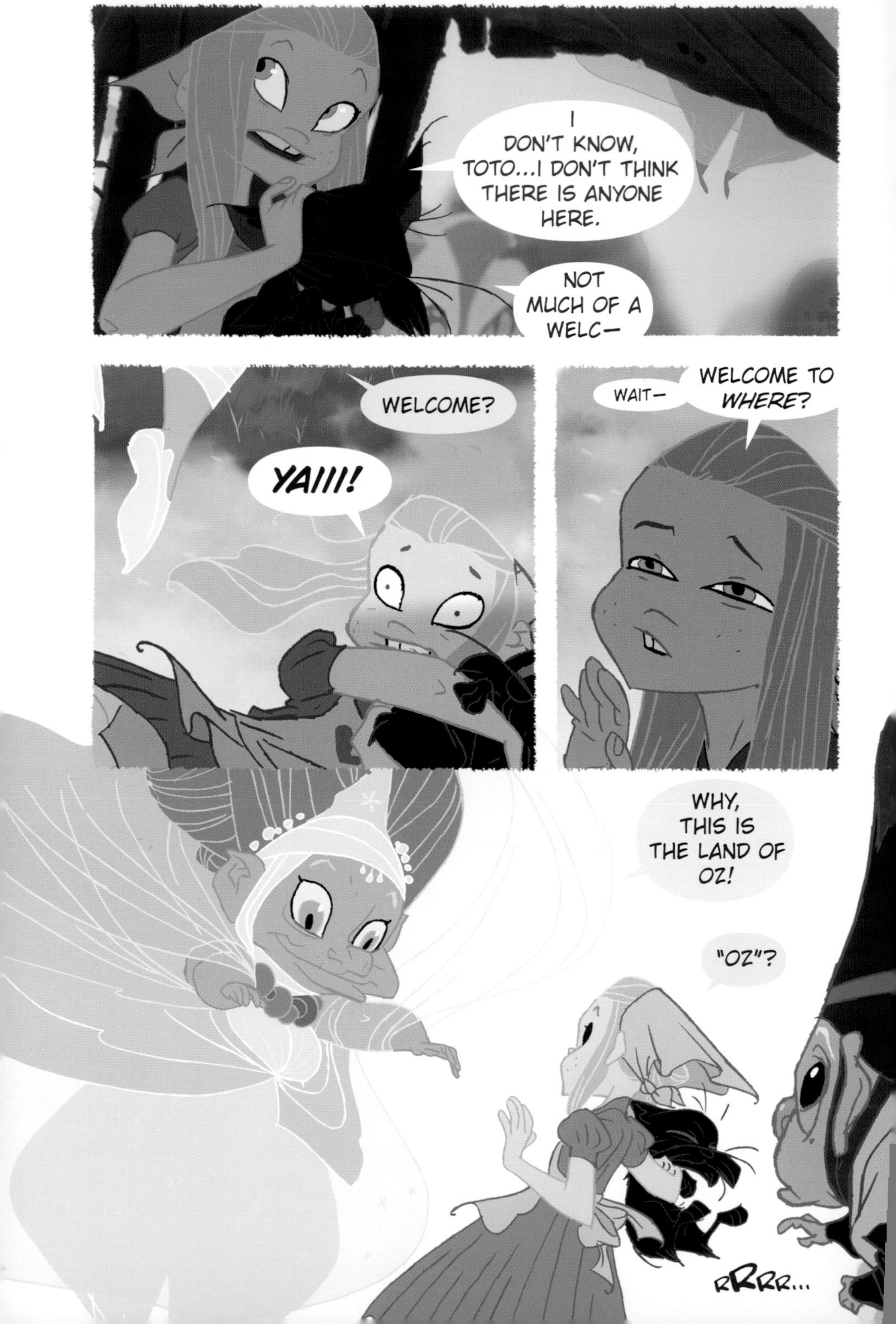

I DON'T KNOW, TOTO...I DON'T THINK THERE IS ANYONE HERE.
NOT MUCH OF A WELC—
WELCOME?
YAIII!
WAIT—
WELCOME TO *WHERE?*
WHY, THIS IS THE LAND OF OZ!
"OZ"?
RRRR...

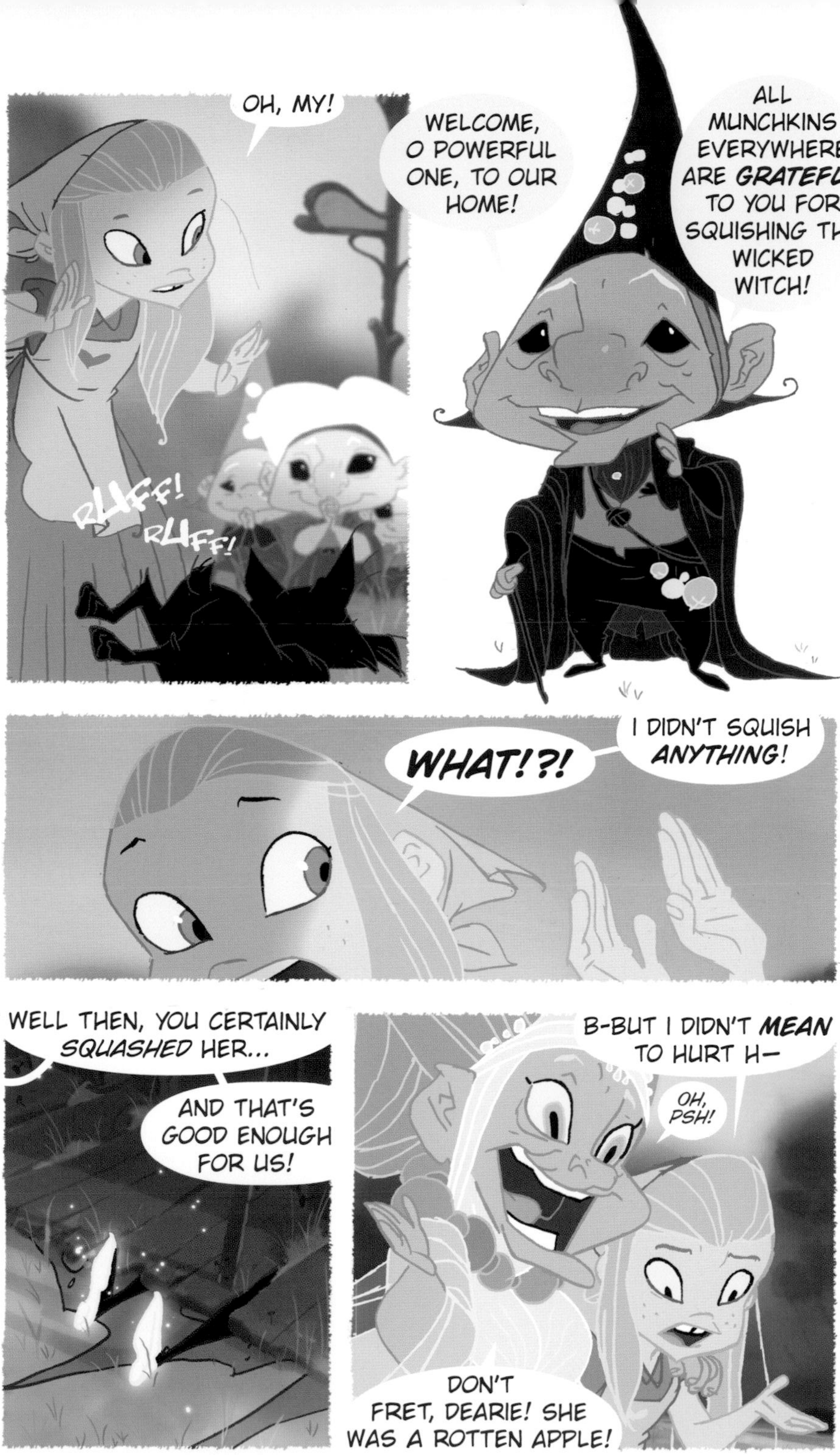
OH, MY!
RUFF! RUFF!
WELCOME, O POWERFUL ONE, TO OUR HOME!
ALL MUNCHKINS EVERYWHERE ARE GRATEFUL TO YOU FOR SQUISHING THE WICKED WITCH!
WHAT!?!
I DIDN'T SQUISH ANYTHING!
WELL THEN, YOU CERTAINLY SQUASHED HER...
AND THAT'S GOOD ENOUGH FOR US!
B-BUT I DIDN'T MEAN TO HURT H—
OH, PSH!
DON'T FRET, DEARIE! SHE WAS A ROTTEN APPLE!

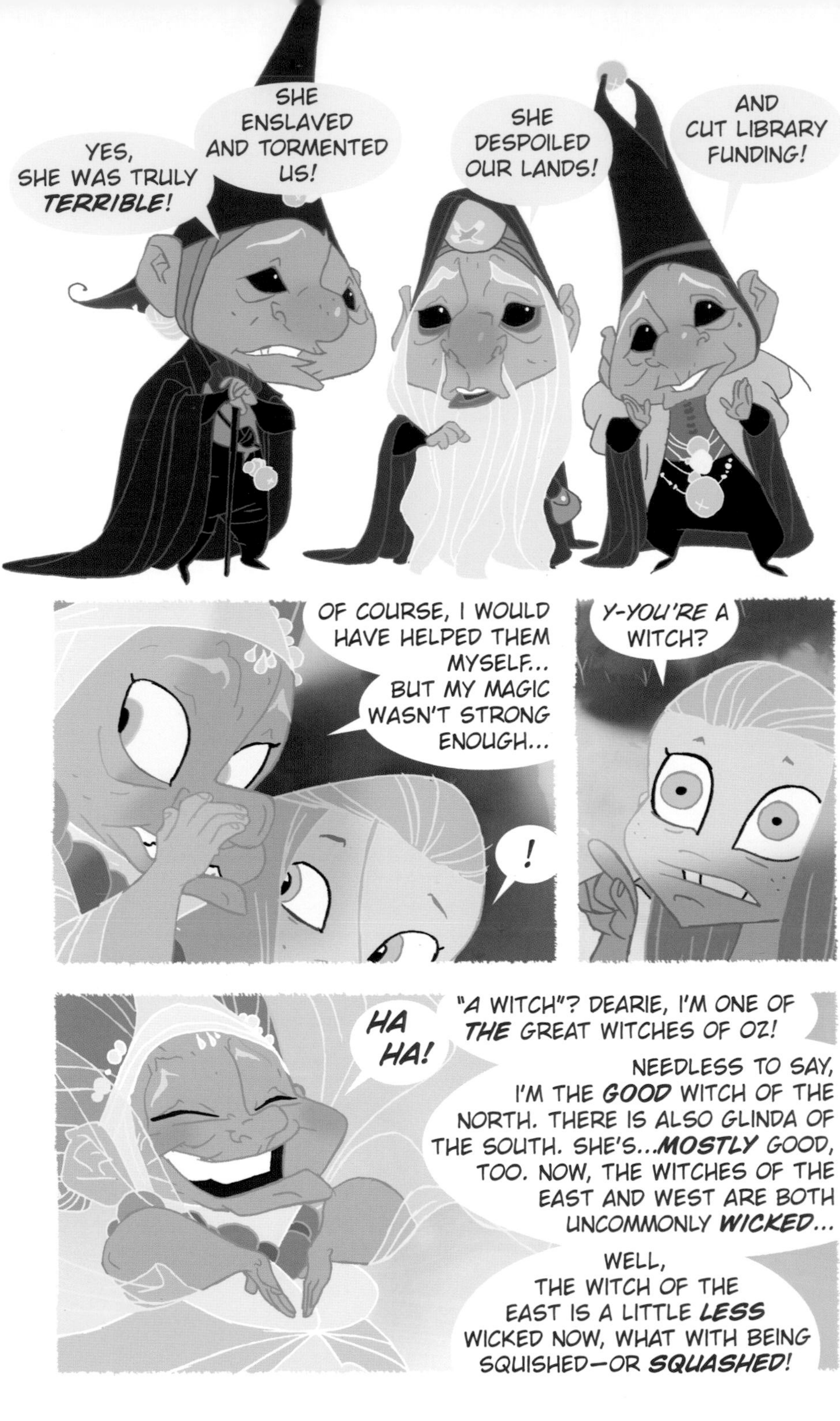
YES, SHE WAS TRULY TERRIBLE!
SHE ENSLAVED AND TORMENTED US!
SHE DESPOILED OUR LANDS!
AND CUT LIBRARY FUNDING!
OF COURSE, I WOULD HAVE HELPED THEM MYSELF... BUT MY MAGIC WASN'T STRONG ENOUGH...
!
Y-YOU'RE A WITCH?
HA HA!
"A WITCH"? DEARIE, I'M ONE OF THE GREAT WITCHES OF OZ!
NEEDLESS TO SAY, I'M THE GOOD WITCH OF THE NORTH. THERE IS ALSO GLINDA OF THE SOUTH. SHE'S...MOSTLY GOOD, TOO. NOW, THE WITCHES OF THE EAST AND WEST ARE BOTH UNCOMMONLY WICKED...
WELL, THE WITCH OF THE EAST IS A LITTLE LESS WICKED NOW, WHAT WITH BEING SQUISHED—OR SQUASHED!

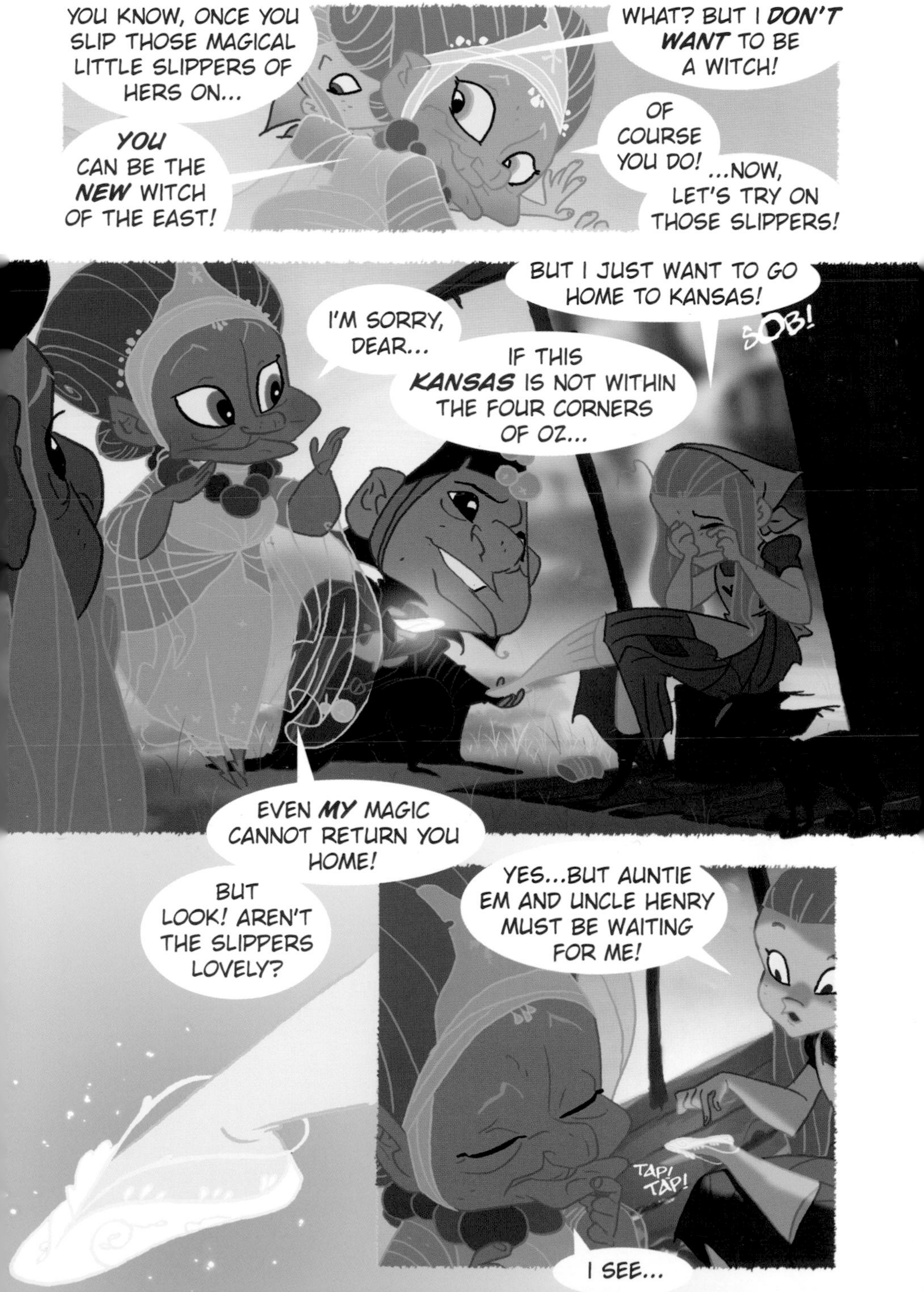

YOU KNOW, ONCE YOU SLIP THOSE MAGICAL LITTLE SLIPPERS OF HERS ON...
YOU CAN BE THE *NEW* WITCH OF THE EAST!
WHAT? BUT I *DON'T WANT* TO BE A WITCH!
OF COURSE YOU DO!
...NOW, LET'S TRY ON THOSE SLIPPERS!
I'M SORRY, DEAR...
IF THIS *KANSAS* IS NOT WITHIN THE FOUR CORNERS OF OZ...
BUT I JUST WANT TO GO HOME TO KANSAS!
SOB!
EVEN *MY* MAGIC CANNOT RETURN YOU HOME!
BUT LOOK! AREN'T THE SLIPPERS LOVELY?
YES...BUT AUNTIE EM AND UNCLE HENRY MUST BE WAITING FOR ME!
TAP! TAP!
I SEE...

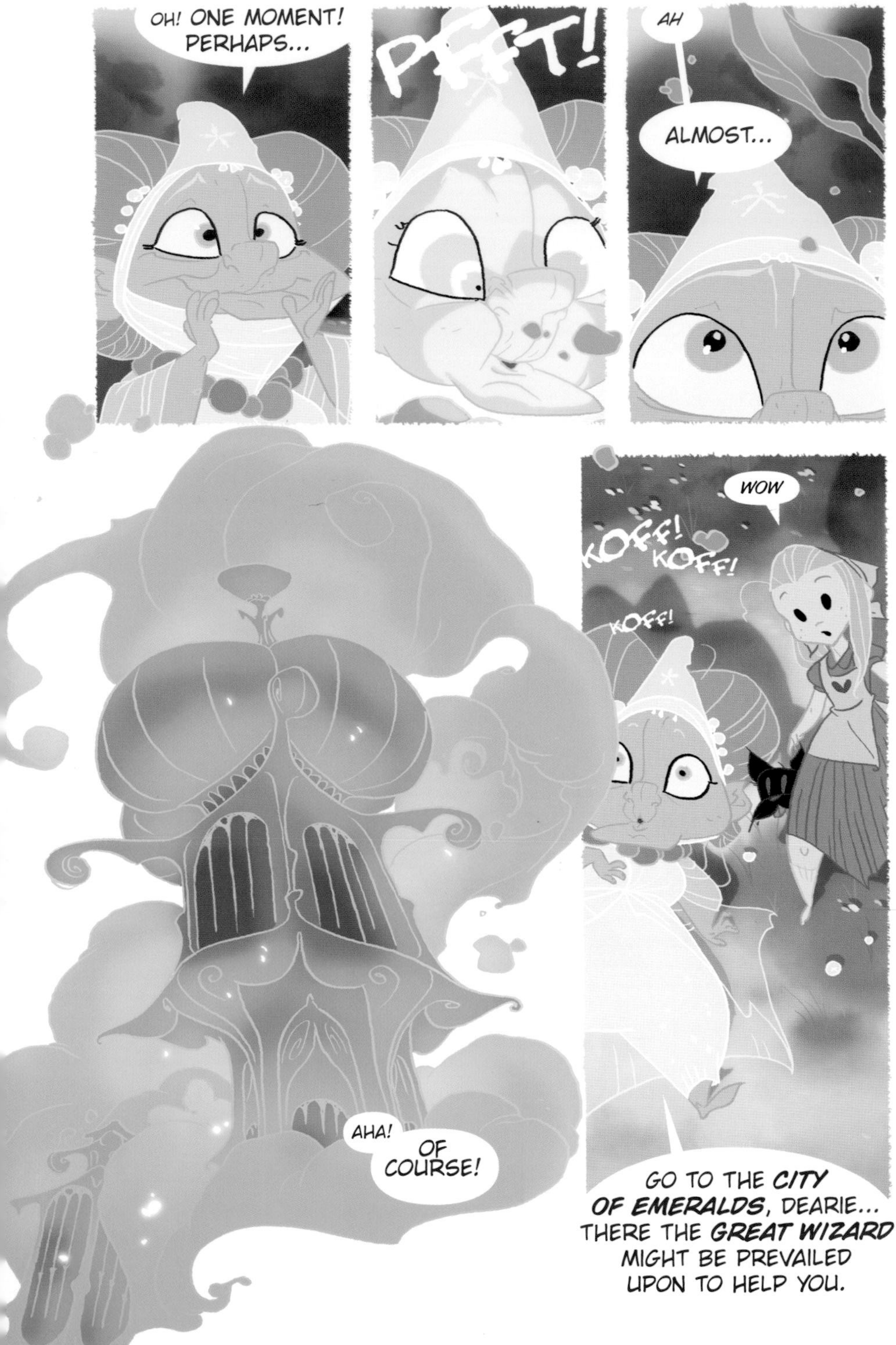
OH! ONE MOMENT! PERHAPS...
PFFT!
AH
ALMOST...
AHA!
OF COURSE!
WOW
KOFF! KOFF!
KOFF!
GO TO THE CITY OF EMERALDS, DEARIE... THERE THE GREAT WIZARD MIGHT BE PREVAILED UPON TO HELP YOU.

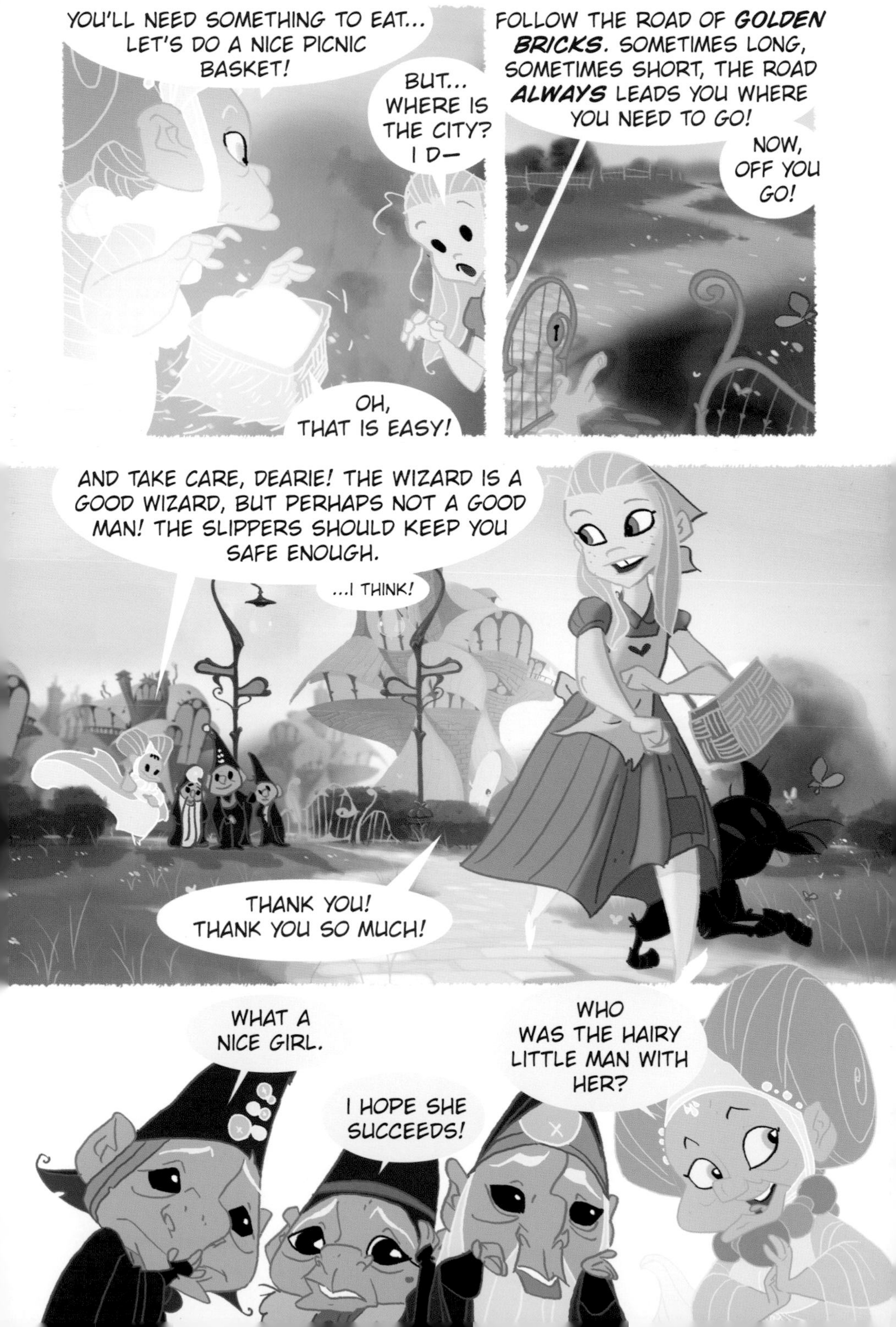
YOU'LL NEED SOMETHING TO EAT... LET'S DO A NICE PICNIC BASKET!
BUT... WHERE IS THE CITY? I D—
OH, THAT IS EASY!
FOLLOW THE ROAD OF **GOLDEN BRICKS**. SOMETIMES LONG, SOMETIMES SHORT, THE ROAD **ALWAYS** LEADS YOU WHERE YOU NEED TO GO!
NOW, OFF YOU GO!
AND TAKE CARE, DEARIE! THE WIZARD IS A GOOD WIZARD, BUT PERHAPS NOT A GOOD MAN! THE SLIPPERS SHOULD KEEP YOU SAFE ENOUGH.
...I THINK!
THANK YOU! THANK YOU SO MUCH!
WHAT A NICE GIRL.
I HOPE SHE SUCCEEDS!
WHO WAS THE HAIRY LITTLE MAN WITH HER?

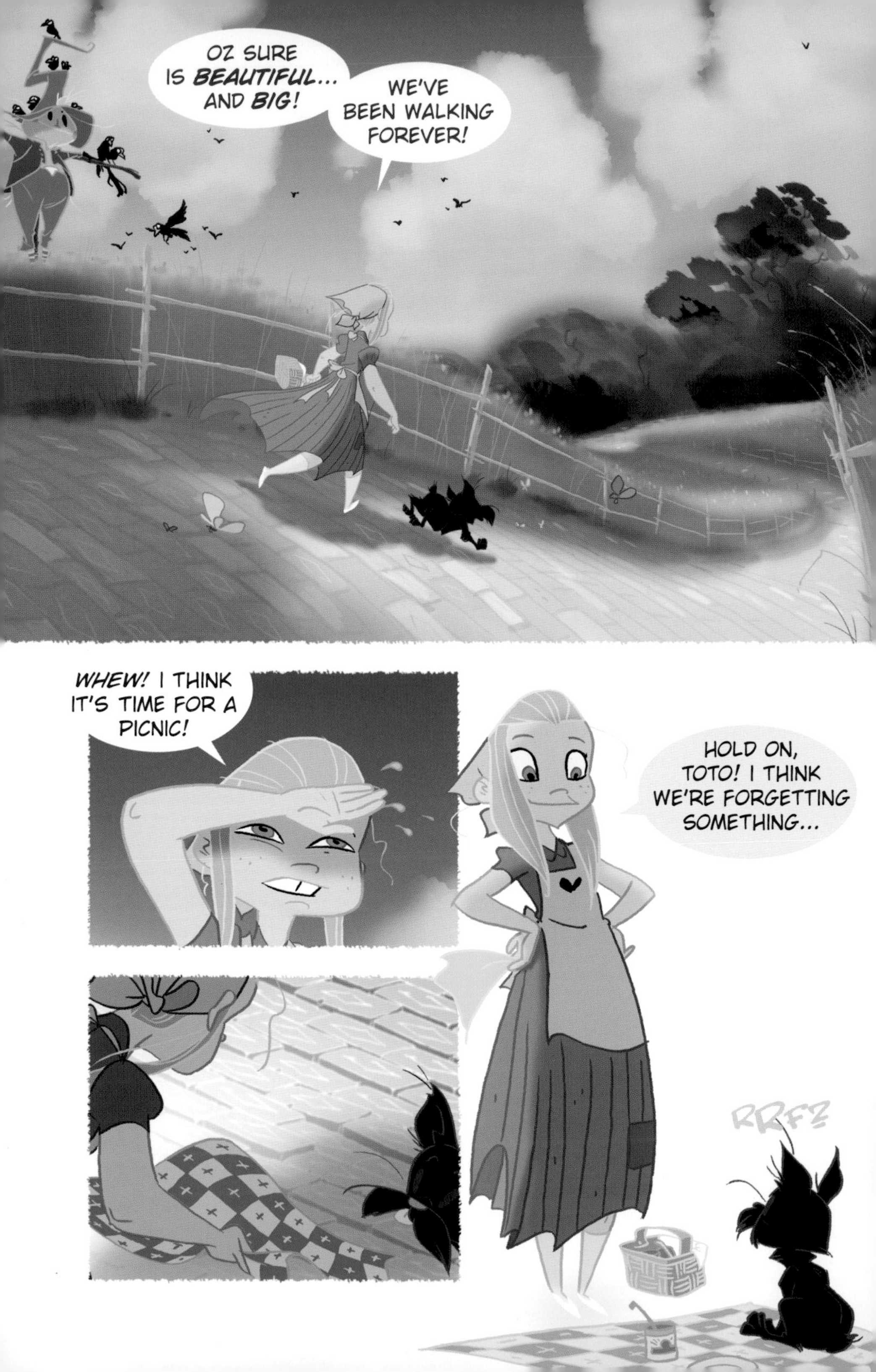
OZ SURE IS *BEAUTIFUL*... AND *BIG*!
WE'VE BEEN WALKING FOREVER!
WHEW! I THINK IT'S TIME FOR A PICNIC!
HOLD ON, TOTO! I THINK WE'RE FORGETTING SOMETHING...
RRF?

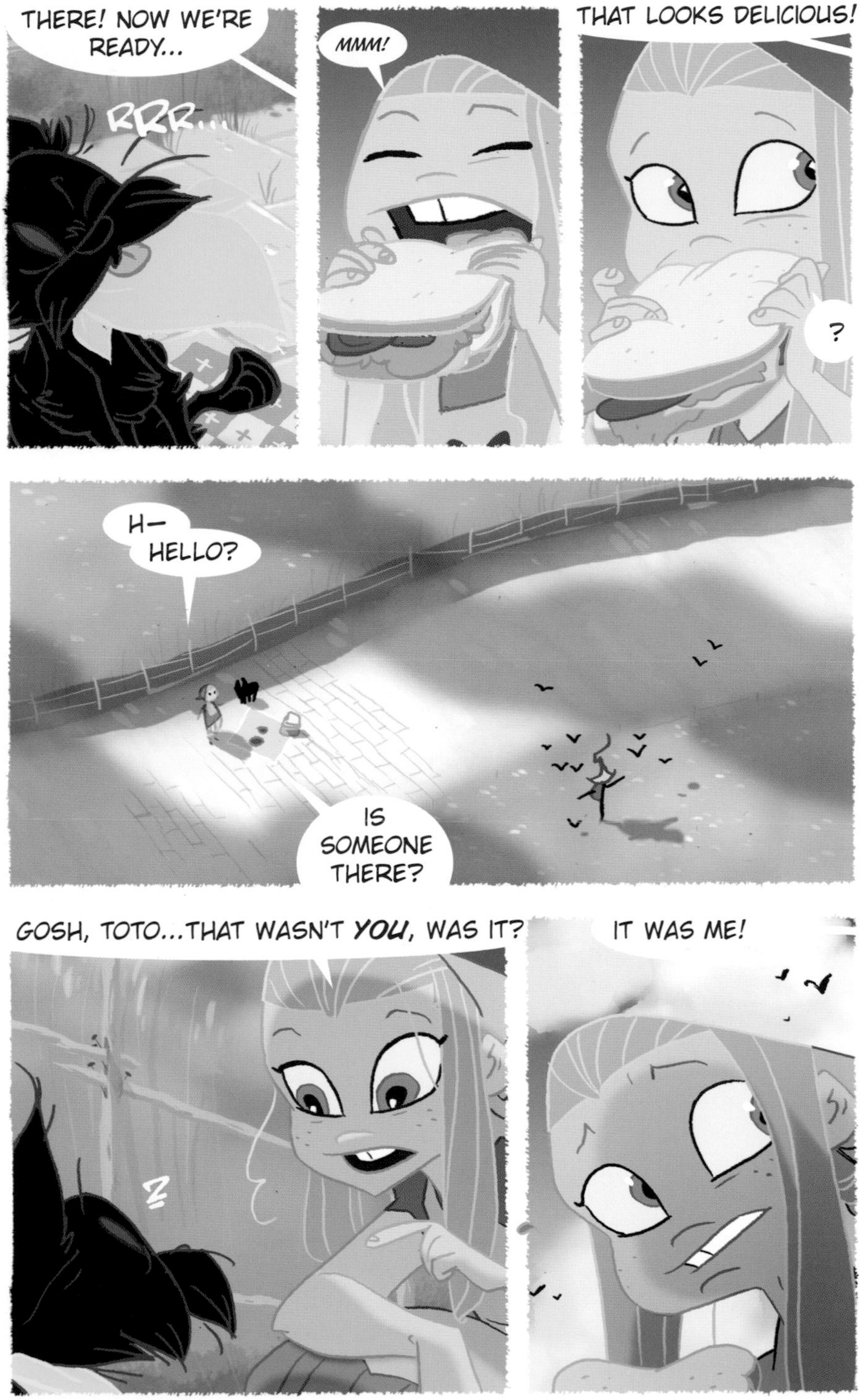
THERE! NOW WE'RE READY...
RRR...
MMM!
THAT LOOKS DELICIOUS!
?
H— HELLO?
IS SOMEONE THERE?
GOSH, TOTO...THAT WASN'T *YOU*, WAS IT?
IT WAS ME!

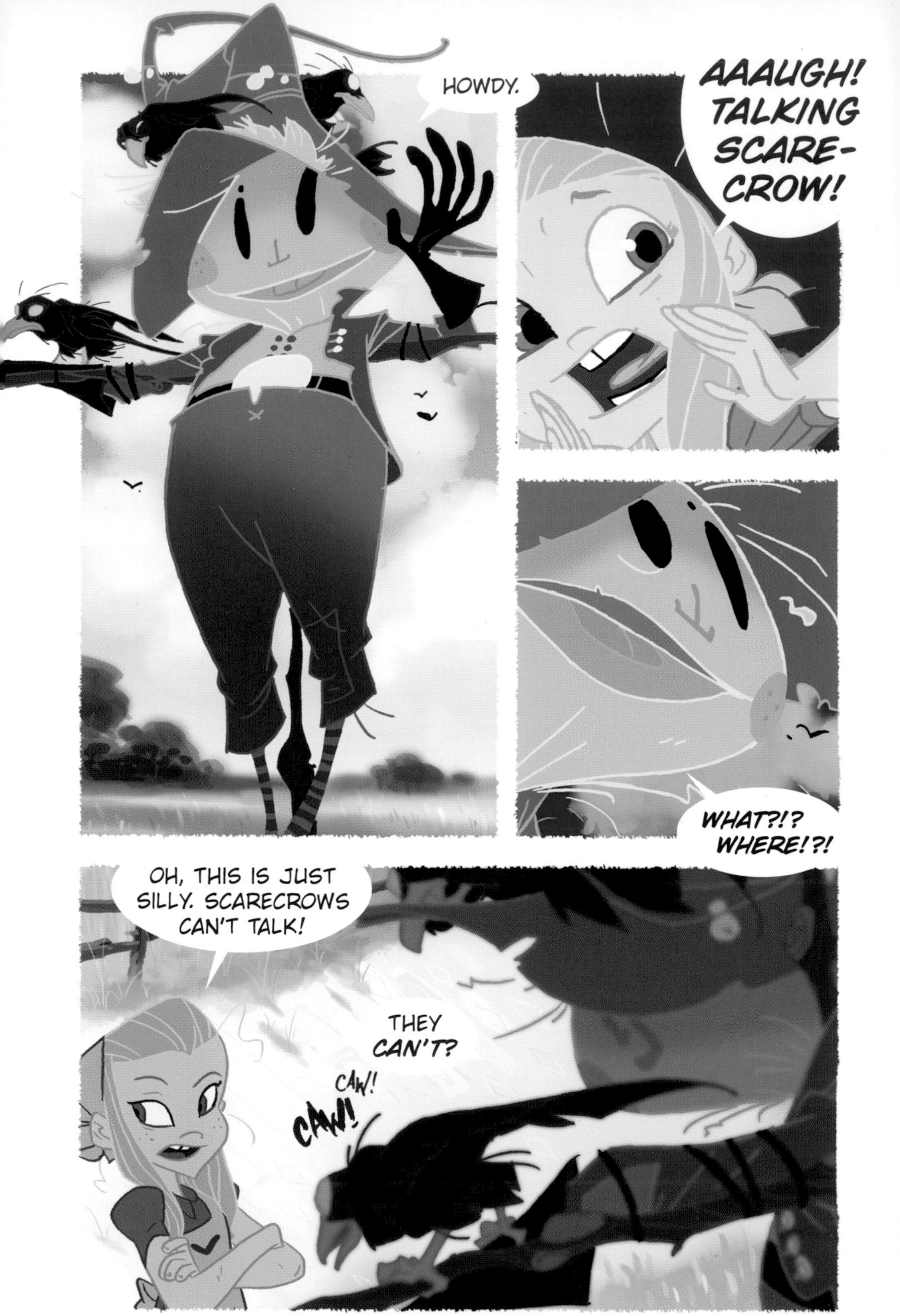
HOWDY.
AAAUGH! TALKING SCARE-CROW!
WHAT?!? WHERE!?!
OH, THIS IS JUST SILLY. SCARECROWS CAN'T TALK!
THEY *CAN'T*?
CAW!
CAW!

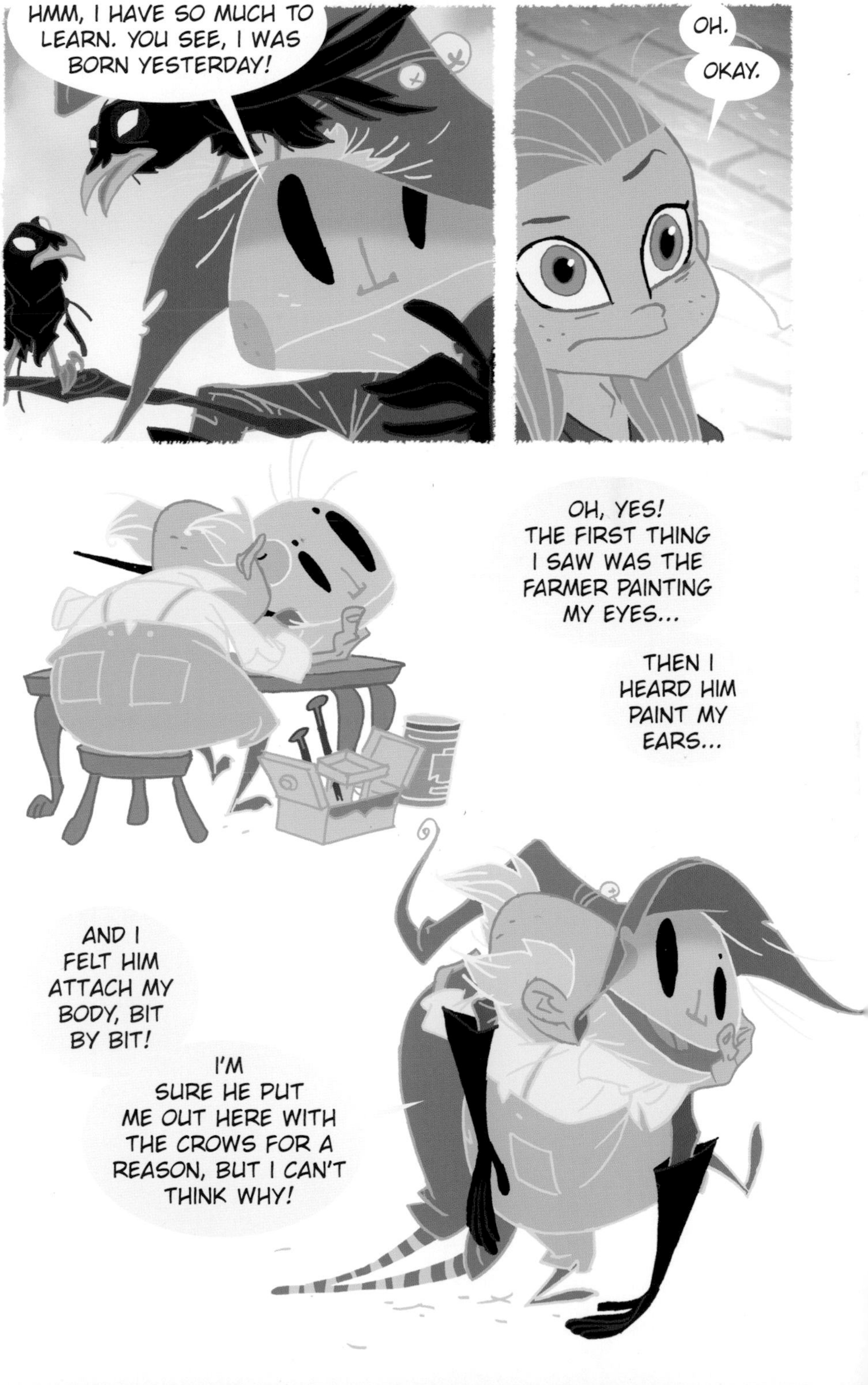

HMM, I HAVE SO MUCH TO LEARN. YOU SEE, I WAS BORN YESTERDAY!
OH.
OKAY.
OH, YES! THE FIRST THING I SAW WAS THE FARMER PAINTING MY EYES...
THEN I HEARD HIM PAINT MY EARS...
AND I FELT HIM ATTACH MY BODY, BIT BY BIT!
I'M SURE HE PUT ME OUT HERE WITH THE CROWS FOR A REASON, BUT I CAN'T THINK WHY!

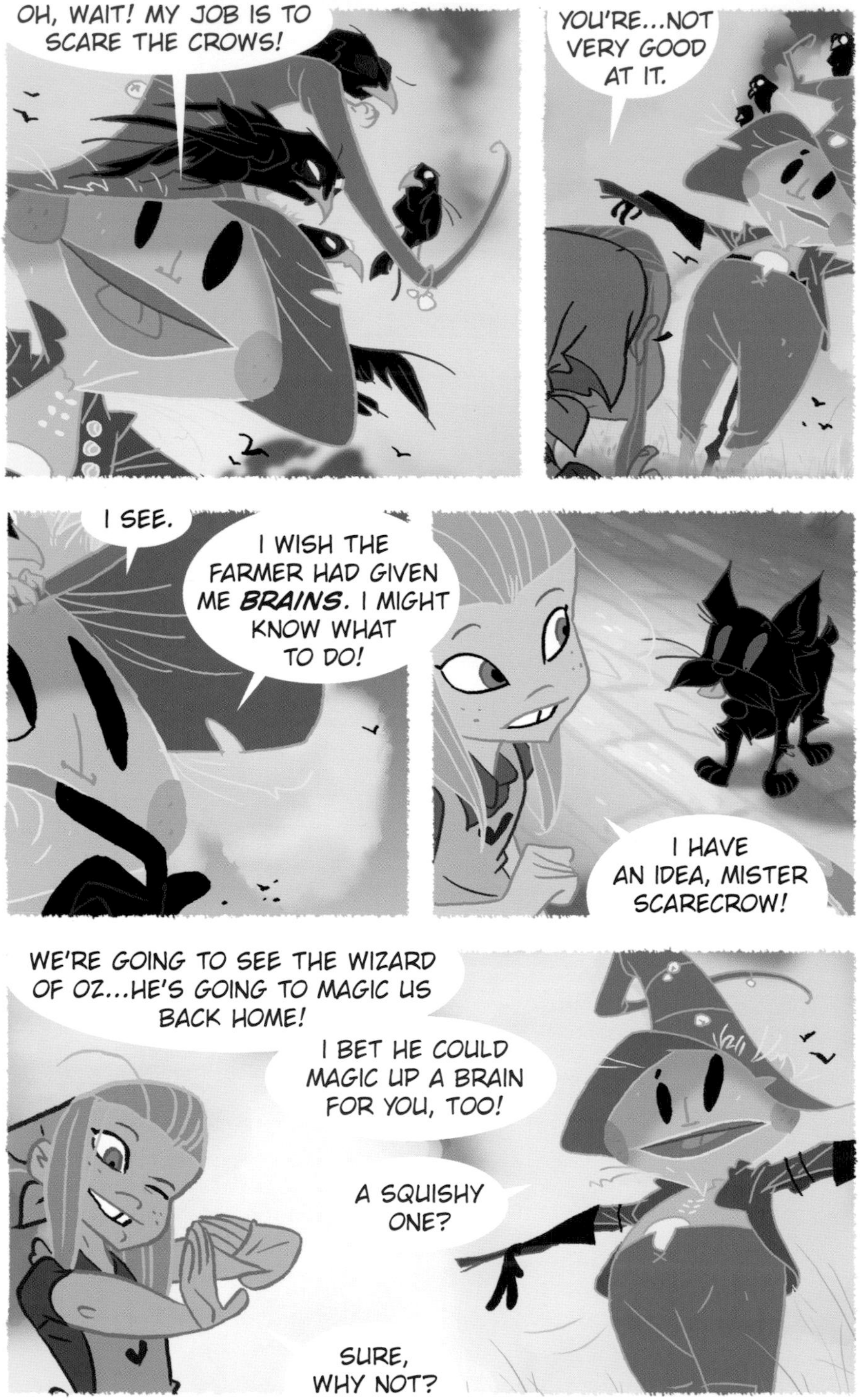
OH, WAIT! MY JOB IS TO SCARE THE CROWS!
YOU'RE...NOT VERY GOOD AT IT.
I SEE.
I WISH THE FARMER HAD GIVEN ME *BRAINS*. I MIGHT KNOW WHAT TO DO!
I HAVE AN IDEA, MISTER SCARECROW!
WE'RE GOING TO SEE THE WIZARD OF OZ...HE'S GOING TO MAGIC US BACK HOME!
I BET HE COULD MAGIC UP A BRAIN FOR YOU, TOO!
A SQUISHY ONE?
SURE, WHY NOT?

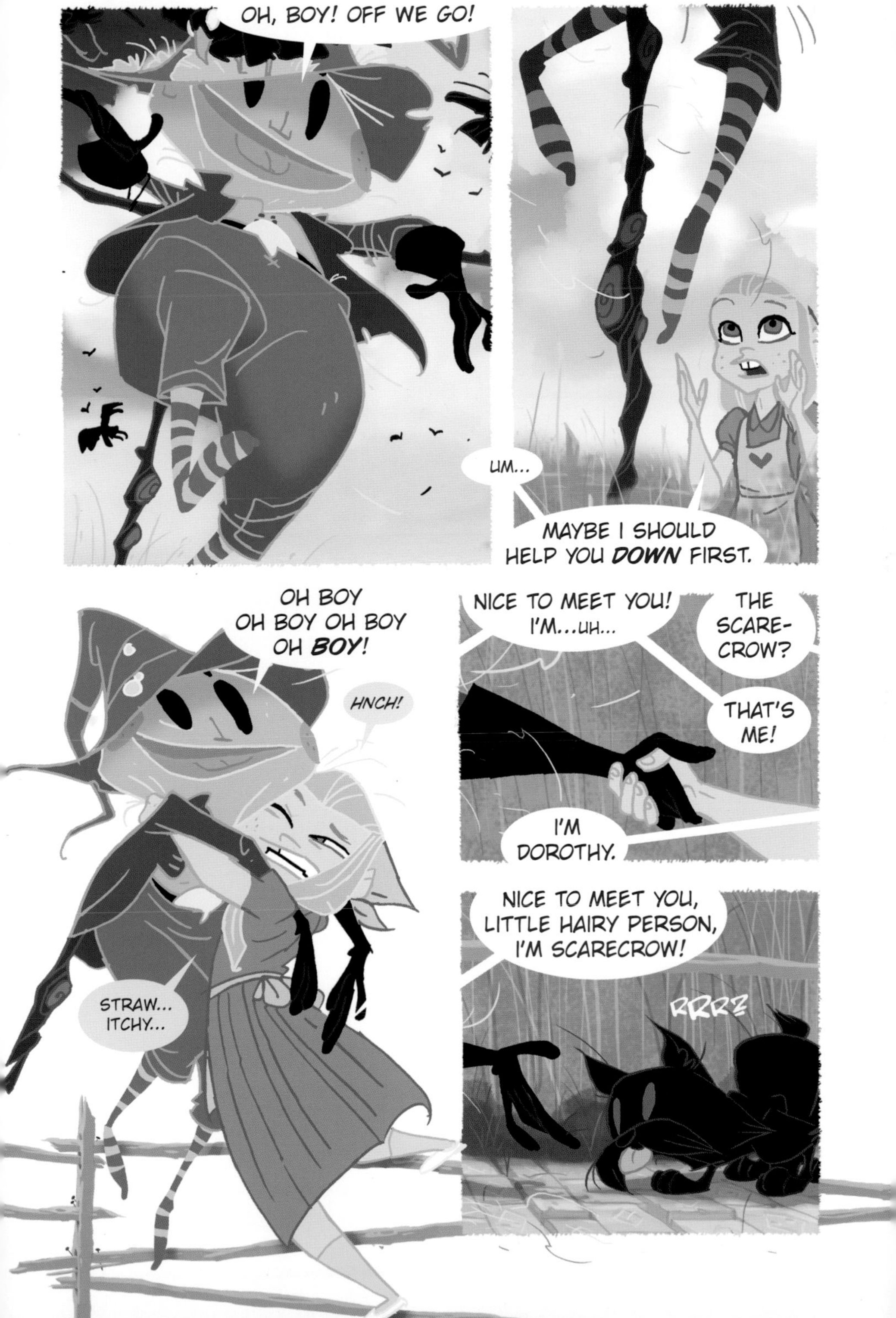
OH, BOY! OFF WE GO!
UM...
MAYBE I SHOULD HELP YOU **DOWN** FIRST.
OH BOY OH BOY OH BOY OH **BOY**!
HNCH!
STRAW... ITCHY...
NICE TO MEET YOU! I'M...UH...
THE SCARE-CROW?
THAT'S ME!
I'M DOROTHY.
NICE TO MEET YOU, LITTLE HAIRY PERSON, I'M SCARECROW!
RRRZ

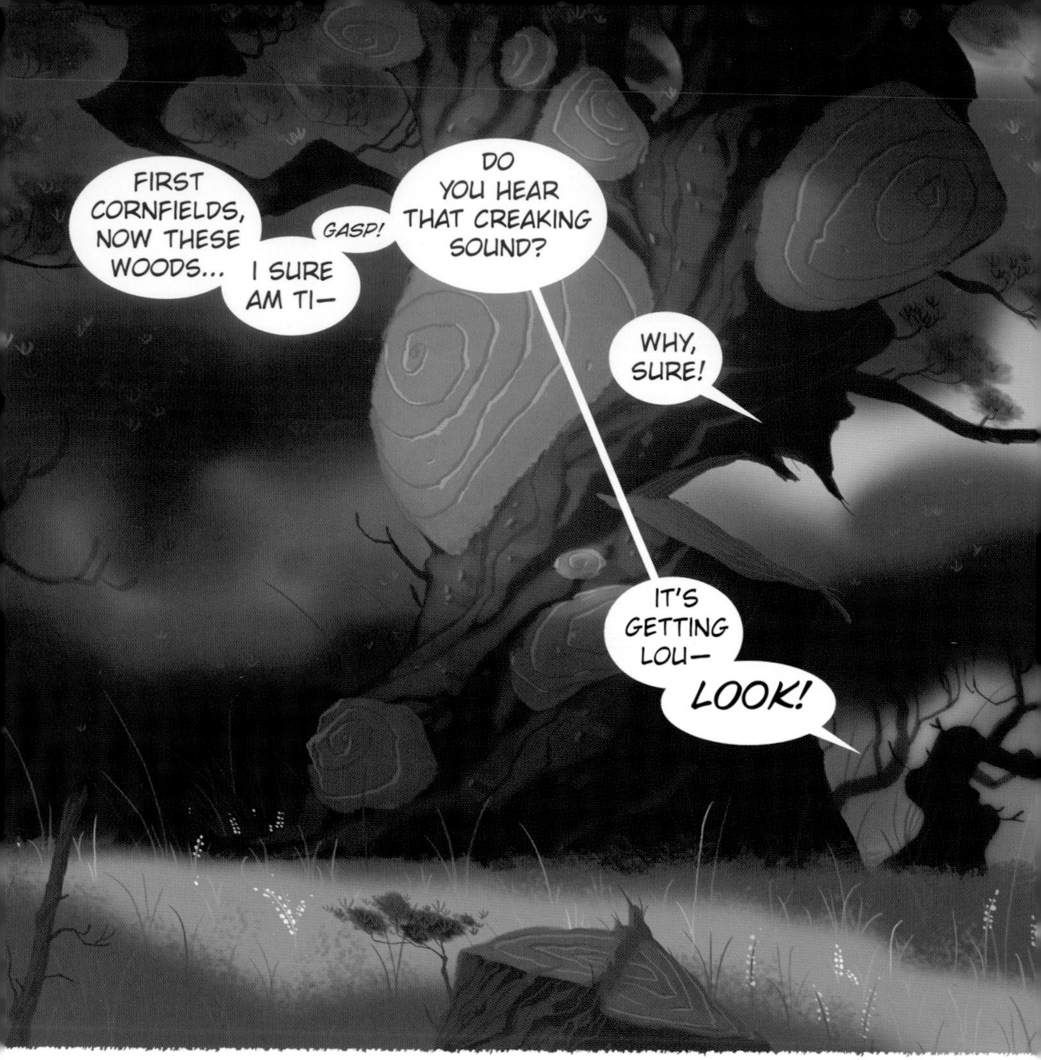
FIRST CORNFIELDS, NOW THESE WOODS...
I SURE AM TI—
GASP!
DO YOU HEAR THAT CREAKING SOUND?
WHY, SURE!
IT'S GETTING LOU—
LOOK!

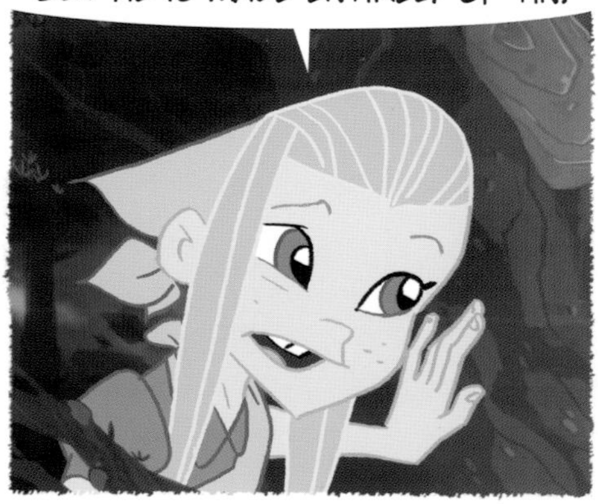
SAY! IT LOOKS LIKE A WOODSMAN... BUT HE IS MADE ENTIRELY OF TIN!

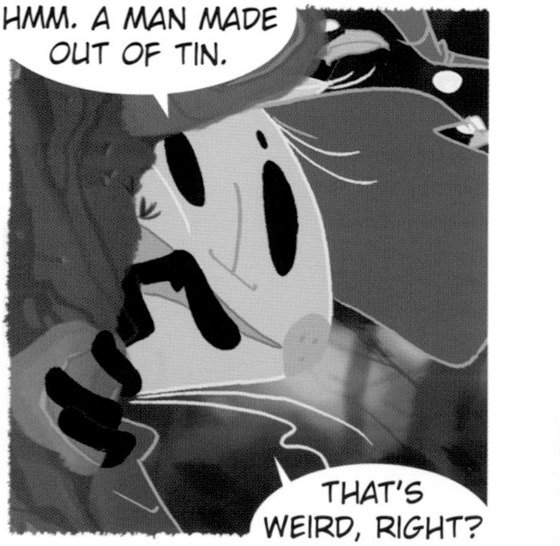
HMM. A MAN MADE OUT OF TIN.
THAT'S WEIRD, RIGHT?

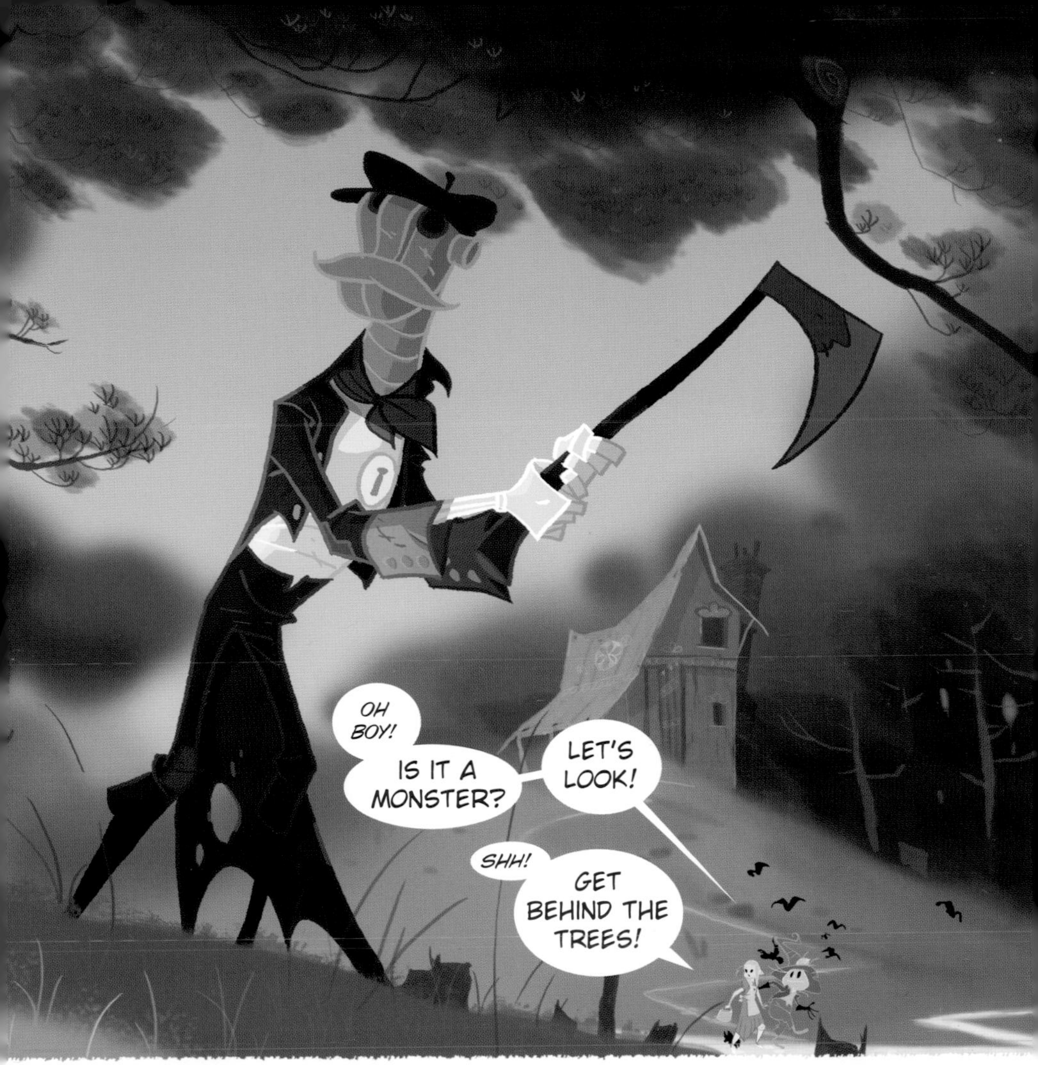
OH BOY!
IS IT A MONSTER?
LET'S LOOK!
SHH!
GET BEHIND THE TREES!

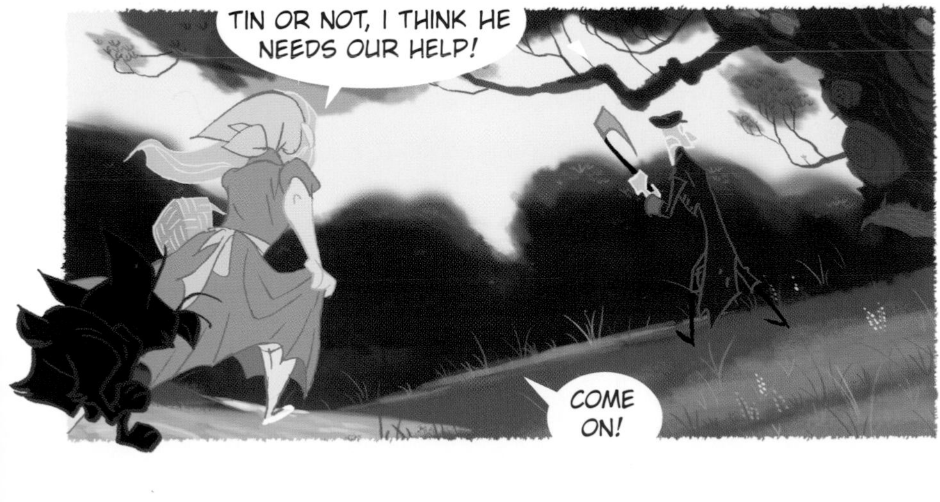
TIN OR NOT, I THINK HE NEEDS OUR HELP!
COME ON!

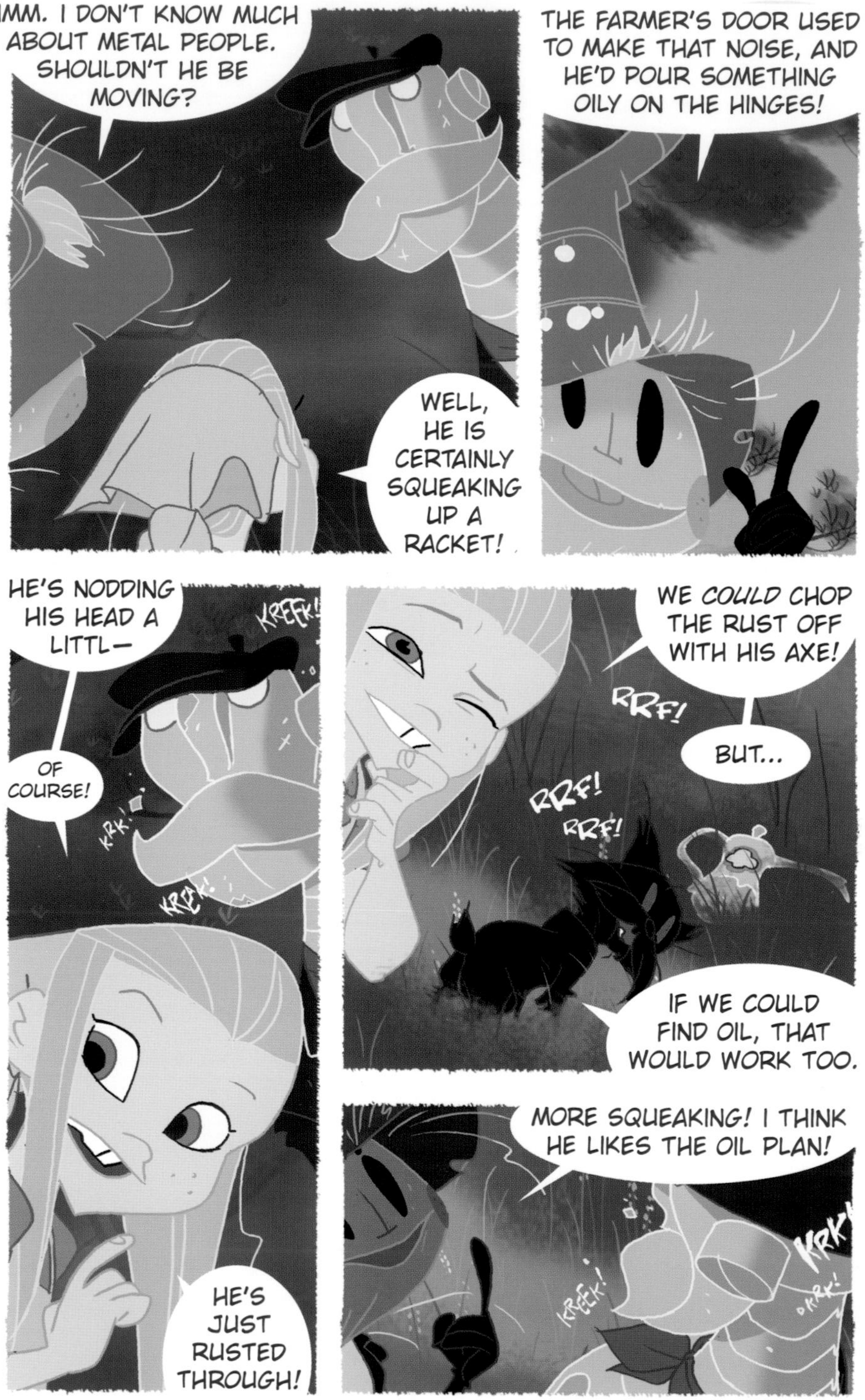
HMM. I DON'T KNOW MUCH ABOUT METAL PEOPLE. SHOULDN'T HE BE MOVING?
WELL, HE IS CERTAINLY SQUEAKING UP A RACKET!
THE FARMER'S DOOR USED TO MAKE THAT NOISE, AND HE'D POUR SOMETHING OILY ON THE HINGES!
HE'S NODDING HIS HEAD A LITTL—
KREEK!
OF COURSE!
KRK!
KREEK!
HE'S JUST RUSTED THROUGH!
WE COULD CHOP THE RUST OFF WITH HIS AXE!
RRF!
BUT...
RRF!
RRF!
IF WE COULD FIND OIL, THAT WOULD WORK TOO.
MORE SQUEAKING! I THINK HE LIKES THE OIL PLAN!
KREEK!
KRK!

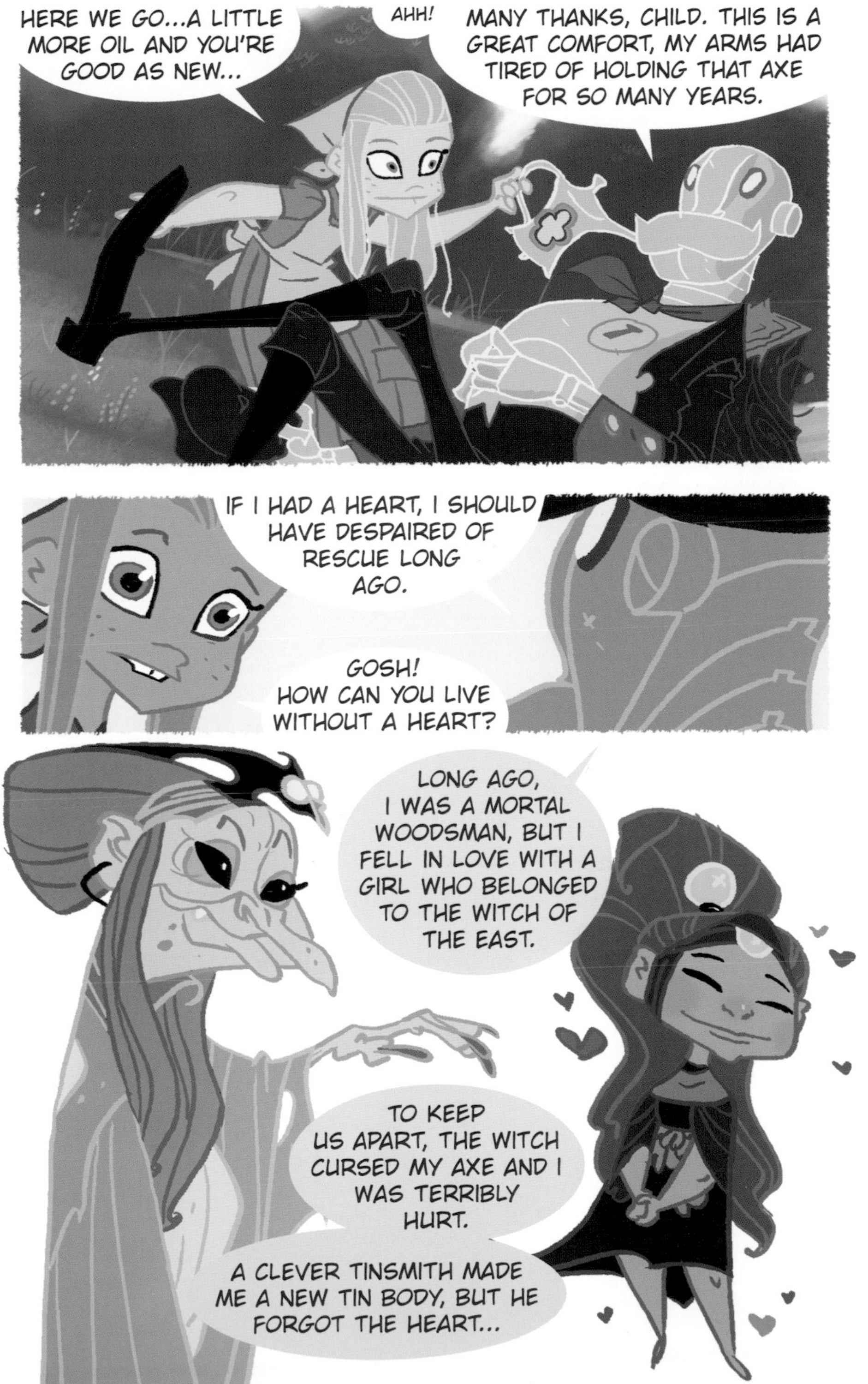
HERE WE GO...A LITTLE MORE OIL AND YOU'RE GOOD AS NEW...
AHH!
MANY THANKS, CHILD. THIS IS A GREAT COMFORT, MY ARMS HAD TIRED OF HOLDING THAT AXE FOR SO MANY YEARS.
IF I HAD A HEART, I SHOULD HAVE DESPAIRED OF RESCUE LONG AGO.
GOSH! HOW CAN YOU LIVE WITHOUT A HEART?
LONG AGO, I WAS A MORTAL WOODSMAN, BUT I FELL IN LOVE WITH A GIRL WHO BELONGED TO THE WITCH OF THE EAST.
TO KEEP US APART, THE WITCH CURSED MY AXE AND I WAS TERRIBLY HURT.
A CLEVER TINSMITH MADE ME A NEW TIN BODY, BUT HE FORGOT THE HEART...

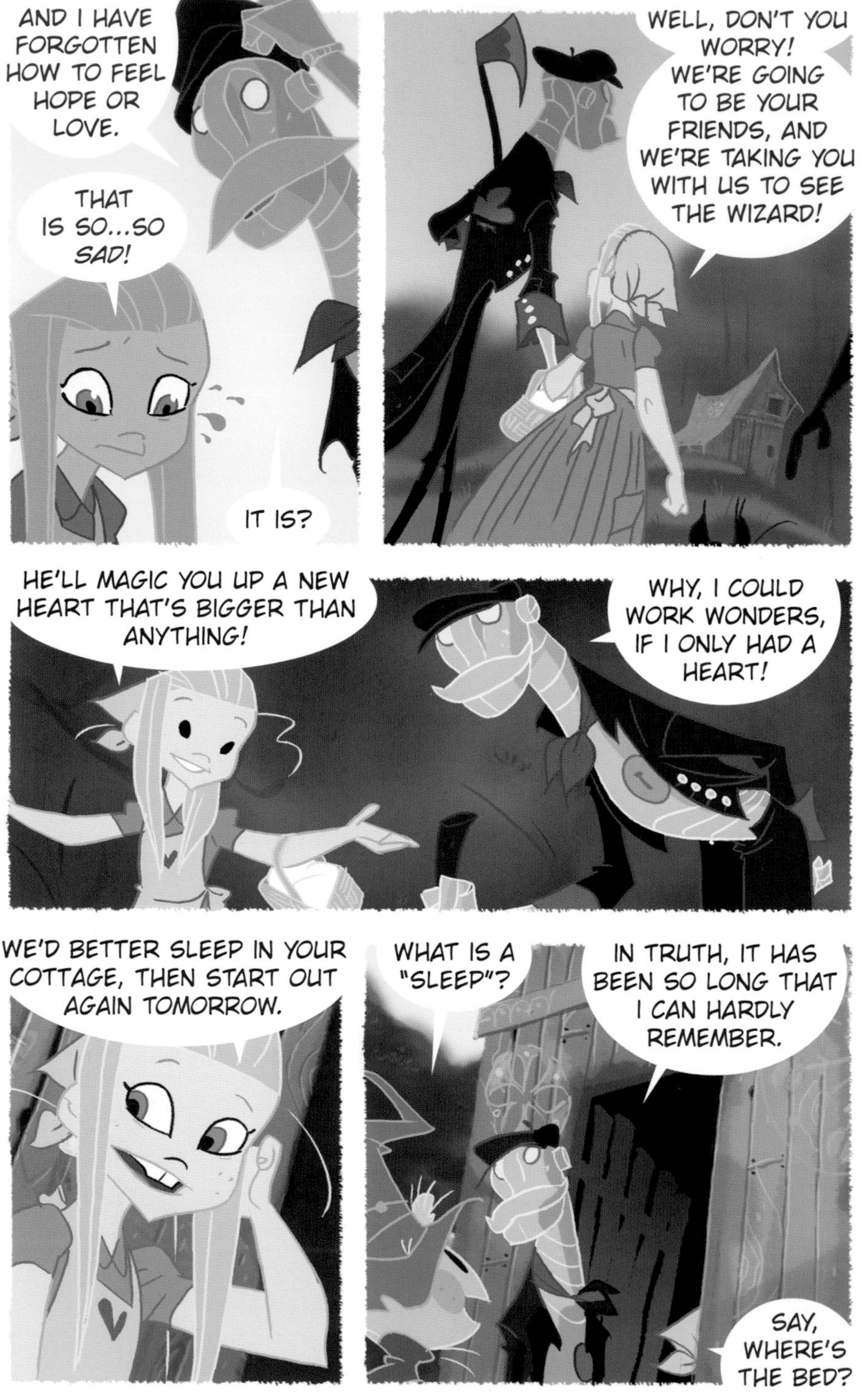
AND I HAVE FORGOTTEN HOW TO FEEL HOPE OR LOVE.
THAT IS SO...SO SAD!
IT IS?
WELL, DON'T YOU WORRY! WE'RE GOING TO BE YOUR FRIENDS, AND WE'RE TAKING YOU WITH US TO SEE THE WIZARD!
HE'LL MAGIC YOU UP A NEW HEART THAT'S BIGGER THAN ANYTHING!
WHY, I COULD WORK WONDERS, IF I ONLY HAD A HEART!
WE'D BETTER SLEEP IN YOUR COTTAGE, THEN START OUT AGAIN TOMORROW.
WHAT IS A "SLEEP"?
IN TRUTH, IT HAS BEEN SO LONG THAT I CAN HARDLY REMEMBER.
SAY, WHERE'S THE BED?

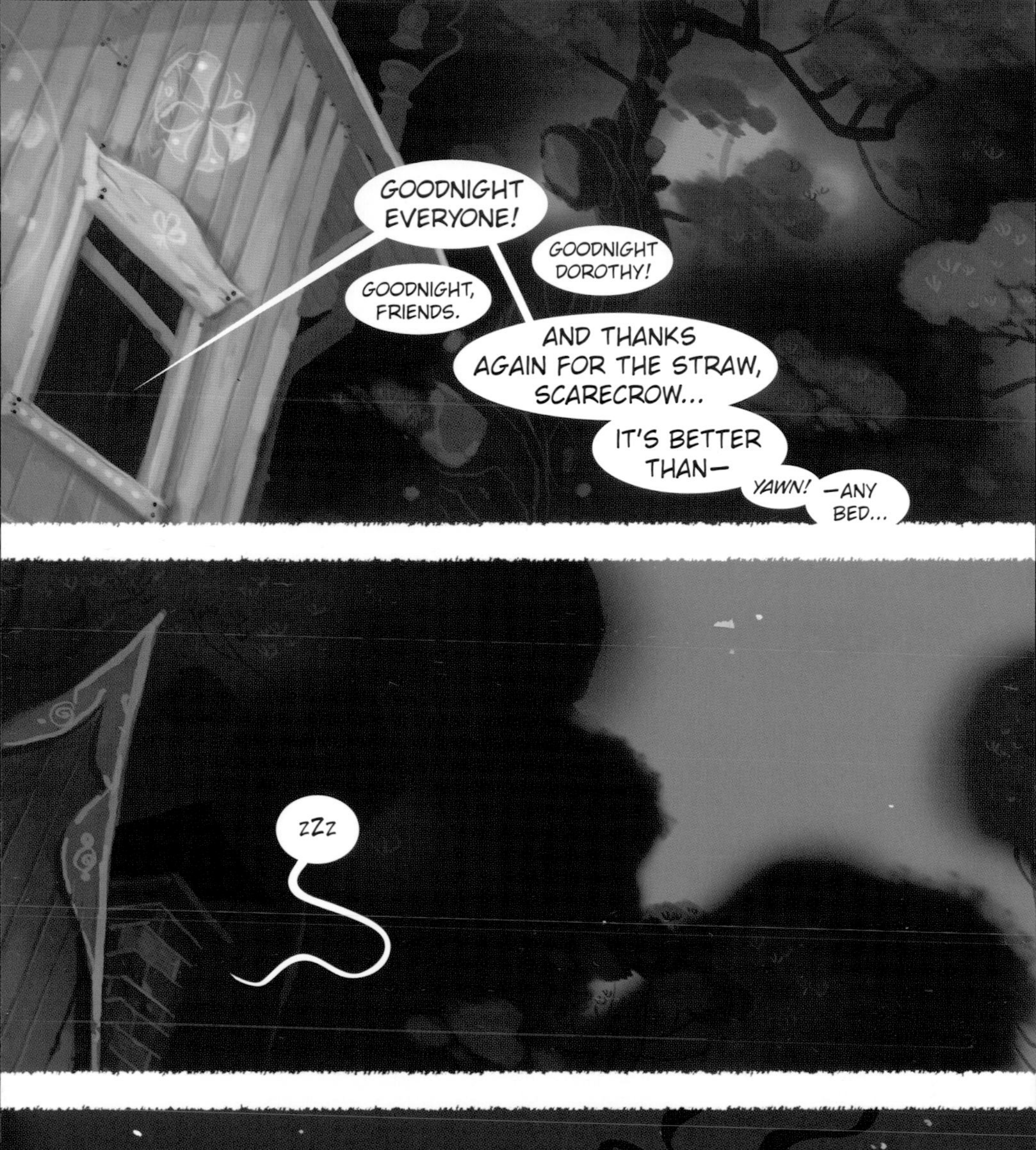
GOODNIGHT EVERYONE!
GOODNIGHT DOROTHY!
GOODNIGHT, FRIENDS.
AND THANKS AGAIN FOR THE STRAW, SCARECROW...
IT'S BETTER THAN—
YAWN!
—ANY BED...
zZz

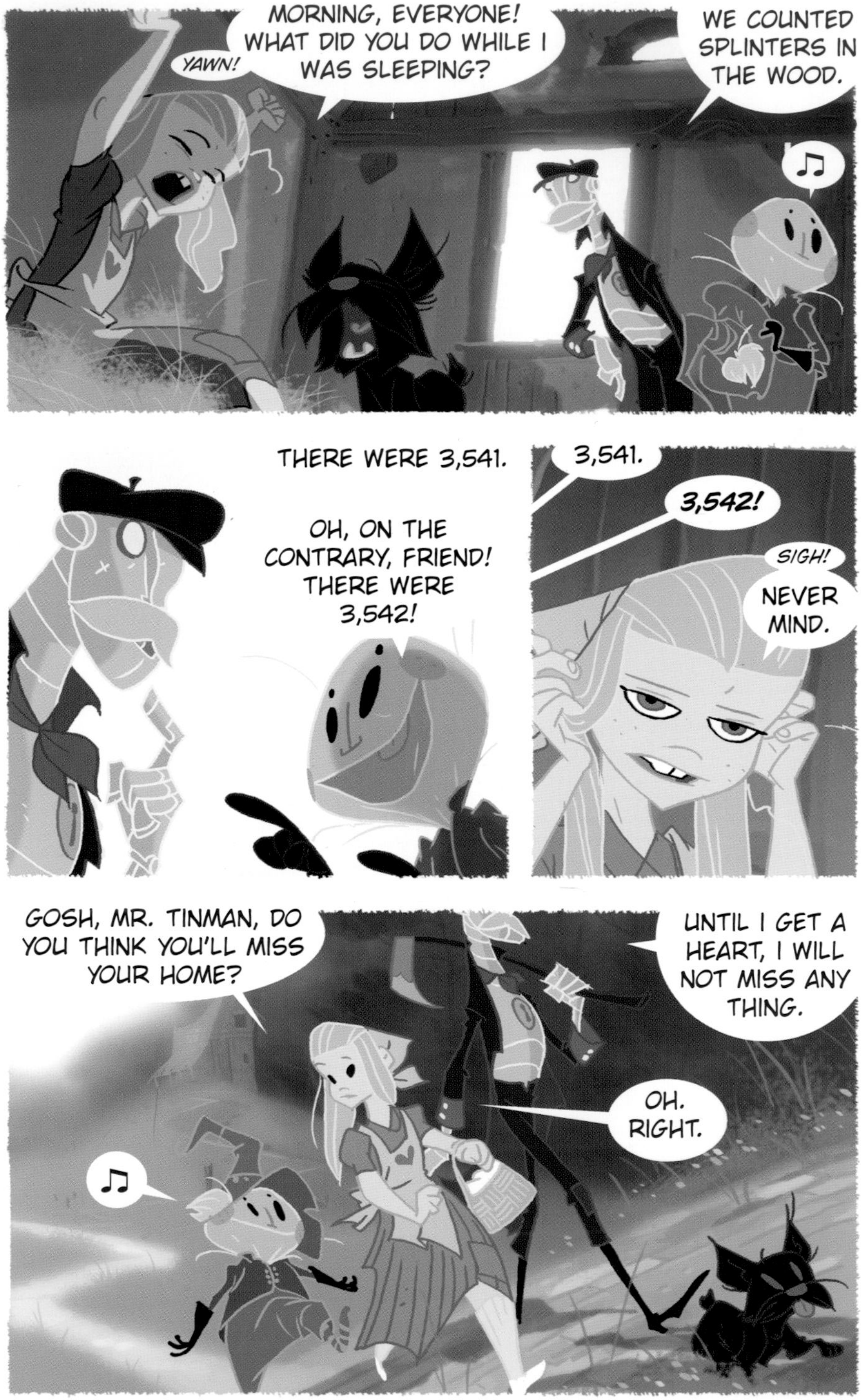
YAWN!
MORNING, EVERYONE! WHAT DID YOU DO WHILE I WAS SLEEPING?
WE COUNTED SPLINTERS IN THE WOOD.
♫
THERE WERE 3,541.
OH, ON THE CONTRARY, FRIEND! THERE WERE 3,542!
3,541.
3,542!
SIGH!
NEVER MIND.
GOSH, MR. TINMAN, DO YOU THINK YOU'LL MISS YOUR HOME?
UNTIL I GET A HEART, I WILL NOT MISS ANY THING.
OH. RIGHT.
♫

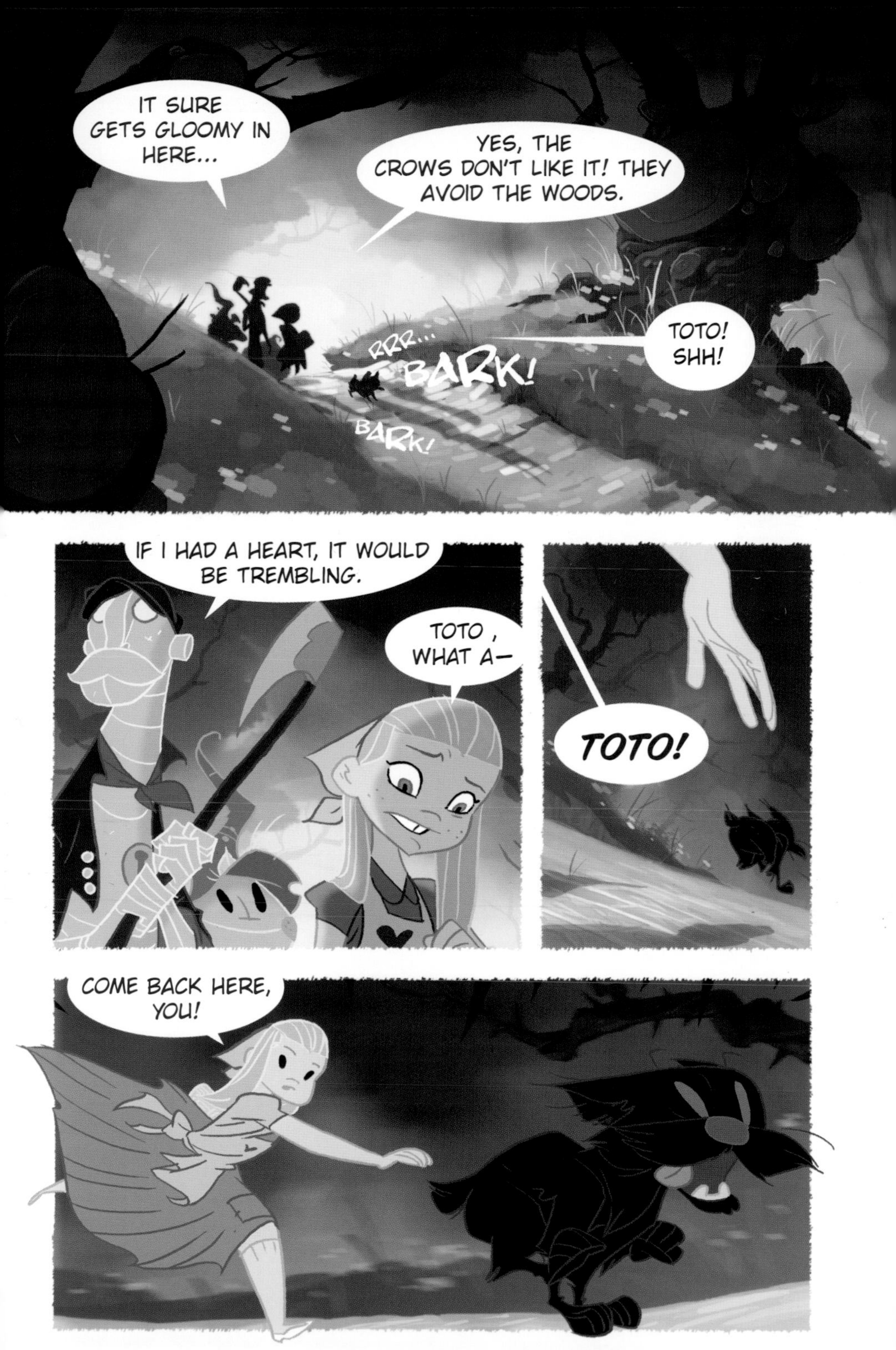
IT SURE GETS GLOOMY IN HERE...
YES, THE CROWS DON'T LIKE IT! THEY AVOID THE WOODS.
RRR...
BARK!
BARK!
TOTO! SHH!
IF I HAD A HEART, IT WOULD BE TREMBLING.
TOTO, WHAT A—
TOTO!
COME BACK HERE, YOU!

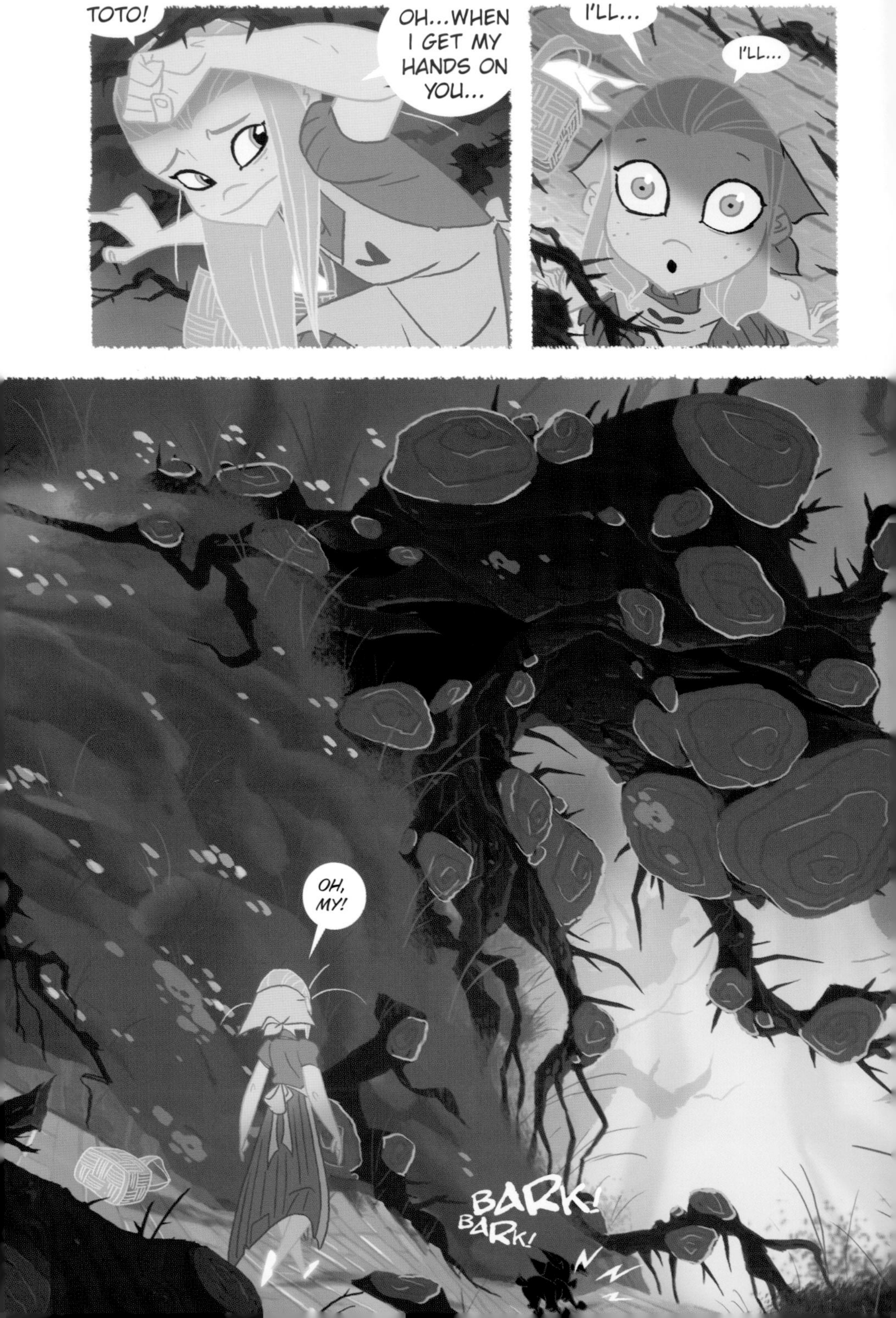
TOTO!
OH...WHEN I GET MY HANDS ON YOU...
I'LL...
I'LL...
OH, MY!
BARK!
BARK!

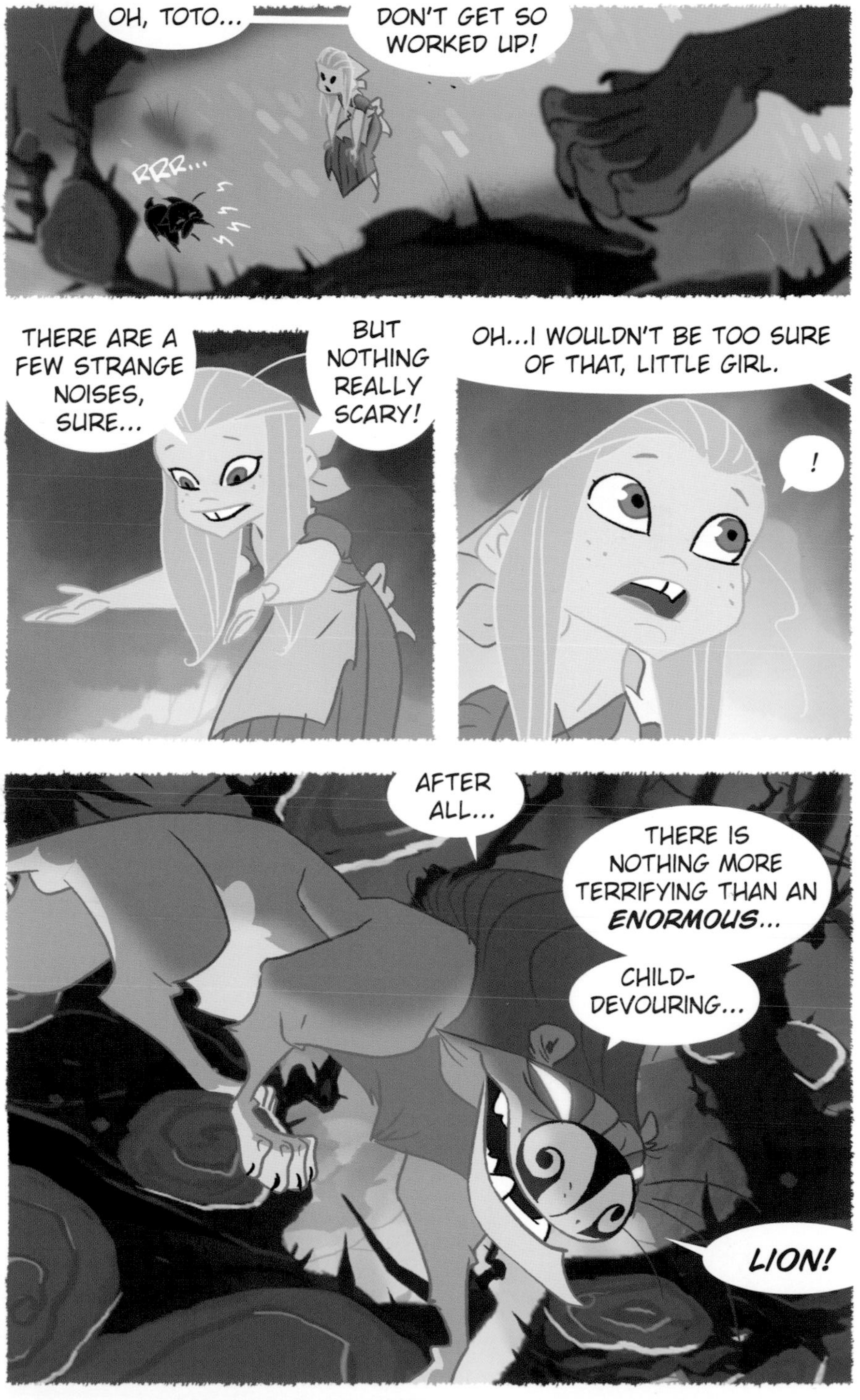
OH, TOTO...
DON'T GET SO WORKED UP!
RRR...
THERE ARE A FEW STRANGE NOISES, SURE...
BUT NOTHING REALLY SCARY!
OH...I WOULDN'T BE TOO SURE OF THAT, LITTLE GIRL.
!
AFTER ALL...
THERE IS NOTHING MORE TERRIFYING THAN AN ENORMOUS...
CHILD-DEVOURING...
LION!

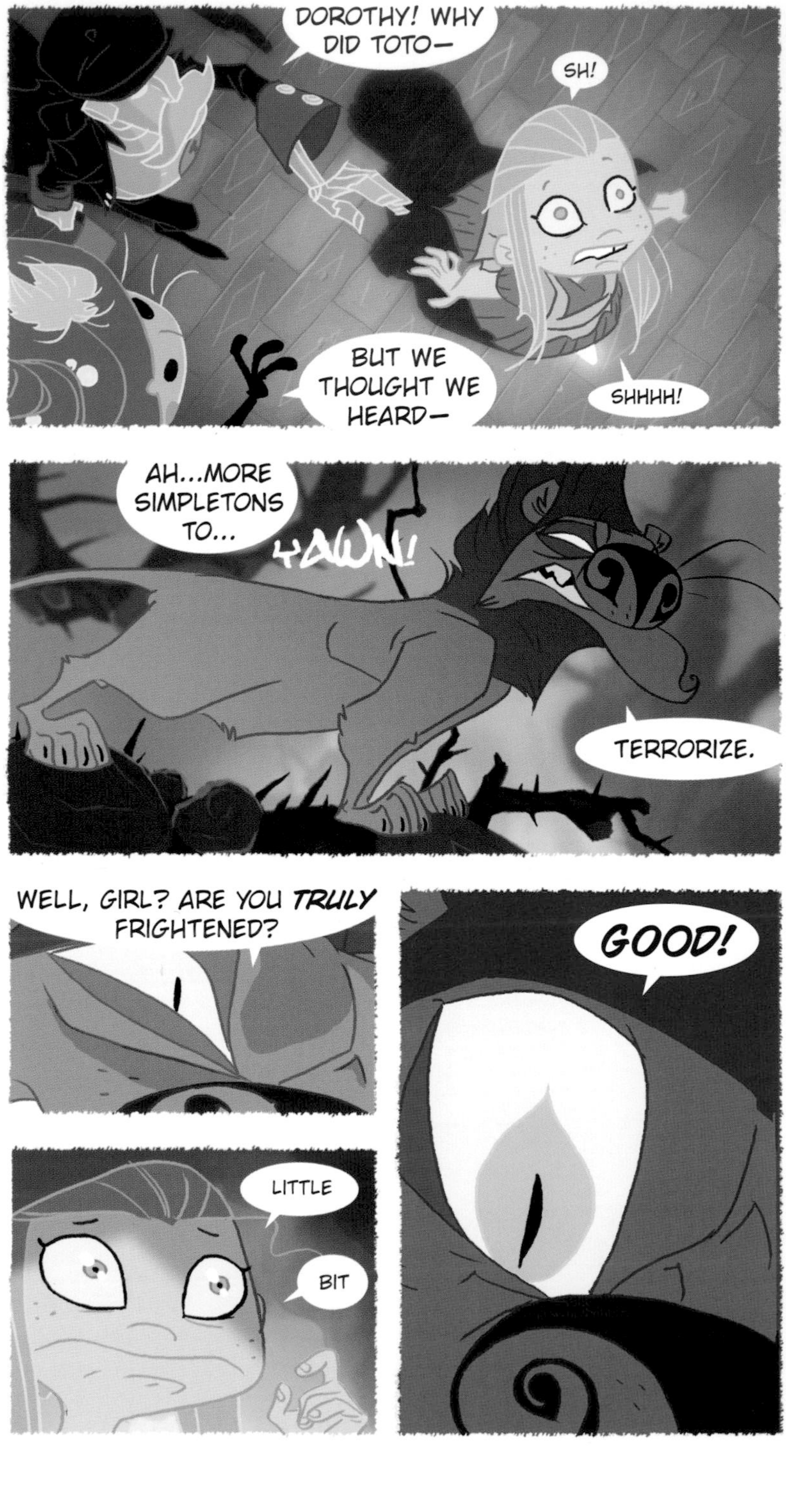
DOROTHY! WHY DID TOTO—
SH!
BUT WE THOUGHT WE HEARD—
SHHHH!
AH...MORE SIMPLETONS TO...
YAWN!
TERRORIZE.
WELL, GIRL? ARE YOU *TRULY* FRIGHTENED?
GOOD!
LITTLE
BIT

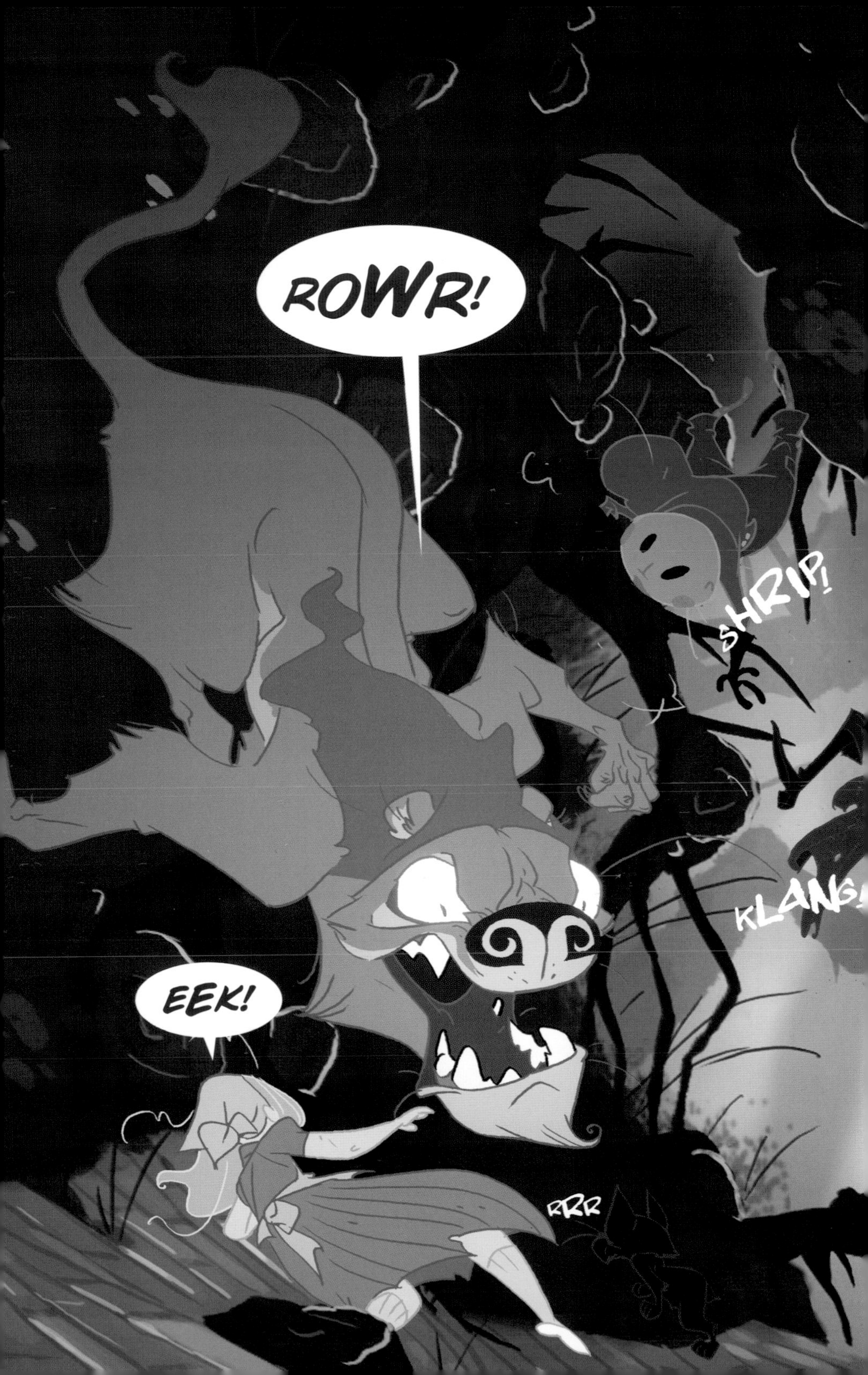
ROWR!
SHRIP!
KLANG!
EEK!
RRR

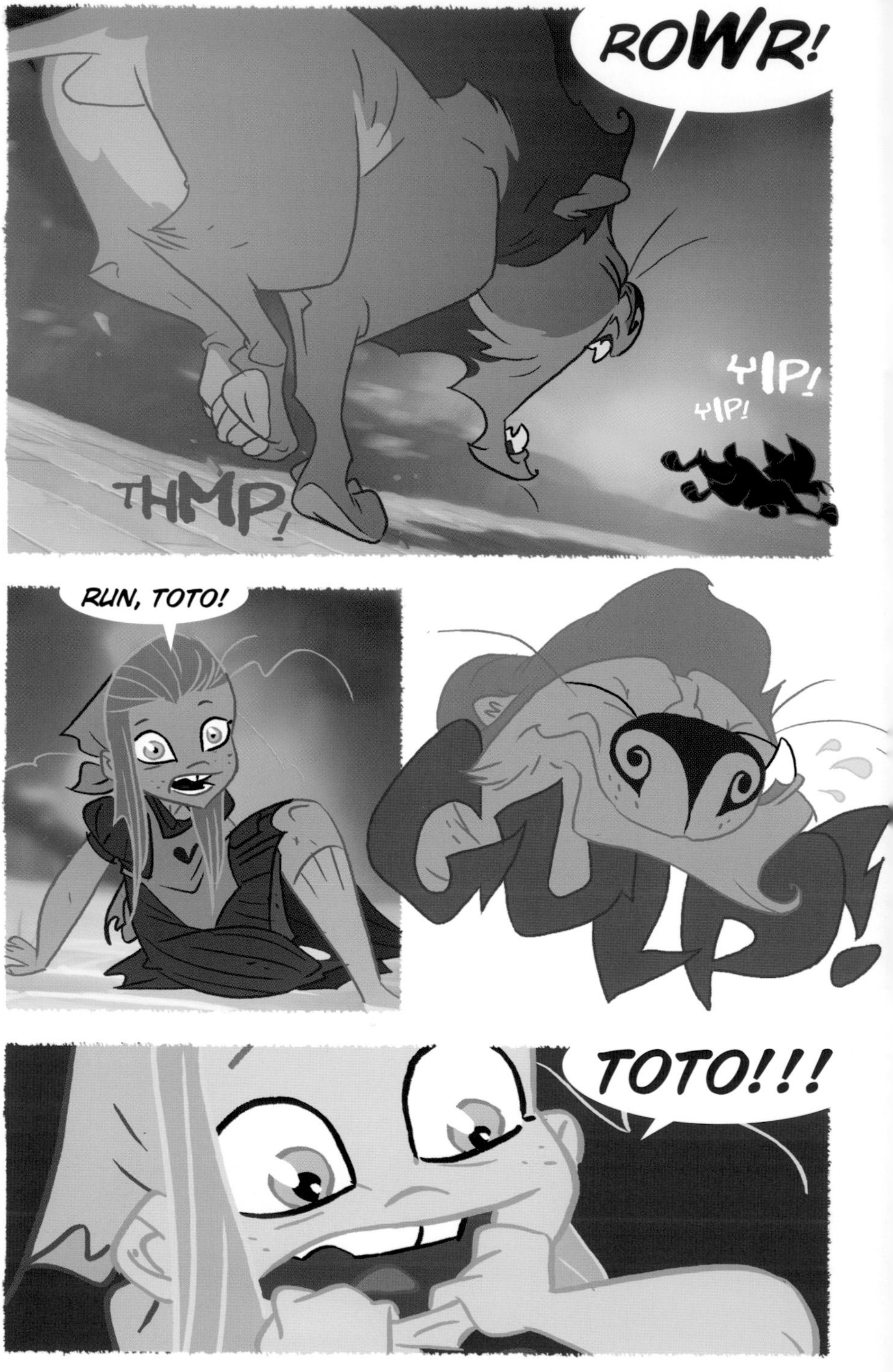
ROWR!
YIP!
YIP!
THMP!
RUN, TOTO!
GULP!
TOTO!!!

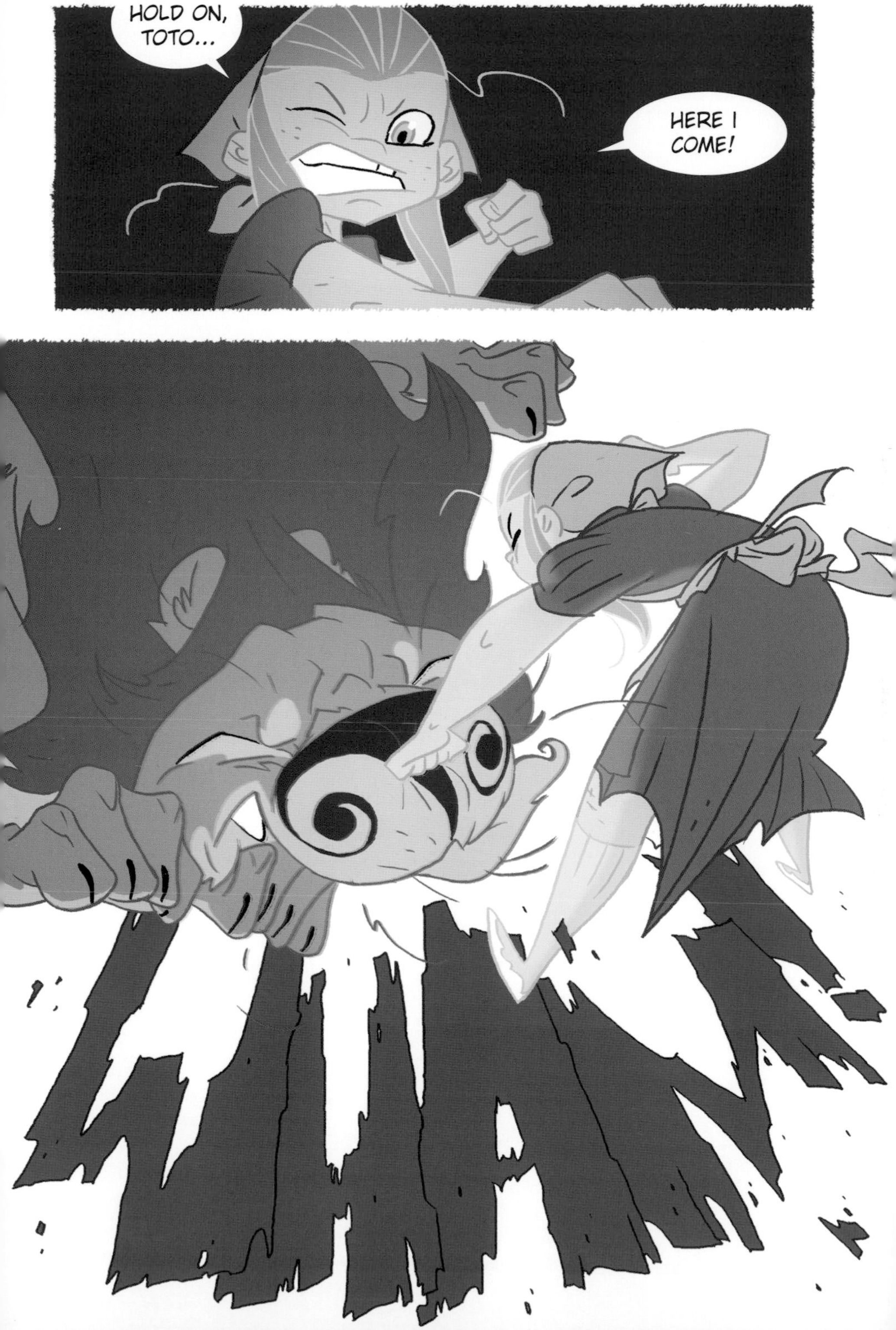

HOLD ON, TOTO...
HERE I COME!
WHAM

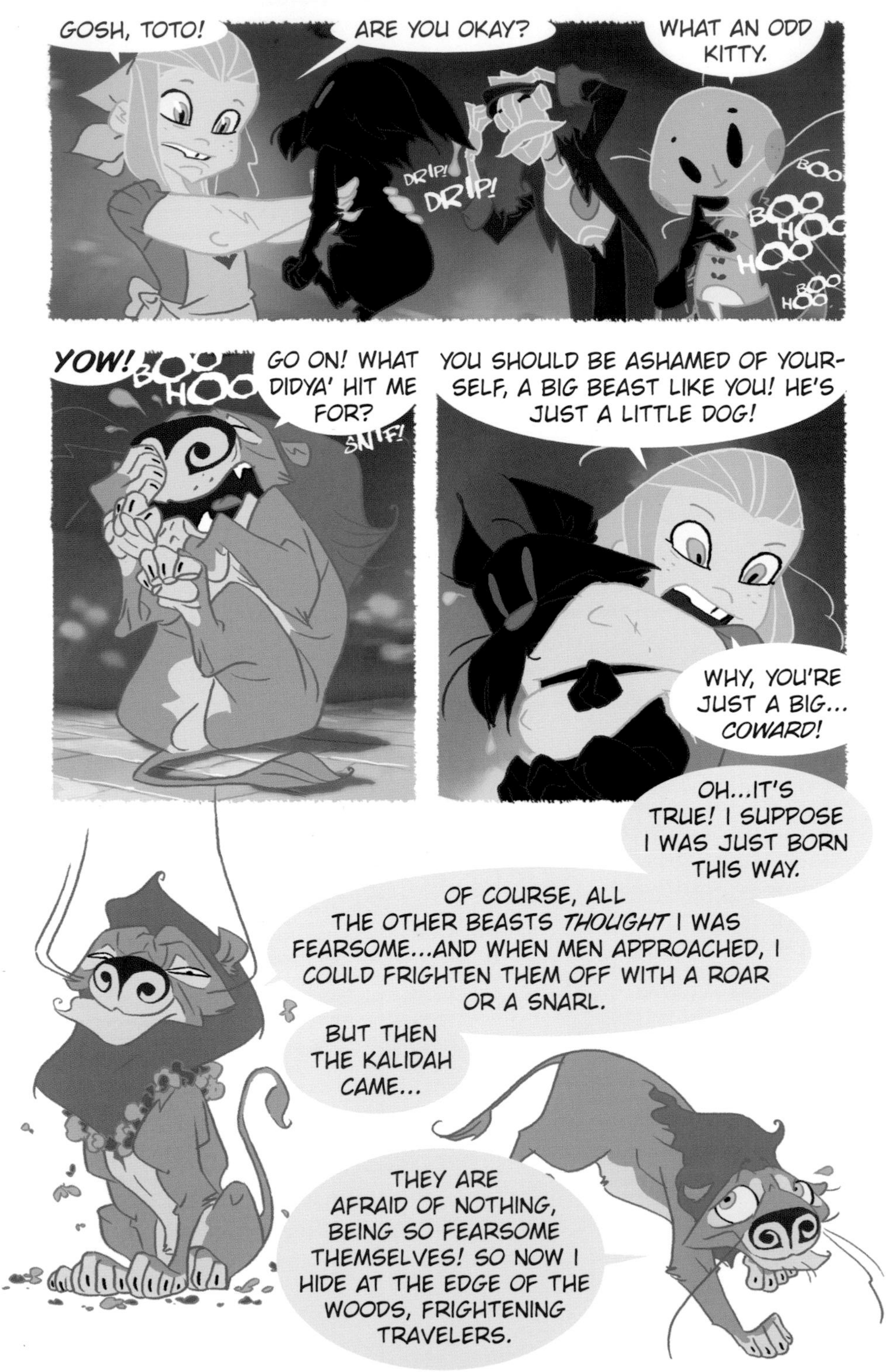

GOSH, TOTO!
ARE YOU OKAY?
DRIP! DRIP!
WHAT AN ODD KITTY.
BOO HOO HOO BOO HOO
YOW! BOO HOO
GO ON! WHAT DIDYA' HIT ME FOR?
SNIF!
YOU SHOULD BE ASHAMED OF YOURSELF, A BIG BEAST LIKE YOU! HE'S JUST A LITTLE DOG!
WHY, YOU'RE JUST A BIG... *COWARD!*
OH...IT'S TRUE! I SUPPOSE I WAS JUST BORN THIS WAY.
OF COURSE, ALL THE OTHER BEASTS *THOUGHT* I WAS FEARSOME...AND WHEN MEN APPROACHED, I COULD FRIGHTEN THEM OFF WITH A ROAR OR A SNARL.
BUT THEN THE KALIDAH CAME...
THEY ARE AFRAID OF NOTHING, BEING SO FEARSOME THEMSELVES! SO NOW I HIDE AT THE EDGE OF THE WOODS, FRIGHTENING TRAVELERS.

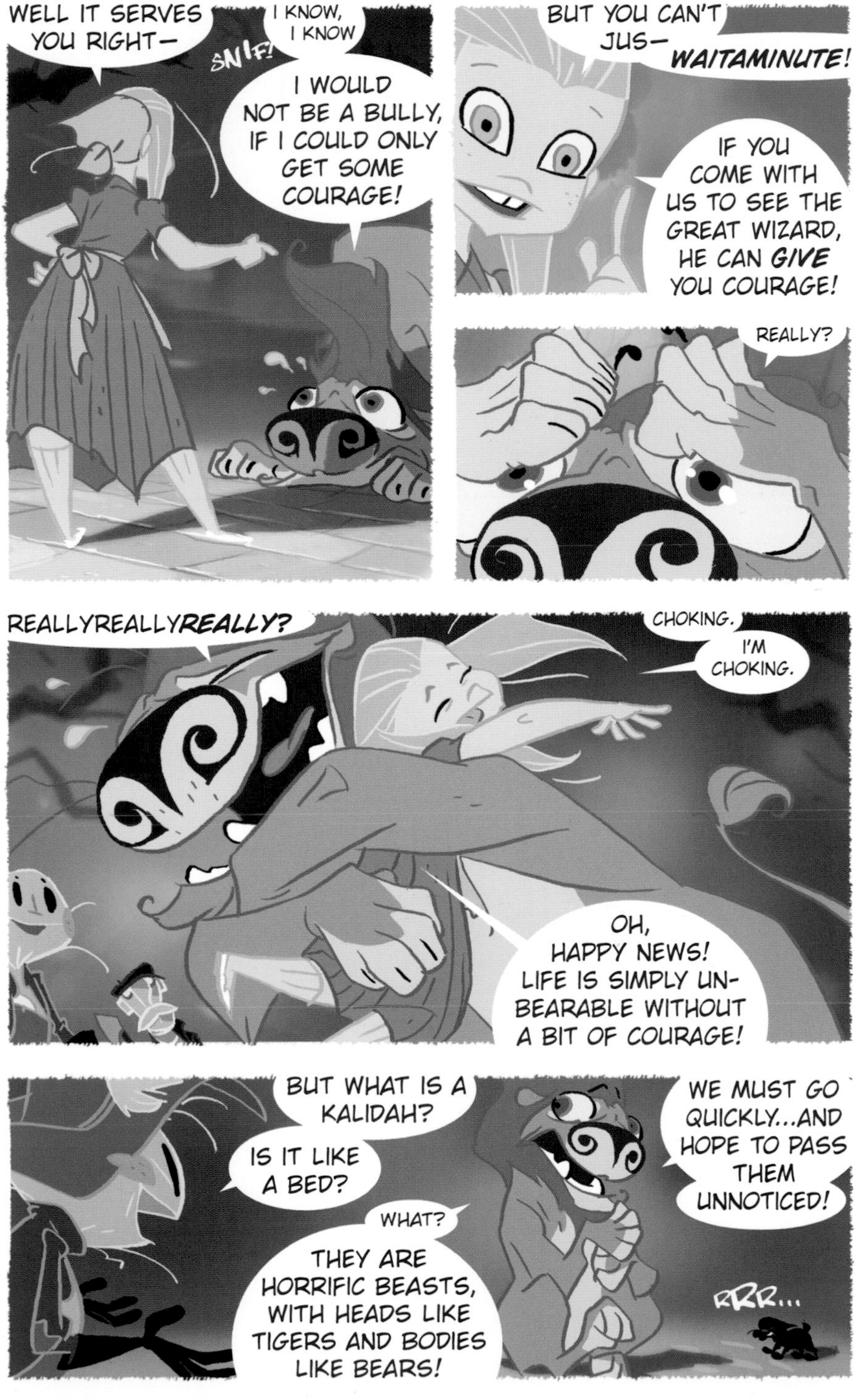
WELL IT SERVES YOU RIGHT—
SNIF!
I KNOW, I KNOW
I WOULD NOT BE A BULLY, IF I COULD ONLY GET SOME COURAGE!
BUT YOU CAN'T JUS—WAITAMINUTE!
IF YOU COME WITH US TO SEE THE GREAT WIZARD, HE CAN GIVE YOU COURAGE!
REALLY?
REALLYREALLYREALLY?
CHOKING.
I'M CHOKING.
OH, HAPPY NEWS! LIFE IS SIMPLY UN-BEARABLE WITHOUT A BIT OF COURAGE!
BUT WHAT IS A KALIDAH?
IS IT LIKE A BED?
WHAT?
THEY ARE HORRIFIC BEASTS, WITH HEADS LIKE TIGERS AND BODIES LIKE BEARS!
WE MUST GO QUICKLY...AND HOPE TO PASS THEM UNNOTICED!
RRR...

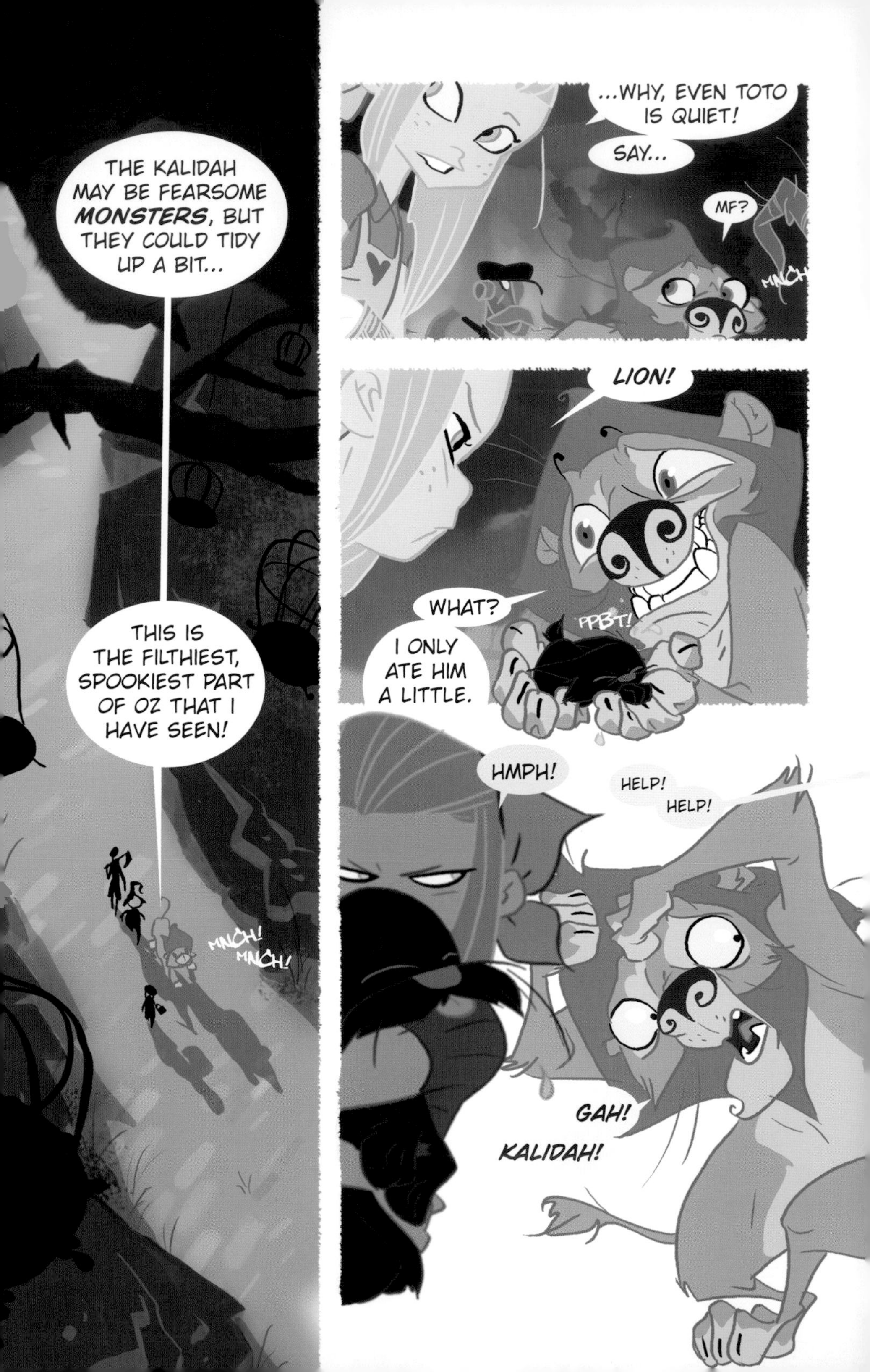
THE KALIDAH MAY BE FEARSOME ***MONSTERS***, BUT THEY COULD TIDY UP A BIT...
THIS IS THE FILTHIEST, SPOOKIEST PART OF OZ THAT I HAVE SEEN!
MNCH! MNCH!
...WHY, EVEN TOTO IS QUIET!
SAY...
MF?
MNCH
LION!
WHAT?
I ONLY ATE HIM A LITTLE.
PPBBT!
HMPH!
HELP!
HELP!
GAH!
KALIDAH!

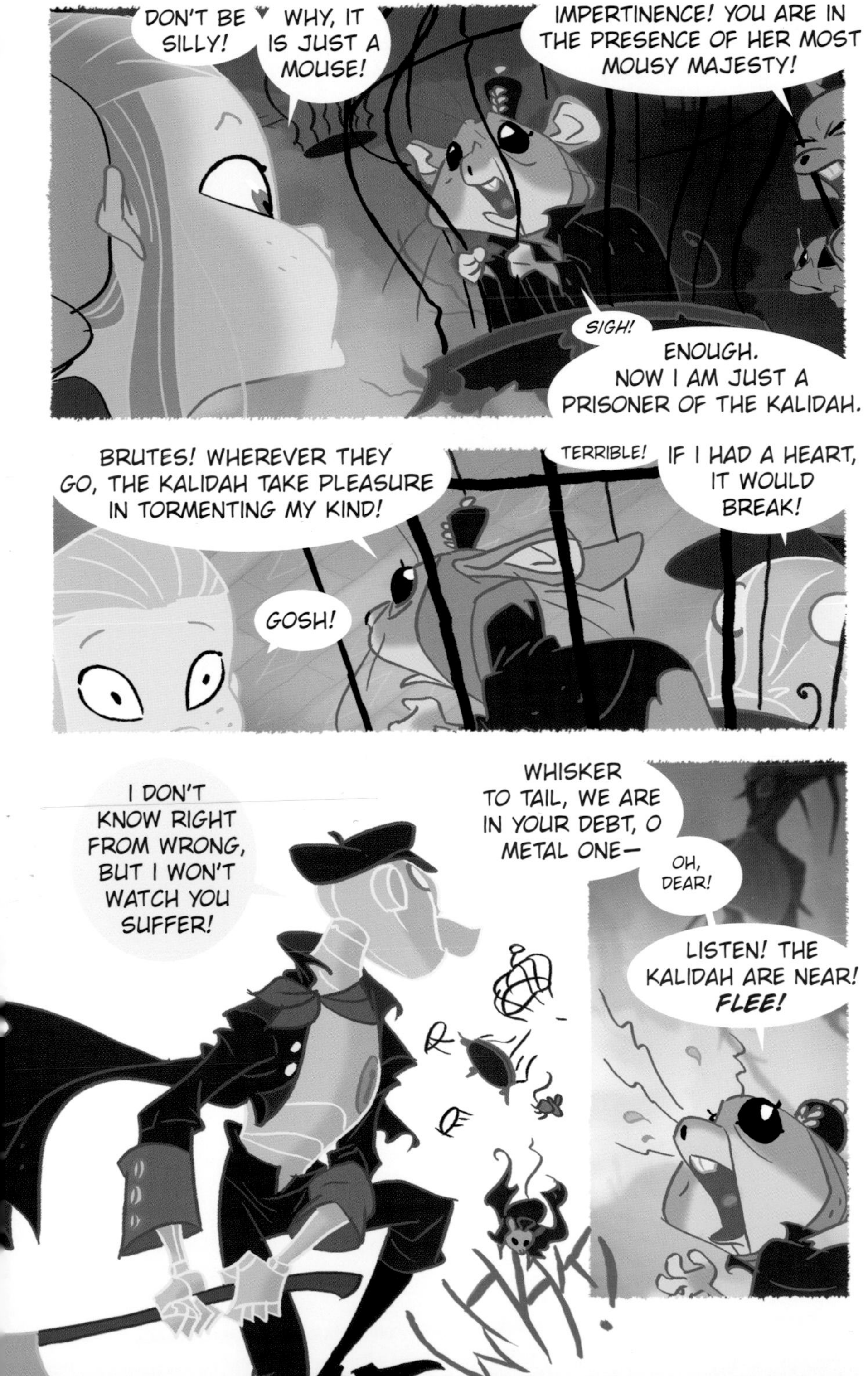
DON'T BE SILLY!
WHY, IT IS JUST A MOUSE!
IMPERTINENCE! YOU ARE IN THE PRESENCE OF HER MOST MOUSY MAJESTY!
SIGH!
ENOUGH. NOW I AM JUST A PRISONER OF THE KALIDAH.
BRUTES! WHEREVER THEY GO, THE KALIDAH TAKE PLEASURE IN TORMENTING MY KIND!
TERRIBLE!
IF I HAD A HEART, IT WOULD BREAK!
GOSH!
I DON'T KNOW RIGHT FROM WRONG, BUT I WON'T WATCH YOU SUFFER!
WHISKER TO TAIL, WE ARE IN YOUR DEBT, O METAL ONE—
OH, DEAR!
LISTEN! THE KALIDAH ARE NEAR! **FLEE!**
WHAK!

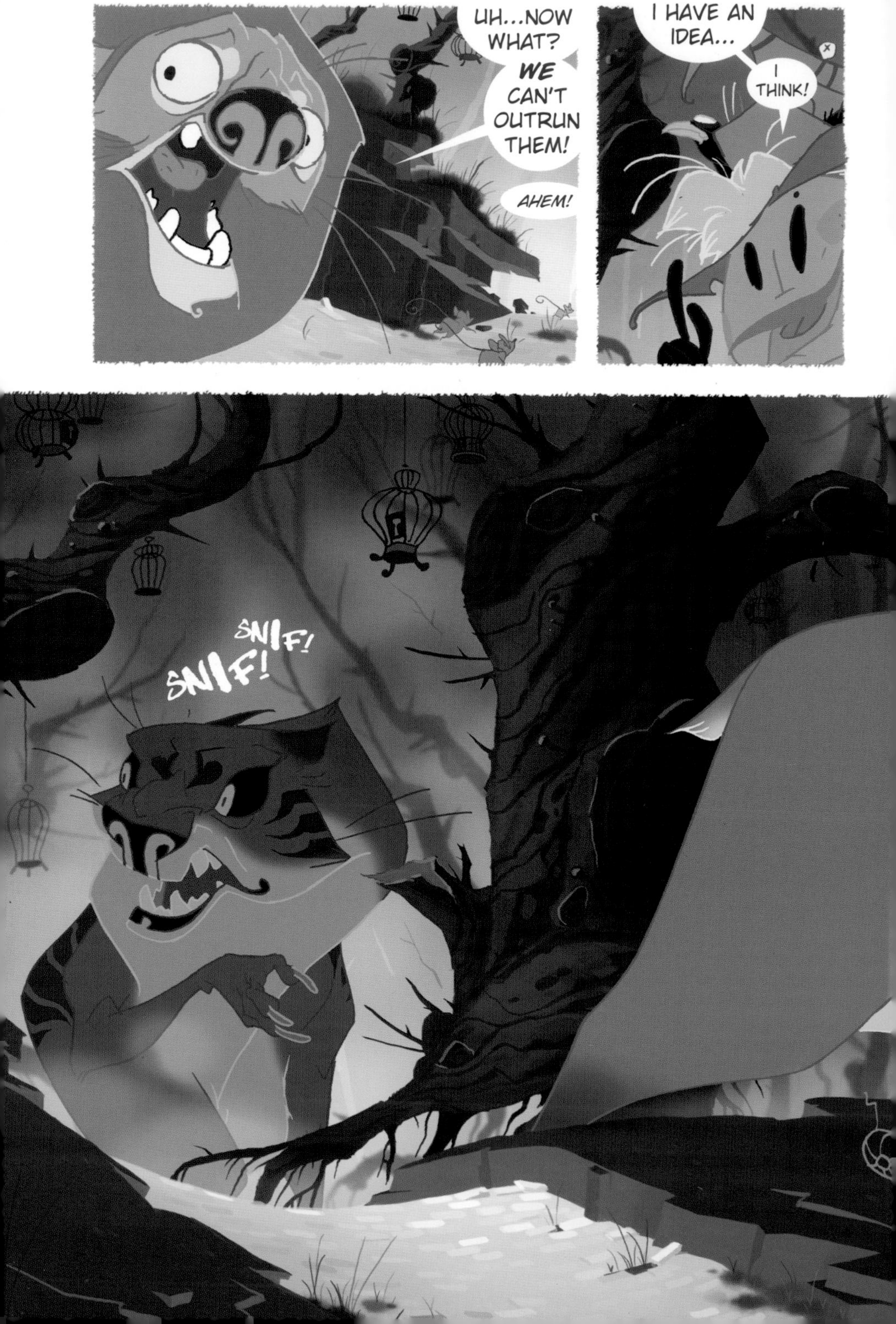
UH...NOW WHAT?
WE CAN'T OUTRUN THEM!
AHEM!
I HAVE AN IDEA...
I THINK!
SNIF!
SNIF!

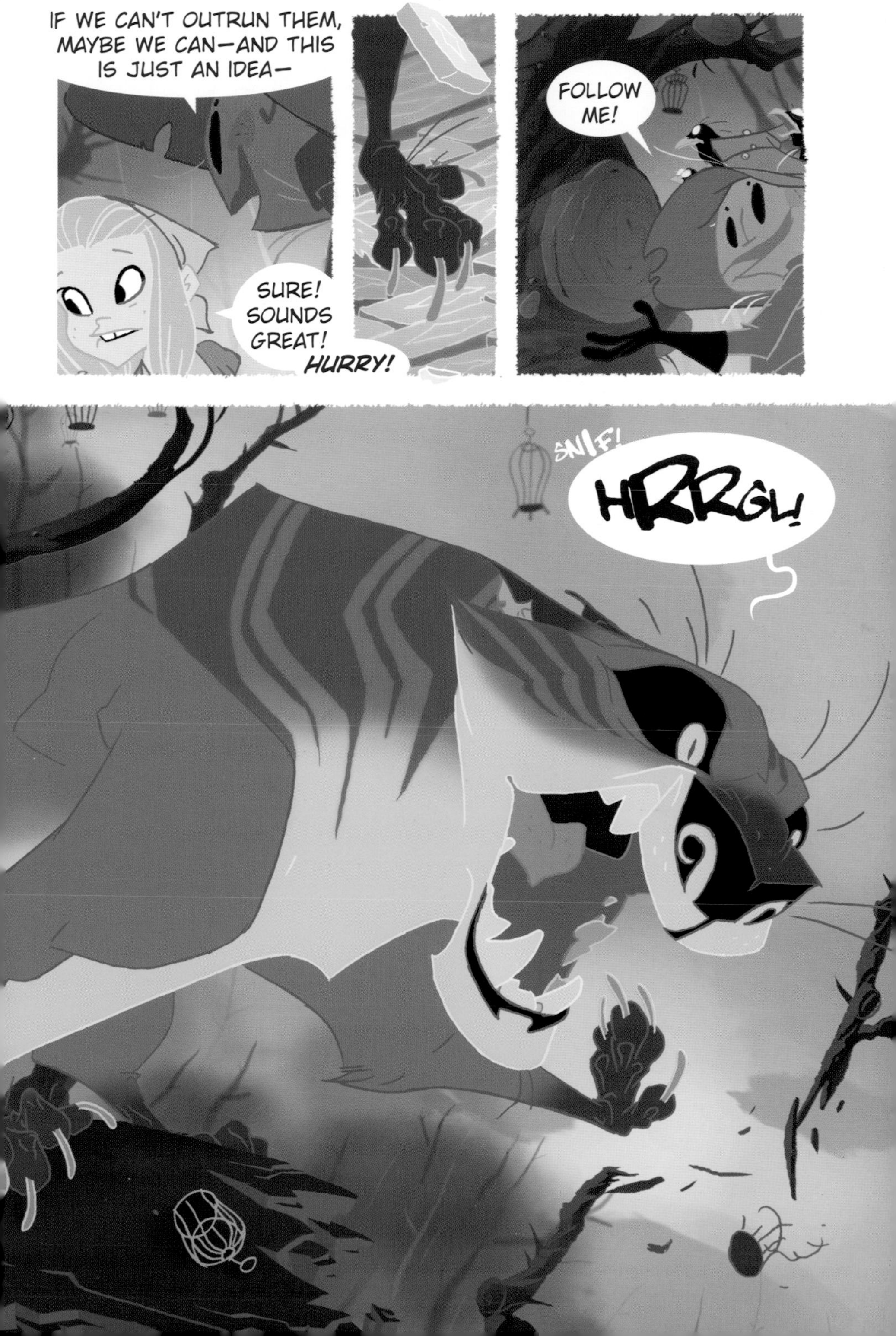
IF WE CAN'T OUTRUN THEM, MAYBE WE CAN—AND THIS IS JUST AN IDEA—
SURE! SOUNDS GREAT!
HURRY!
FOLLOW ME!
SNIF!
HRRGL!

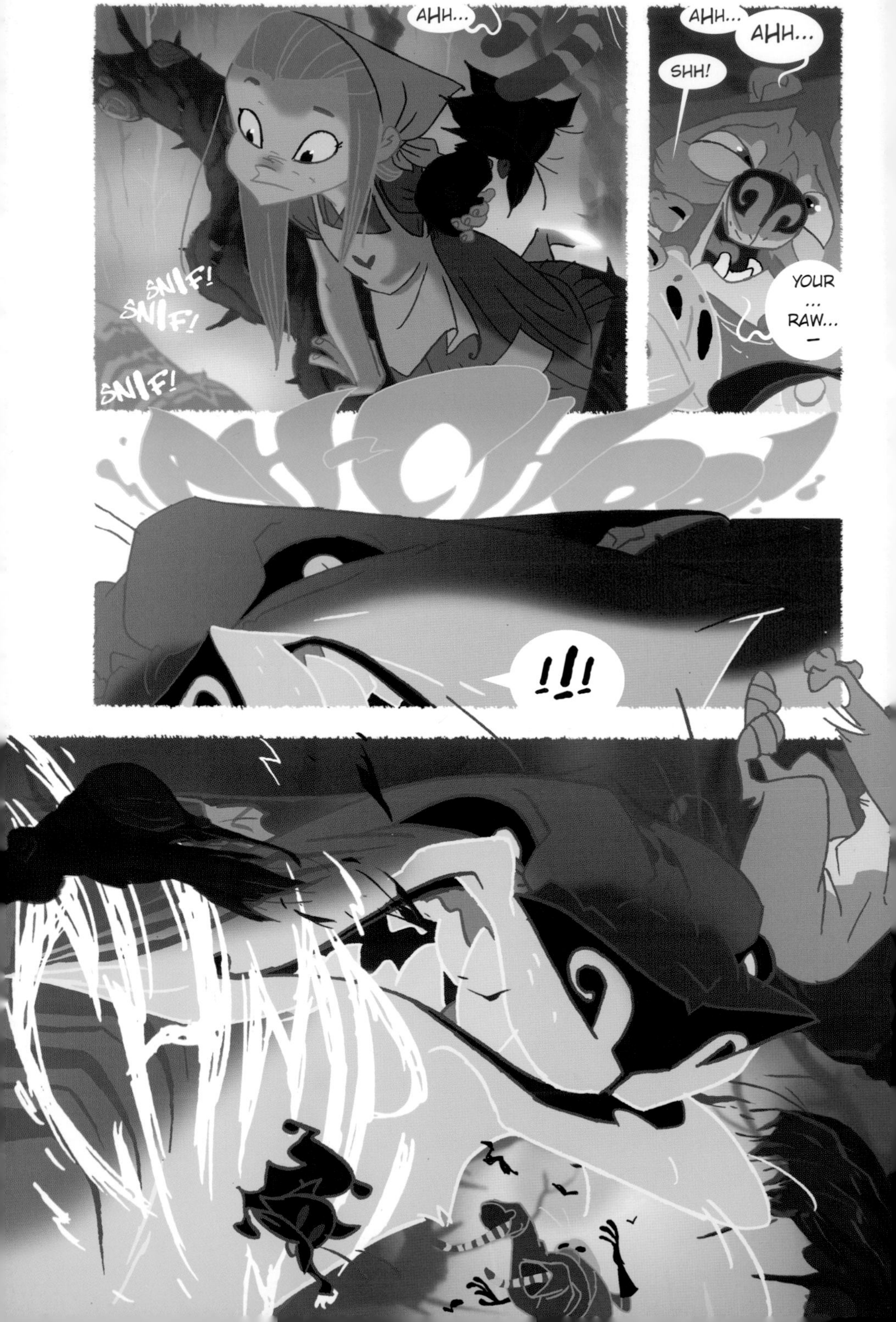
AHH...
SNIF!
SNIF!
SNIF!
AHH...
AHH...
SHH!
YOUR ... RAW... —
!!!

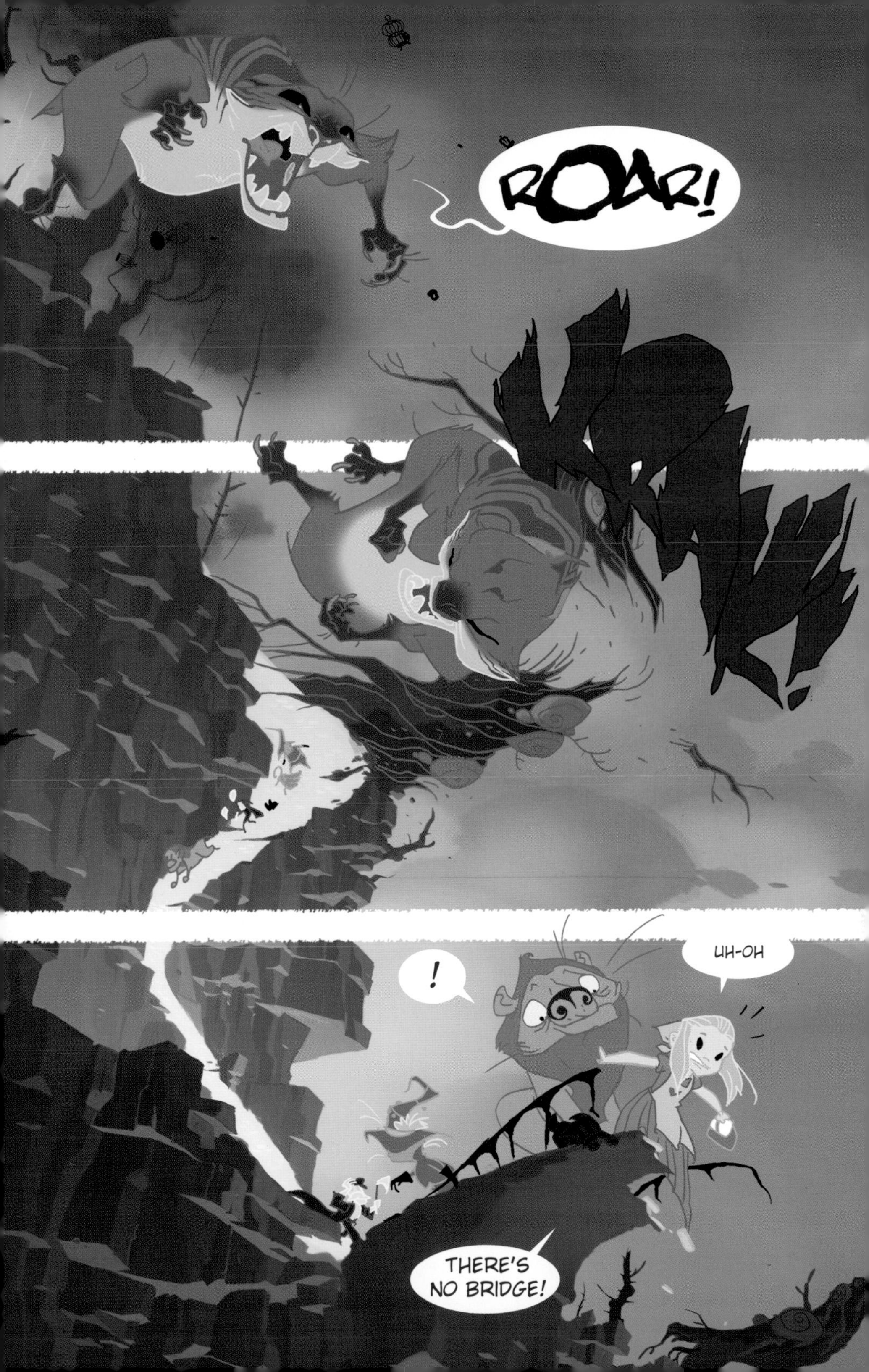
ROAR!
!
UH-OH
THERE'S NO BRIDGE!

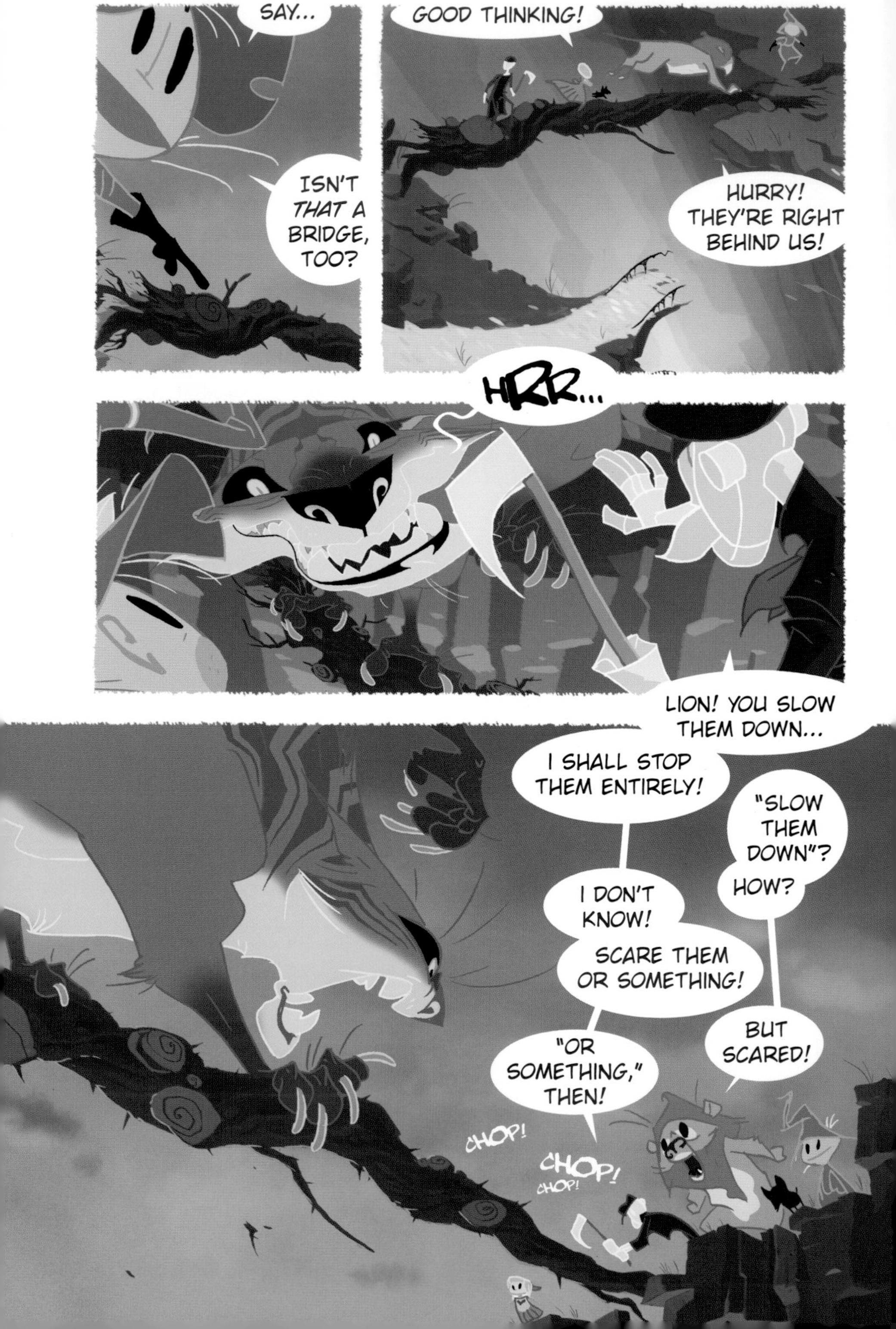
SAY...
ISN'T THAT A BRIDGE, TOO?
GOOD THINKING!
HURRY! THEY'RE RIGHT BEHIND US!
HRR...
LION! YOU SLOW THEM DOWN...
I SHALL STOP THEM ENTIRELY!
"SLOW THEM DOWN"? HOW?
I DON'T KNOW!
SCARE THEM OR SOMETHING!
BUT SCARED!
"OR SOMETHING," THEN!
CHOP!
CHOP!
CHOP!

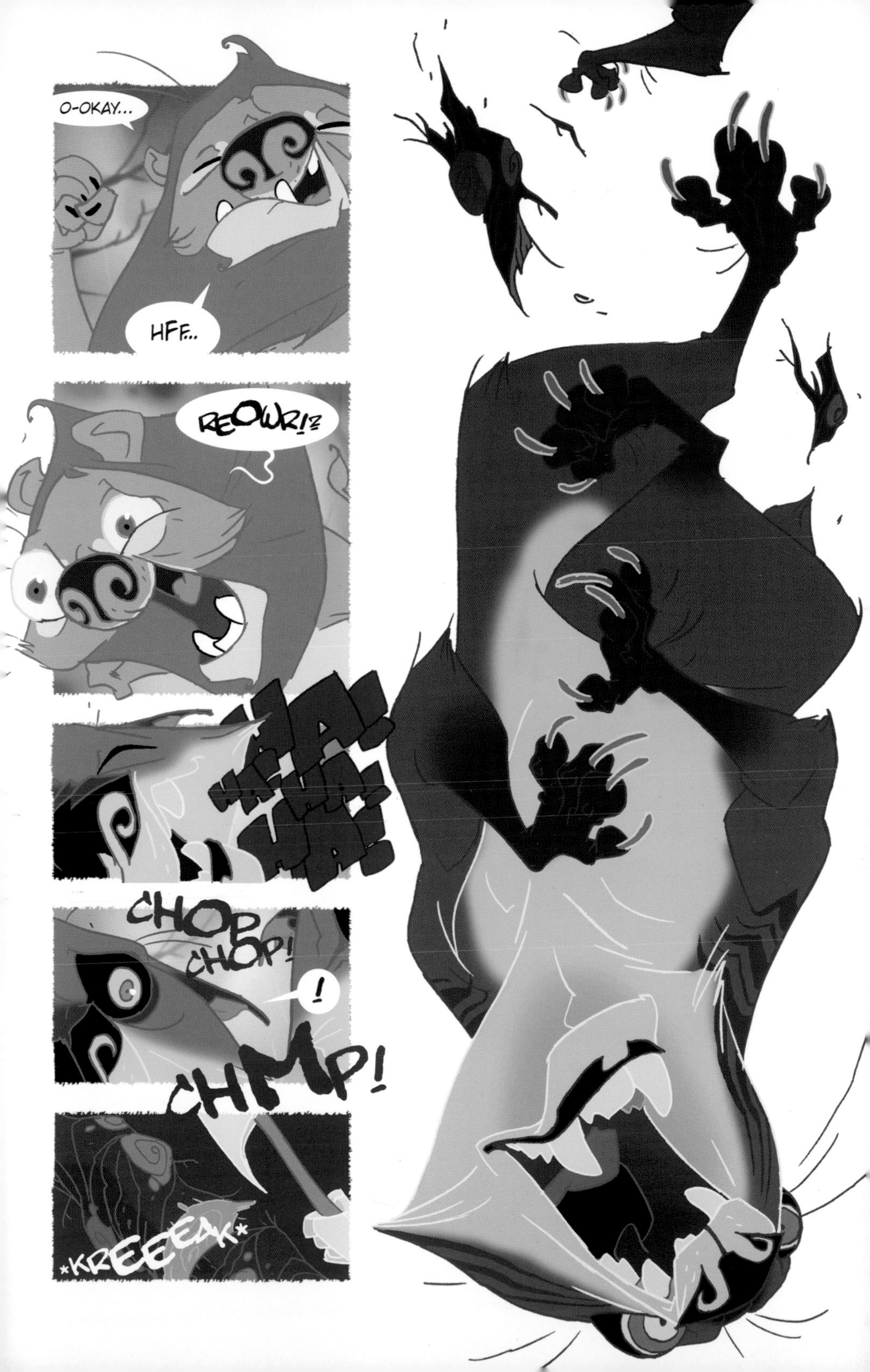
O-OKAY...
HFF...
REOWR!?
HA! HA! HA! HA! HA!
CHOP CHOP!
!
CHMP!
KREEEAK

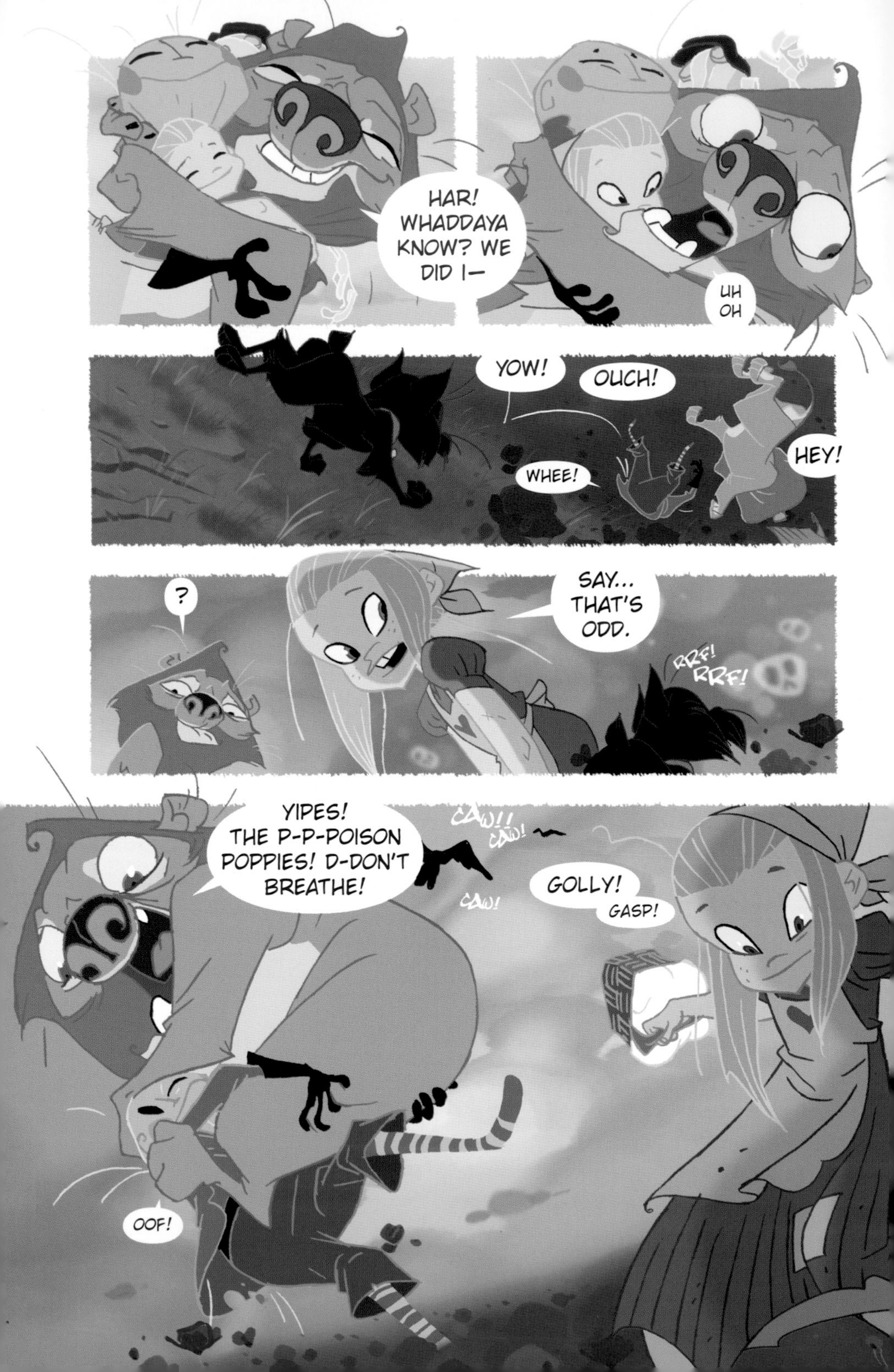

HAR! WHADDAYA KNOW? WE DID I—
UH OH
YOW!
OUCH!
WHEE!
HEY!
?
SAY... THAT'S ODD.
RRF! RRF!
YIPES! THE P-P-POISON POPPIES! D-DON'T BREATHE!
CAW!! CAW!
CAW!
GOLLY!
GASP!
OOF!

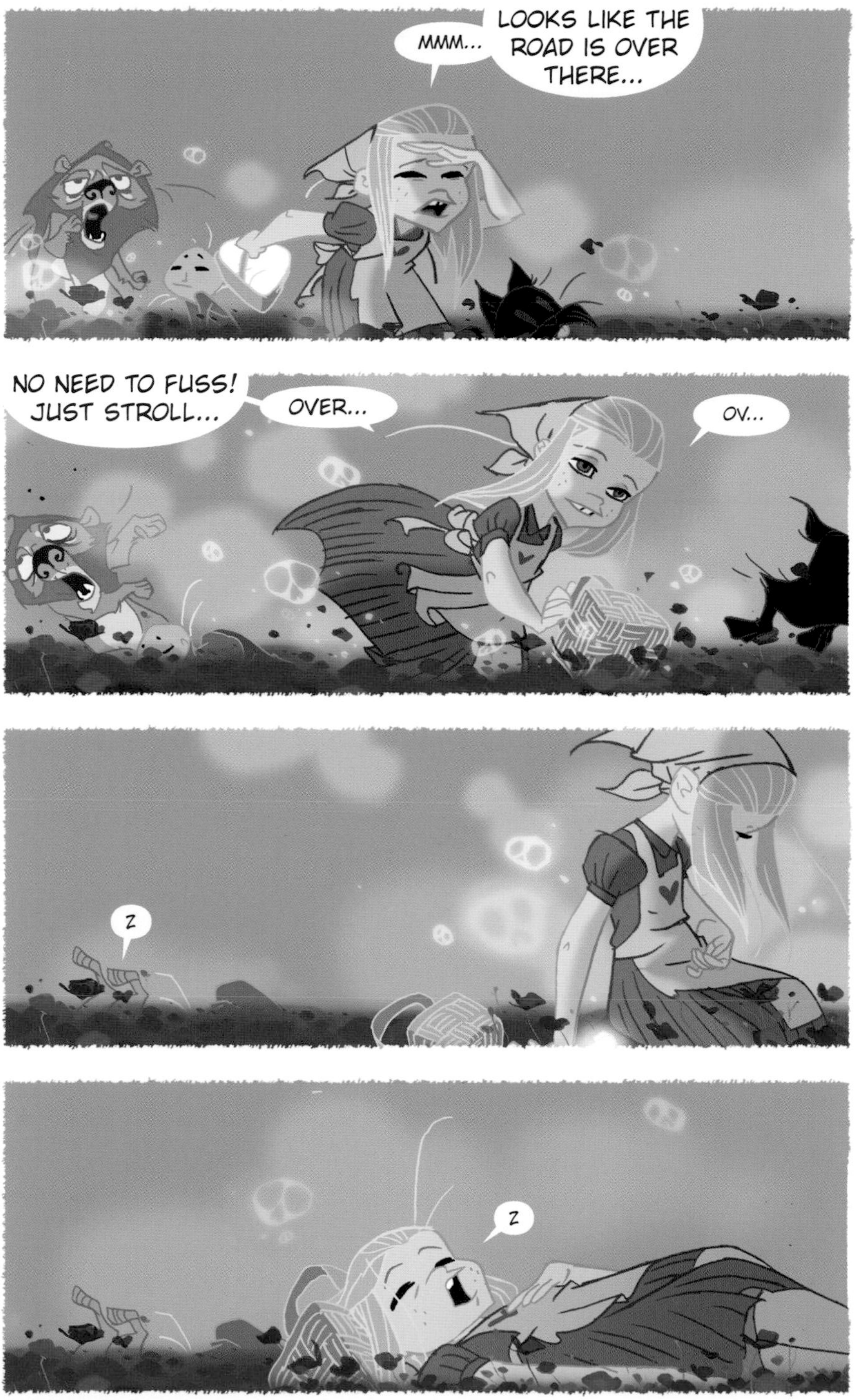
MMM...
LOOKS LIKE THE ROAD IS OVER THERE...
NO NEED TO FUSS! JUST STROLL...
OVER...
OV...
Z
Z

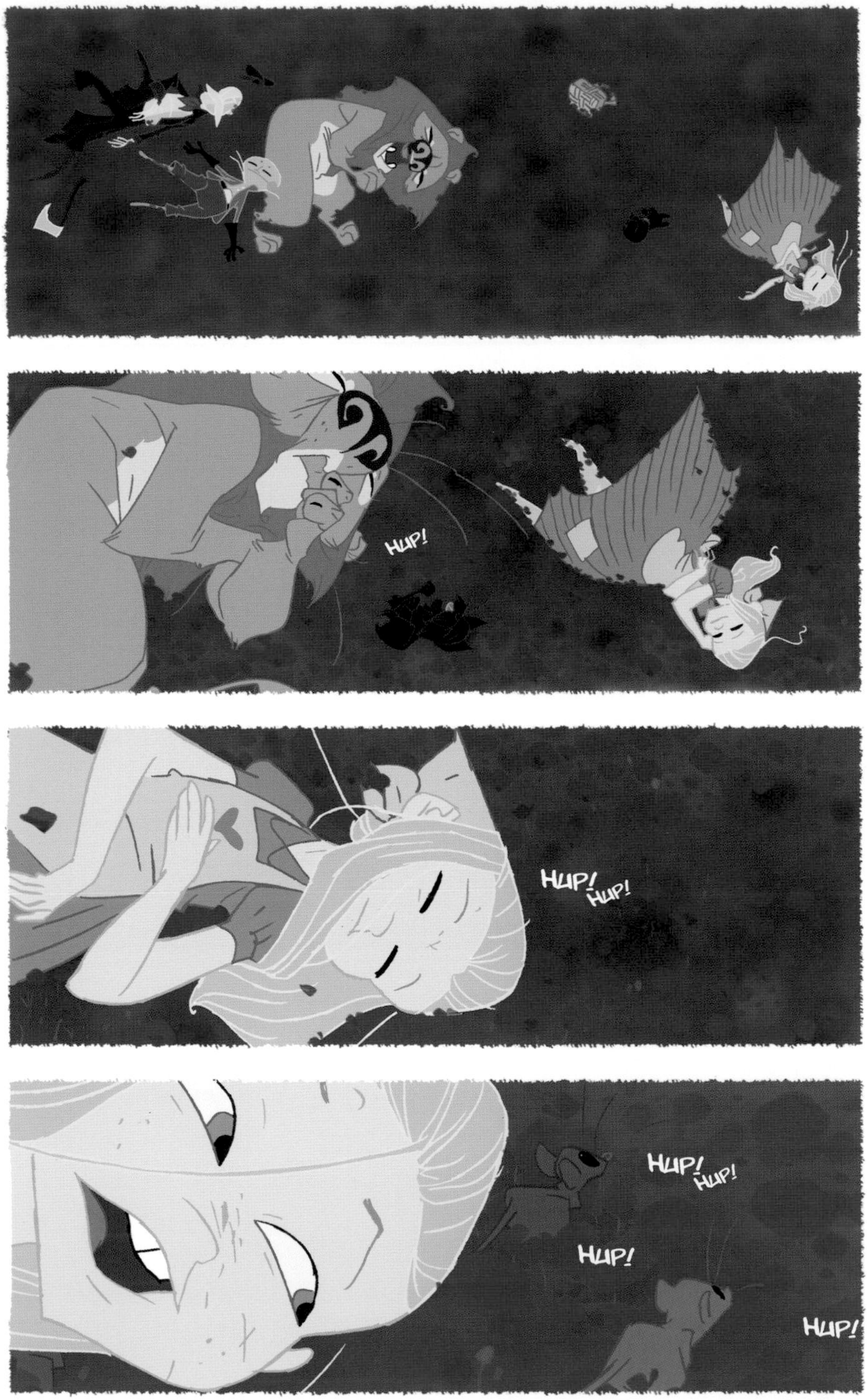
HUP!
HUP!
HUP!
HUP!
HUP!
HUP!
HUP!

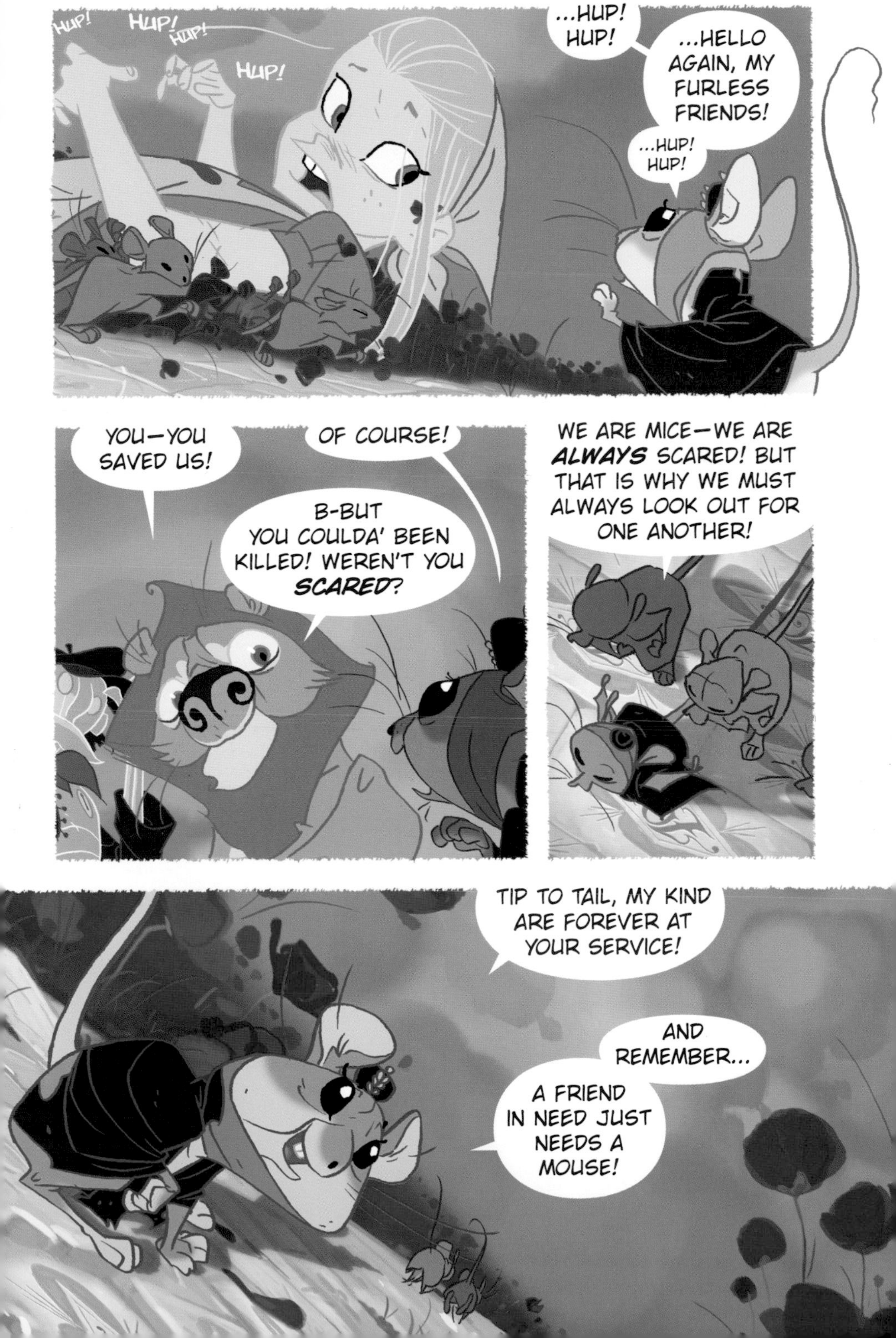
HUP!
HUP!
HUP!
HUP!
...HUP!
HUP!
...HELLO
AGAIN, MY
FURLESS
FRIENDS!
...HUP!
HUP!
YOU—YOU
SAVED US!
OF COURSE!
B-BUT
YOU COULDA' BEEN
KILLED! WEREN'T YOU
SCARED?
WE ARE MICE—WE ARE
ALWAYS SCARED! BUT
THAT IS WHY WE MUST
ALWAYS LOOK OUT FOR
ONE ANOTHER!
TIP TO TAIL, MY KIND
ARE FOREVER AT
YOUR SERVICE!
AND
REMEMBER...
A FRIEND
IN NEED JUST
NEEDS A
MOUSE!

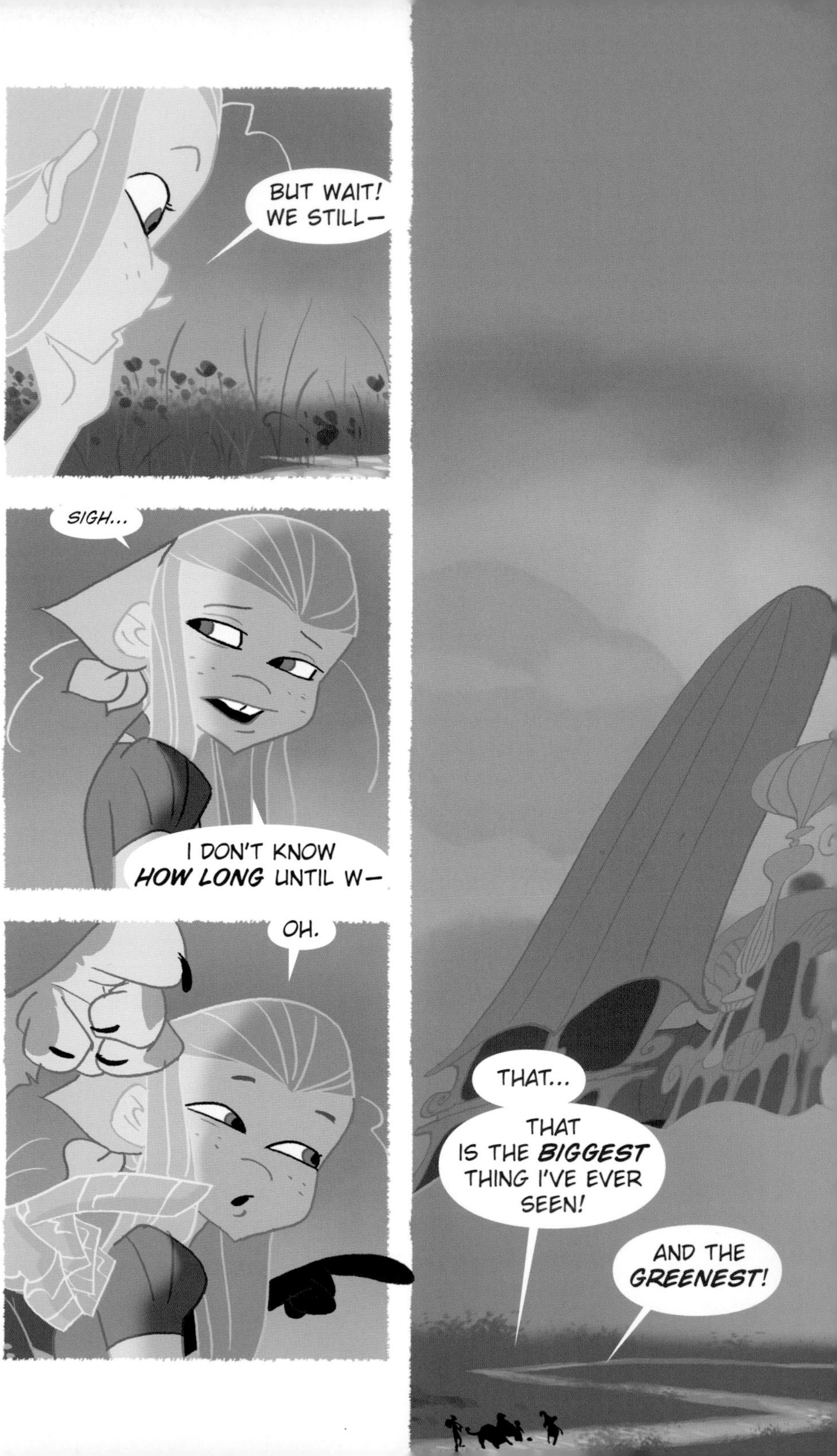
BUT WAIT! WE STILL—
SIGH...
I DON'T KNOW HOW LONG UNTIL W—
OH.
THAT...
THAT IS THE BIGGEST THING I'VE EVER SEEN!
AND THE GREENEST!

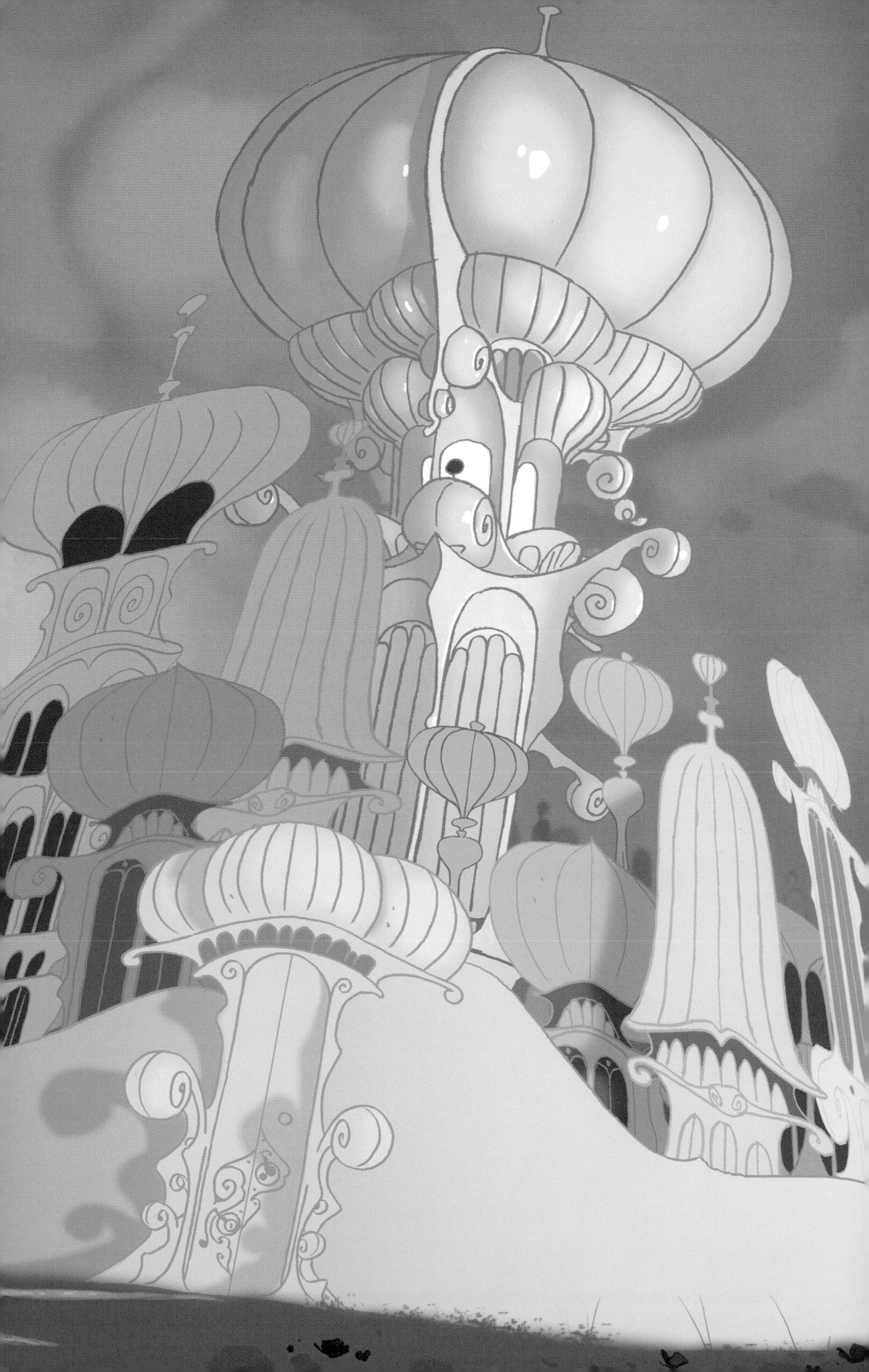

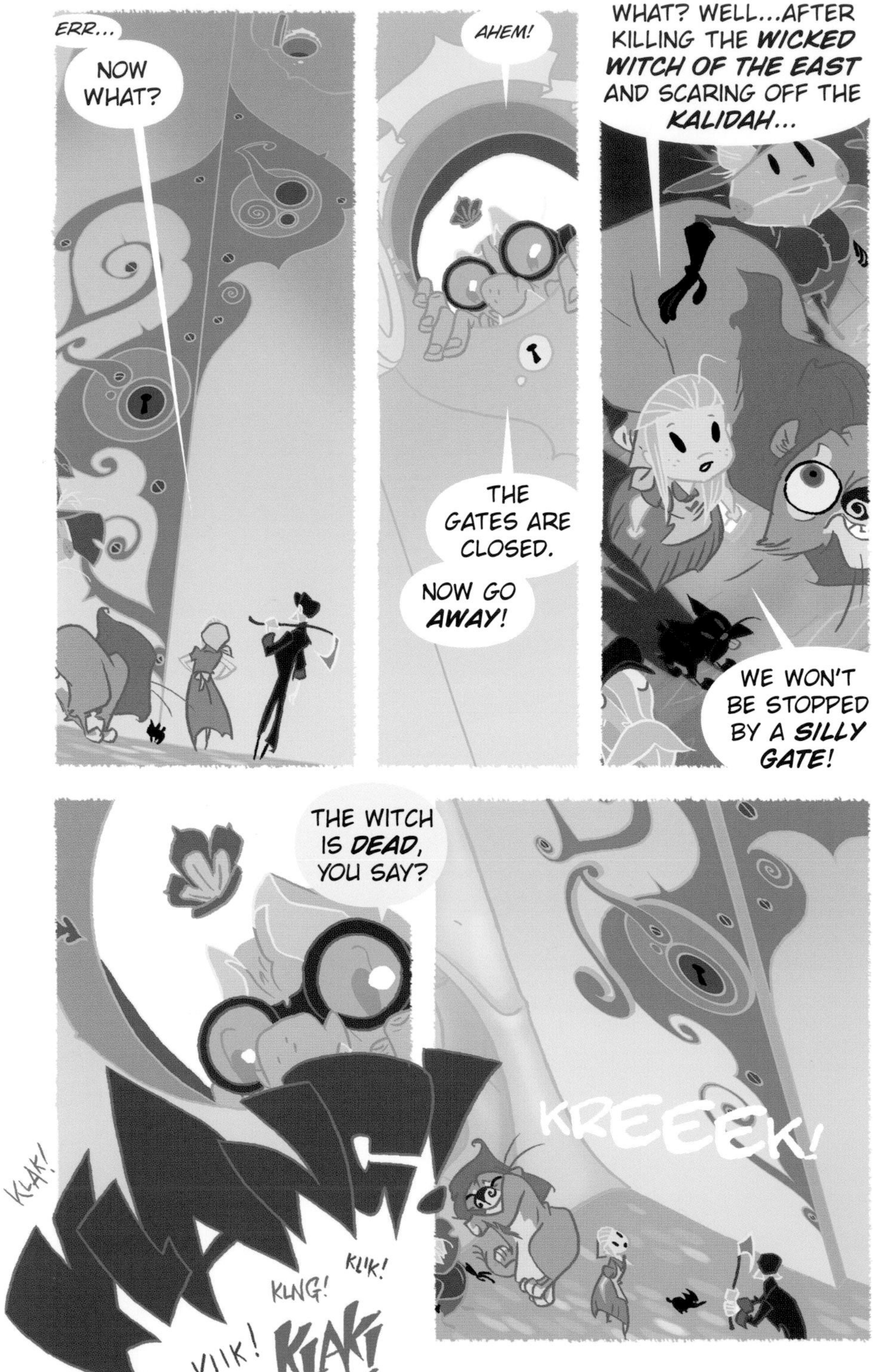
ERR...
NOW WHAT?
AHEM!
THE GATES ARE CLOSED.
NOW GO AWAY!
WHAT? WELL...AFTER KILLING THE WICKED WITCH OF THE EAST AND SCARING OFF THE KALIDAH...
WE WON'T BE STOPPED BY A SILLY GATE!
THE WITCH IS DEAD, YOU SAY?
KLAK!
KLIK!
KLNG!
KLIK!
KLAK!
KREEEEK!

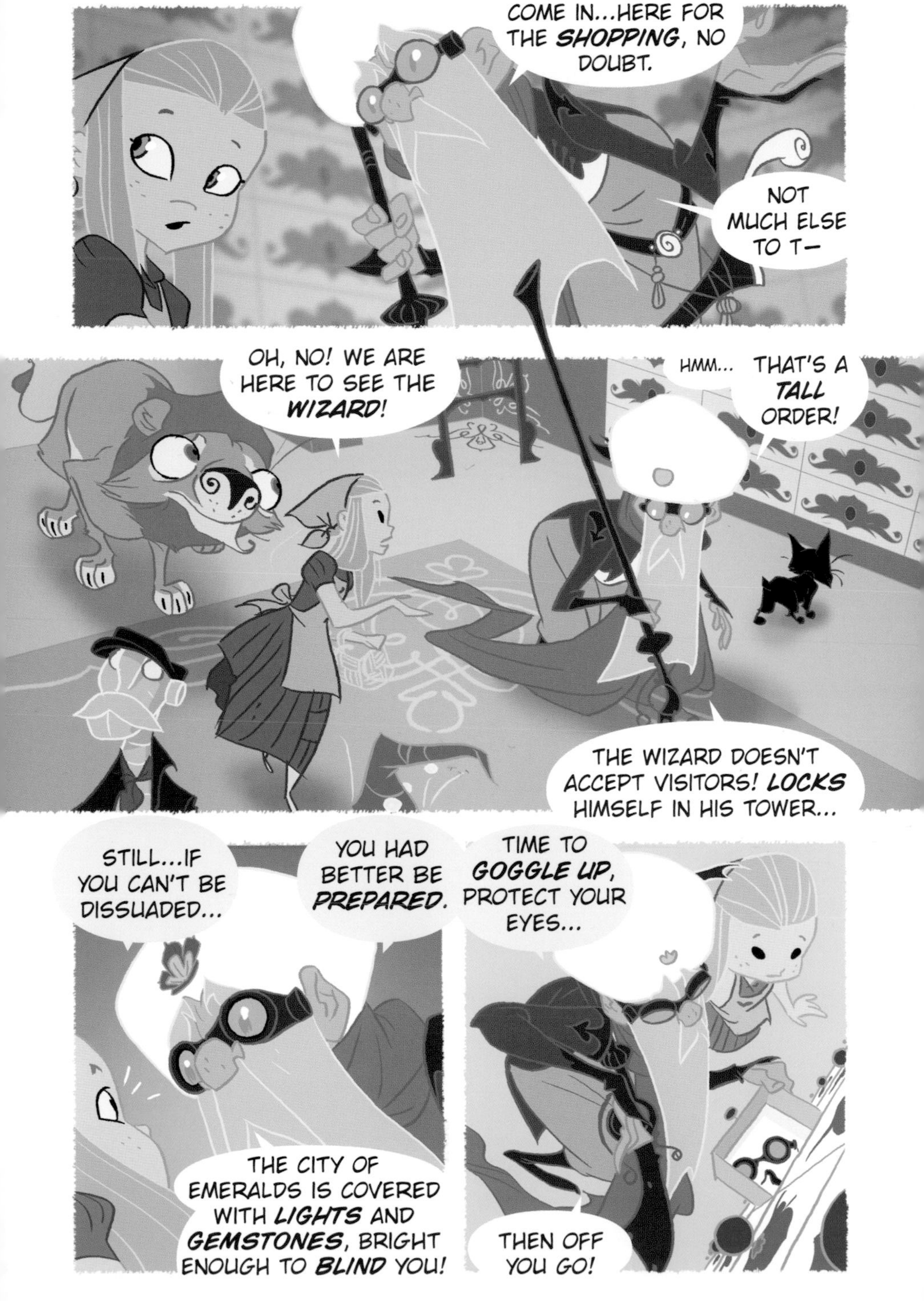
COME IN...HERE FOR THE *SHOPPING*, NO DOUBT.
NOT MUCH ELSE TO T—
OH, NO! WE ARE HERE TO SEE THE *WIZARD*!
HMM...
THAT'S A *TALL* ORDER!
THE WIZARD DOESN'T ACCEPT VISITORS! *LOCKS* HIMSELF IN HIS TOWER...
STILL...IF YOU CAN'T BE DISSUADED...
YOU HAD BETTER BE *PREPARED*.
THE CITY OF EMERALDS IS COVERED WITH *LIGHTS* AND *GEMSTONES*, BRIGHT ENOUGH TO *BLIND* YOU!
TIME TO *GOGGLE UP*, PROTECT YOUR EYES...
THEN OFF YOU GO!

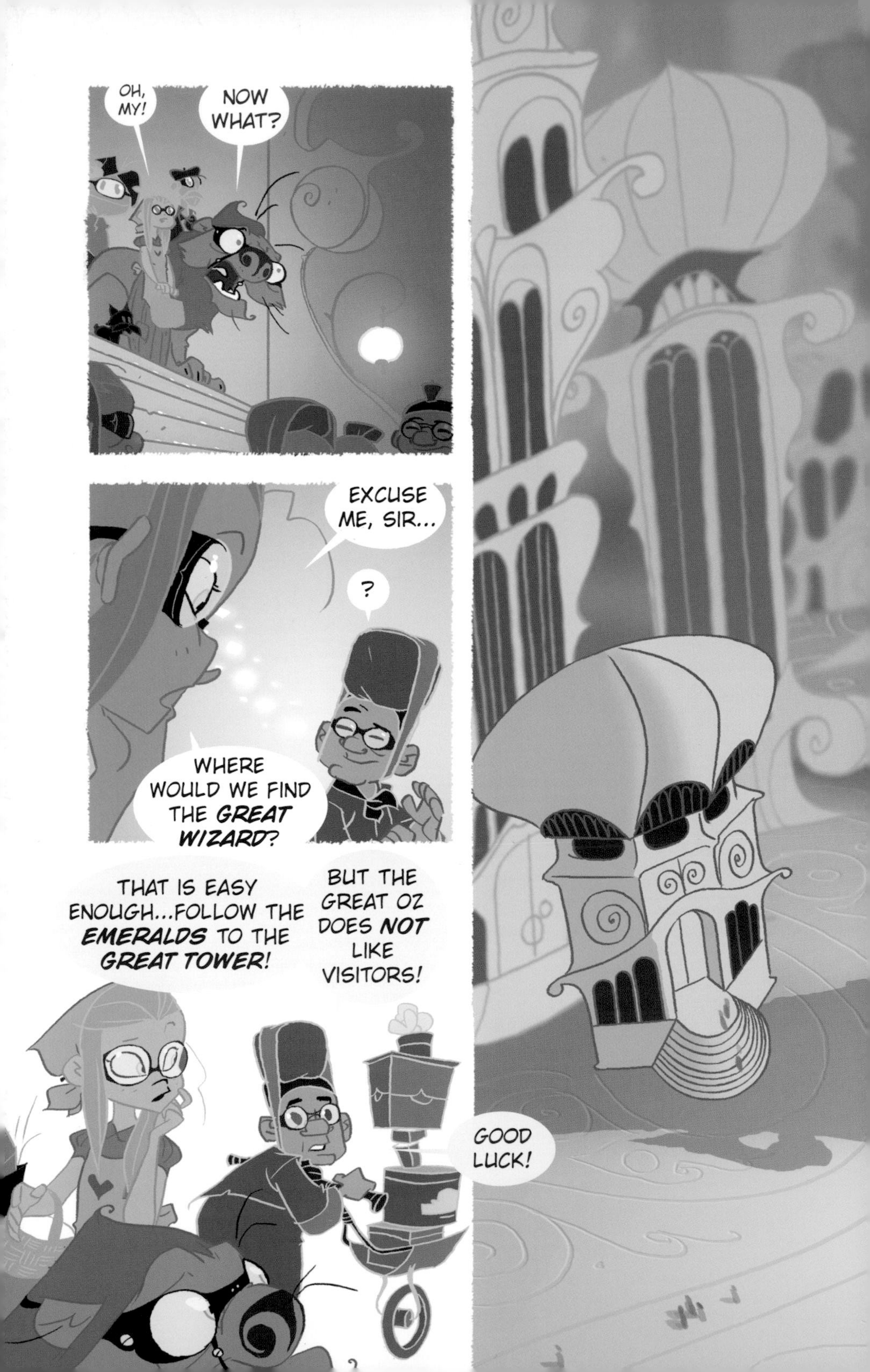
OH, MY!
NOW WHAT?
EXCUSE ME, SIR...
?
WHERE WOULD WE FIND THE GREAT WIZARD?
THAT IS EASY ENOUGH...FOLLOW THE EMERALDS TO THE GREAT TOWER!
BUT THE GREAT OZ DOES NOT LIKE VISITORS!
GOOD LUCK!

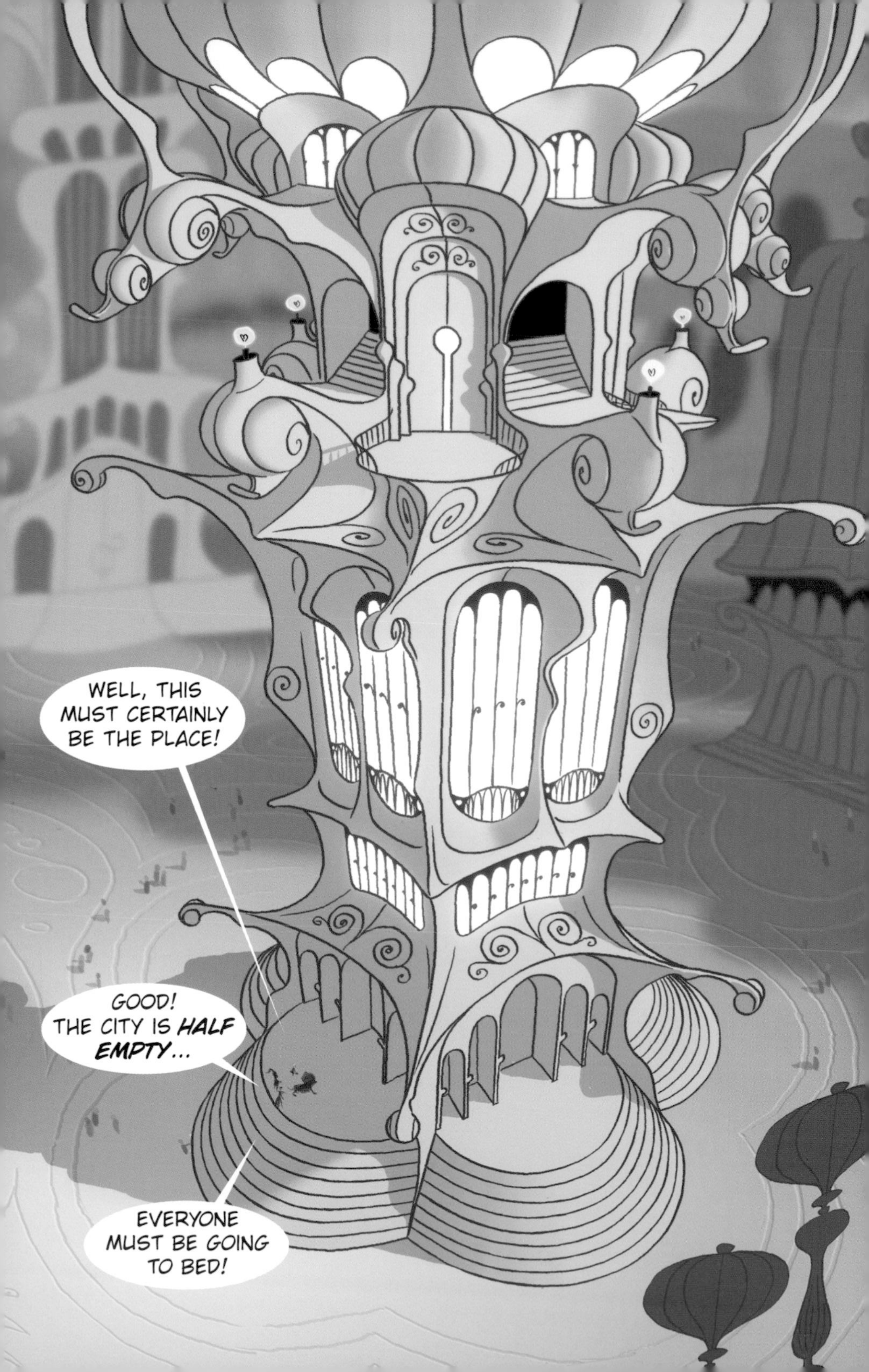
WELL, THIS MUST CERTAINLY BE THE PLACE!
GOOD! THE CITY IS *HALF EMPTY*...
EVERYONE MUST BE GOING TO BED!

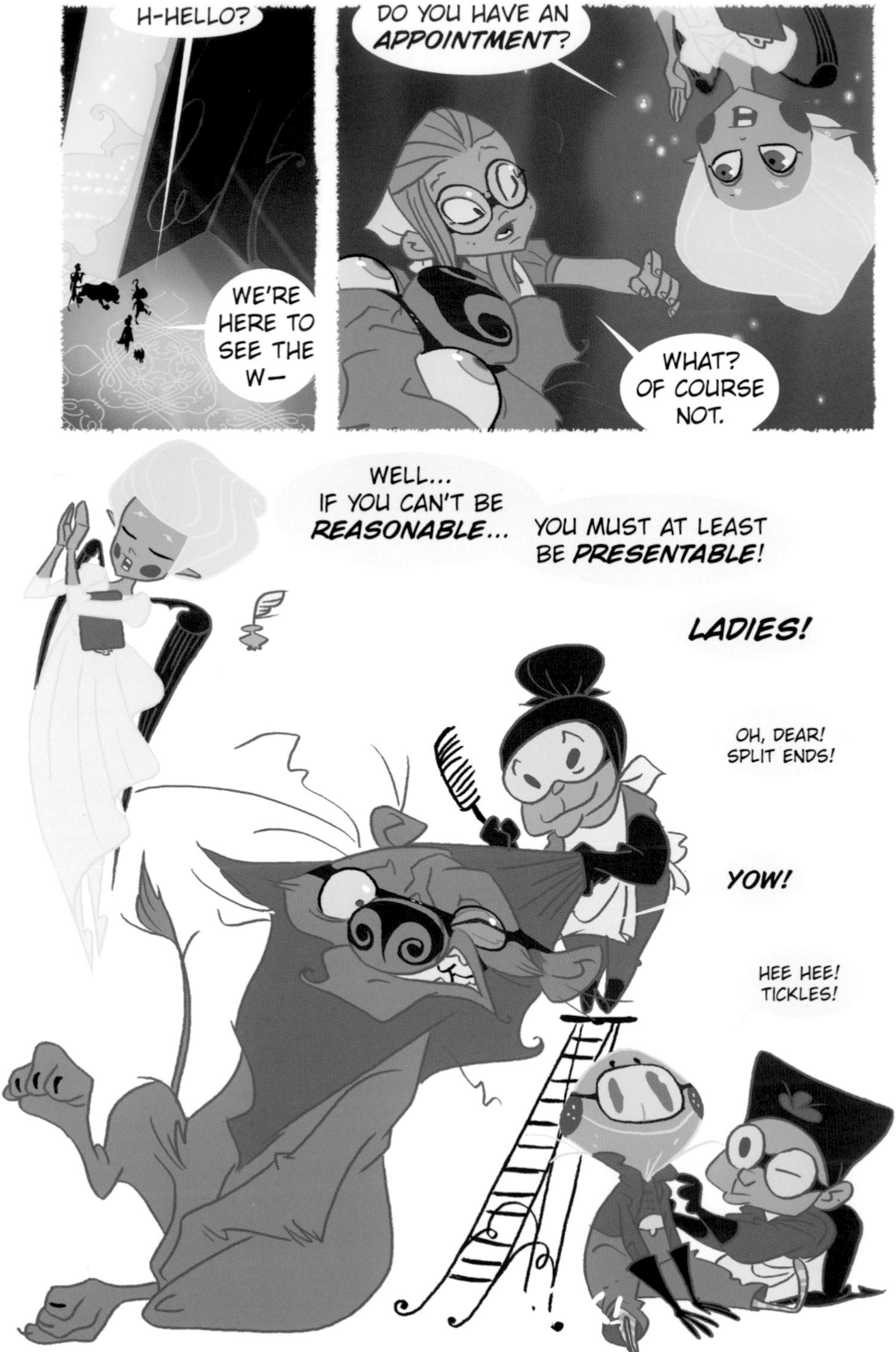
H-HELLO?
WE'RE HERE TO SEE THE W—
DO YOU HAVE AN APPOINTMENT?
WHAT? OF COURSE NOT.
WELL... IF YOU CAN'T BE REASONABLE...
YOU MUST AT LEAST BE PRESENTABLE!
LADIES!
OH, DEAR! SPLIT ENDS!
YOW!
HEE HEE! TICKLES!

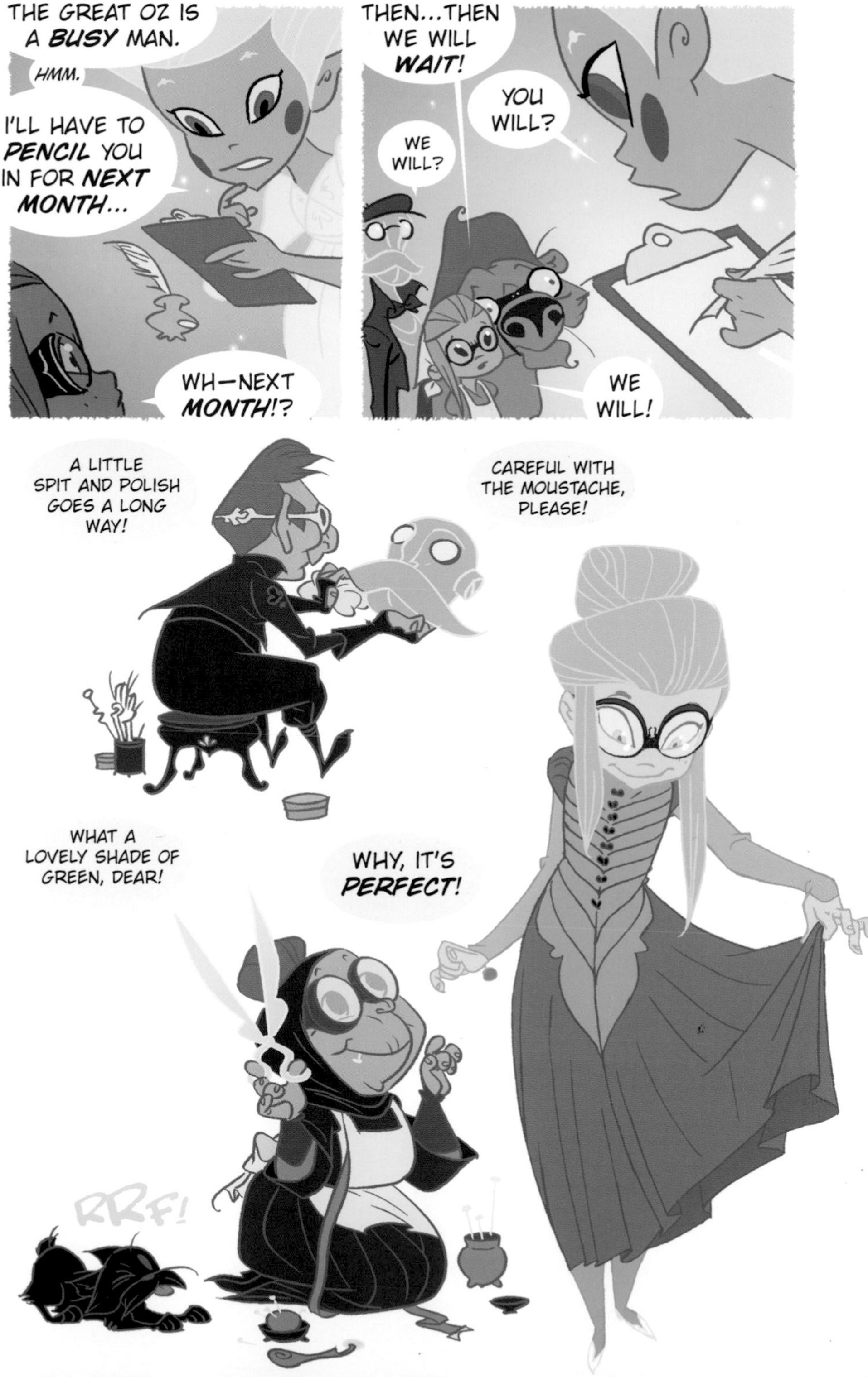

THE GREAT OZ IS A *BUSY* MAN.
HMM.
I'LL HAVE TO *PENCIL* YOU IN FOR *NEXT MONTH*...
WH—NEXT *MONTH*!?
THEN...THEN WE WILL *WAIT*!
WE WILL?
YOU WILL?
WE WILL!
A LITTLE SPIT AND POLISH GOES A LONG WAY!
CAREFUL WITH THE MOUSTACHE, PLEASE!
WHAT A LOVELY SHADE OF GREEN, DEAR!
WHY, IT'S *PERFECT*!
RRF!

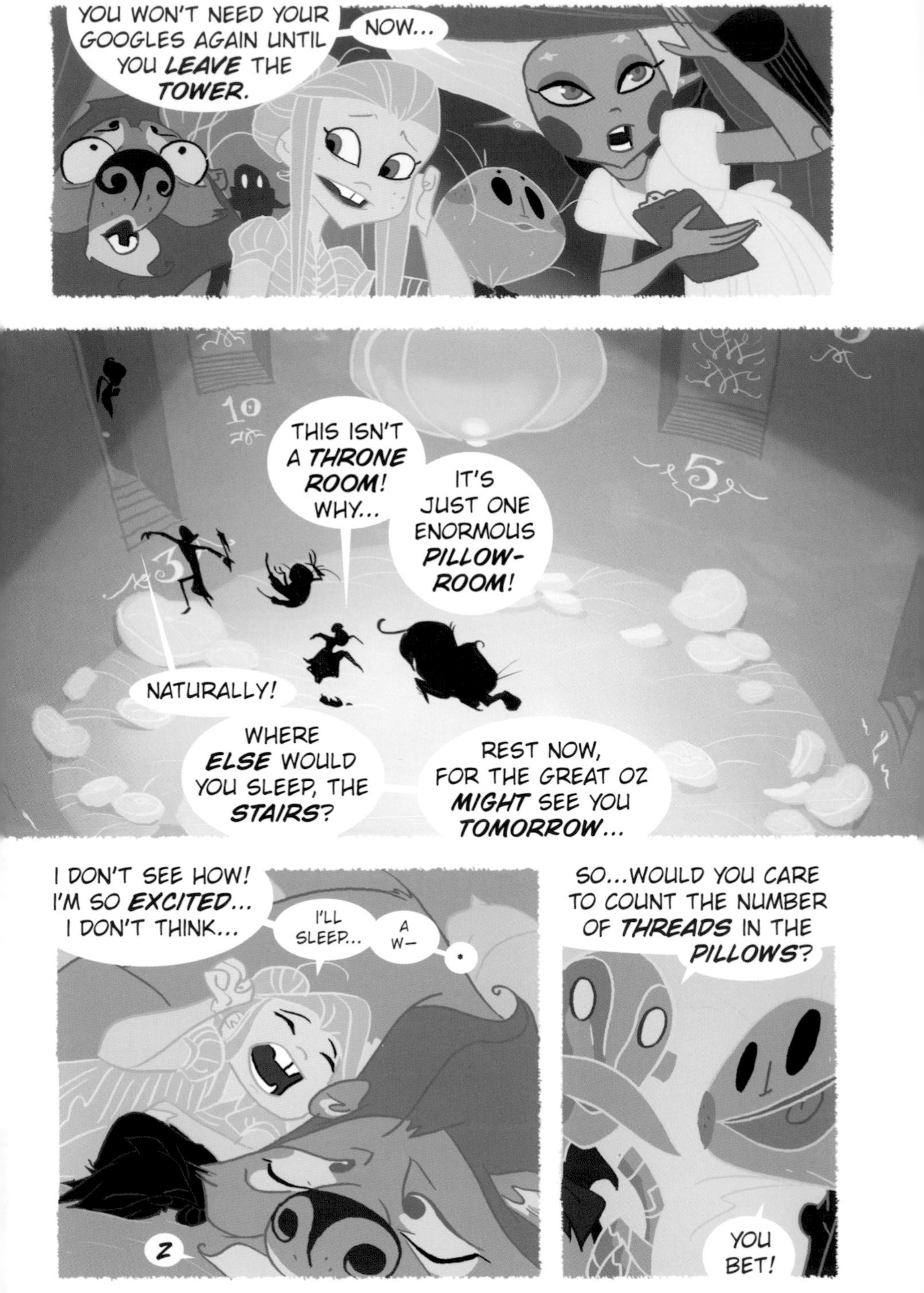
YOU WON'T NEED YOUR GOOGLES AGAIN UNTIL YOU LEAVE THE TOWER.
NOW...
THIS ISN'T A THRONE ROOM! WHY...
IT'S JUST ONE ENORMOUS PILLOW-ROOM!
NATURALLY!
WHERE ELSE WOULD YOU SLEEP, THE STAIRS?
REST NOW, FOR THE GREAT OZ MIGHT SEE YOU TOMORROW...
10
5
3
I DON'T SEE HOW! I'M SO EXCITED... I DON'T THINK...
I'LL SLEEP...
A W—
*
Z
SO...WOULD YOU CARE TO COUNT THE NUMBER OF THREADS IN THE PILLOWS?
YOU BET!

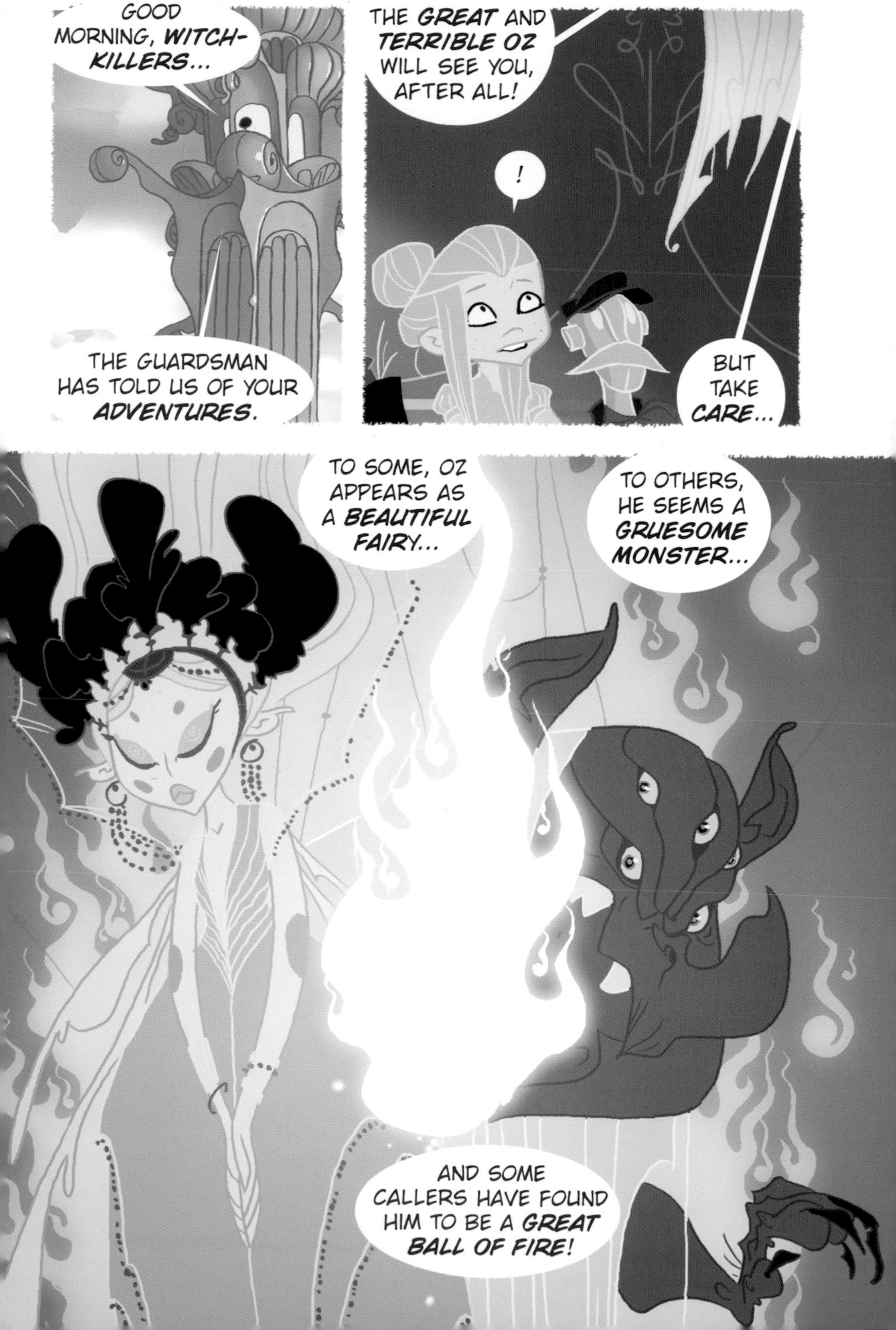
GOOD MORNING, WITCH-KILLERS...
THE GUARDSMAN HAS TOLD US OF YOUR ADVENTURES.
THE GREAT AND TERRIBLE OZ WILL SEE YOU, AFTER ALL!
!
BUT TAKE CARE...
TO SOME, OZ APPEARS AS A BEAUTIFUL FAIRY...
TO OTHERS, HE SEEMS A GRUESOME MONSTER...
AND SOME CALLERS HAVE FOUND HIM TO BE A GREAT BALL OF FIRE!

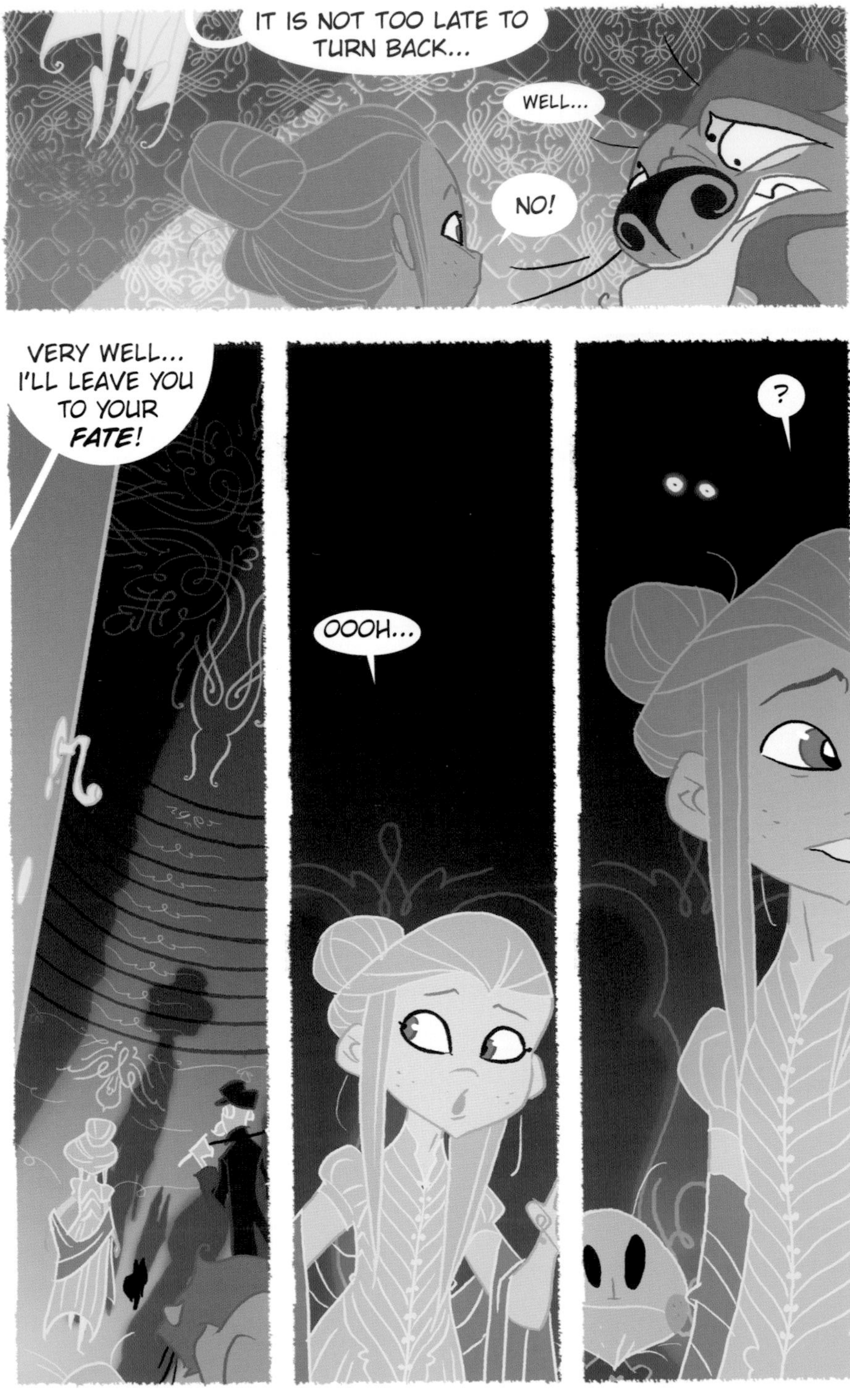
IT IS NOT TOO LATE TO TURN BACK...
WELL...
NO!
VERY WELL... I'LL LEAVE YOU TO YOUR *FATE*!
OOOH...
?

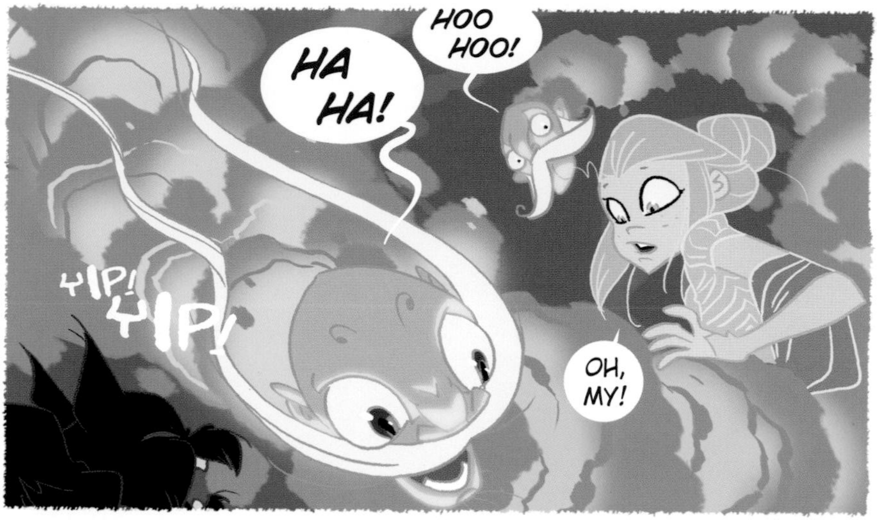
HA HA!
HOO HOO!
YIP! YIP!
OH, MY!
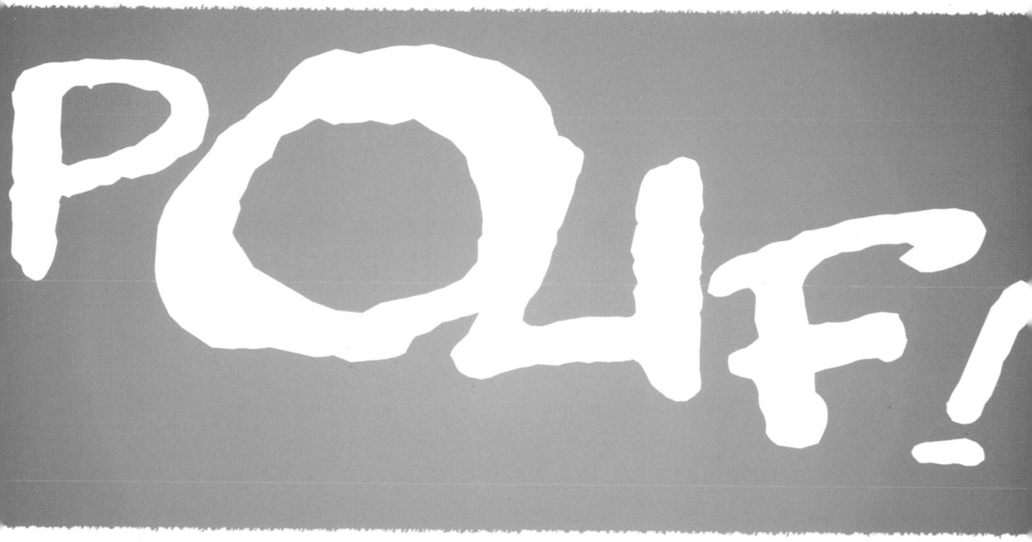
POUF!
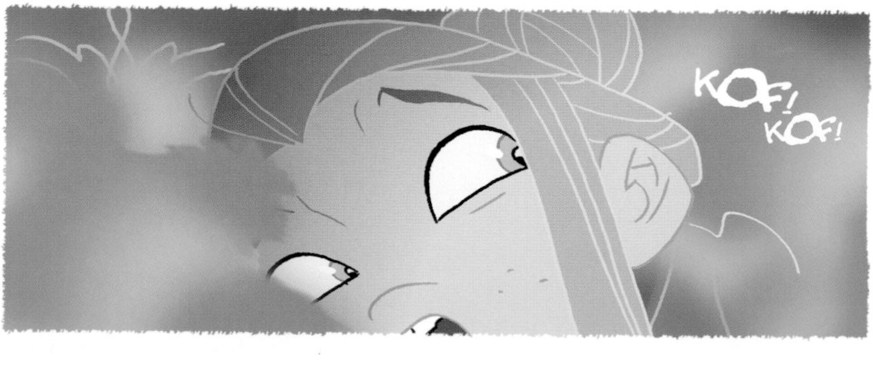
KOF! KOF!

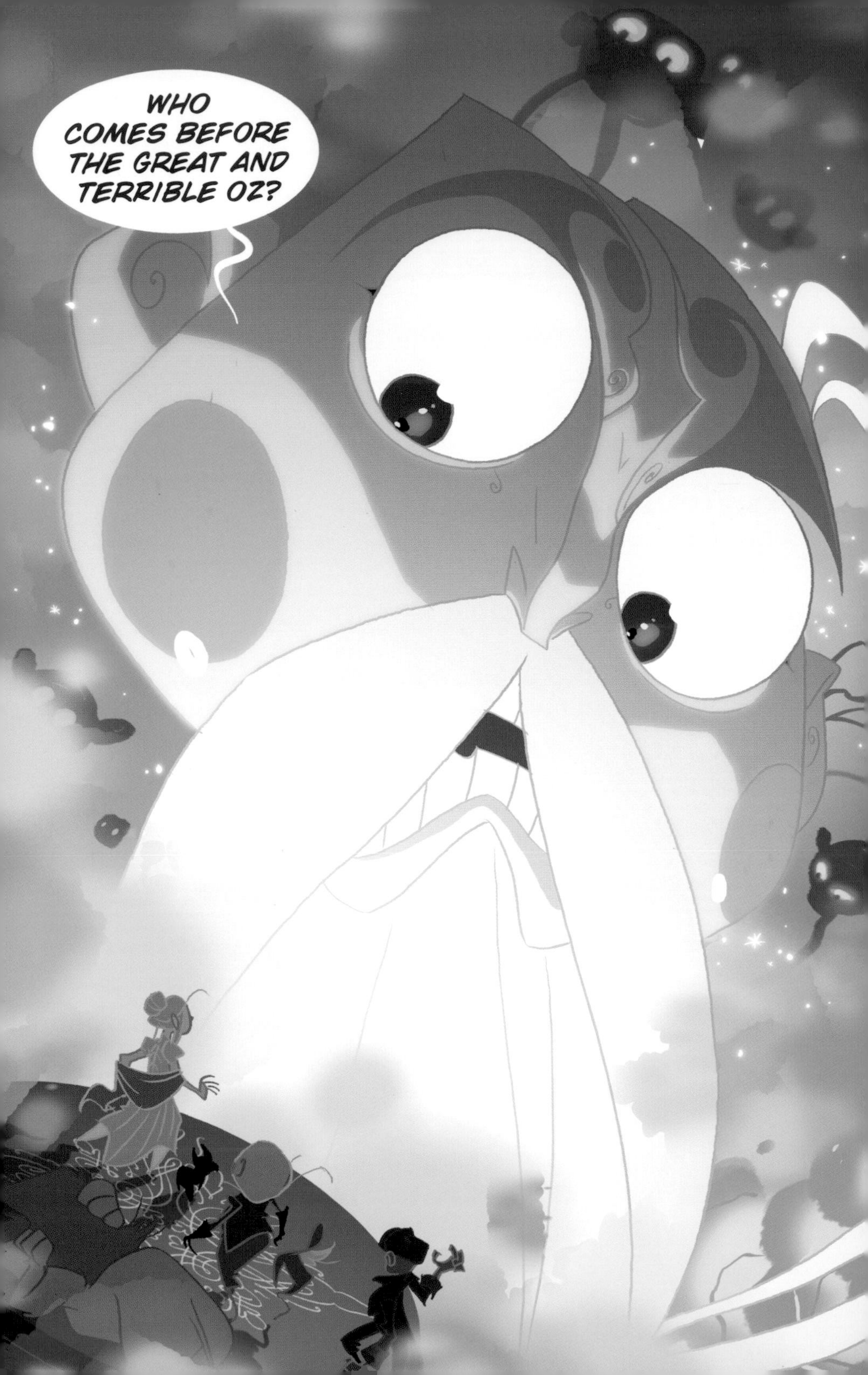
WHO COMES BEFORE THE GREAT AND TERRIBLE OZ?

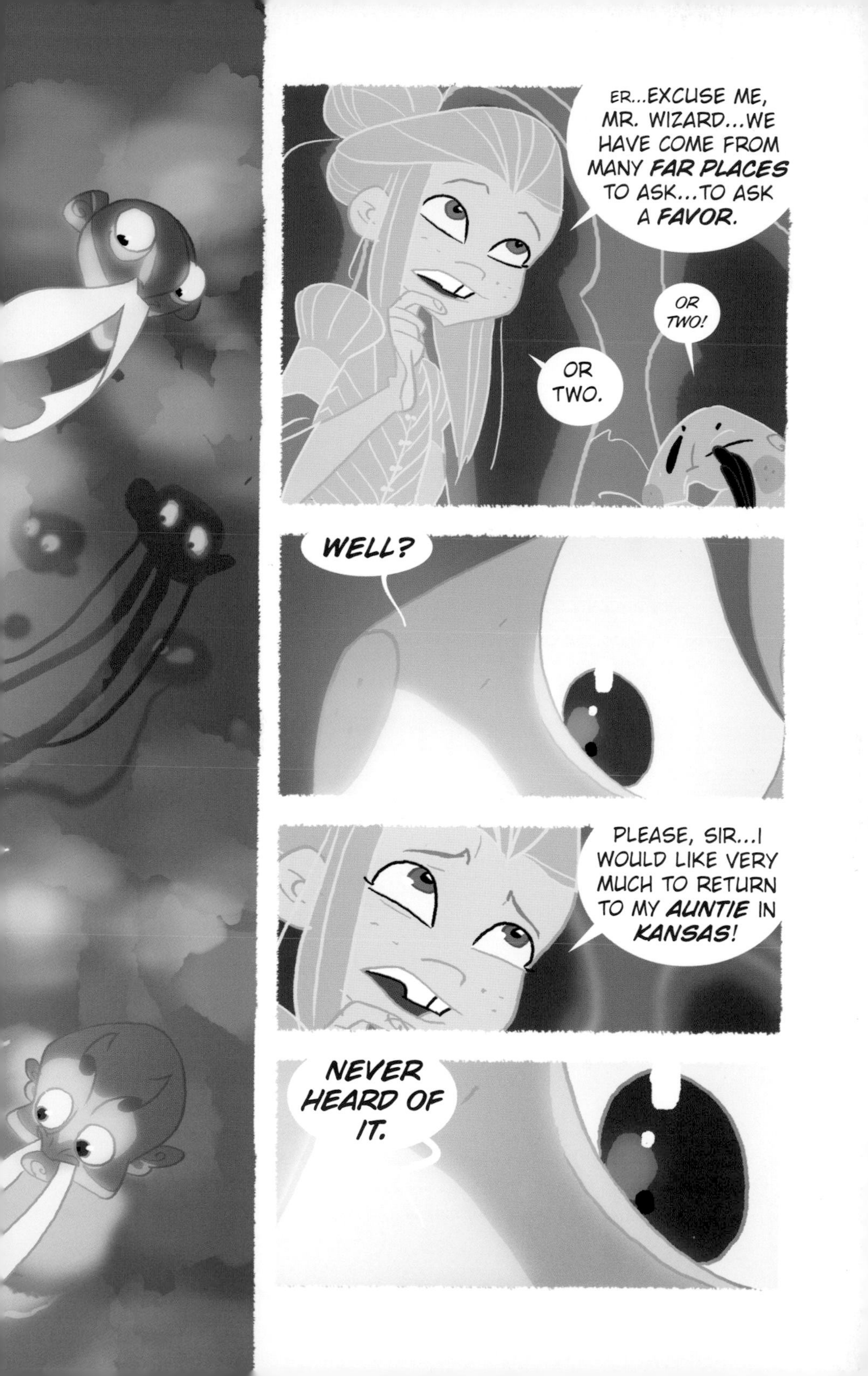
ER...EXCUSE ME, MR. WIZARD...WE HAVE COME FROM MANY **FAR PLACES** TO ASK...TO ASK A **FAVOR**.
OR TWO.
OR TWO!
WELL?
PLEASE, SIR...I WOULD LIKE VERY MUCH TO RETURN TO MY **AUNTIE** IN **KANSAS**!
NEVER HEARD OF IT.

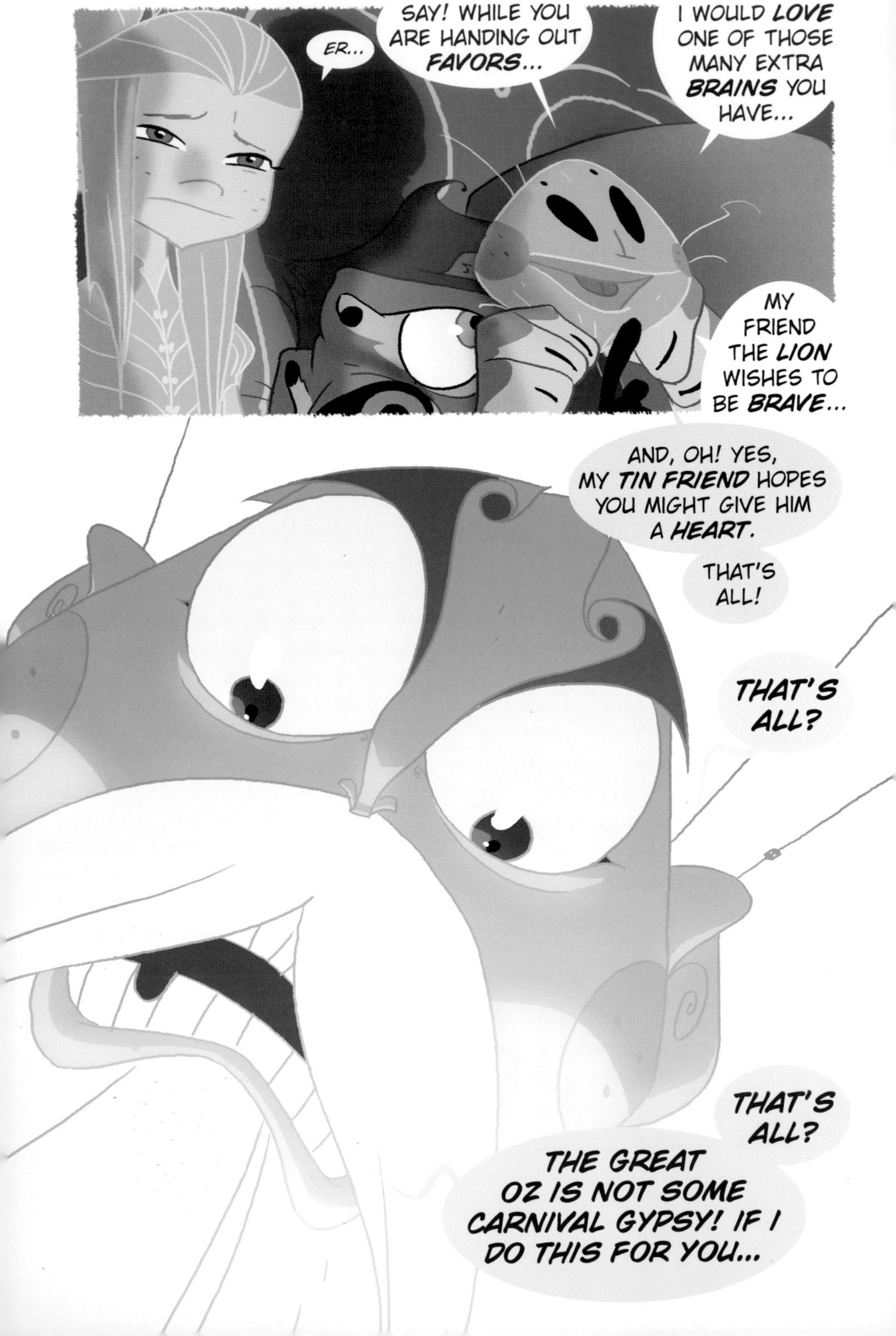
ER...
SAY! WHILE YOU ARE HANDING OUT FAVORS...
I WOULD LOVE ONE OF THOSE MANY EXTRA BRAINS YOU HAVE...
MY FRIEND THE LION WISHES TO BE BRAVE...
AND, OH! YES, MY TIN FRIEND HOPES YOU MIGHT GIVE HIM A HEART.
THAT'S ALL!
THAT'S ALL?
THAT'S ALL?
THE GREAT OZ IS NOT SOME CARNIVAL GYPSY! IF I DO THIS FOR YOU...

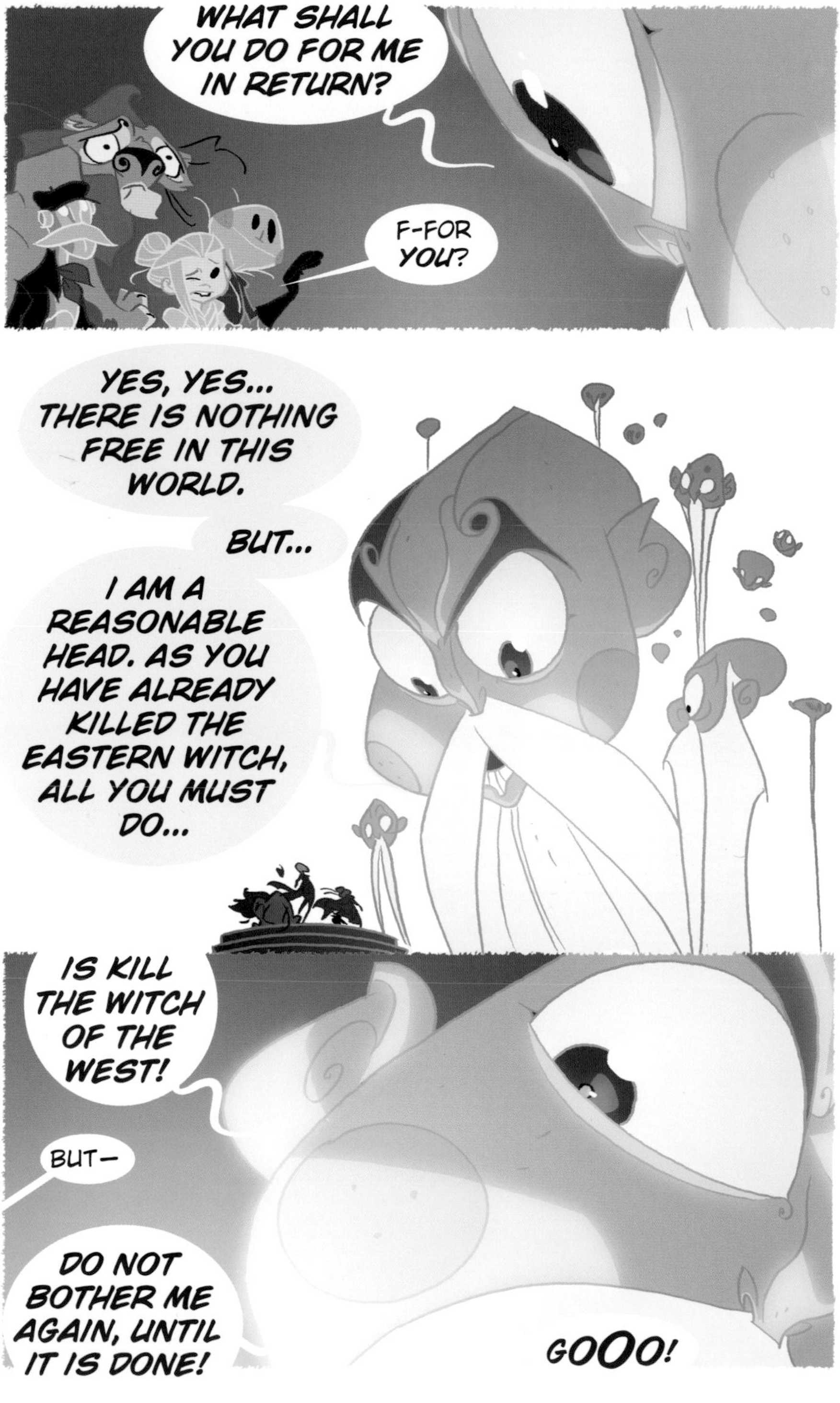
WHAT SHALL YOU DO FOR ME IN RETURN?
F-FOR YOU?
YES, YES... THERE IS NOTHING FREE IN THIS WORLD.
BUT...
I AM A REASONABLE HEAD. AS YOU HAVE ALREADY KILLED THE EASTERN WITCH, ALL YOU MUST DO...
IS KILL THE WITCH OF THE WEST!
BUT—
DO NOT BOTHER ME AGAIN, UNTIL IT IS DONE!
GOOO!

KREE-EEAK!

SH!

QUICKLY...

THIS IS THE PATH TO THE **WESTERN WITCH**...UN-LESS, OF COURSE, YOU DECIDE TO TURN **BACK!**

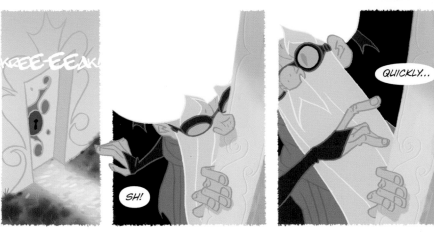

MY CLOTHES!

GOOD-BYE!

SLAM!

YES, YES... THE EMERALD MAGIC **FADES** OUTSIDE OF THE CITY.

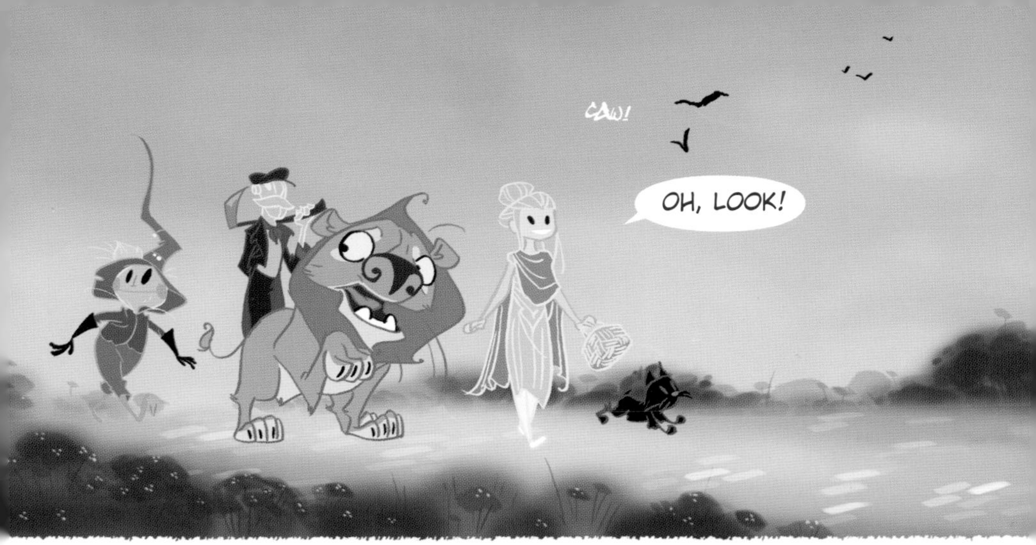
CAW!
OH, LOOK!
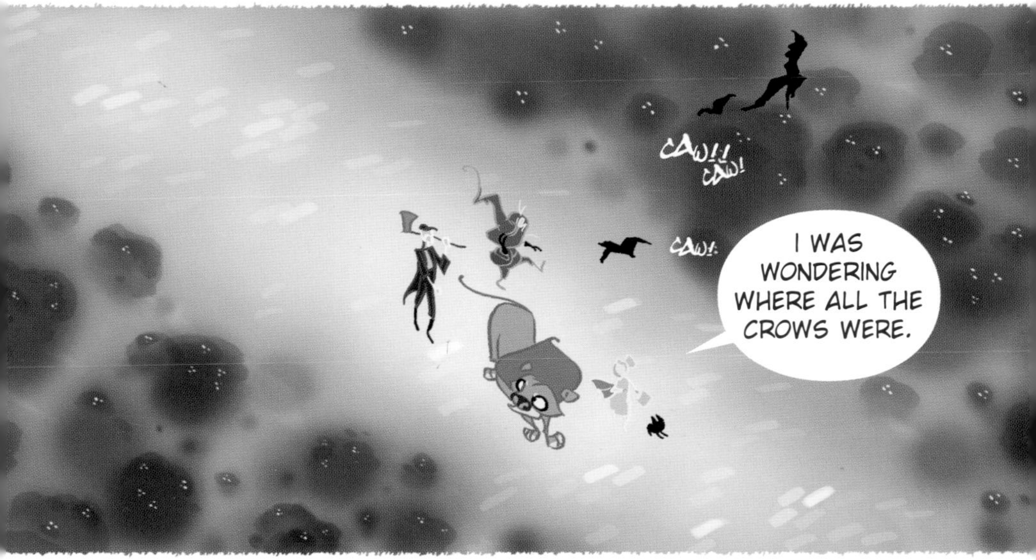
CAW!!
CAW!
CAW!
I WAS WONDERING WHERE ALL THE CROWS WERE.
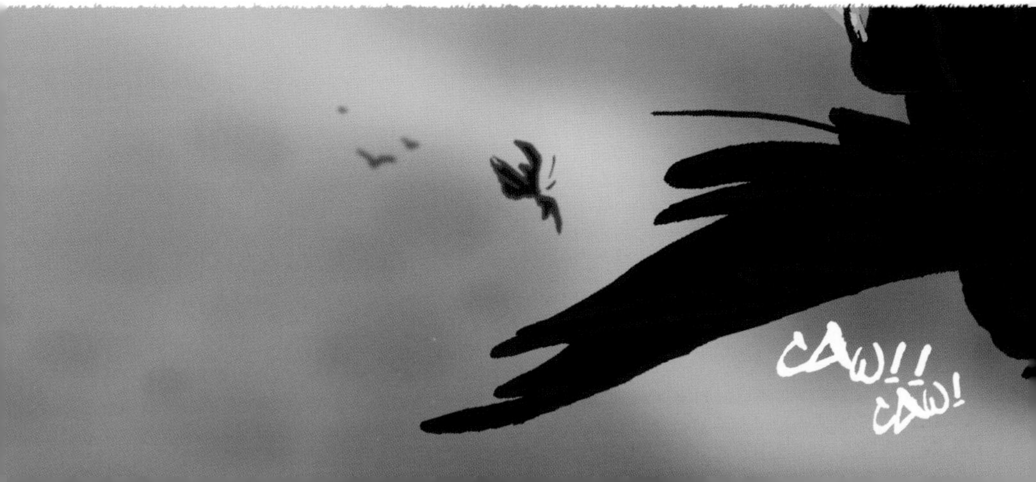
CAW!!
CAW!

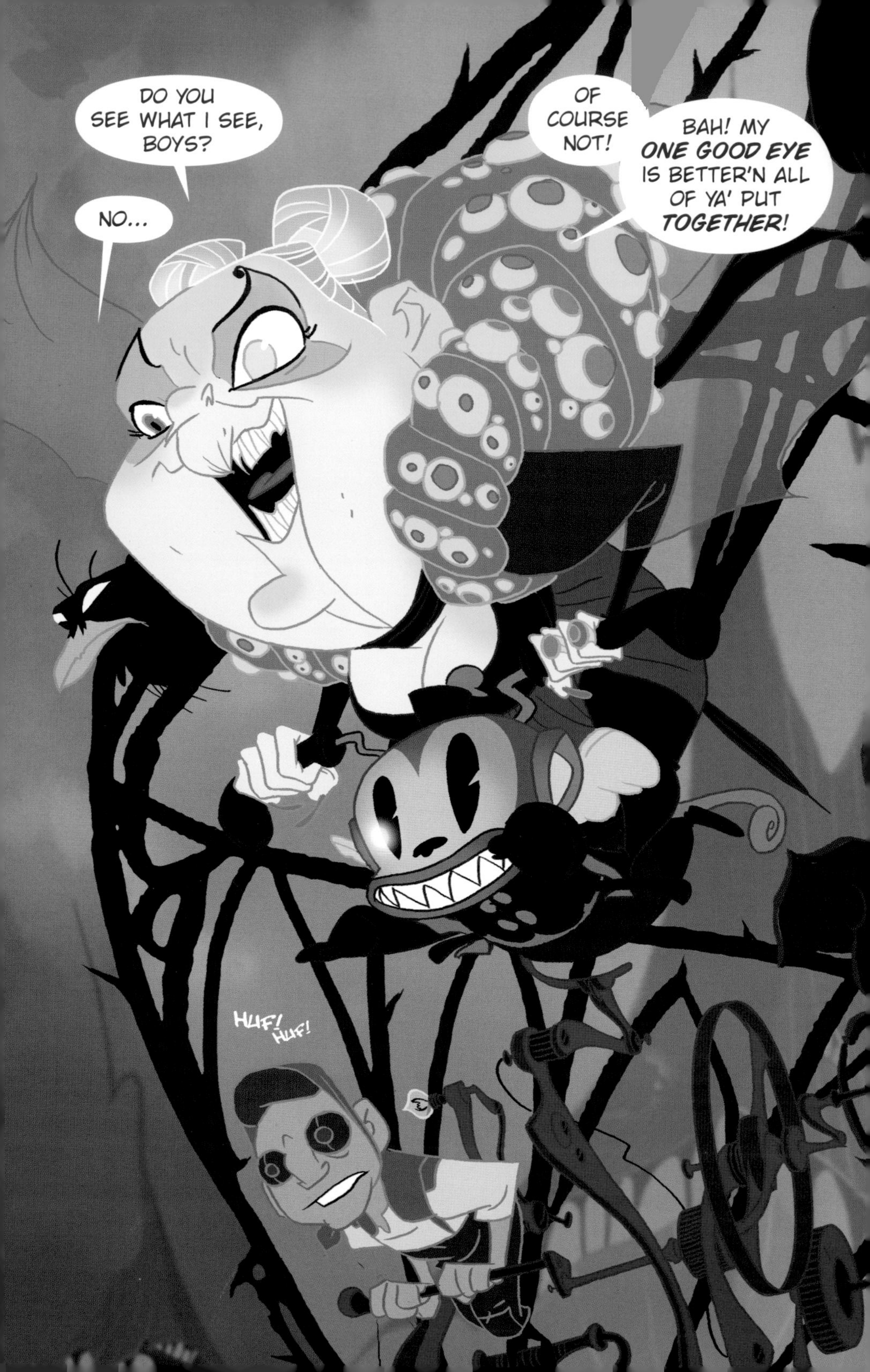
DO YOU SEE WHAT I SEE, BOYS?
NO...
OF COURSE NOT!
BAH! MY ONE GOOD EYE IS BETTER'N ALL OF YA' PUT TOGETHER!
HUF! HUF!

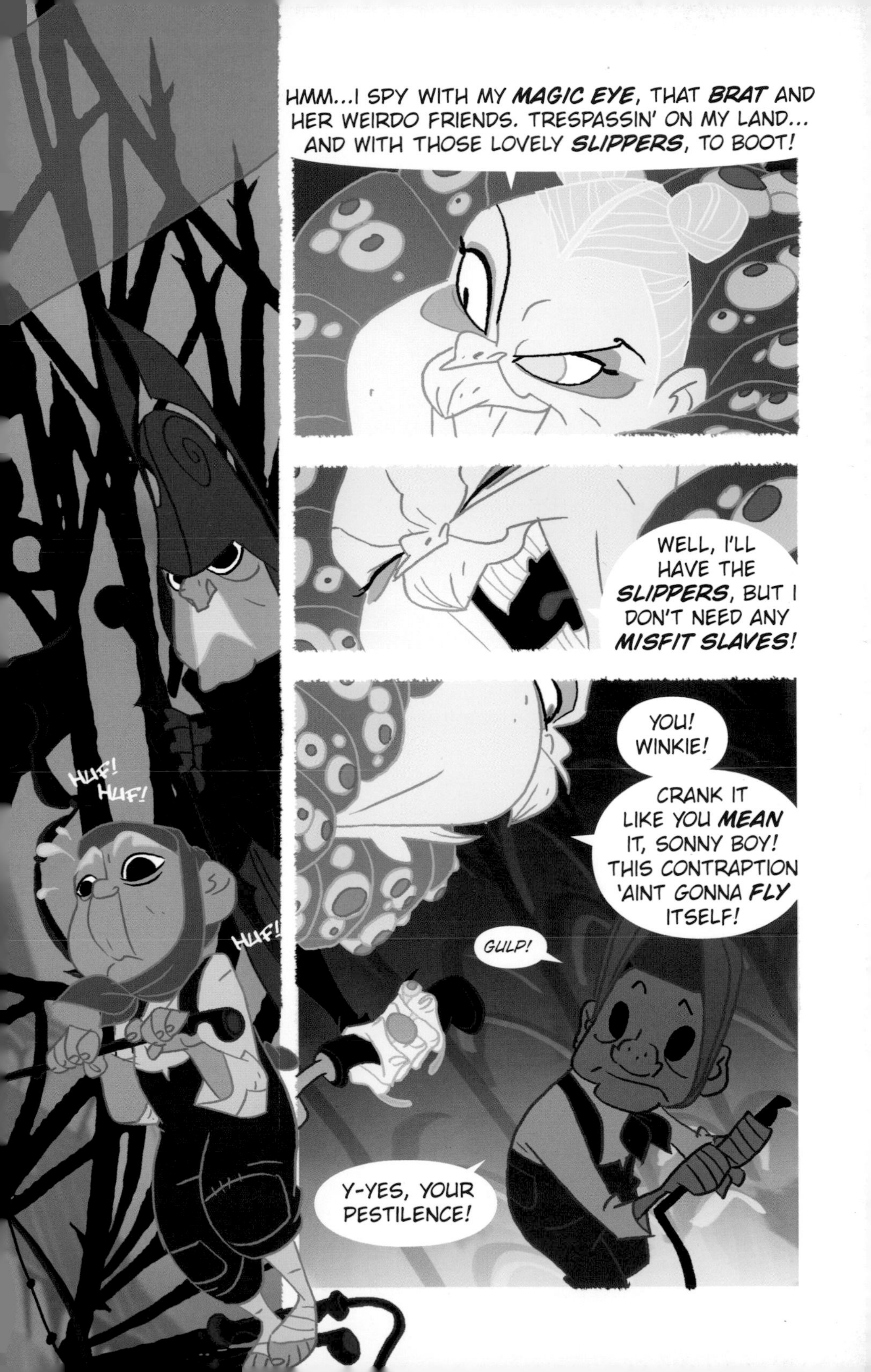
HMM...I SPY WITH MY MAGIC EYE, THAT BRAT AND HER WEIRDO FRIENDS. TRESPASSIN' ON MY LAND... AND WITH THOSE LOVELY SLIPPERS, TO BOOT!
WELL, I'LL HAVE THE SLIPPERS, BUT I DON'T NEED ANY MISFIT SLAVES!
HUF! HUF!
HUF!
YOU! WINKIE!
CRANK IT LIKE YOU MEAN IT, SONNY BOY! THIS CONTRAPTION 'AINT GONNA FLY ITSELF!
GULP!
Y-YES, YOUR PESTILENCE!

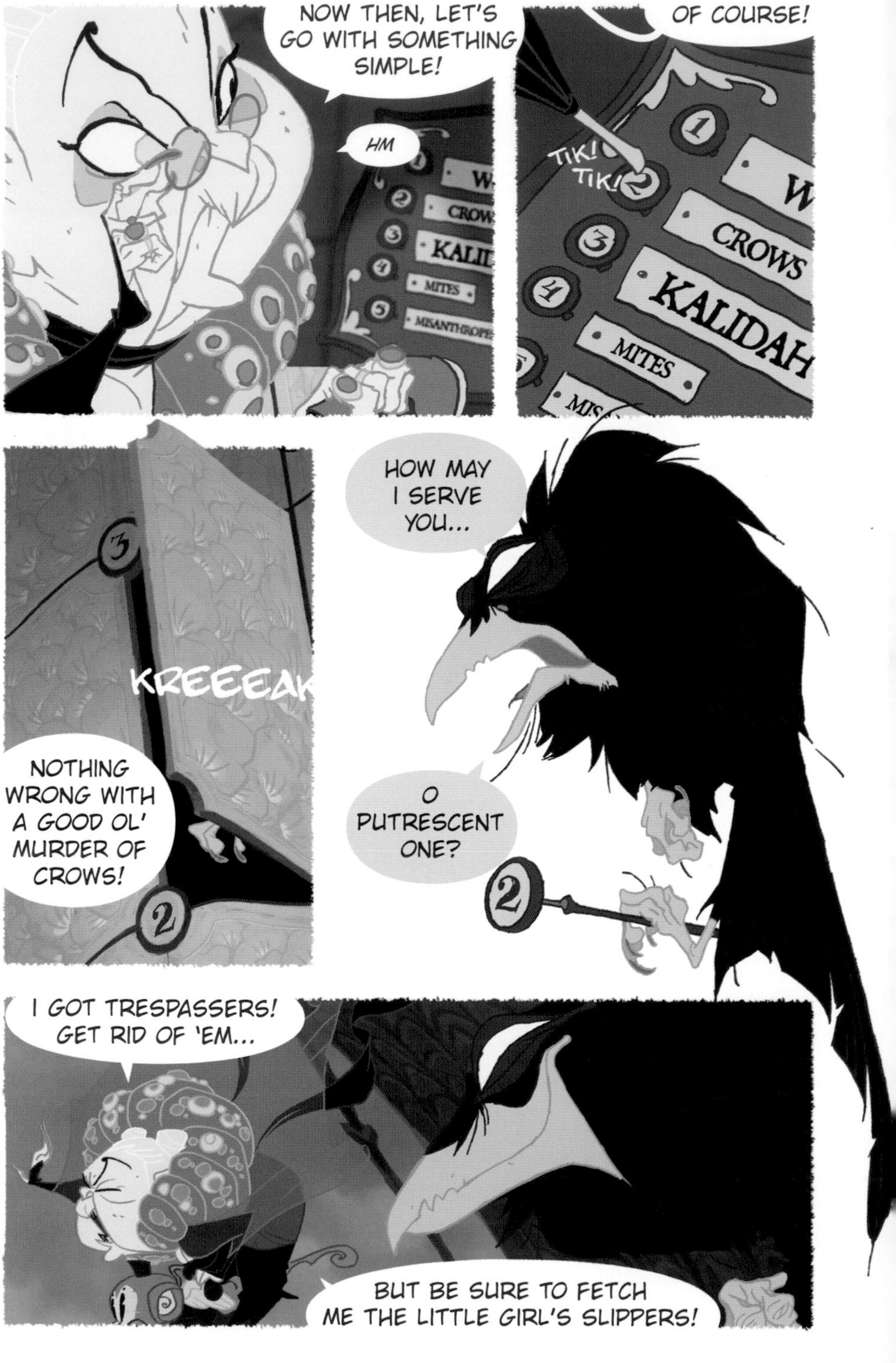
NOW THEN, LET'S GO WITH SOMETHING SIMPLE!
HM
W
CROWS
KALID
MITES
MISANTHROPES
OF COURSE!
TIK! TIK!
CROWS
KALIDAH
MITES
KREEEAK
NOTHING WRONG WITH A GOOD OL' MURDER OF CROWS!
HOW MAY I SERVE YOU...
O PUTRESCENT ONE?
I GOT TRESPASSERS! GET RID OF 'EM...
BUT BE SURE TO FETCH ME THE LITTLE GIRL'S SLIPPERS!

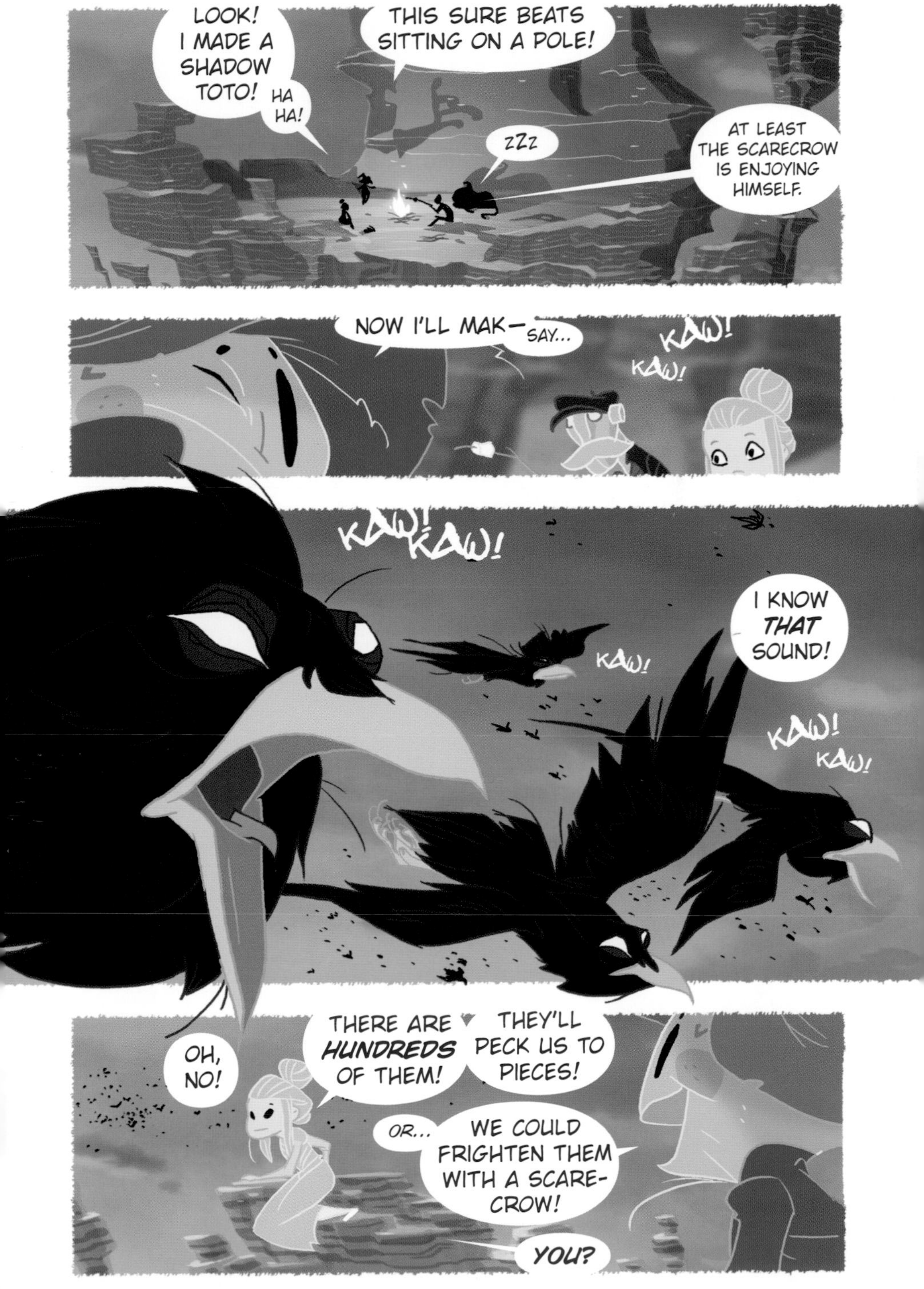
LOOK! I MADE A SHADOW TOTO!
HA HA!
THIS SURE BEATS SITTING ON A POLE!
ZZz
AT LEAST THE SCARECROW IS ENJOYING HIMSELF.
NOW I'LL MAK—
SAY...
KAW!
KAW!
KAW! KAW!
I KNOW *THAT* SOUND!
KAW!
KAW!
KAW!
OH, NO!
THERE ARE ***HUNDREDS*** OF THEM!
THEY'LL PECK US TO PIECES!
OR...
WE COULD FRIGHTEN THEM WITH A SCARE-CROW!
YOU?

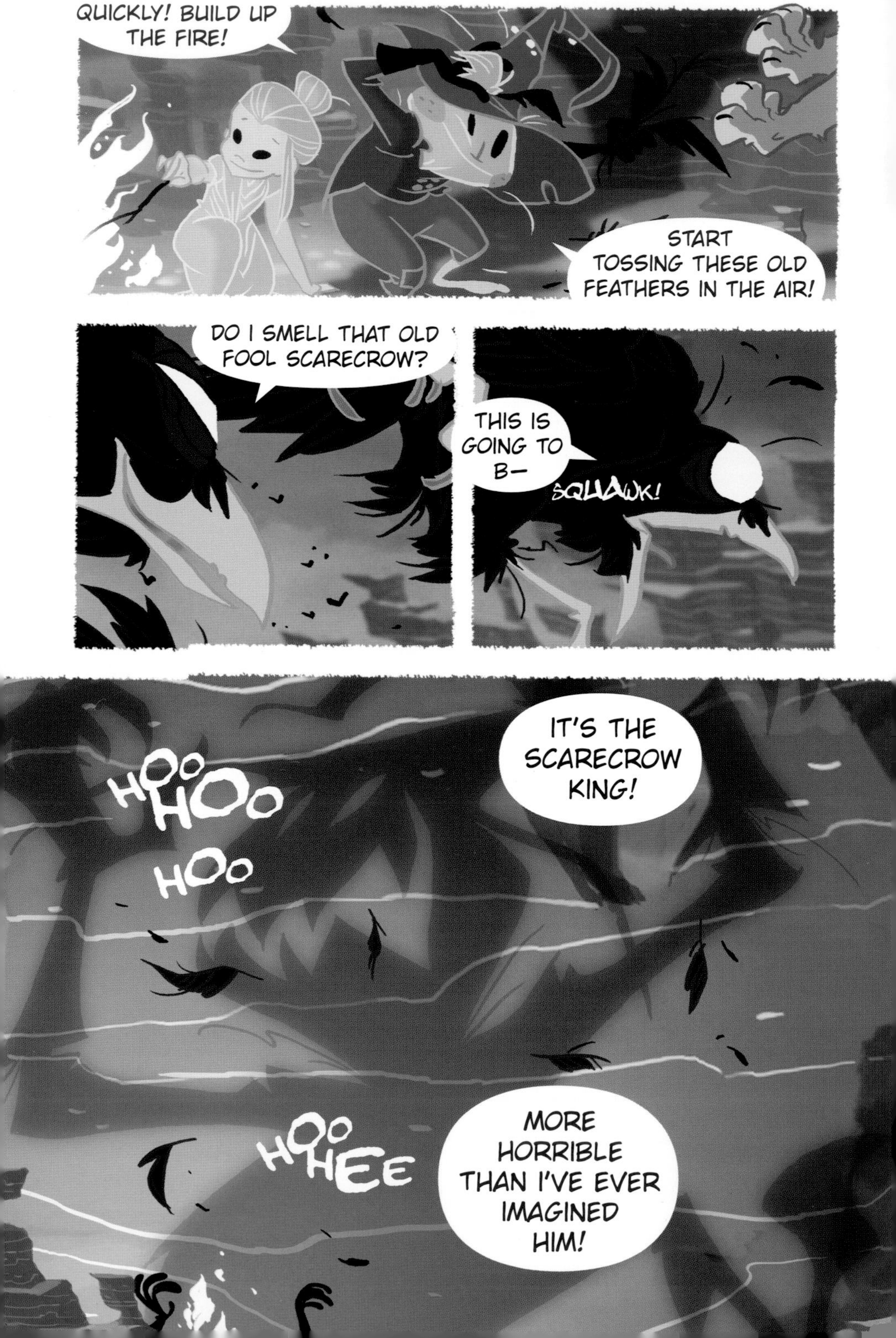
QUICKLY! BUILD UP THE FIRE!
START TOSSING THESE OLD FEATHERS IN THE AIR!
DO I SMELL THAT OLD FOOL SCARECROW?
THIS IS GOING TO B—
SQUAWK!
IT'S THE SCARECROW KING!
HOO HOO HOO
HOO HEE
MORE HORRIBLE THAN I'VE EVER IMAGINED HIM!

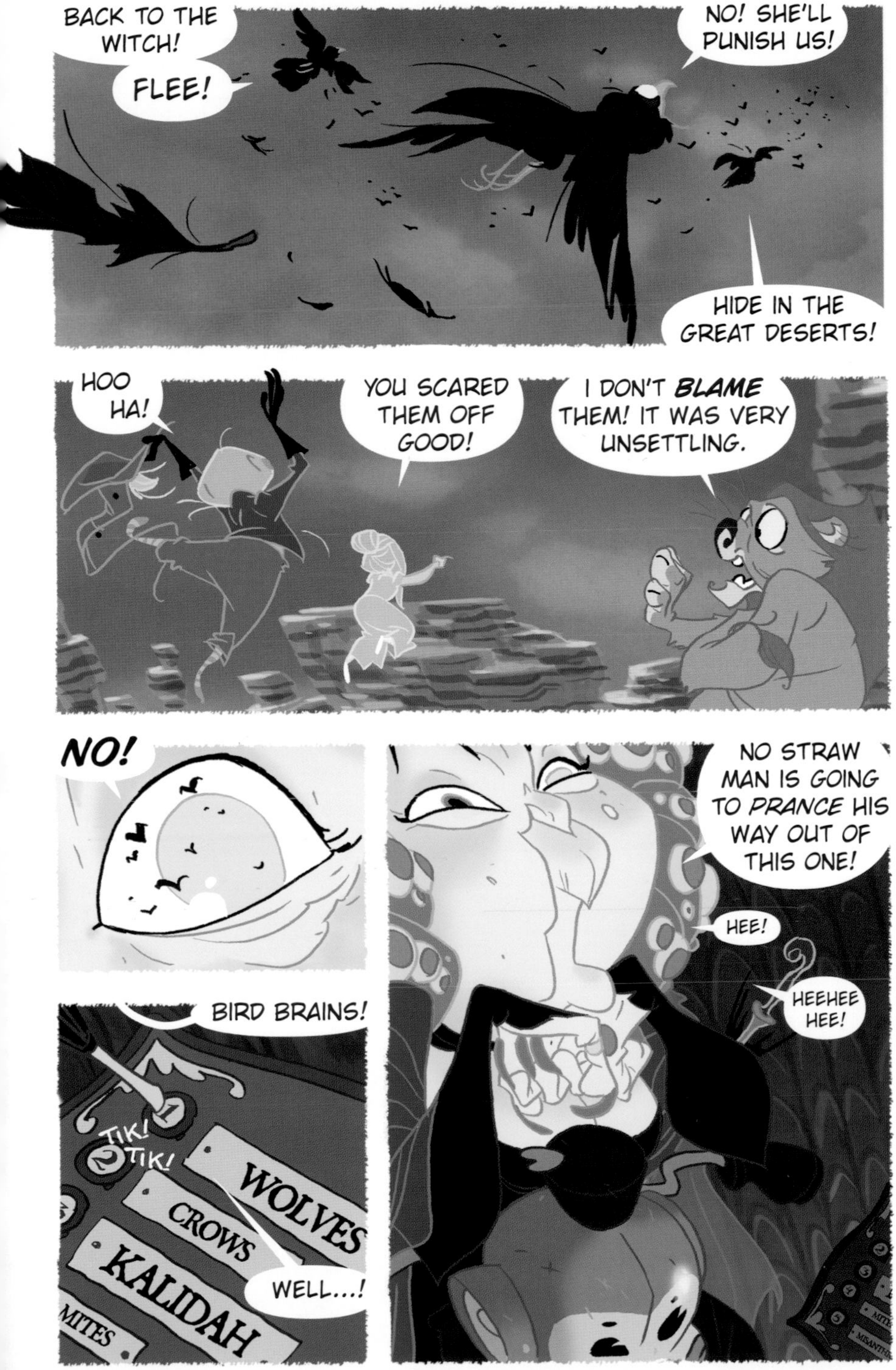
BACK TO THE WITCH!
FLEE!
NO! SHE'LL PUNISH US!
HIDE IN THE GREAT DESERTS!
HOO HA!
YOU SCARED THEM OFF GOOD!
I DON'T BLAME THEM! IT WAS VERY UNSETTLING.
NO!
NO STRAW MAN IS GOING TO PRANCE HIS WAY OUT OF THIS ONE!
HEE!
HEEHEE HEE!
BIRD BRAINS!
TIK!
TIK!
WOLVES
CROWS
KALIDAH
MITES
WELL...!

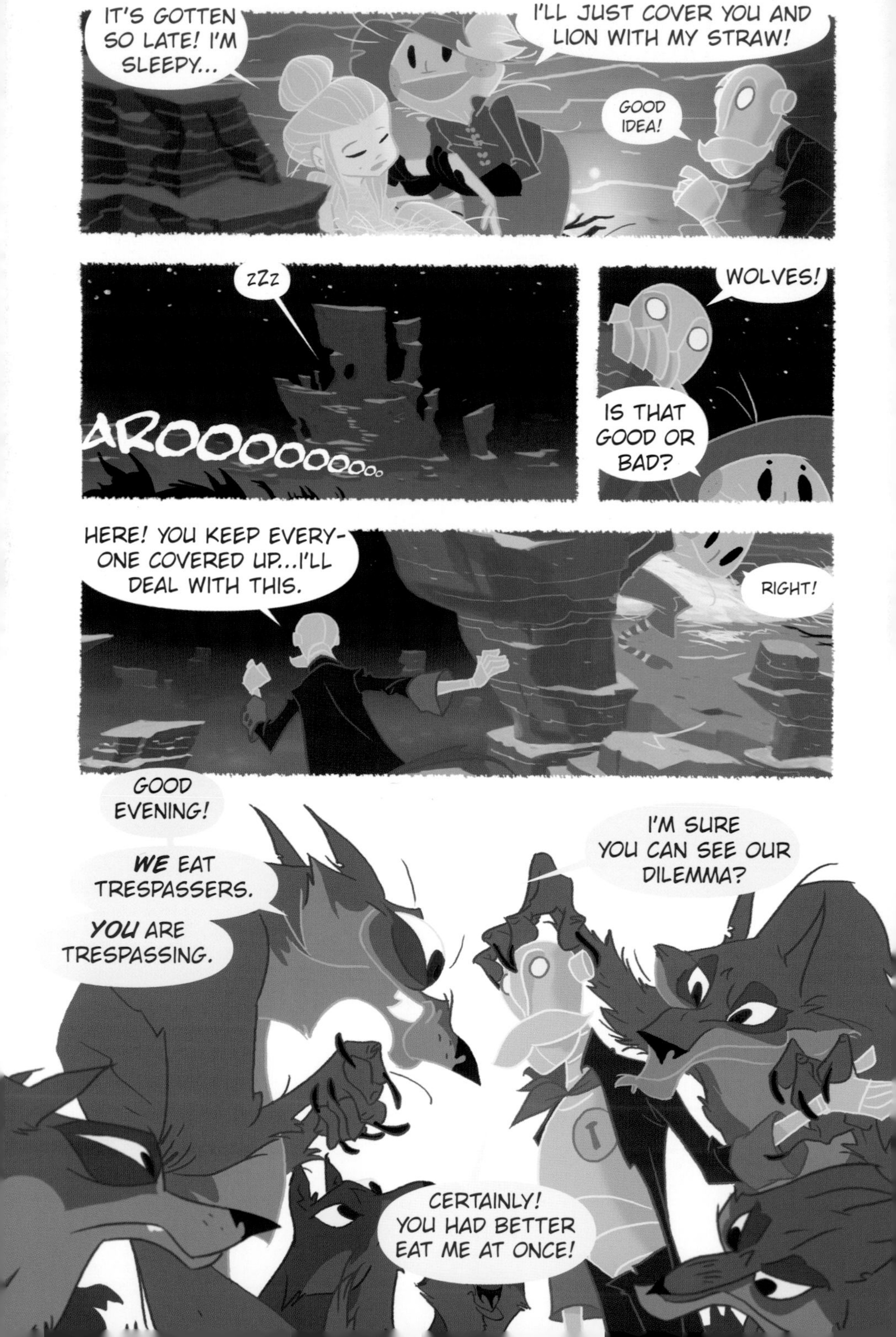
IT'S GOTTEN SO LATE! I'M SLEEPY...
I'LL JUST COVER YOU AND LION WITH MY STRAW!
GOOD IDEA!
ZZZ
AROOOOOOOOoo
WOLVES!
IS THAT GOOD OR BAD?
HERE! YOU KEEP EVERY-ONE COVERED UP...I'LL DEAL WITH THIS.
RIGHT!
GOOD EVENING!
WE EAT TRESPASSERS.
YOU ARE TRESPASSING.
I'M SURE YOU CAN SEE OUR DILEMMA?
CERTAINLY! YOU HAD BETTER EAT ME AT ONCE!

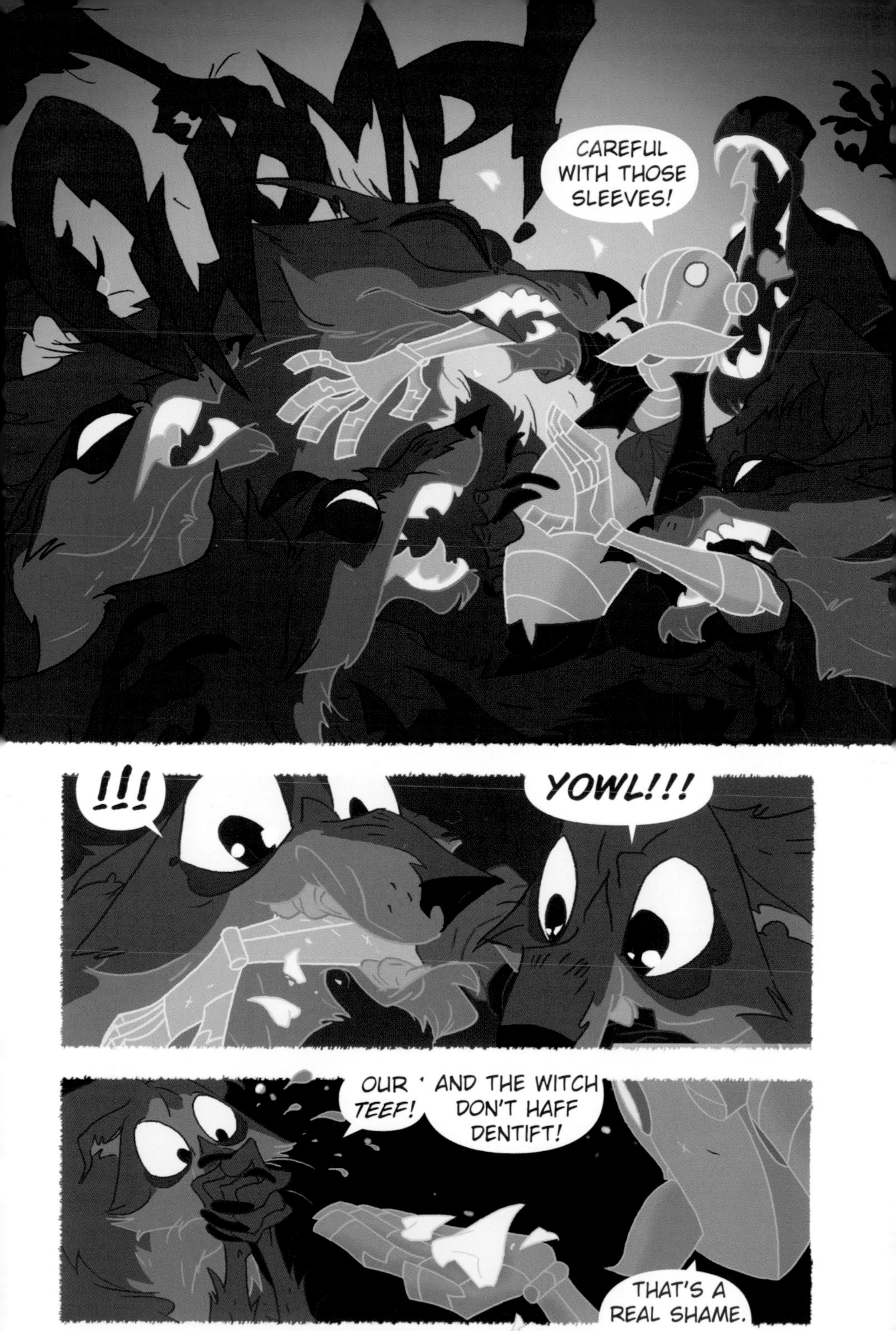
CAREFUL WITH THOSE SLEEVES!
!!!
YOWL!!!
OUR TEEF!
AND THE WITCH DON'T HAFF DENTIFT!
THAT'S A REAL SHAME.

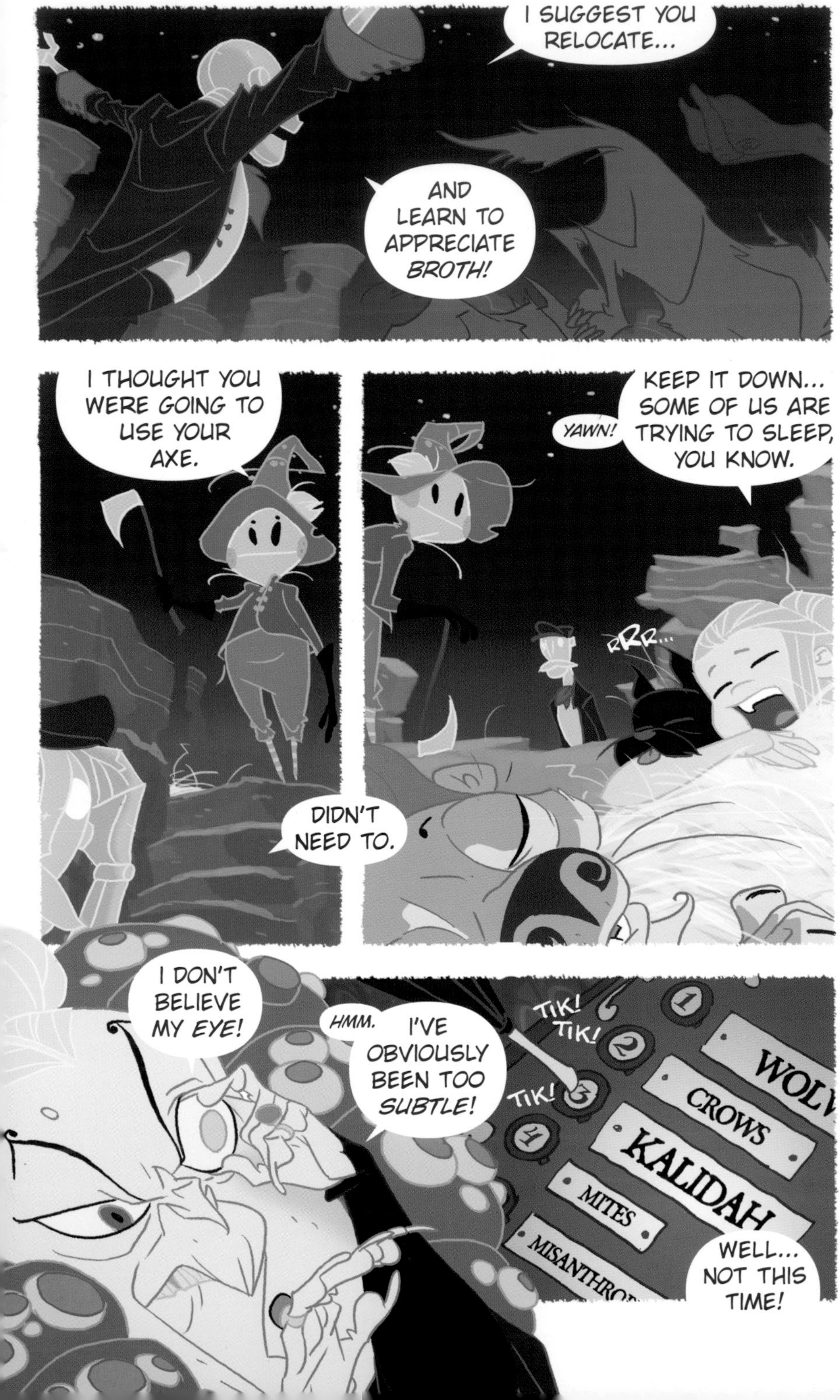
I SUGGEST YOU RELOCATE...
AND LEARN TO APPRECIATE *BROTH!*
I THOUGHT YOU WERE GOING TO USE YOUR AXE.
DIDN'T NEED TO.
YAWN!
KEEP IT DOWN... SOME OF US ARE TRYING TO SLEEP, YOU KNOW.
RRR...
I DON'T BELIEVE MY *EYE!*
HMM.
I'VE OBVIOUSLY BEEN TOO *SUBTLE!*
TIK! TIK!
TIK!
WOLV
CROWS
KALIDAH
MITES
WELL... NOT THIS *TIME!*

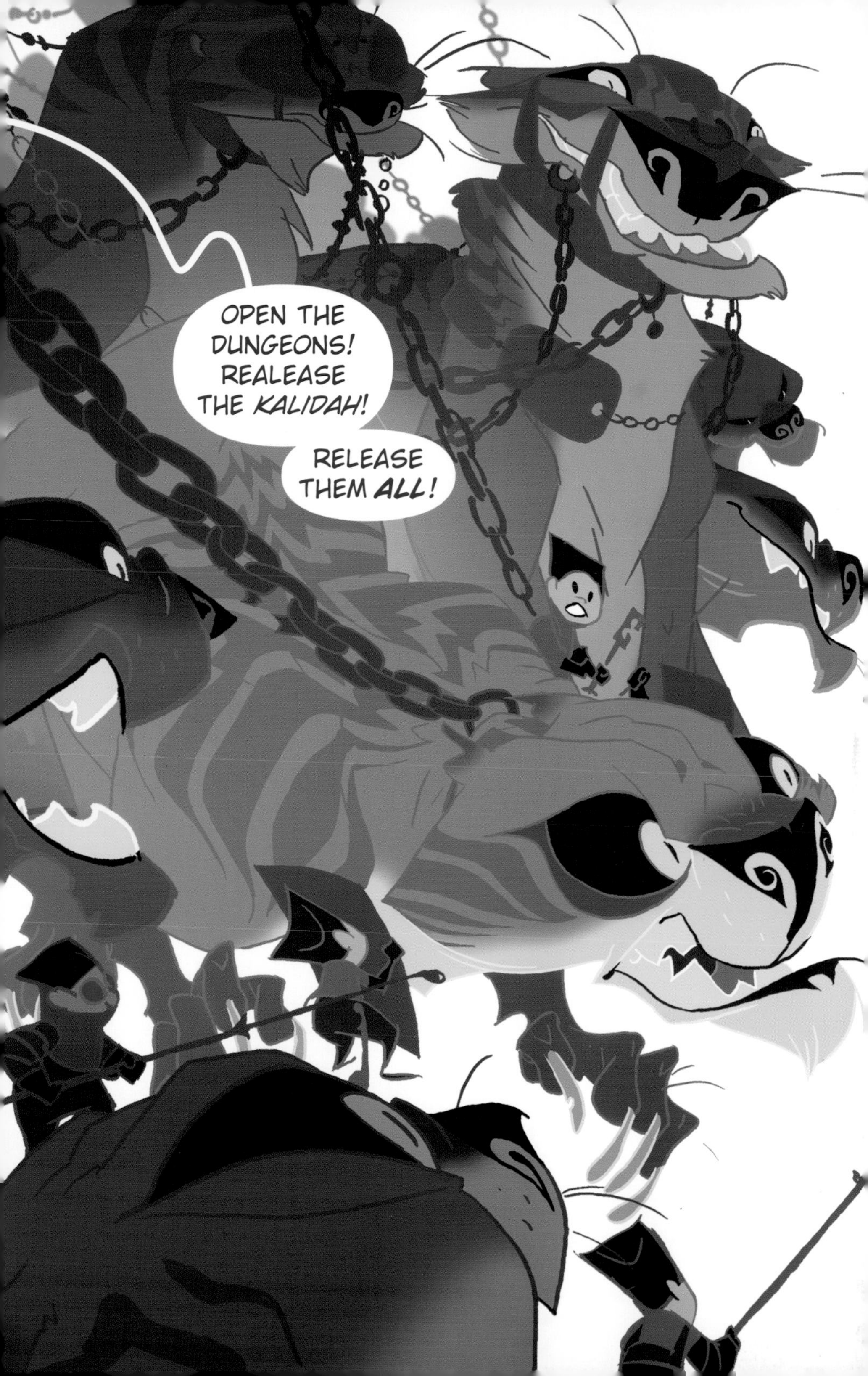
OPEN THE DUNGEONS! REALEASE THE KALIDAH!
RELEASE THEM ALL!

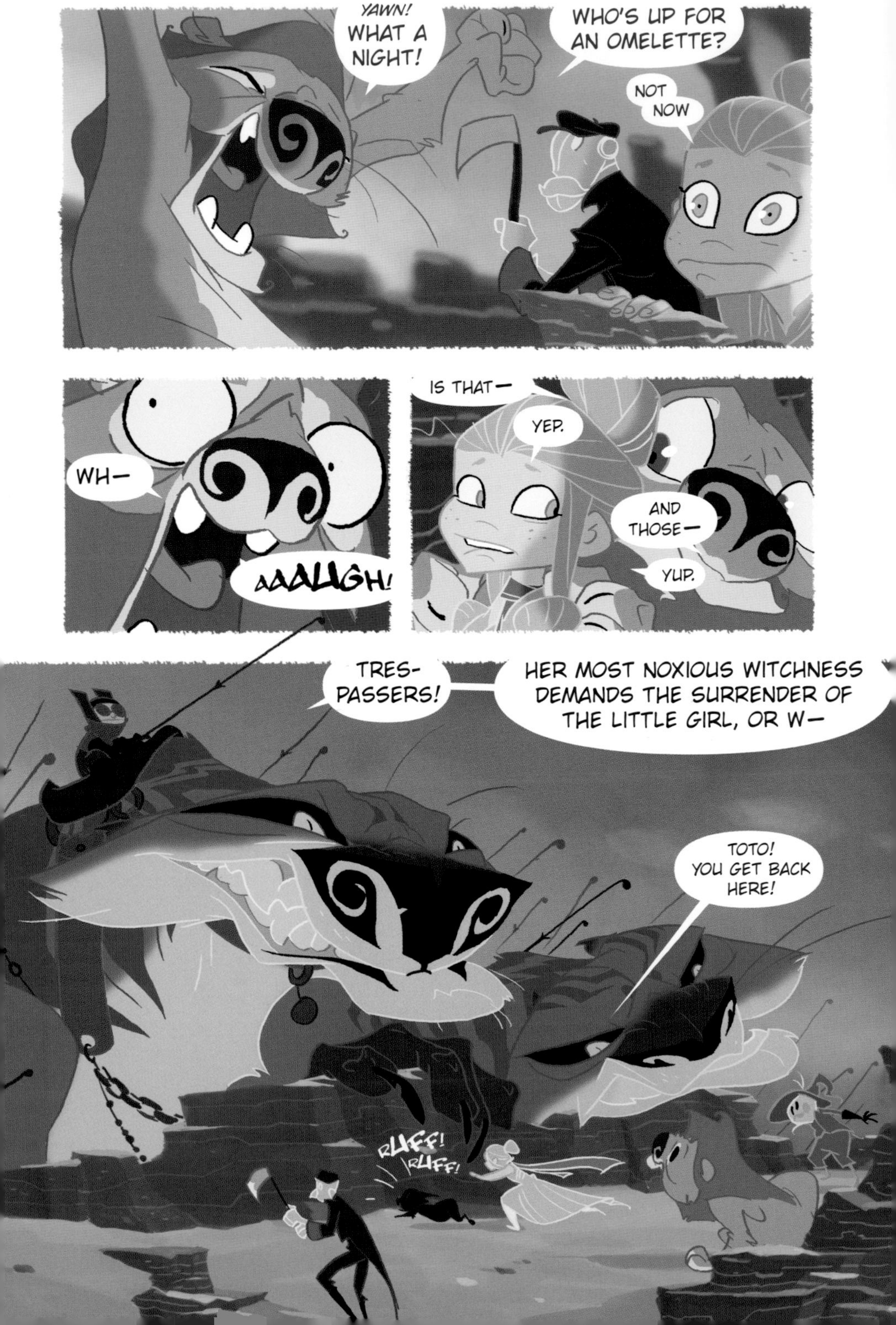
YAWN! WHAT A NIGHT!
WHO'S UP FOR AN OMELETTE?
NOT NOW
WH—
AAAUGH!
IS THAT—
YEP.
AND THOSE—
YUP.
TRES-PASSERS!
HER MOST NOXIOUS WITCHNESS DEMANDS THE SURRENDER OF THE LITTLE GIRL, OR W—
TOTO! YOU GET BACK HERE!
RUFF! RUFF!

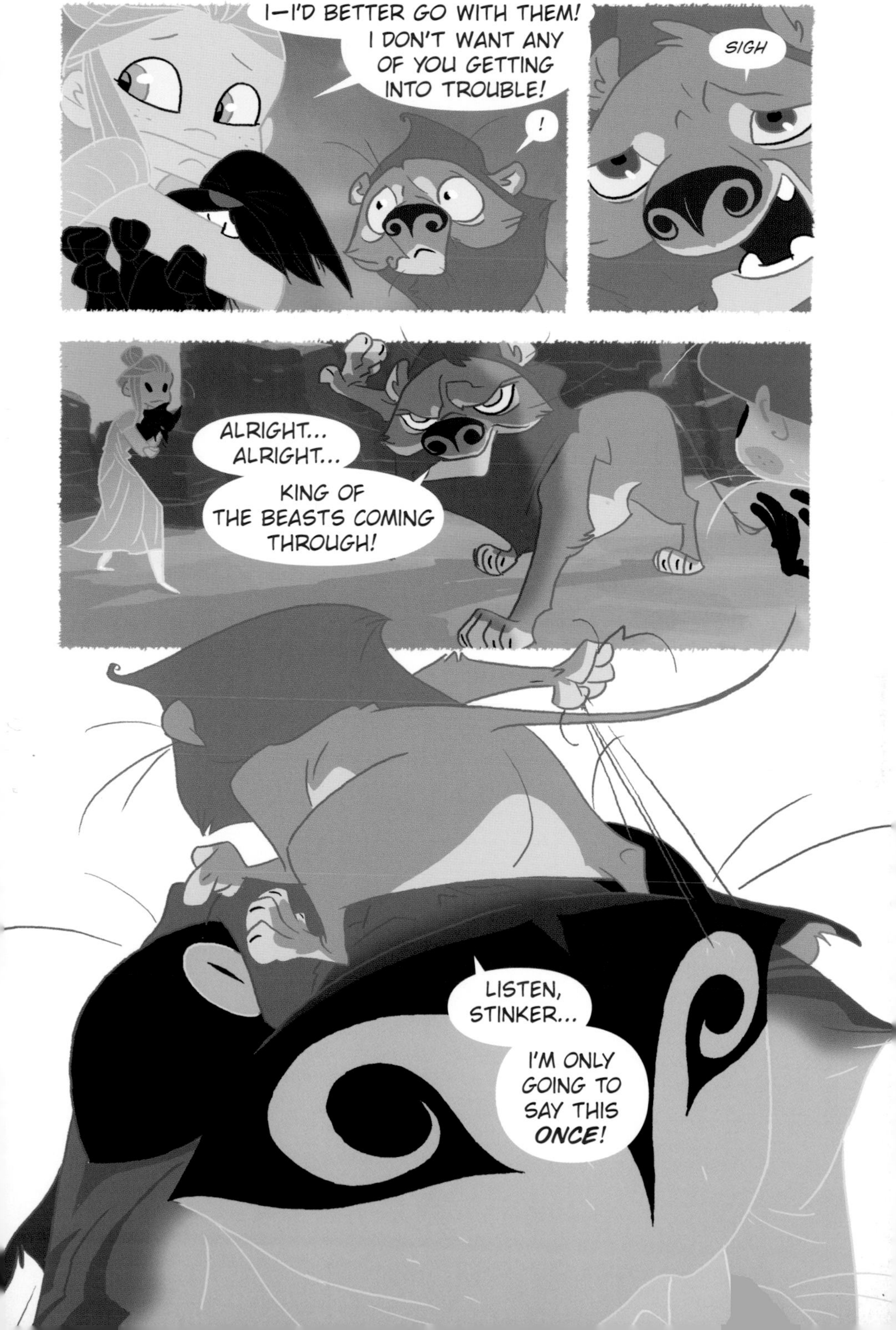
I—I'D BETTER GO WITH THEM! I DON'T WANT ANY OF YOU GETTING INTO TROUBLE!
!
SIGH
ALRIGHT... ALRIGHT...
KING OF THE BEASTS COMING THROUGH!
LISTEN, STINKER...
I'M ONLY GOING TO SAY THIS *ONCE*!

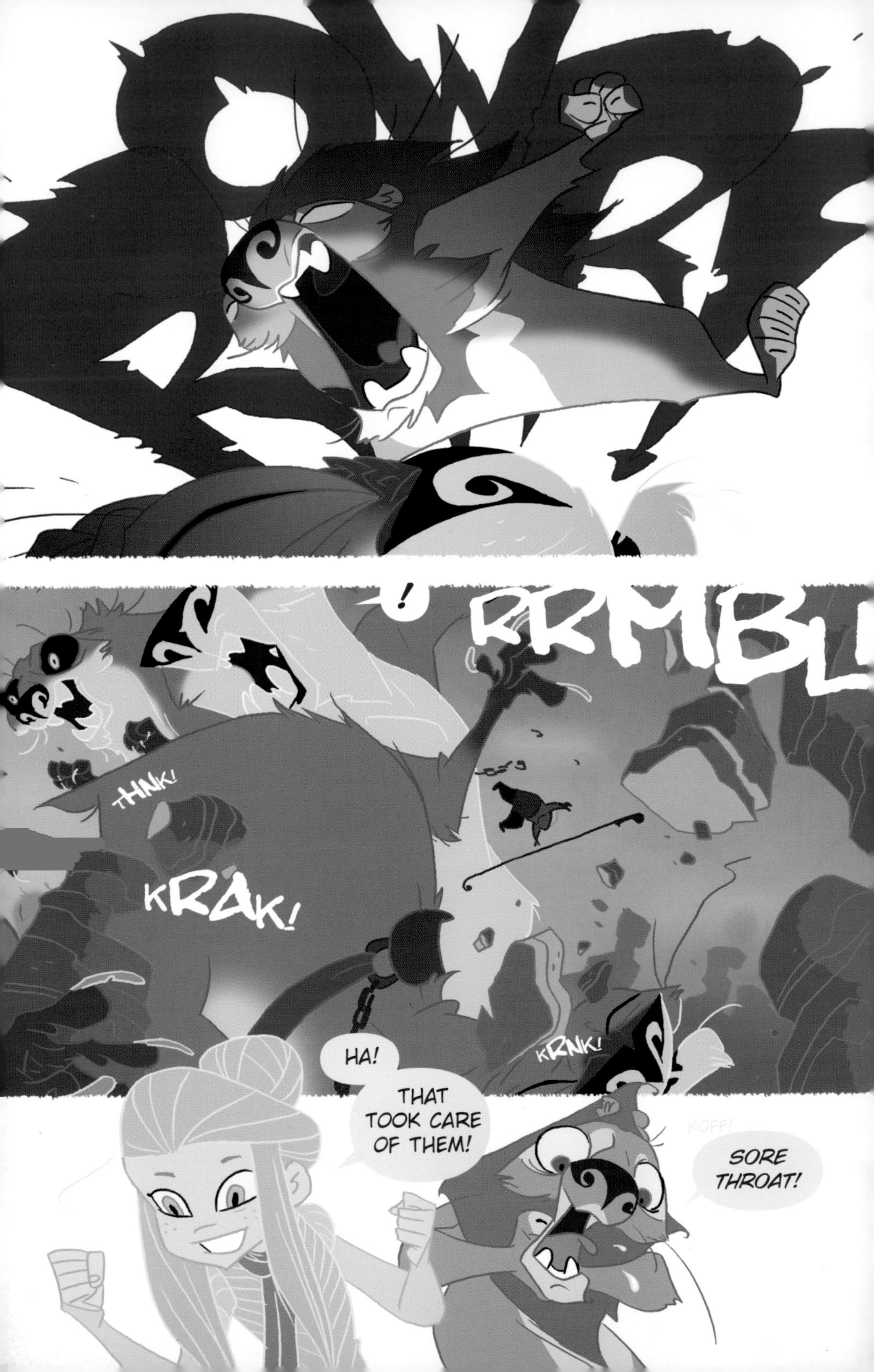
!
RRMBL
THNK!
KRAK!
KRNK!
HA!
THAT TOOK CARE OF THEM!
KOFF!
SORE THROAT!

I DON'T BELIEVE IT!

GRR...

GET OUT, CABBAGES!

SLAM!

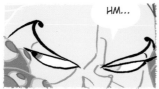

HM...

!

WELL... THERE'S MORE THAN ONE WAY TO SKIN A CAT!

AND A SCARECROW, AND A TIN MAN...

AND A LITTLE GIRL!

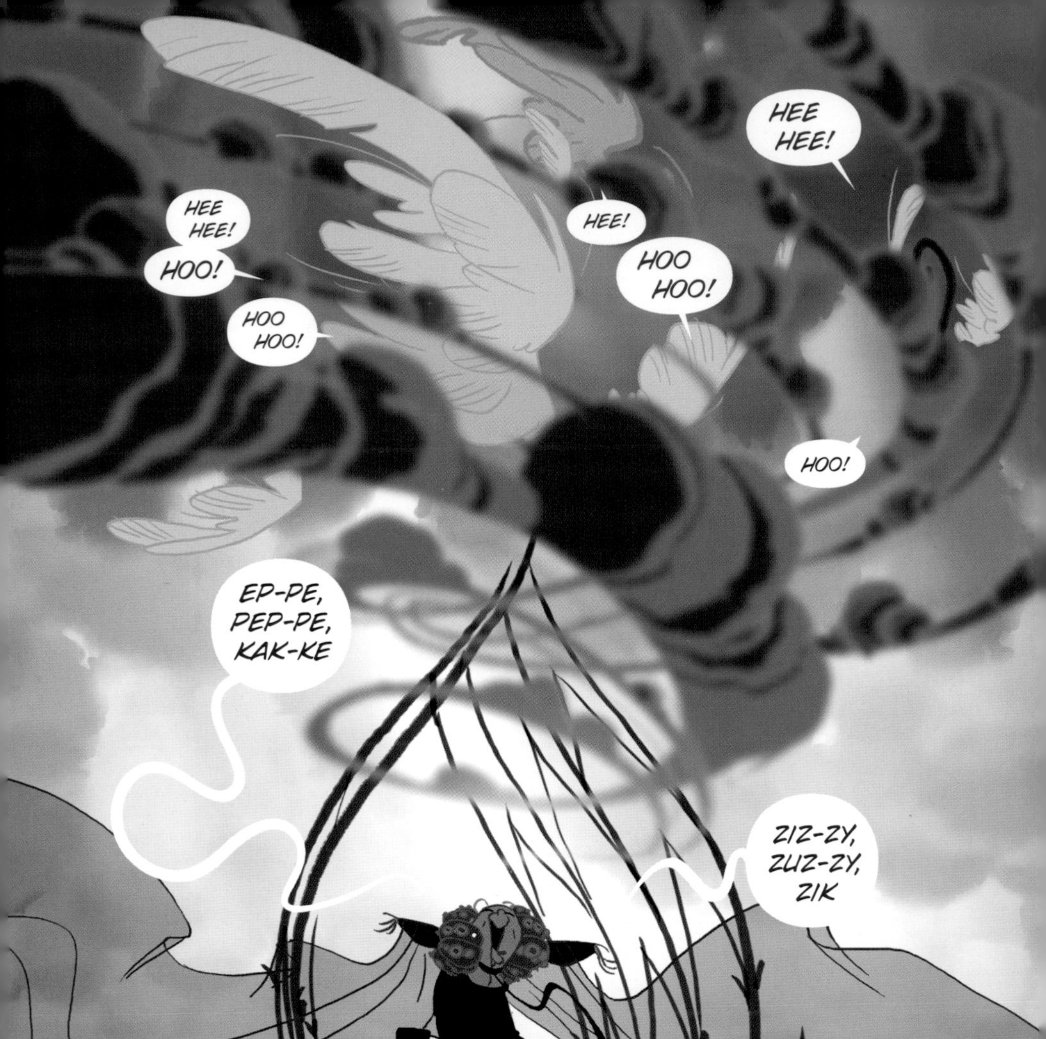
HEE HEE!
HOO!
HOO HOO!
HEE!
HOO HOO!
HEE HEE!
HOO!
EP-PE, PEP-PE, KAK-KE
ZIZ-ZY, ZUZ-ZY, ZIK

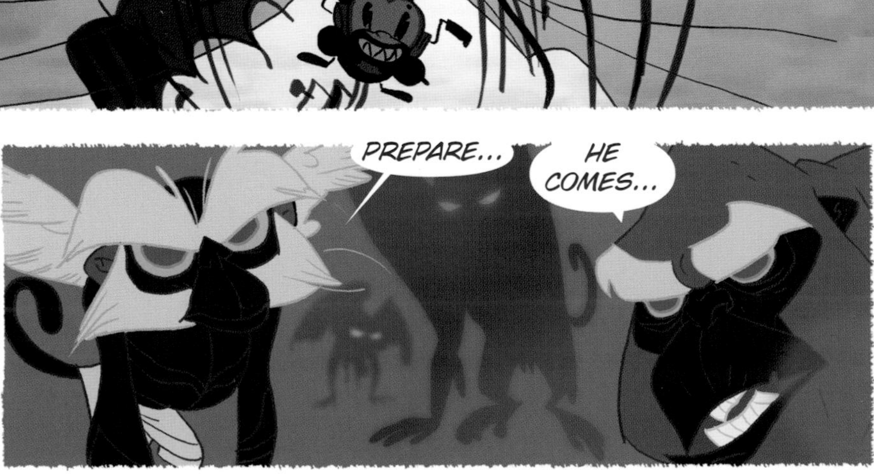
PREPARE...
HE COMES...

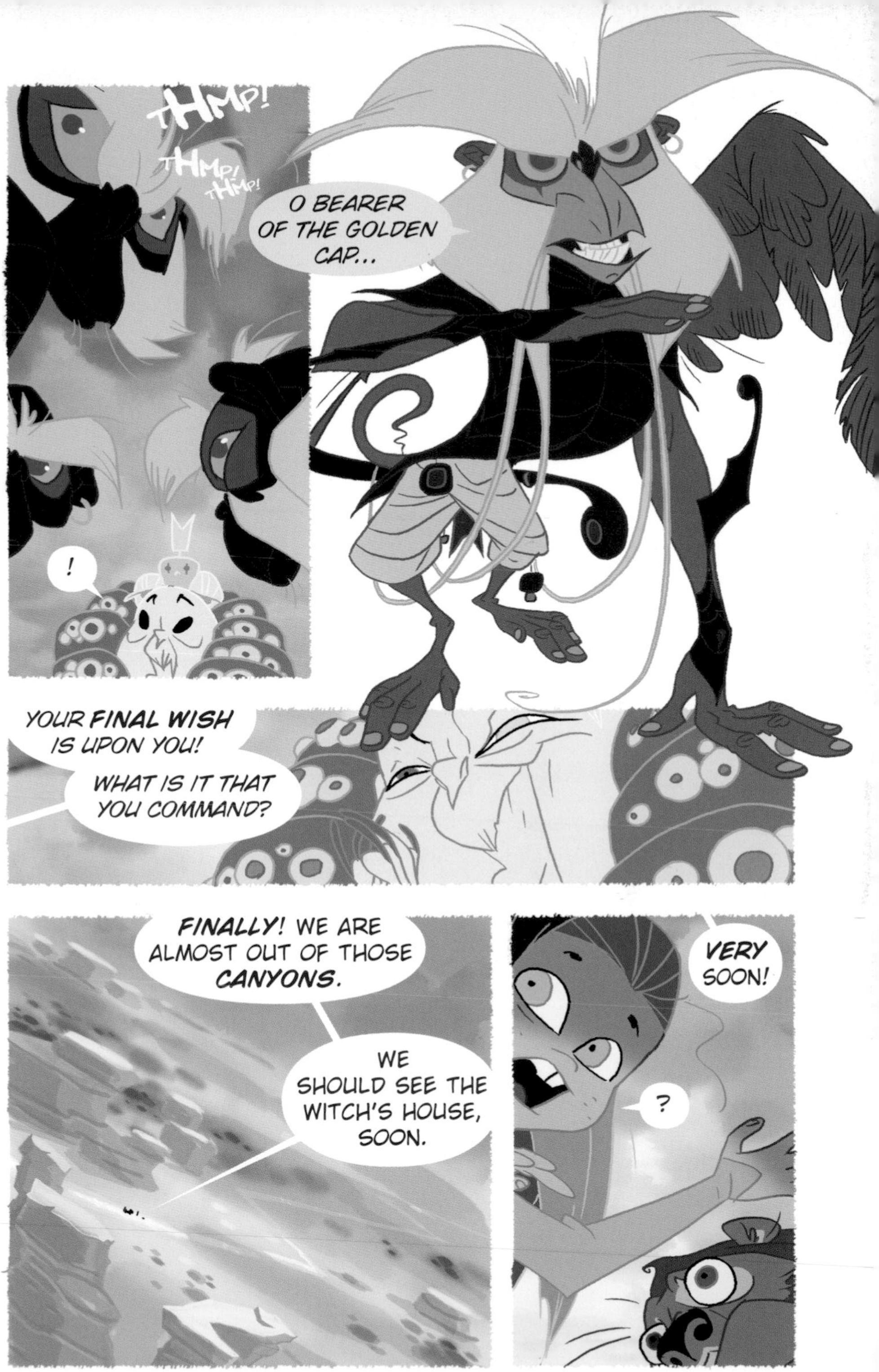
tHMp!
tHMp!
tHMp!
O BEARER OF THE GOLDEN CAP...
!
YOUR FINAL WISH IS UPON YOU!
WHAT IS IT THAT YOU COMMAND?
FINALLY! WE ARE ALMOST OUT OF THOSE CANYONS.
WE SHOULD SEE THE WITCH'S HOUSE, SOON.
VERY SOON!
?

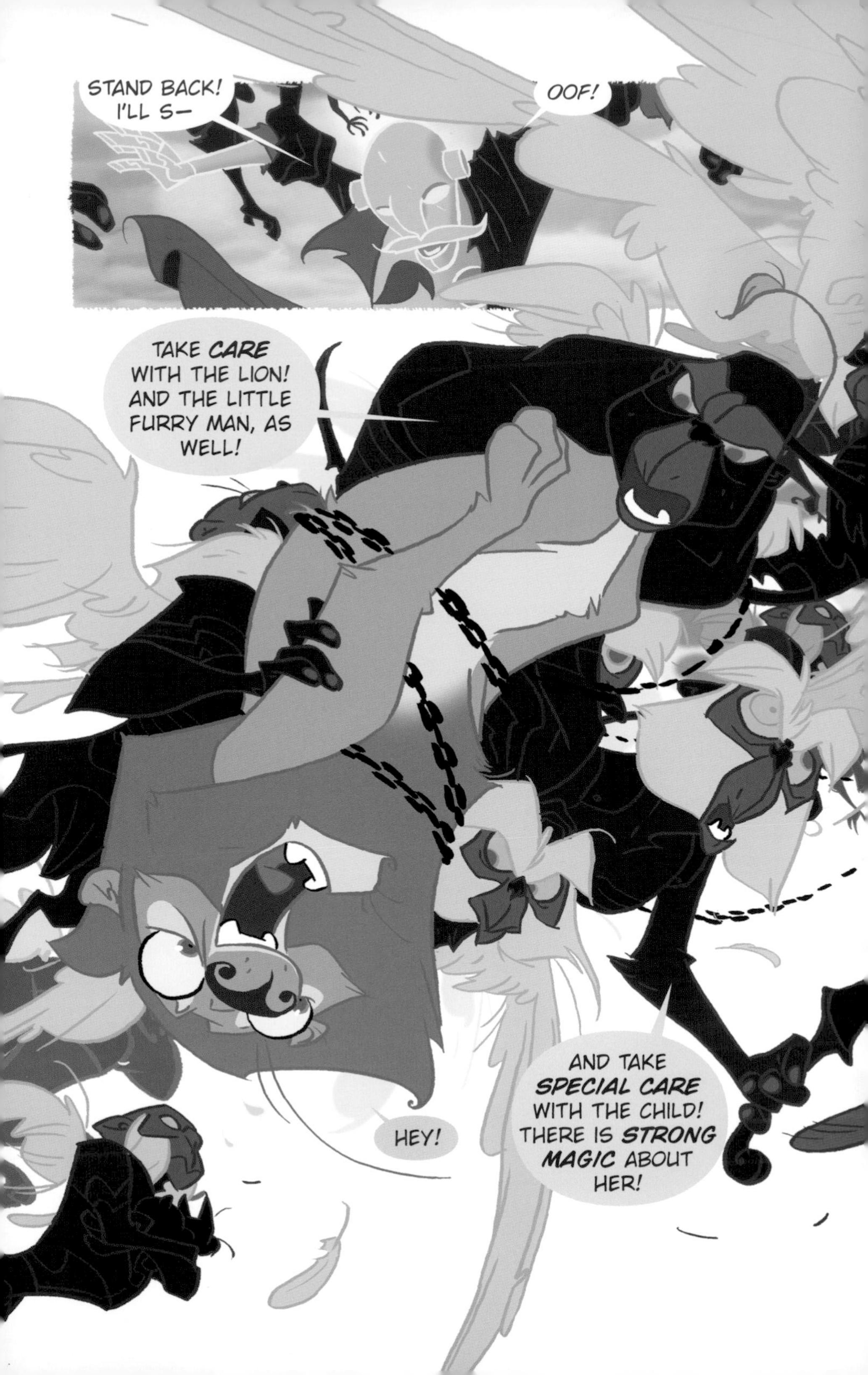
STAND BACK! I'LL S—
OOF!
TAKE CARE WITH THE LION! AND THE LITTLE FURRY MAN, AS WELL!
HEY!
AND TAKE SPECIAL CARE WITH THE CHILD! THERE IS STRONG MAGIC ABOUT HER!

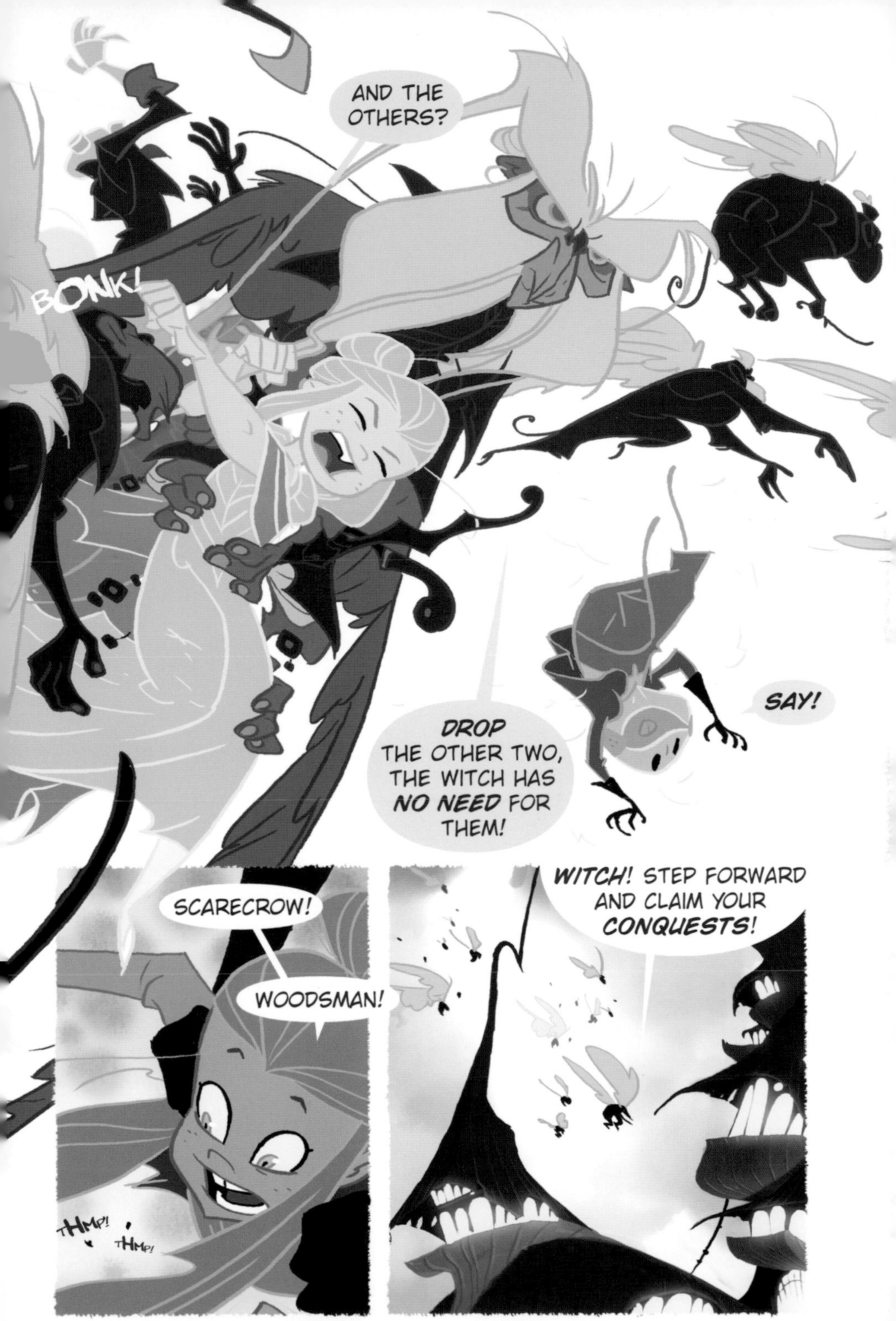
AND THE OTHERS?
BONK!
DROP THE OTHER TWO, THE WITCH HAS NO NEED FOR THEM!
SAY!
SCARECROW!
WOODSMAN!
THMP! THMP!
WITCH! STEP FORWARD AND CLAIM YOUR CONQUESTS!

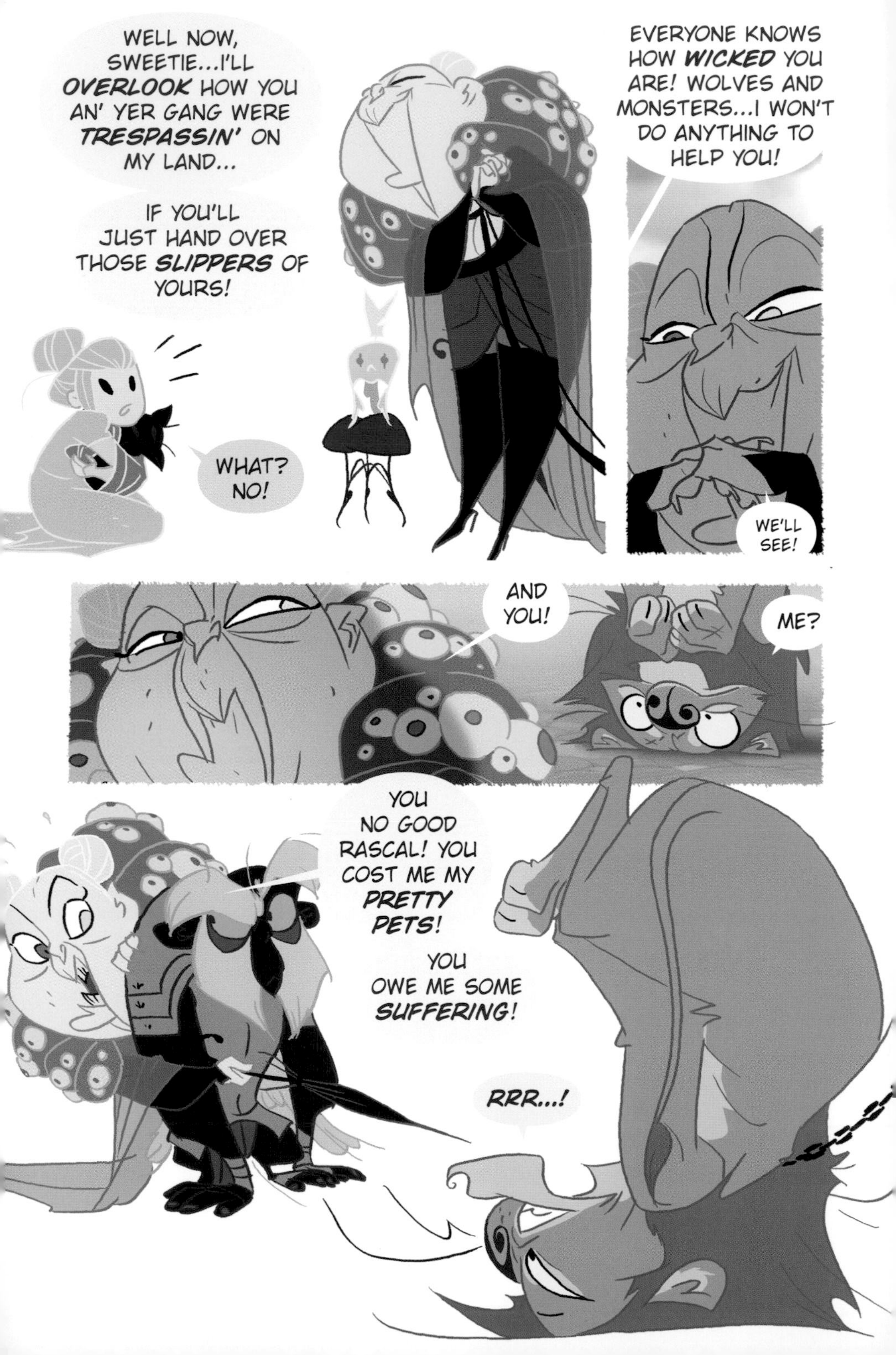
WELL NOW, SWEETIE...I'LL OVERLOOK HOW YOU AN' YER GANG WERE TRESPASSIN' ON MY LAND...
IF YOU'LL JUST HAND OVER THOSE SLIPPERS OF YOURS!
WHAT? NO!
EVERYONE KNOWS HOW WICKED YOU ARE! WOLVES AND MONSTERS...I WON'T DO ANYTHING TO HELP YOU!
WE'LL SEE!
AND YOU!
ME?
YOU NO GOOD RASCAL! YOU COST ME MY PRETTY PETS!
YOU OWE ME SOME SUFFERING!
RRR...!

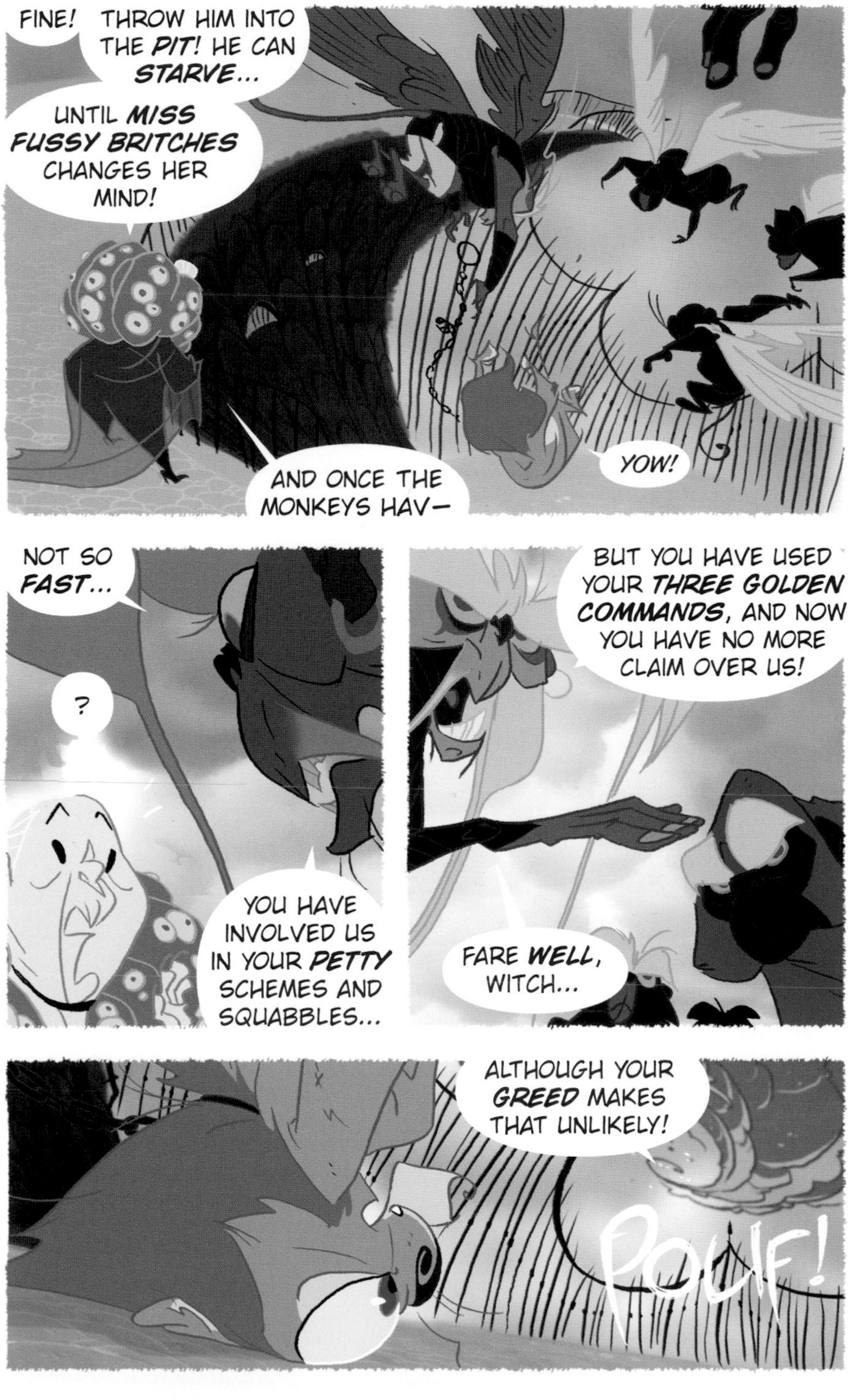
FINE!
THROW HIM INTO THE PIT! HE CAN STARVE...
UNTIL MISS FUSSY BRITCHES CHANGES HER MIND!
AND ONCE THE MONKEYS HAV—
YOW!
NOT SO FAST...
?
YOU HAVE INVOLVED US IN YOUR PETTY SCHEMES AND SQUABBLES...
BUT YOU HAVE USED YOUR THREE GOLDEN COMMANDS, AND NOW YOU HAVE NO MORE CLAIM OVER US!
FARE WELL, WITCH...
ALTHOUGH YOUR GREED MAKES THAT UNLIKELY!
POUF!

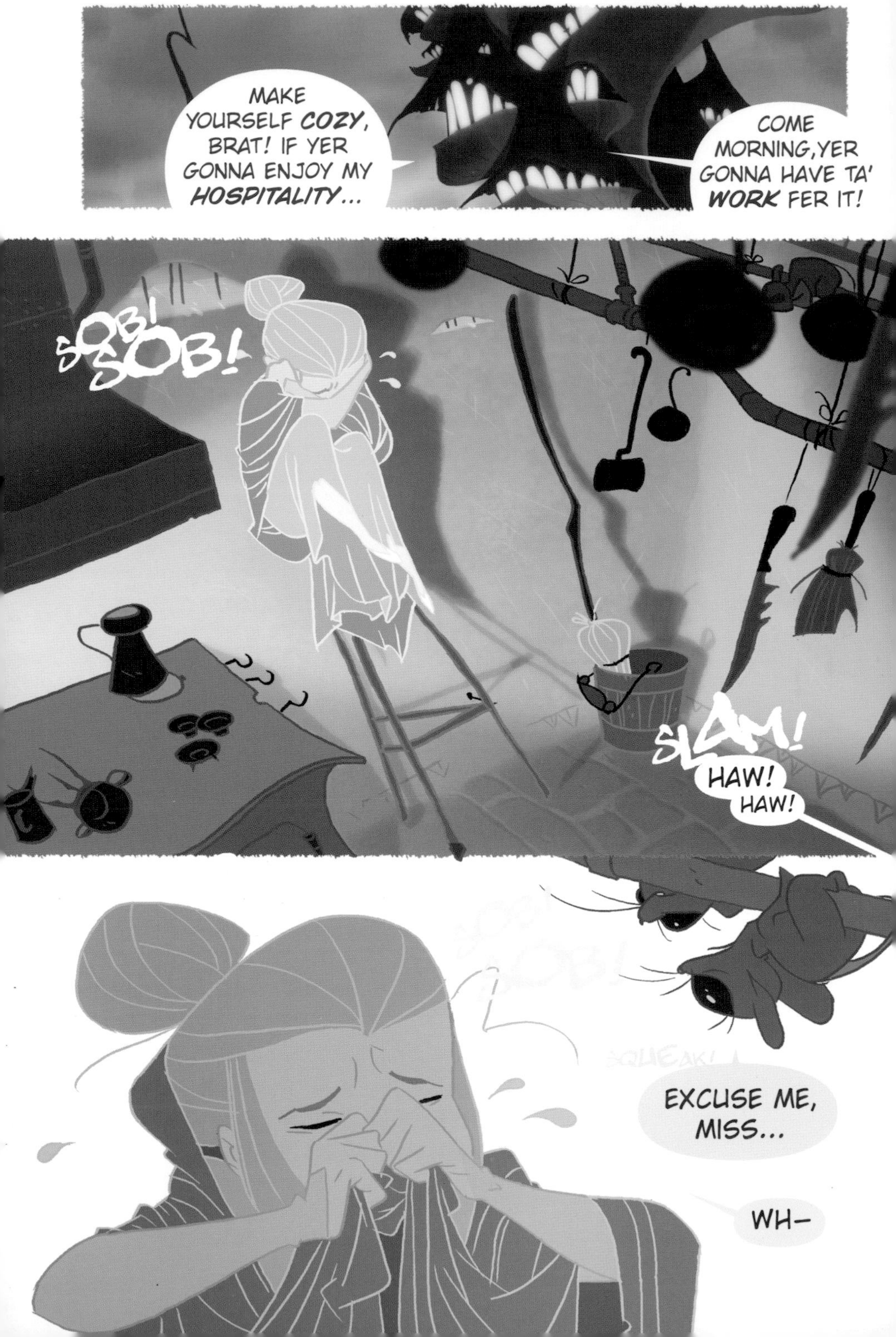
MAKE YOURSELF COZY, BRAT! IF YER GONNA ENJOY MY HOSPITALITY...
COME MORNING, YER GONNA HAVE TA' WORK FER IT!
SOB! SOB!
SLAM!
HAW! HAW!
EXCUSE ME, MISS...
WH–

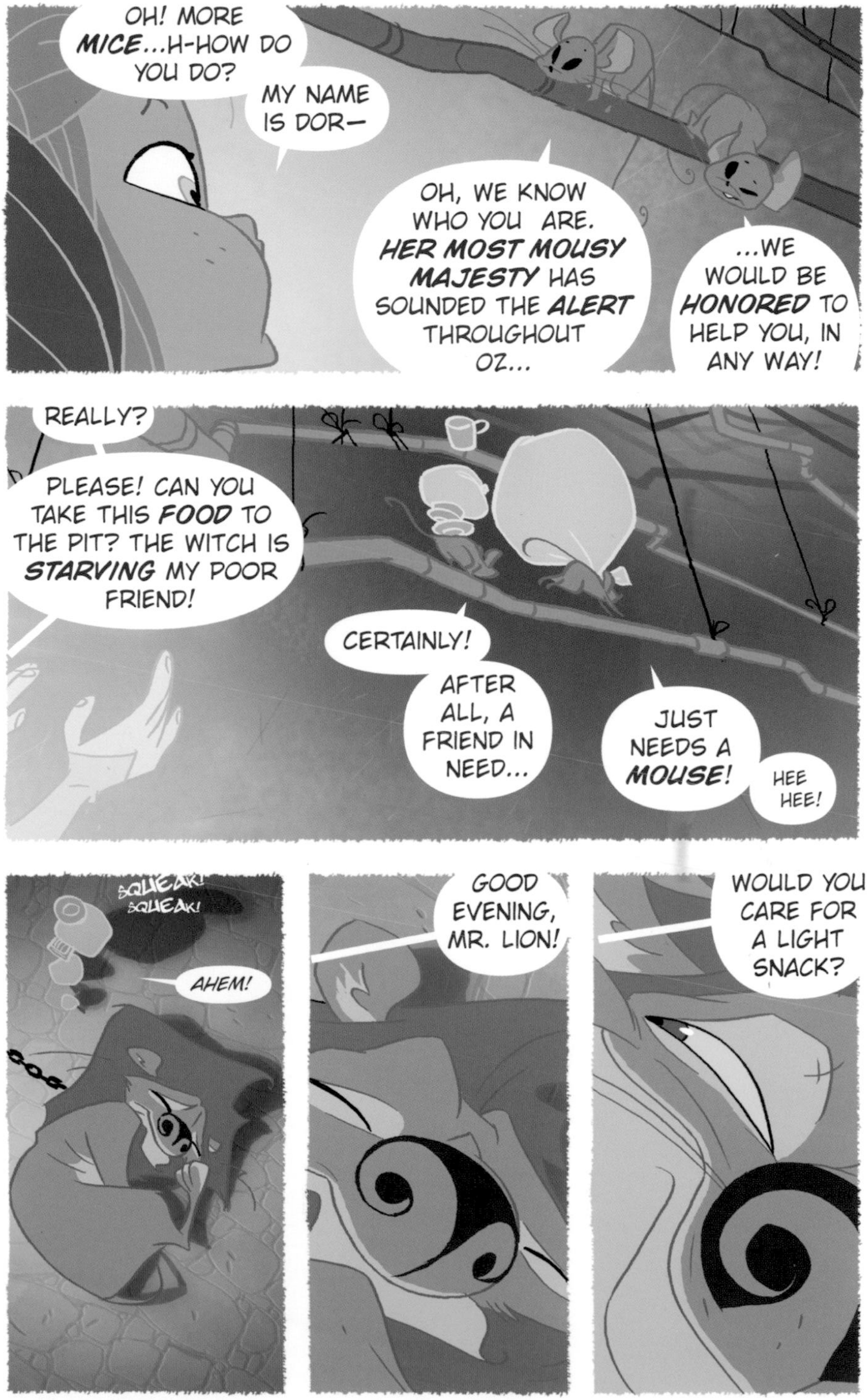
OH! MORE MICE...H-HOW DO YOU DO?
MY NAME IS DOR—
OH, WE KNOW WHO YOU ARE. HER MOST MOUSY MAJESTY HAS SOUNDED THE ALERT THROUGHOUT OZ...
...WE WOULD BE HONORED TO HELP YOU, IN ANY WAY!
REALLY?
PLEASE! CAN YOU TAKE THIS FOOD TO THE PIT? THE WITCH IS STARVING MY POOR FRIEND!
CERTAINLY!
AFTER ALL, A FRIEND IN NEED...
JUST NEEDS A MOUSE!
HEE HEE!
SQUEAK! SQUEAK!
AHEM!
GOOD EVENING, MR. LION!
WOULD YOU CARE FOR A LIGHT SNACK?

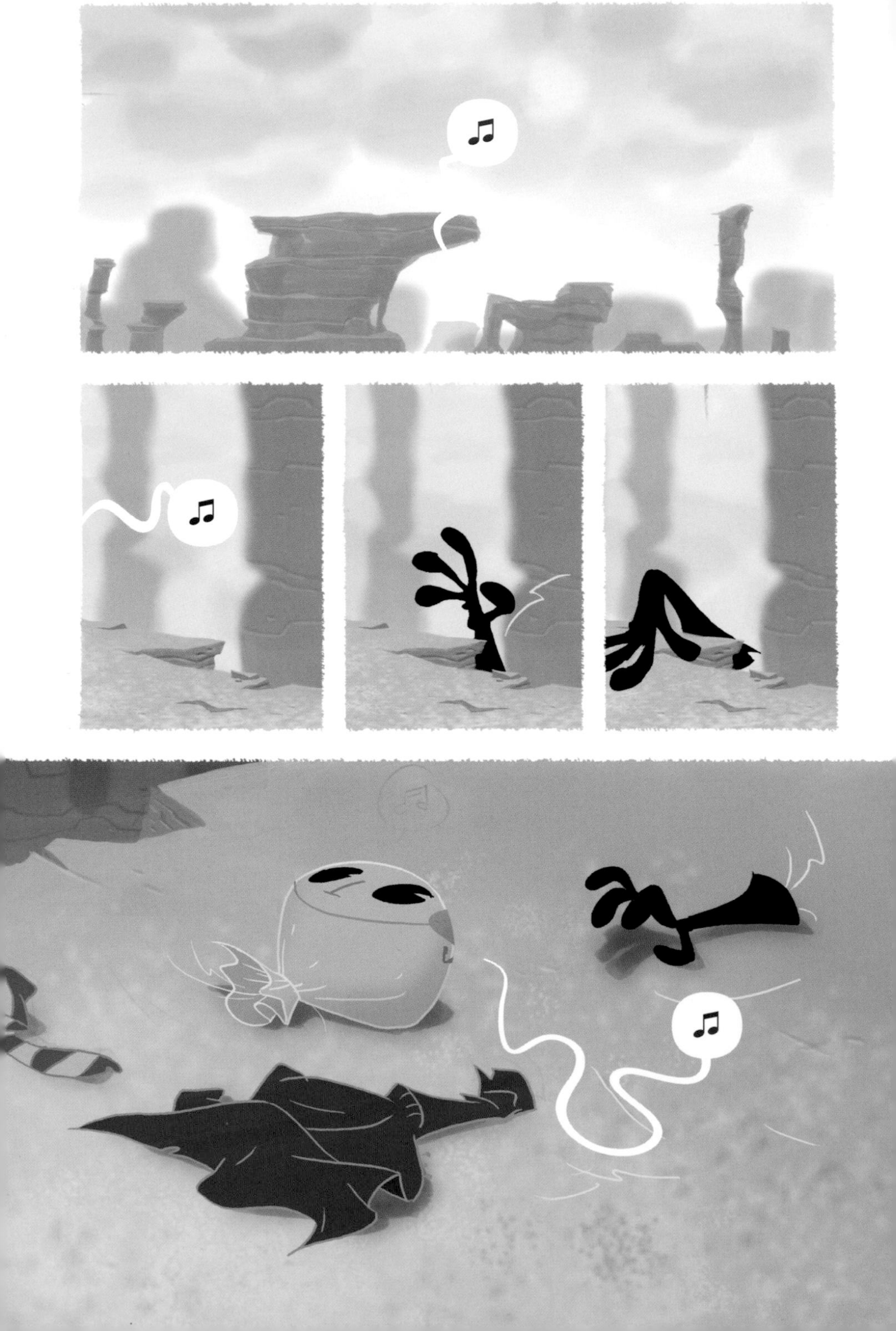

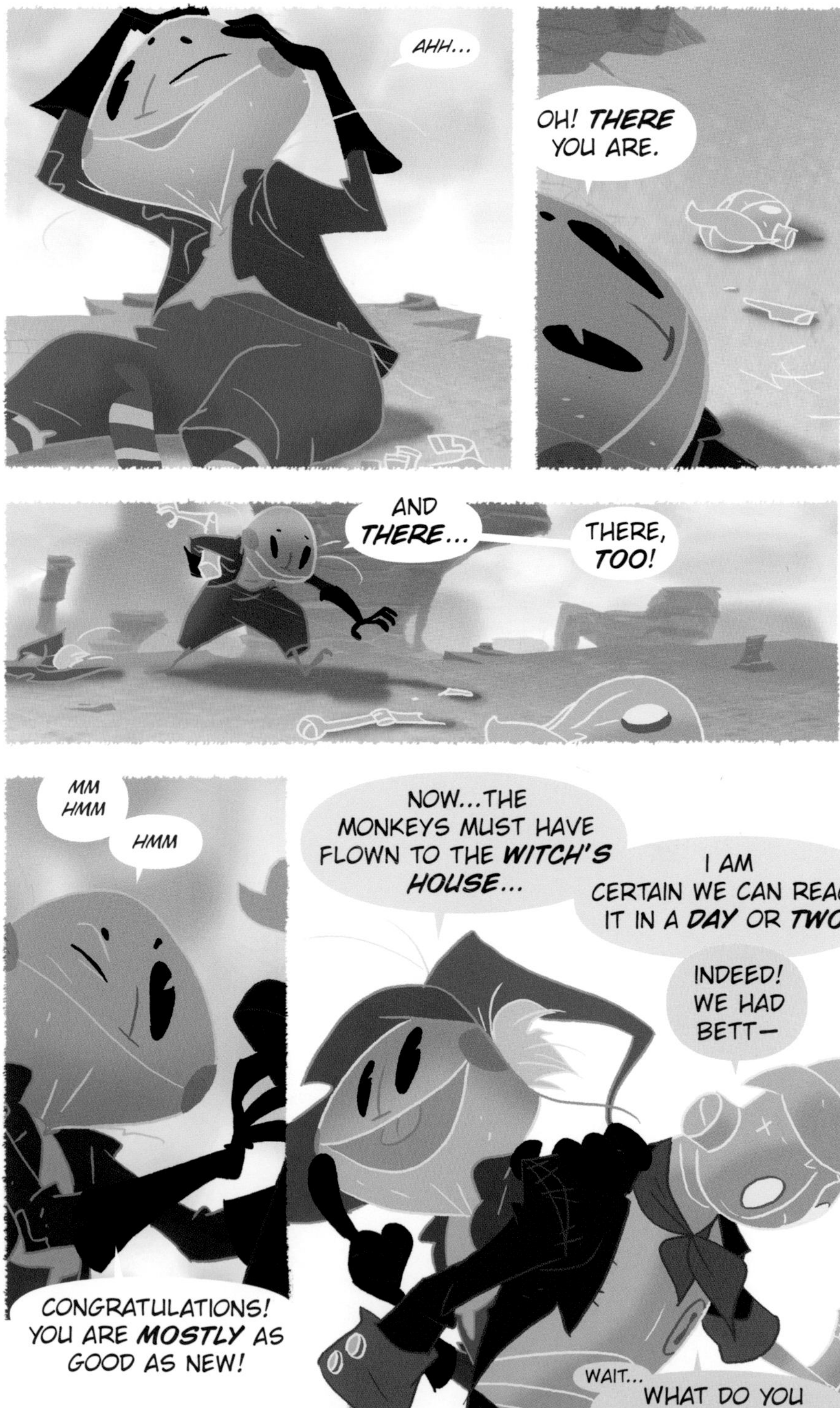
AHH...
OH! THERE YOU ARE.
AND THERE...
THERE, TOO!
MM HMM
HMM
CONGRATULATIONS! YOU ARE MOSTLY AS GOOD AS NEW!
NOW...THE MONKEYS MUST HAVE FLOWN TO THE WITCH'S HOUSE...
I AM CERTAIN WE CAN REACH IT IN A DAY OR TWO.
INDEED! WE HAD BETT—
WAIT... WHAT DO YOU MEAN, "MOSTLY"?

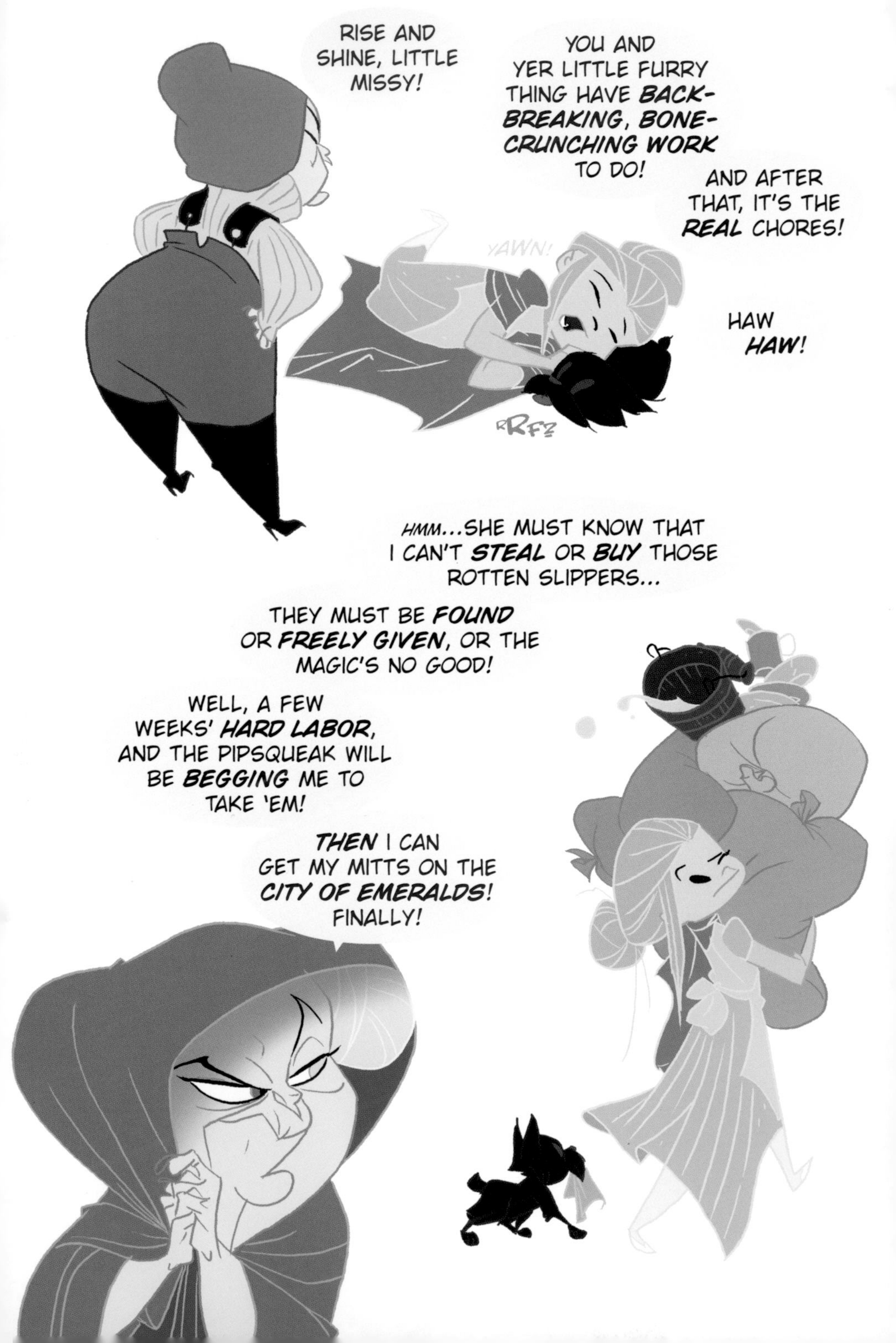
RISE AND SHINE, LITTLE MISSY!
YOU AND YER LITTLE FURRY THING HAVE BACK-BREAKING, BONE-CRUNCHING WORK TO DO!
AND AFTER THAT, IT'S THE REAL CHORES!
YAWN!
HAW HAW!
RRF?
HMM...SHE MUST KNOW THAT I CAN'T STEAL OR BUY THOSE ROTTEN SLIPPERS...
THEY MUST BE FOUND OR FREELY GIVEN, OR THE MAGIC'S NO GOOD!
WELL, A FEW WEEKS' HARD LABOR, AND THE PIPSQUEAK WILL BE BEGGING ME TO TAKE 'EM!
THEN I CAN GET MY MITTS ON THE CITY OF EMERALDS! FINALLY!

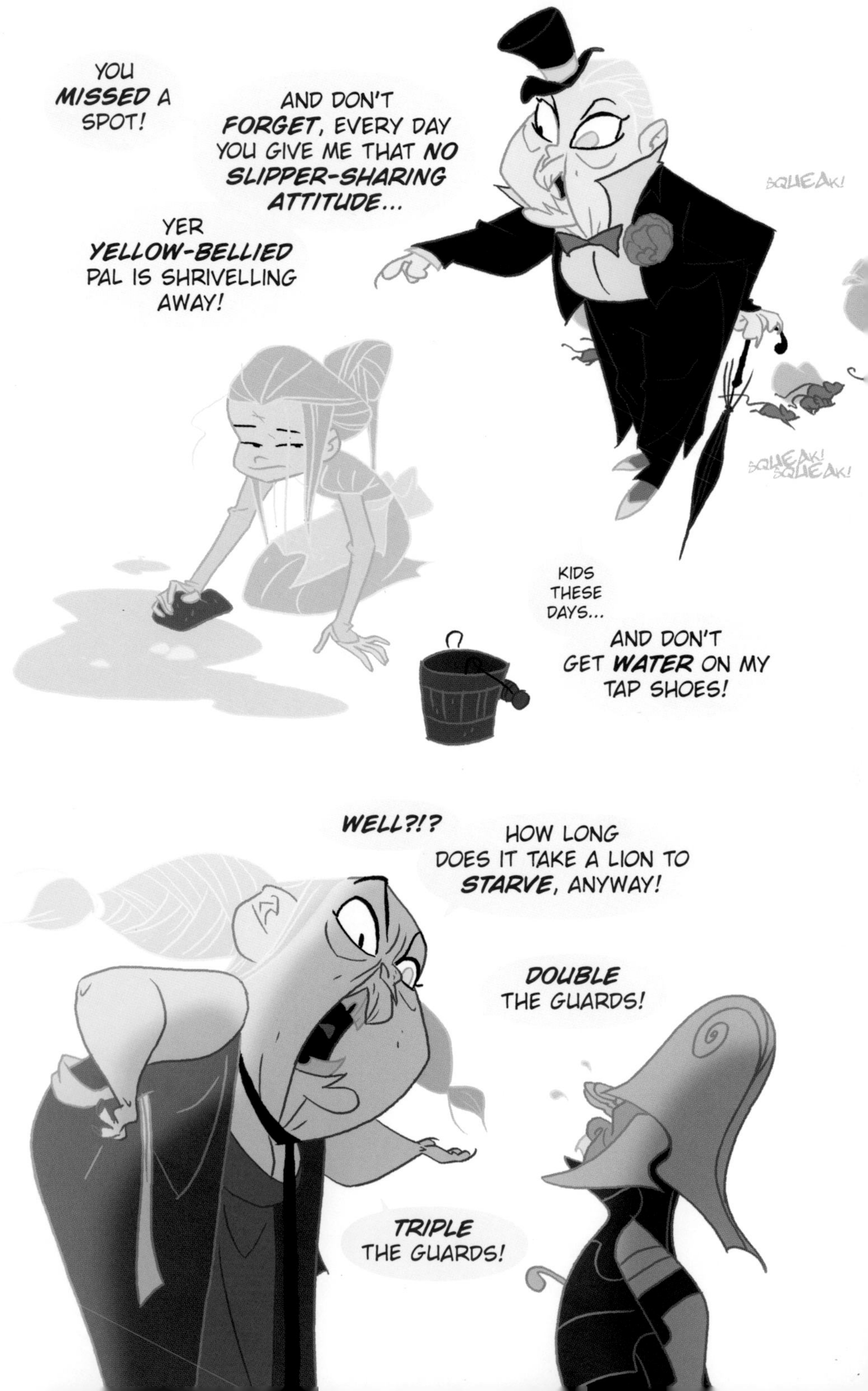
YOU MISSED A SPOT!
AND DON'T FORGET, EVERY DAY YOU GIVE ME THAT NO SLIPPER-SHARING ATTITUDE...
YER YELLOW-BELLIED PAL IS SHRIVELLING AWAY!
SQUEAK!
SQUEAK! SQUEAK!
KIDS THESE DAYS...
AND DON'T GET WATER ON MY TAP SHOES!
WELL?!?
HOW LONG DOES IT TAKE A LION TO STARVE, ANYWAY!
DOUBLE THE GUARDS!
TRIPLE THE GUARDS!

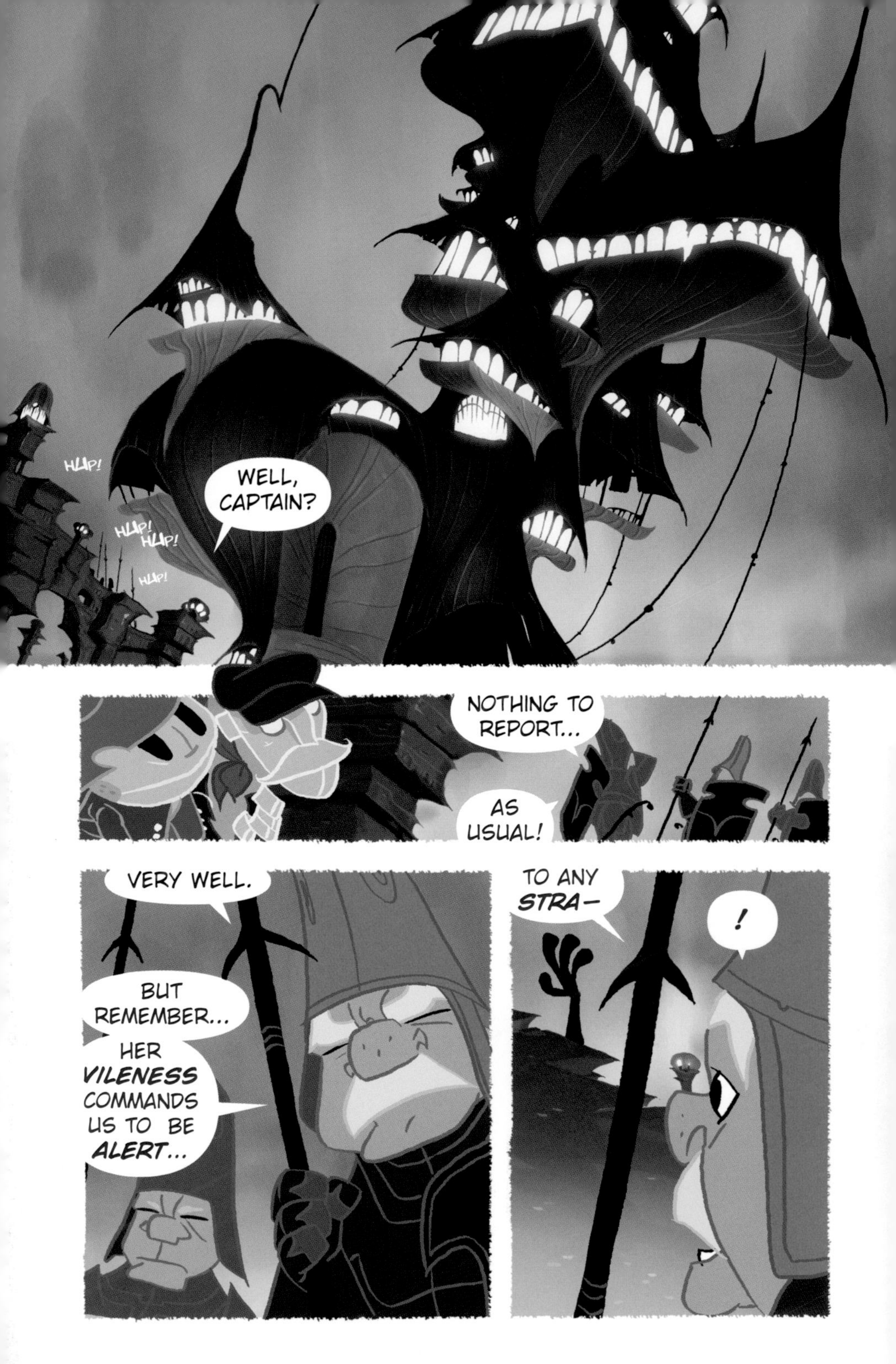
HUP!
WELL, CAPTAIN?
HUP!
HUP!
HUP!
NOTHING TO REPORT...
AS USUAL!
VERY WELL.
BUT REMEMBER...
HER VILENESS COMMANDS US TO BE ALERT...
TO ANY STRA—
!

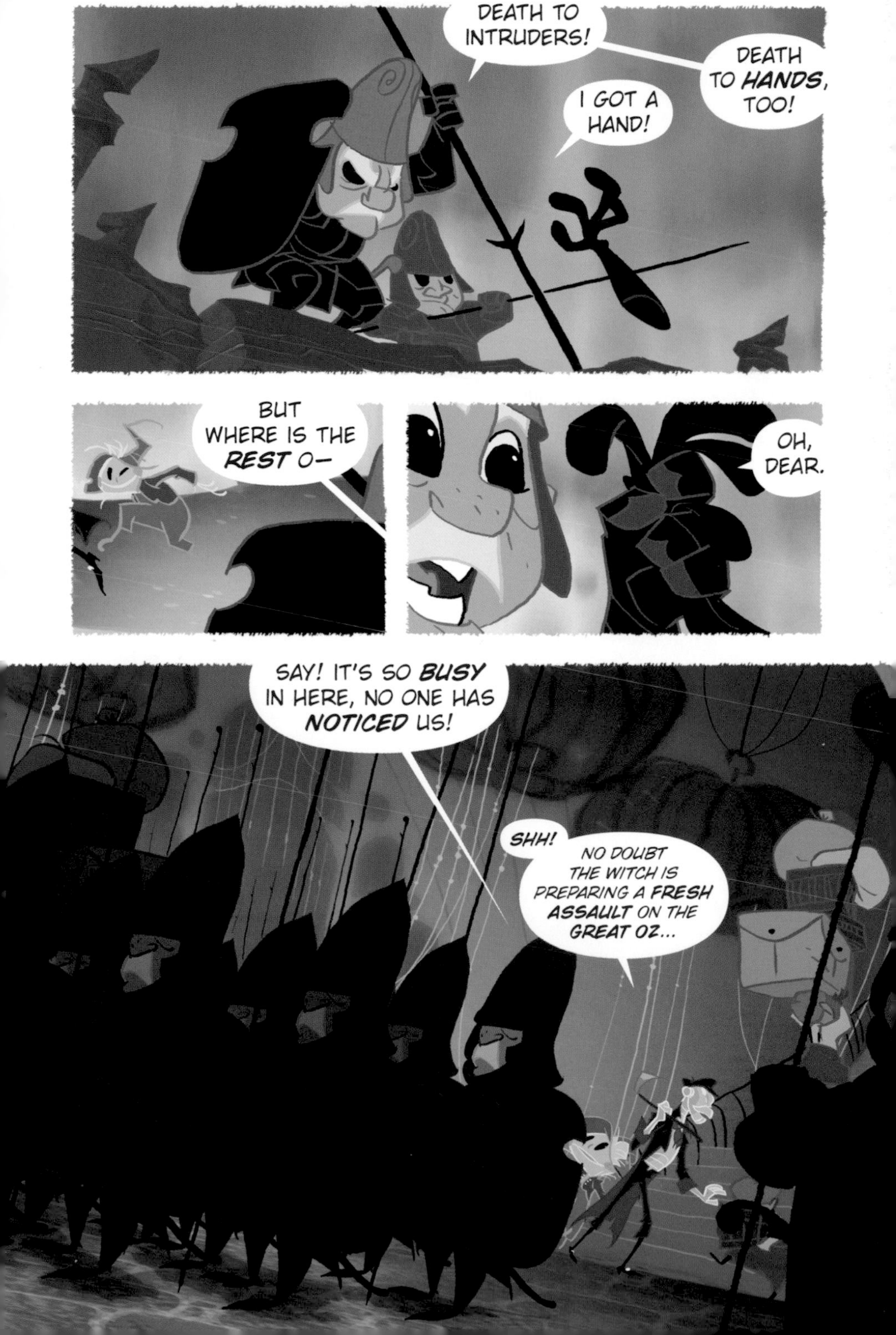
DEATH TO INTRUDERS!
DEATH TO HANDS, TOO!
I GOT A HAND!
BUT WHERE IS THE REST O—
OH, DEAR.
SAY! IT'S SO BUSY IN HERE, NO ONE HAS NOTICED US!
SHH!
NO DOUBT THE WITCH IS PREPARING A FRESH ASSAULT ON THE GREAT OZ...

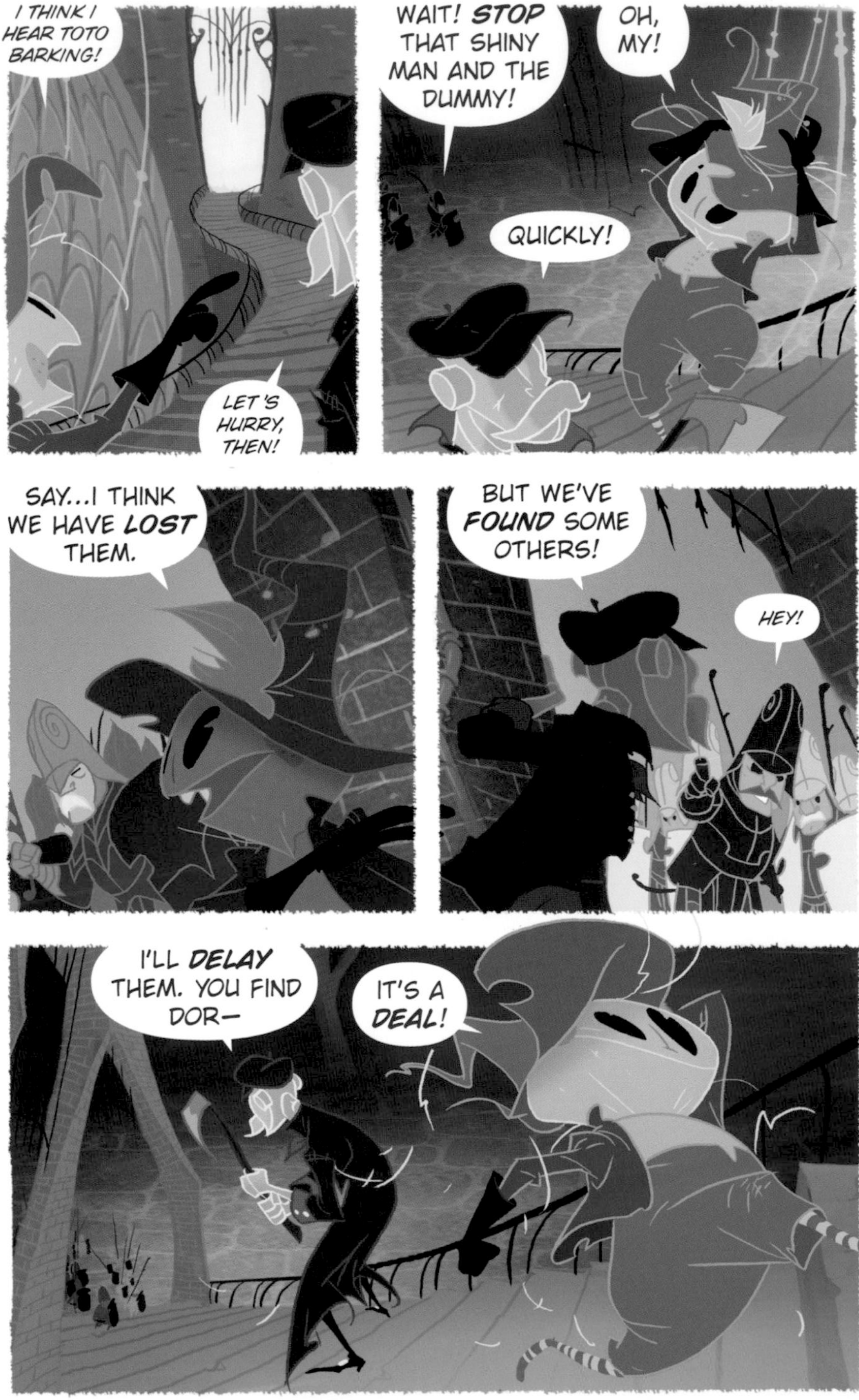
I THINK I HEAR TOTO BARKING!
LET'S HURRY, THEN!
WAIT! STOP THAT SHINY MAN AND THE DUMMY!
OH, MY!
QUICKLY!
SAY...I THINK WE HAVE LOST THEM.
BUT WE'VE FOUND SOME OTHERS!
HEY!
I'LL DELAY THEM. YOU FIND DOR—
IT'S A DEAL!

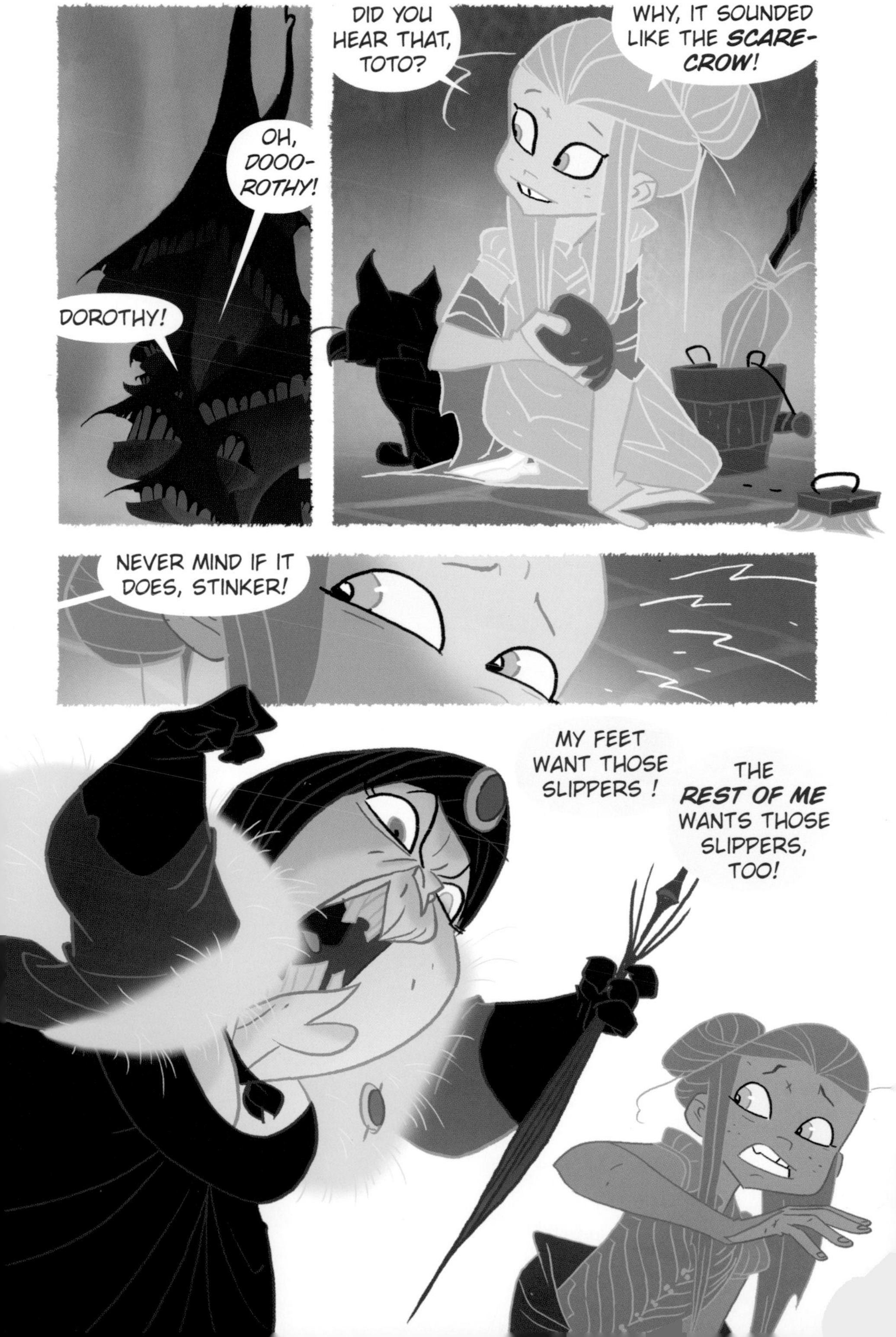

OH, DOOO-ROTHY!
DOROTHY!
DID YOU HEAR THAT, TOTO?
WHY, IT SOUNDED LIKE THE **SCARE-CROW**!
NEVER MIND IF IT DOES, STINKER!
MY FEET WANT THOSE SLIPPERS !
THE **REST OF ME** WANTS THOSE SLIPPERS, TOO!

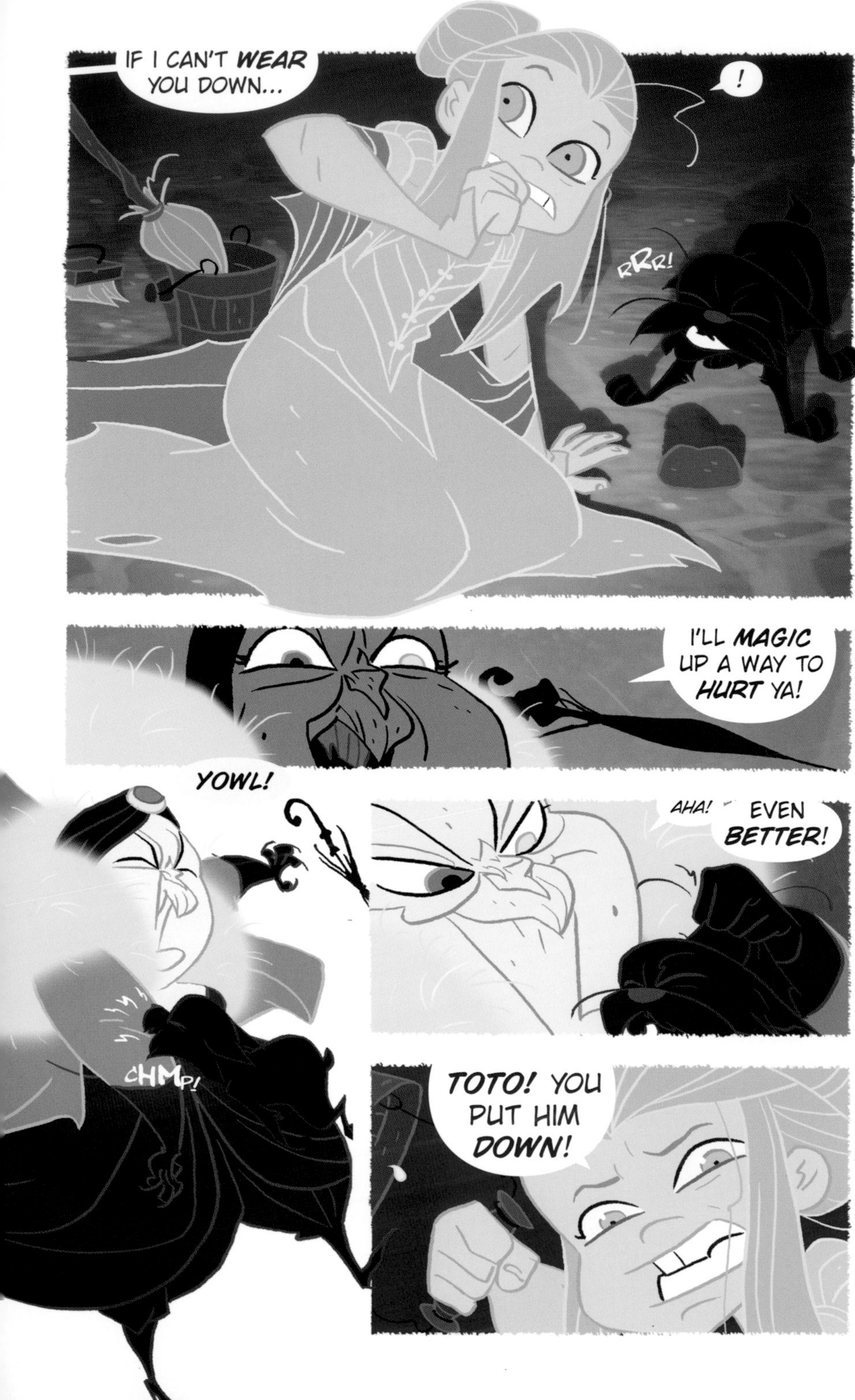
IF I CAN'T WEAR YOU DOWN...
!
RRR!
I'LL MAGIC UP A WAY TO HURT YA!
YOWL!
AHA!
EVEN BETTER!
CHMP!
TOTO! YOU PUT HIM DOWN!

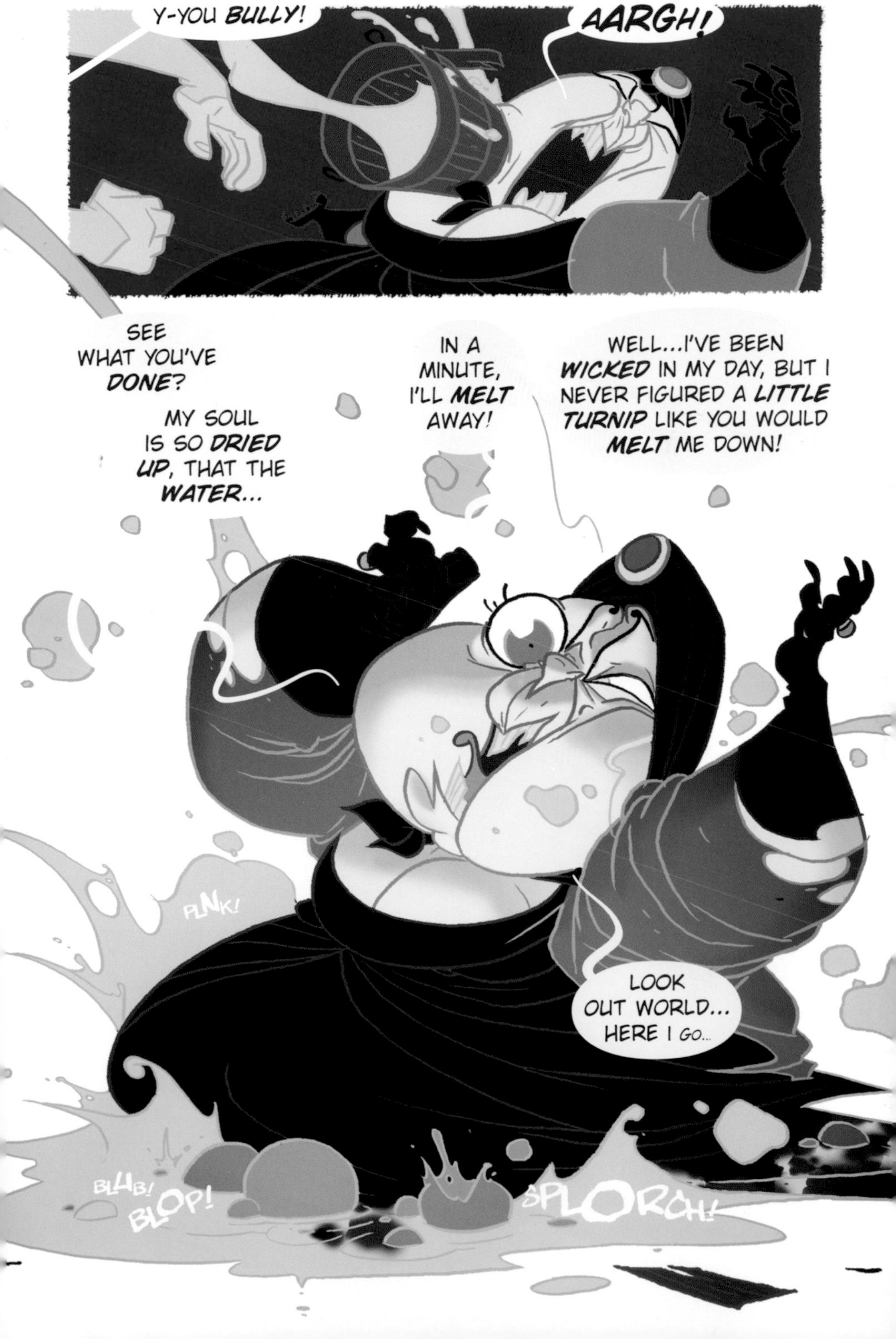
Y-YOU BULLY!
AARGH!
SEE WHAT YOU'VE DONE?
MY SOUL IS SO DRIED UP, THAT THE WATER...
IN A MINUTE, I'LL MELT AWAY!
WELL...I'VE BEEN WICKED IN MY DAY, BUT I NEVER FIGURED A LITTLE TURNIP LIKE YOU WOULD MELT ME DOWN!
PLINK!
LOOK OUT WORLD... HERE I GO...
BLUB! BLOP!
SPLORCH!

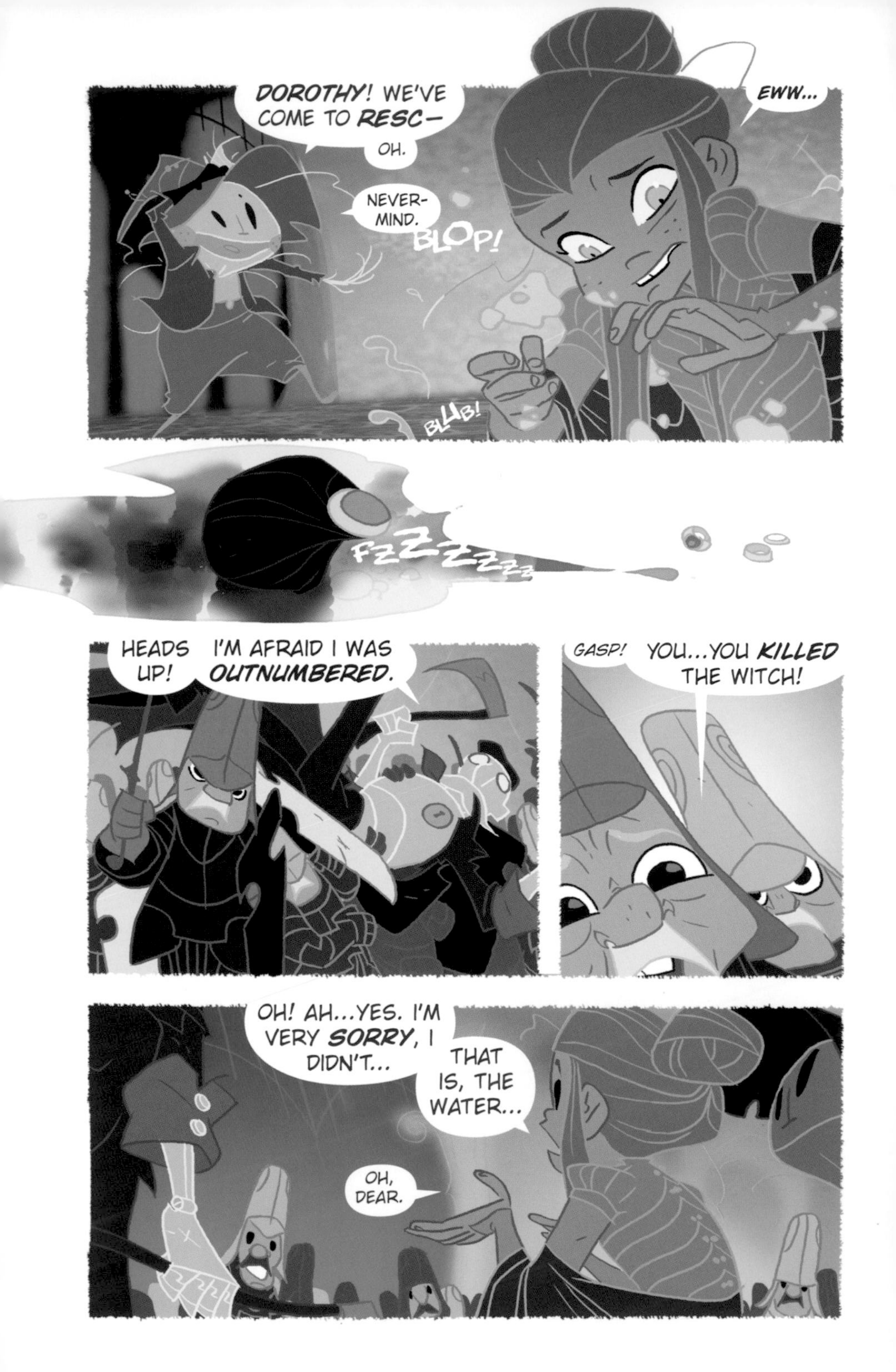
DOROTHY! WE'VE COME TO RESC—
OH.
NEVER-MIND.
BLOP!
EWW...
BLUB!
FZZZZZZZZ
HEADS UP!
I'M AFRAID I WAS OUTNUMBERED.
GASP!
YOU...YOU KILLED THE WITCH!
OH! AH...YES. I'M VERY SORRY, I DIDN'T...
THAT IS, THE WATER...
OH, DEAR.

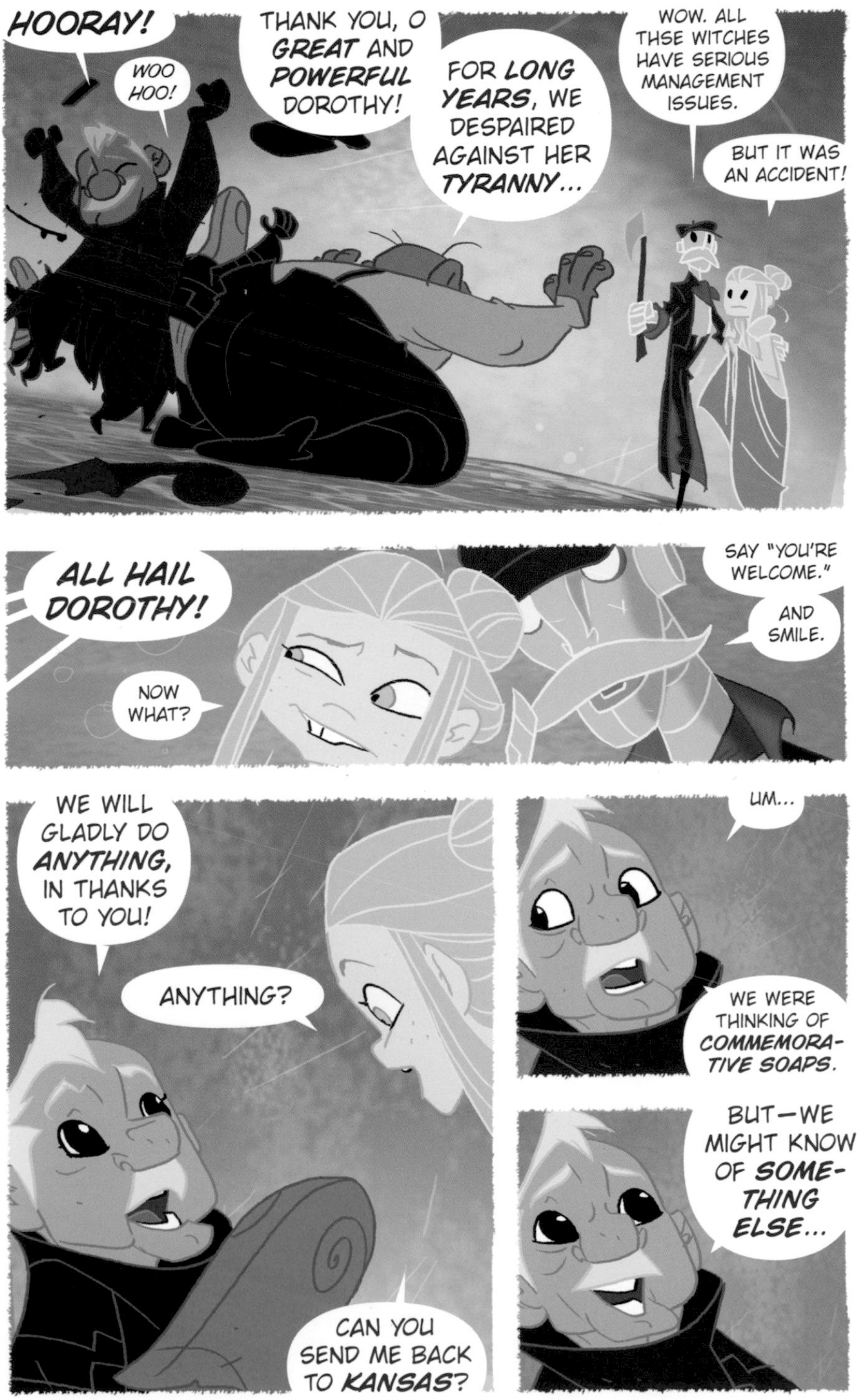
HOORAY!
WOO HOO!
THANK YOU, O GREAT AND POWERFUL DOROTHY!
FOR LONG YEARS, WE DESPAIRED AGAINST HER TYRANNY...
WOW. ALL THSE WITCHES HAVE SERIOUS MANAGEMENT ISSUES.
BUT IT WAS AN ACCIDENT!
ALL HAIL DOROTHY!
NOW WHAT?
SAY "YOU'RE WELCOME."
AND SMILE.
WE WILL GLADLY DO ANYTHING, IN THANKS TO YOU!
ANYTHING?
CAN YOU SEND ME BACK TO KANSAS?
UM...
WE WERE THINKING OF COMMEMORA-TIVE SOAPS.
BUT—WE MIGHT KNOW OF SOME-THING ELSE...

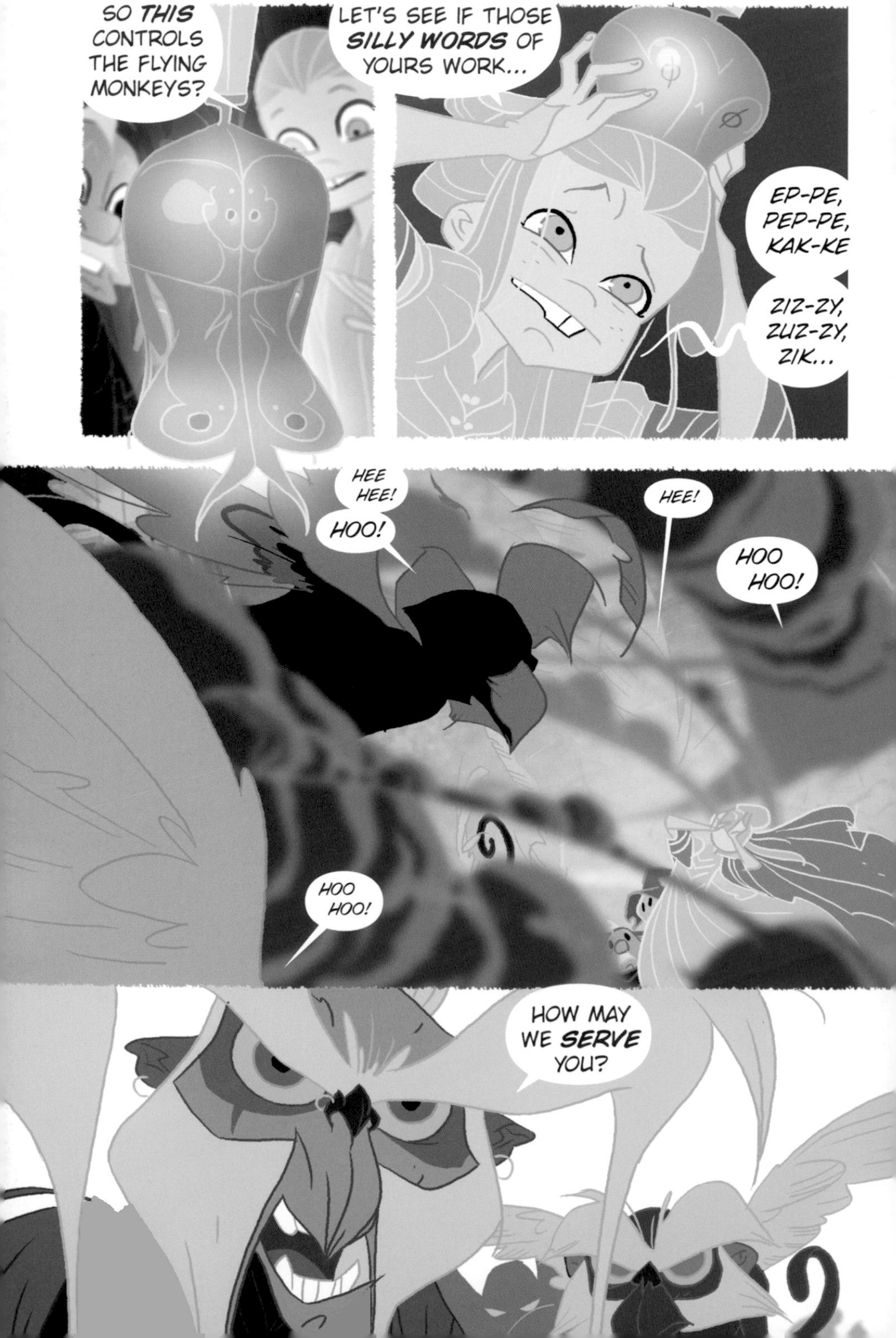
SO THIS CONTROLS THE FLYING MONKEYS?
LET'S SEE IF THOSE SILLY WORDS OF YOURS WORK...
EP-PE, PEP-PE, KAK-KE
ZIZ-ZY, ZUZ-ZY, ZIK...
HEE HEE!
HOO!
HEE!
HOO HOO!
HOO HOO!
HOW MAY WE SERVE YOU?

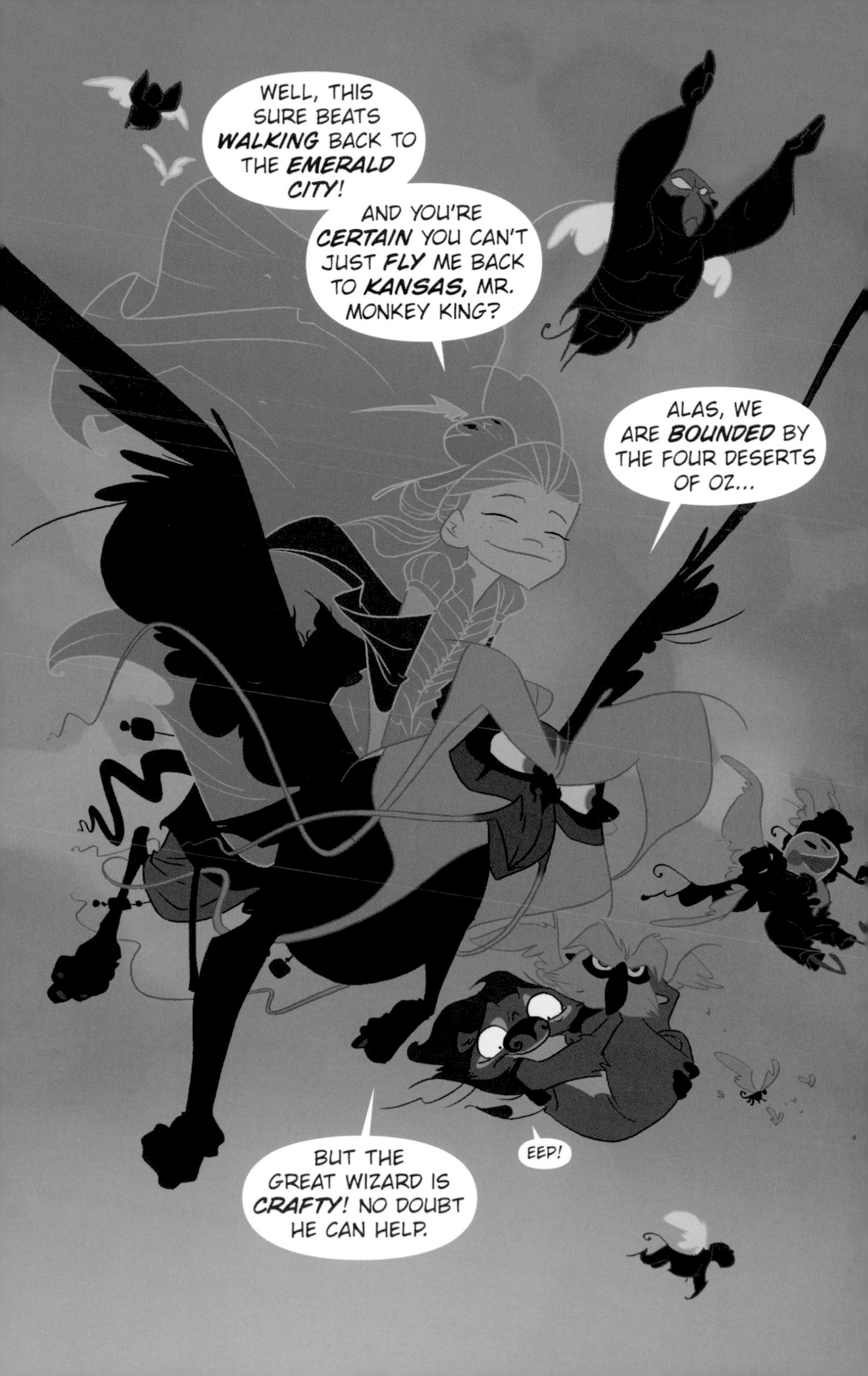
WELL, THIS SURE BEATS **WALKING** BACK TO THE **EMERALD CITY**!
AND YOU'RE **CERTAIN** YOU CAN'T JUST **FLY** ME BACK TO **KANSAS,** MR. MONKEY KING?
ALAS, WE ARE **BOUNDED** BY THE FOUR DESERTS OF OZ...
BUT THE GREAT WIZARD IS **CRAFTY!** NO DOUBT HE CAN HELP.
EEP!

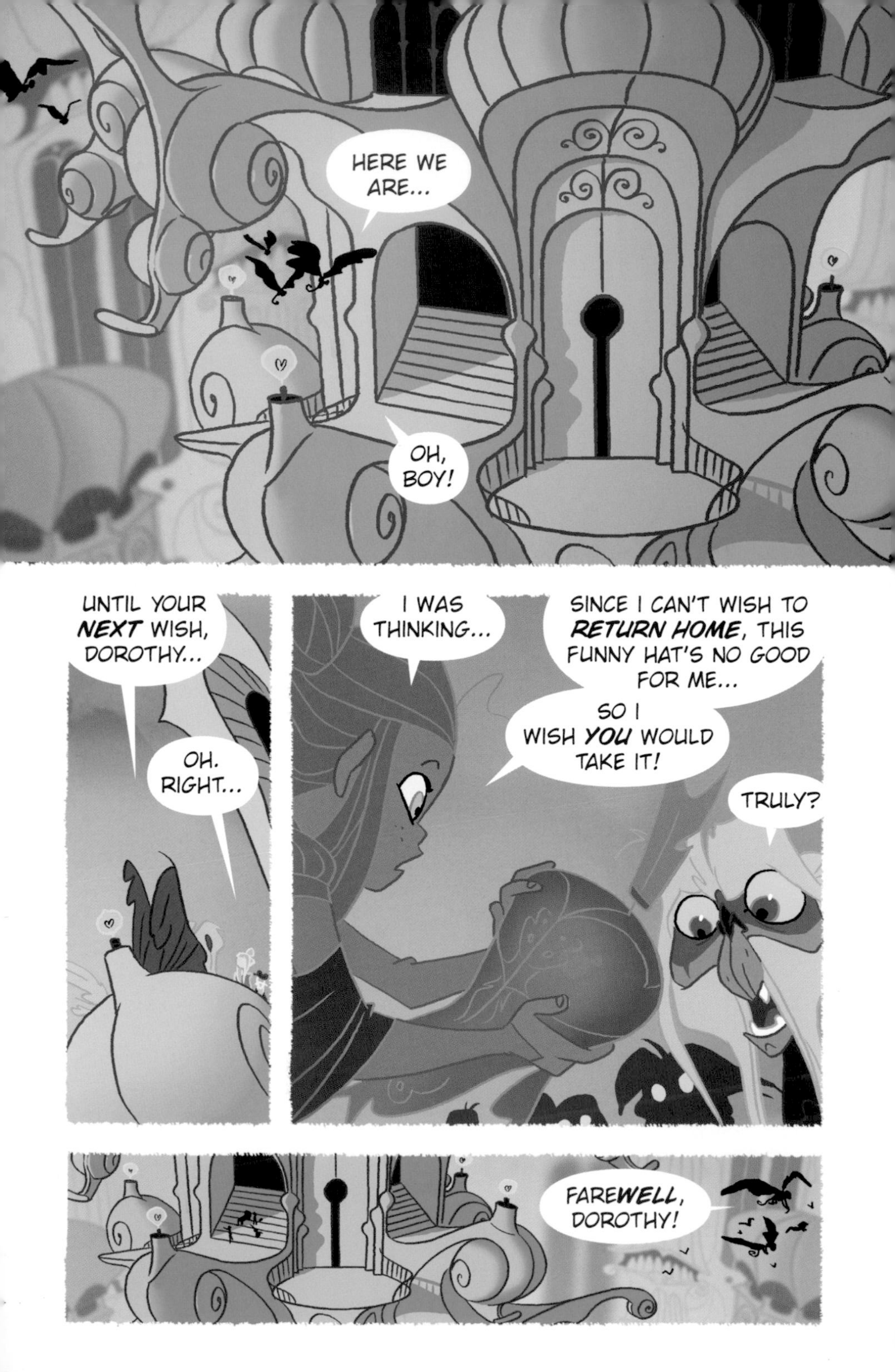
HERE WE ARE...
OH, BOY!
UNTIL YOUR **NEXT** WISH, DOROTHY...
OH. RIGHT...
I WAS THINKING...
SINCE I CAN'T WISH TO **RETURN HOME**, THIS FUNNY HAT'S NO GOOD FOR ME...
SO I WISH **YOU** WOULD TAKE IT!
TRULY?
FARE**WELL**, DOROTHY!

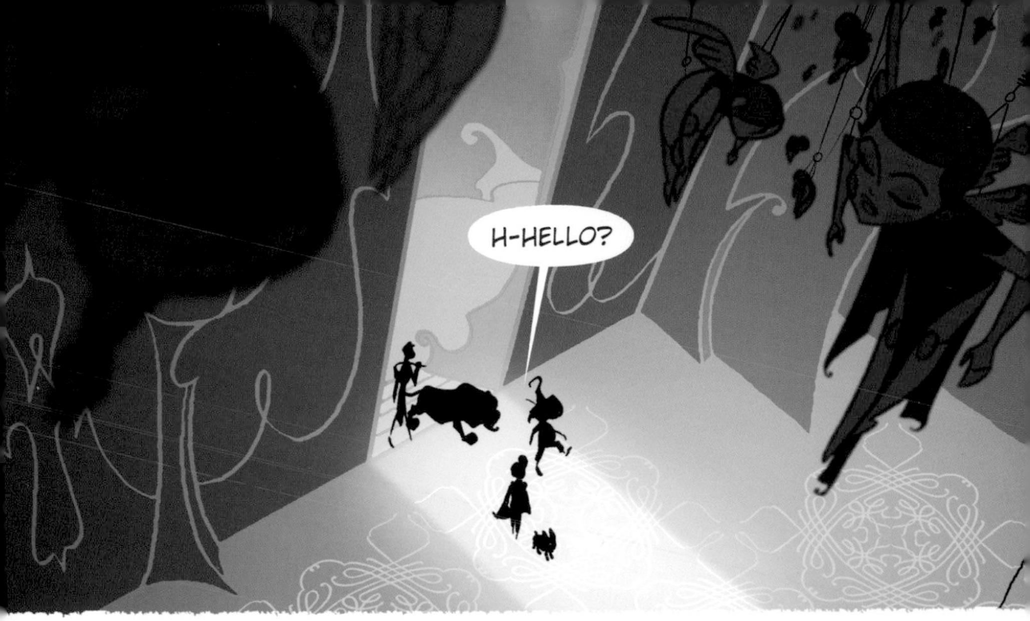
H-HELLO?

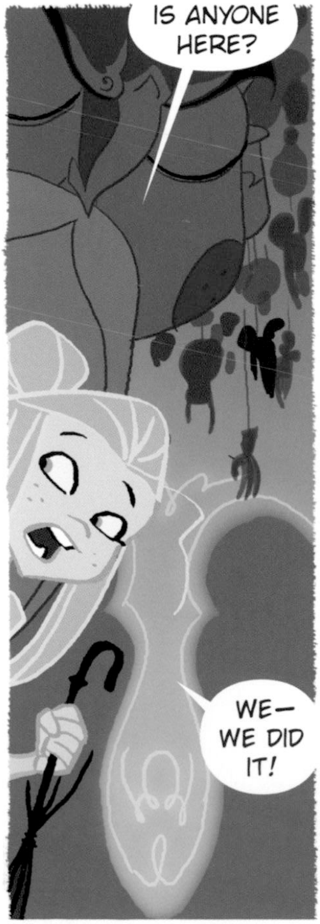
IS ANYONE HERE?
WE—
WE DID IT!

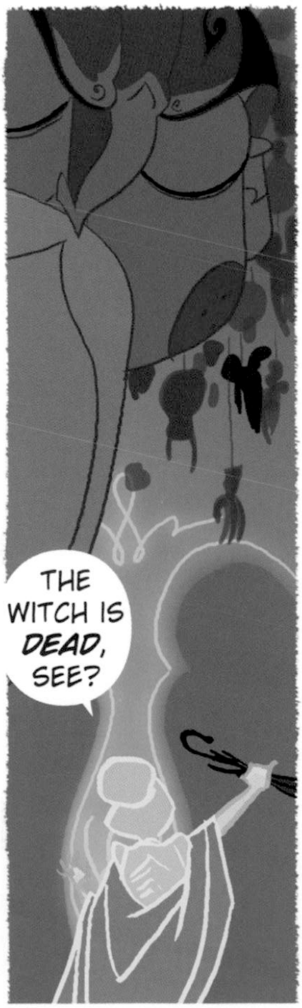
THE WITCH IS *DEAD*, SEE?

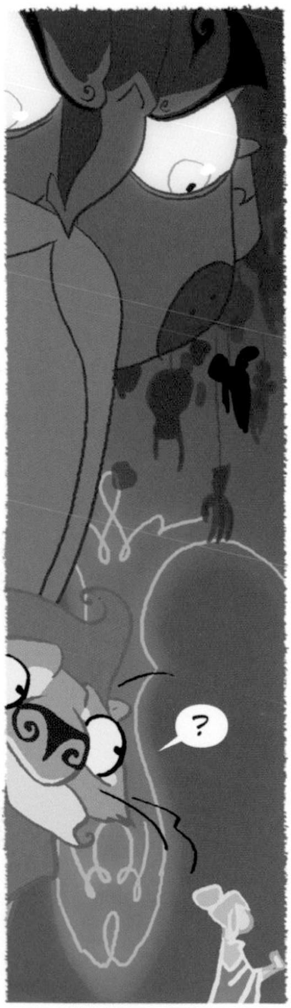
?

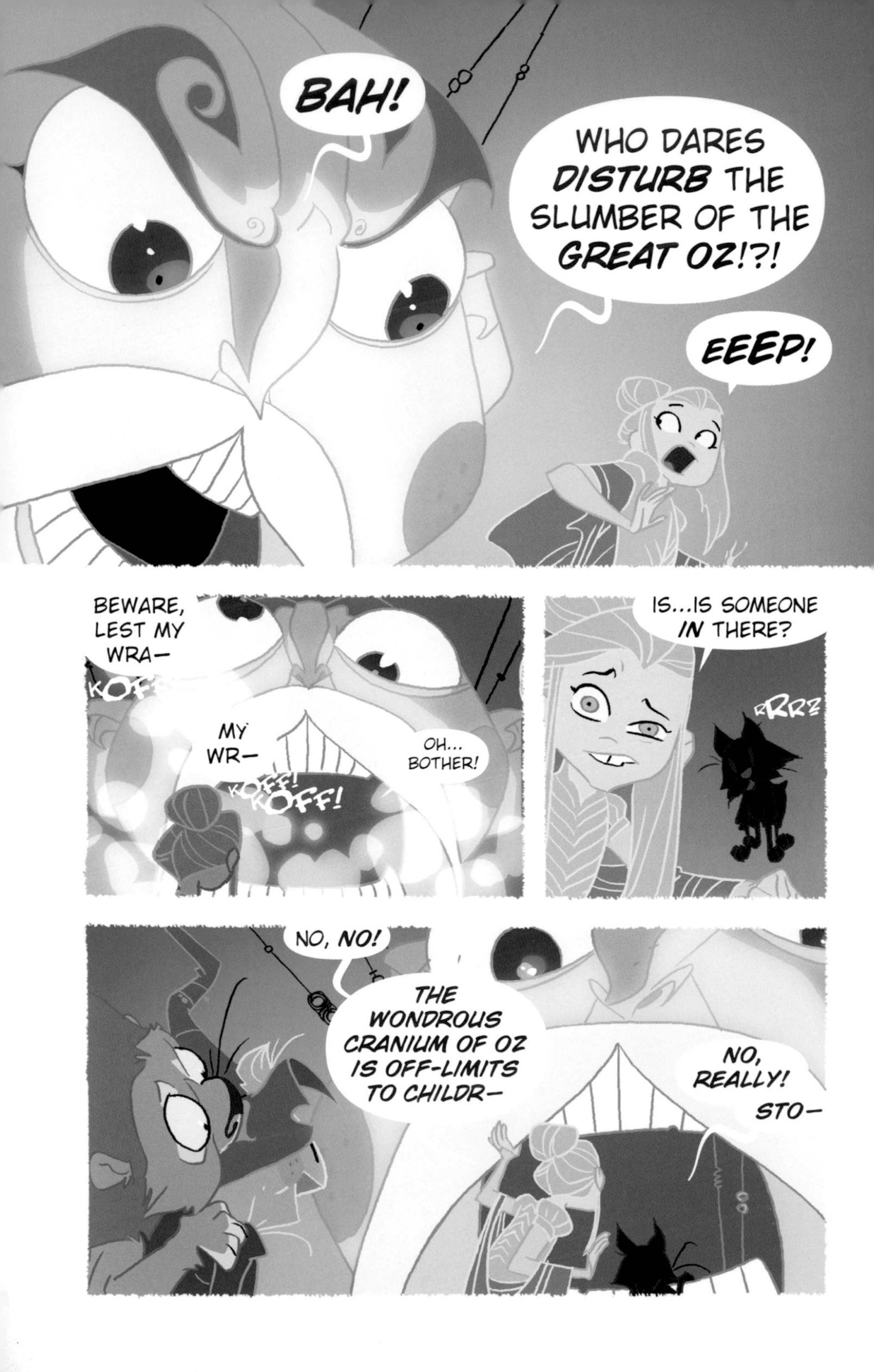
BAH!
WHO DARES DISTURB THE SLUMBER OF THE GREAT OZ!?!
EEEP!
BEWARE, LEST MY WRA—
KOFF!
MY WR—
KOFF! KOFF!
OH... BOTHER!
IS...IS SOMEONE IN THERE?
RRR?
NO, NO!
THE WONDROUS CRANIUM OF OZ IS OFF-LIMITS TO CHILDR—
NO, REALLY!
STO—

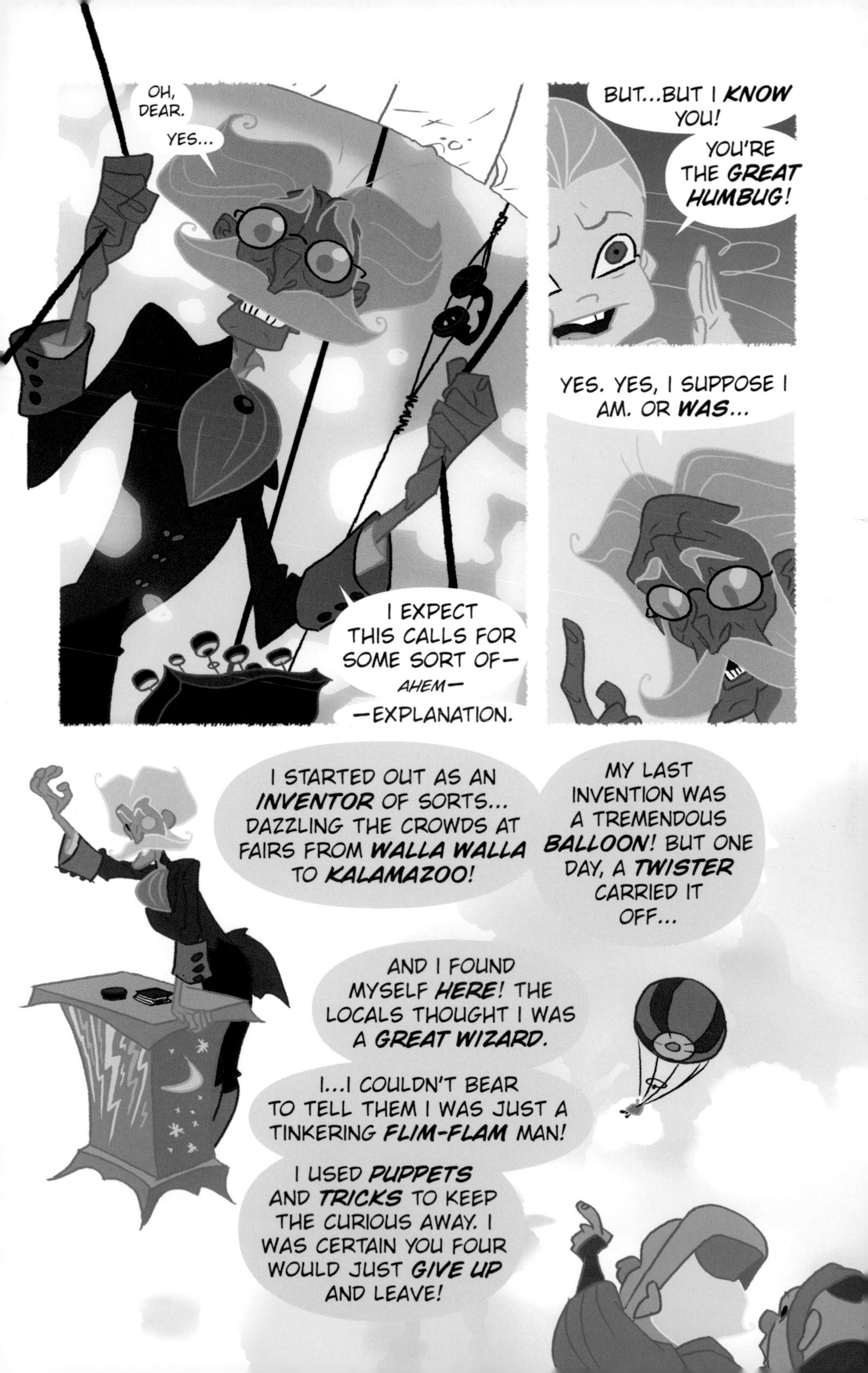
OH, DEAR.
YES...
I EXPECT THIS CALLS FOR SOME SORT OF—
AHEM—
—EXPLANATION.
BUT...BUT I KNOW YOU!
YOU'RE THE GREAT HUMBUG!
YES. YES, I SUPPOSE I AM. OR WAS...
I STARTED OUT AS AN INVENTOR OF SORTS... DAZZLING THE CROWDS AT FAIRS FROM WALLA WALLA TO KALAMAZOO!
MY LAST INVENTION WAS A TREMENDOUS BALLOON! BUT ONE DAY, A TWISTER CARRIED IT OFF...
AND I FOUND MYSELF HERE! THE LOCALS THOUGHT I WAS A GREAT WIZARD.
I...I COULDN'T BEAR TO TELL THEM I WAS JUST A TINKERING FLIM-FLAM MAN!
I USED PUPPETS AND TRICKS TO KEEP THE CURIOUS AWAY. I WAS CERTAIN YOU FOUR WOULD JUST GIVE UP AND LEAVE!

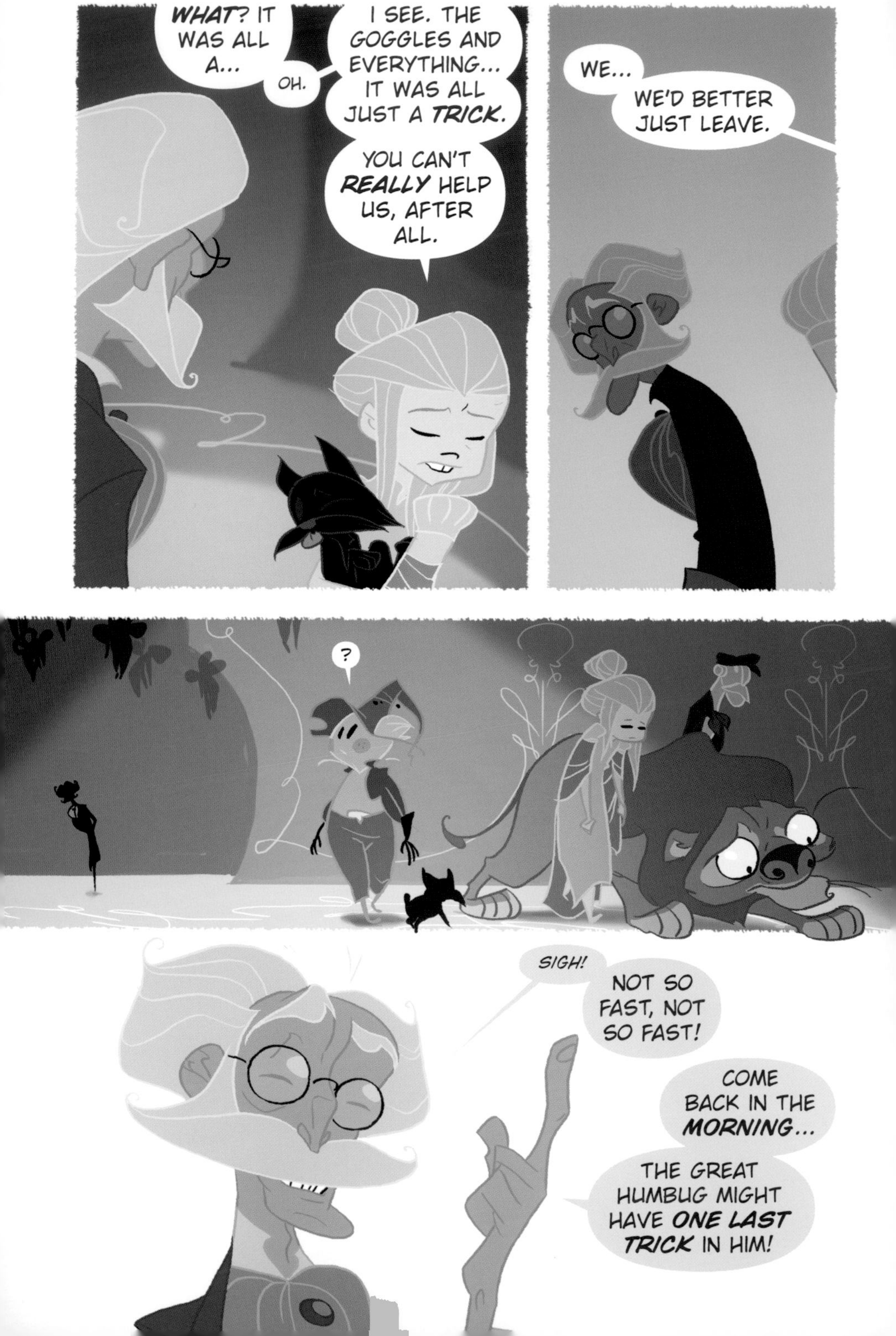
WHAT? IT WAS ALL A...
OH.
I SEE. THE GOGGLES AND EVERYTHING... IT WAS ALL JUST A TRICK.
YOU CAN'T REALLY HELP US, AFTER ALL.
WE...
WE'D BETTER JUST LEAVE.
?
SIGH!
NOT SO FAST, NOT SO FAST!
COME BACK IN THE MORNING...
THE GREAT HUMBUG MIGHT HAVE ONE LAST TRICK IN HIM!

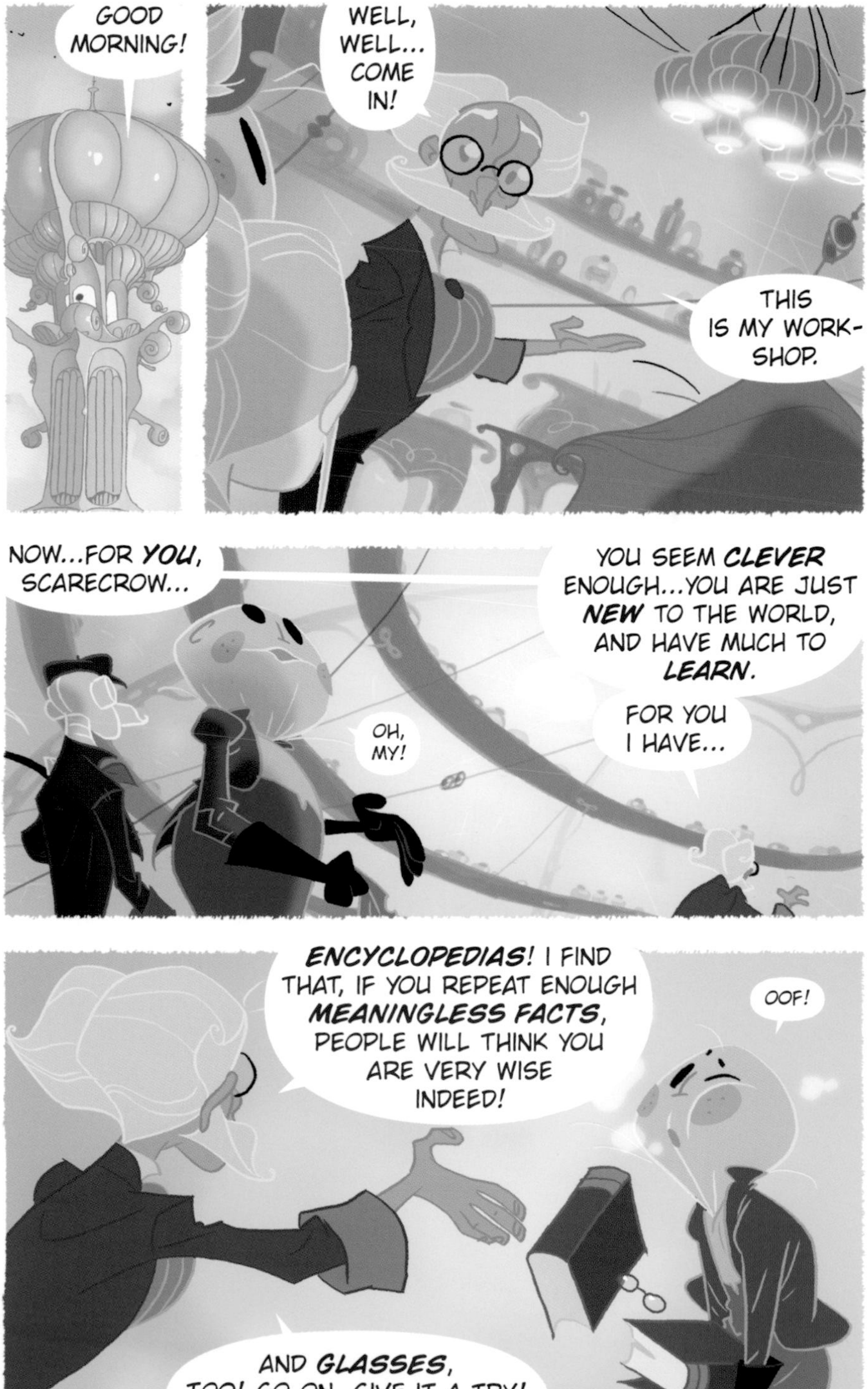
GOOD MORNING!
WELL, WELL... COME IN!
THIS IS MY WORK-SHOP.
NOW...FOR YOU, SCARECROW...
YOU SEEM CLEVER ENOUGH...YOU ARE JUST NEW TO THE WORLD, AND HAVE MUCH TO LEARN.
OH, MY!
FOR YOU I HAVE...
ENCYCLOPEDIAS! I FIND THAT, IF YOU REPEAT ENOUGH MEANINGLESS FACTS, PEOPLE WILL THINK YOU ARE VERY WISE INDEED!
OOF!
AND GLASSES, TOO! GO ON, GIVE IT A TRY!

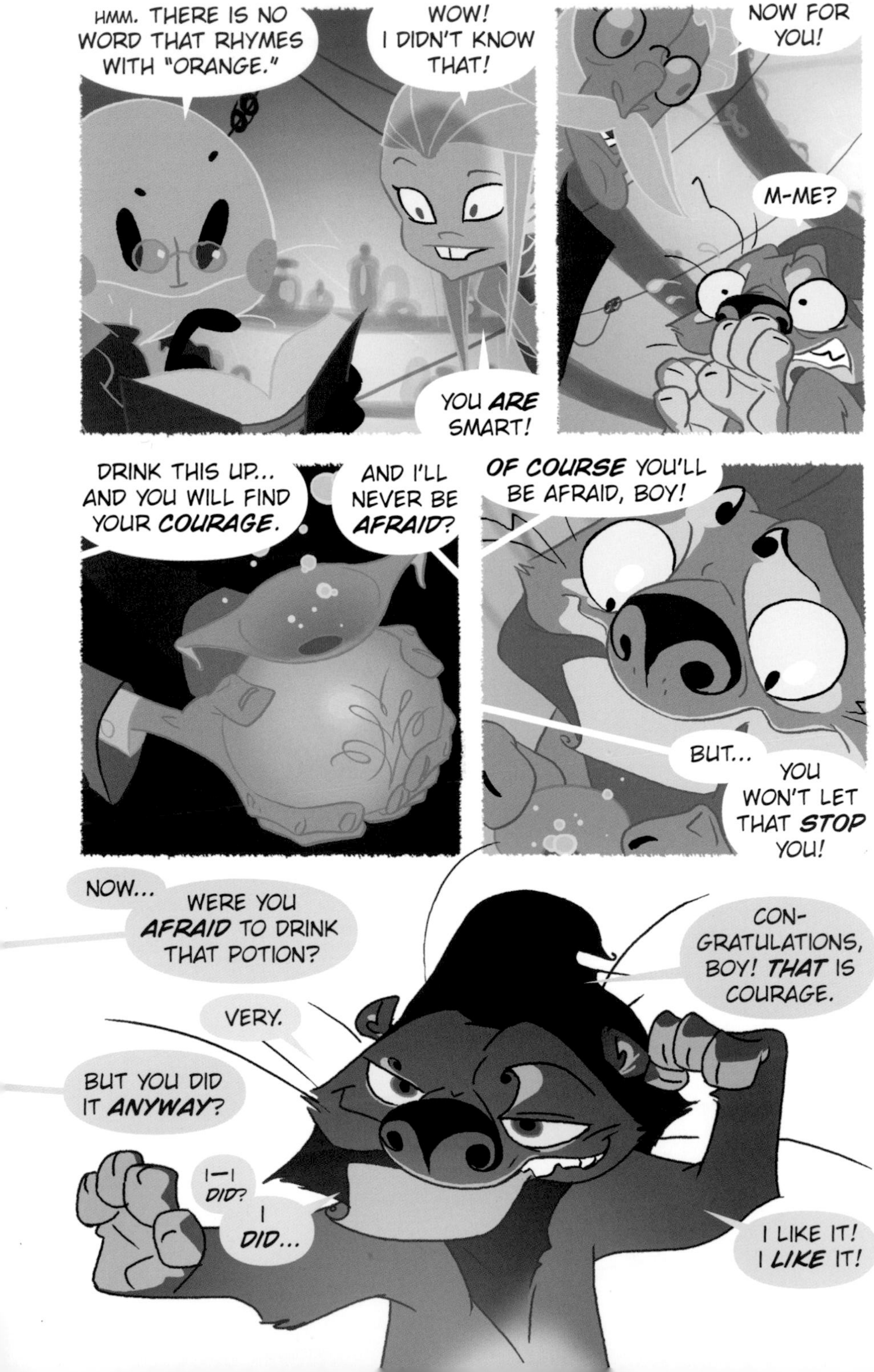
HMM. THERE IS NO WORD THAT RHYMES WITH "ORANGE."
WOW! I DIDN'T KNOW THAT!
YOU ARE SMART!
NOW FOR YOU!
M-ME?
DRINK THIS UP... AND YOU WILL FIND YOUR COURAGE.
AND I'LL NEVER BE AFRAID?
OF COURSE YOU'LL BE AFRAID, BOY!
BUT...
YOU WON'T LET THAT STOP YOU!
NOW...
WERE YOU AFRAID TO DRINK THAT POTION?
VERY.
BUT YOU DID IT ANYWAY?
CON-GRATULATIONS, BOY! THAT IS COURAGE.
I—I DID?
I DID...
I LIKE IT! I LIKE IT!

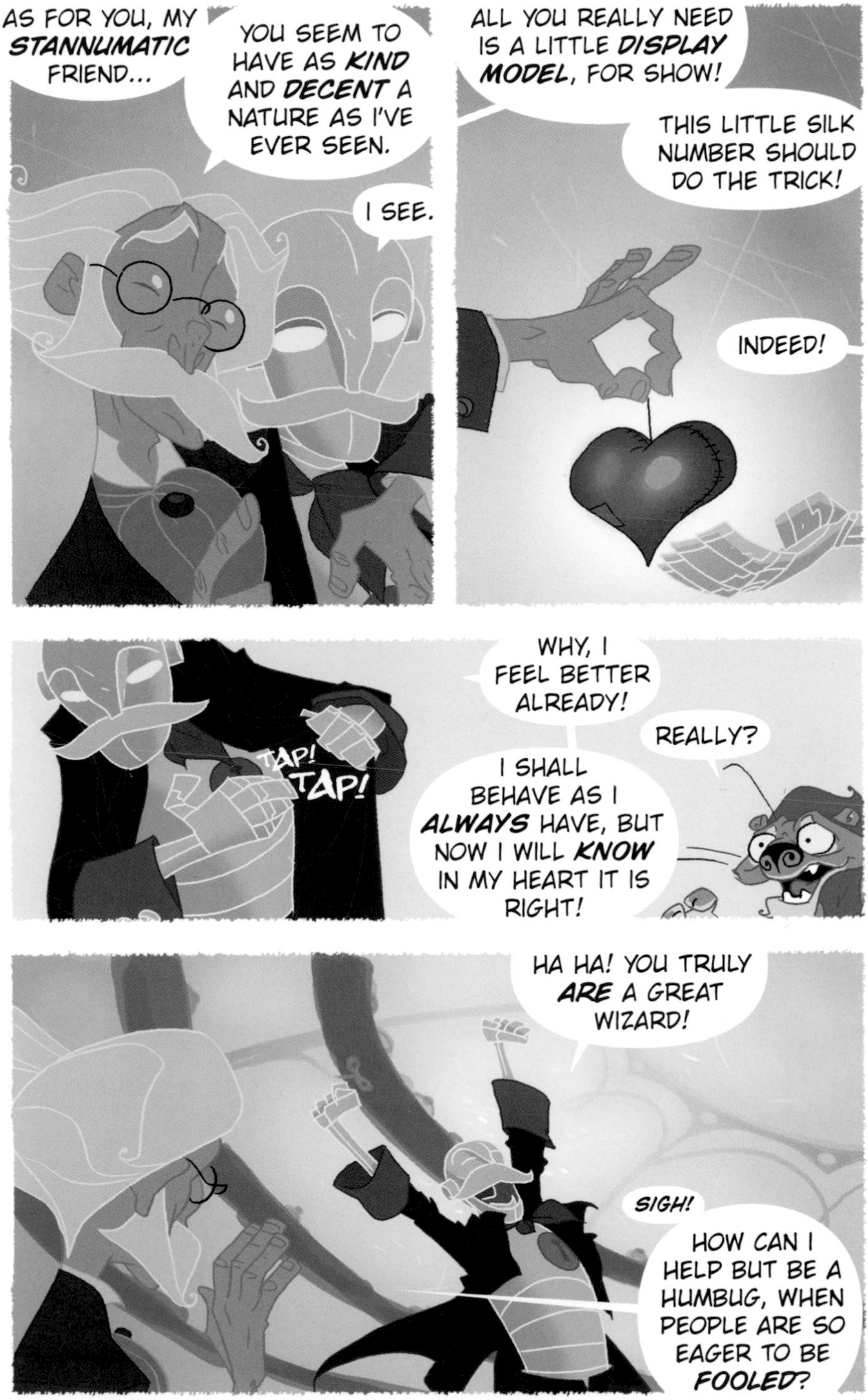
AS FOR YOU, MY STANNUMATIC FRIEND...
YOU SEEM TO HAVE AS KIND AND DECENT A NATURE AS I'VE EVER SEEN.
I SEE.
ALL YOU REALLY NEED IS A LITTLE DISPLAY MODEL, FOR SHOW!
THIS LITTLE SILK NUMBER SHOULD DO THE TRICK!
INDEED!
TAP! TAP!
WHY, I FEEL BETTER ALREADY!
I SHALL BEHAVE AS I ALWAYS HAVE, BUT NOW I WILL KNOW IN MY HEART IT IS RIGHT!
REALLY?
HA HA! YOU TRULY ARE A GREAT WIZARD!
SIGH!
HOW CAN I HELP BUT BE A HUMBUG, WHEN PEOPLE ARE SO EAGER TO BE FOOLED?

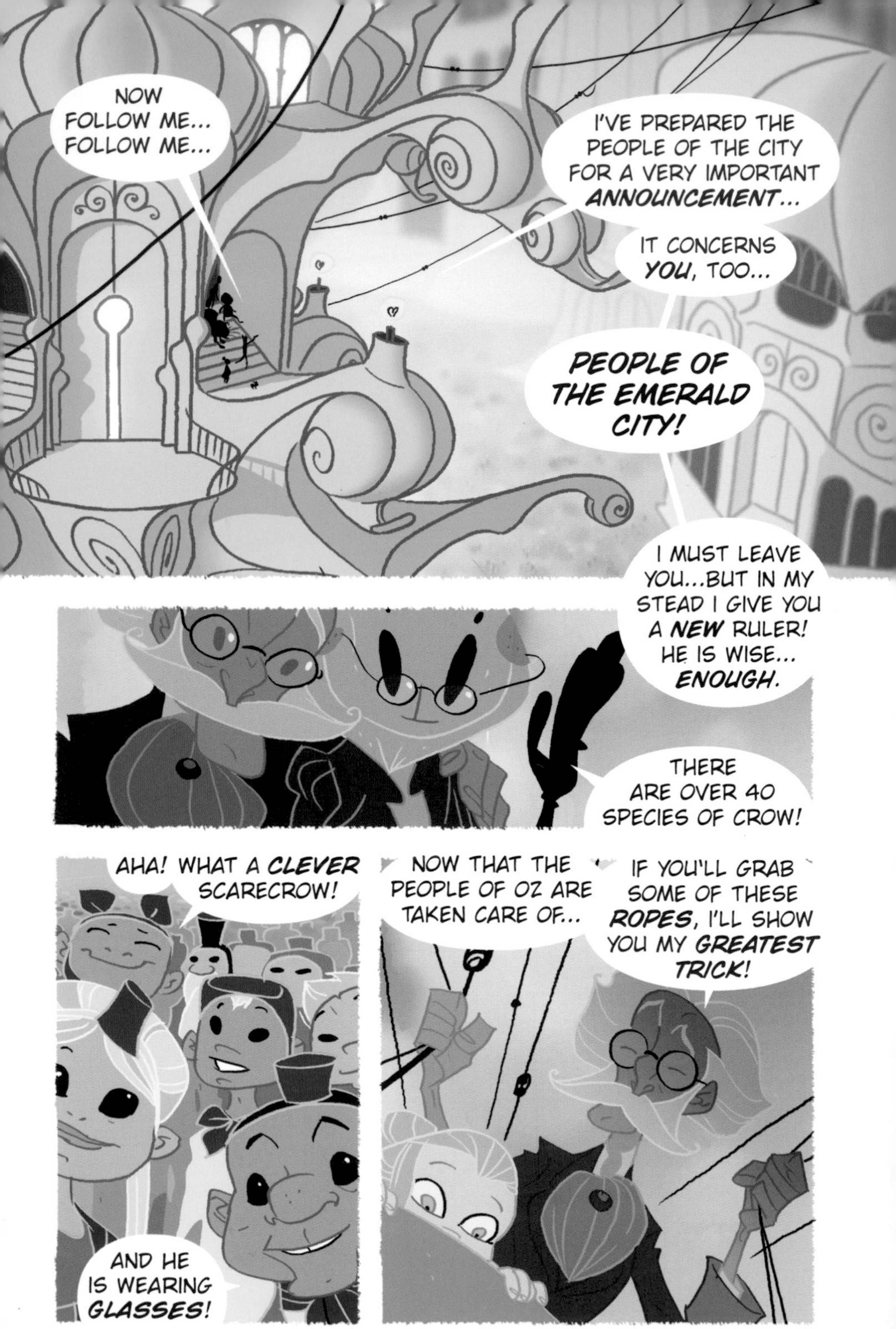
NOW FOLLOW ME... FOLLOW ME...
I'VE PREPARED THE PEOPLE OF THE CITY FOR A VERY IMPORTANT ANNOUNCEMENT...
IT CONCERNS YOU, TOO...
PEOPLE OF THE EMERALD CITY!
I MUST LEAVE YOU...BUT IN MY STEAD I GIVE YOU A NEW RULER! HE IS WISE... ENOUGH.
THERE ARE OVER 40 SPECIES OF CROW!
AHA! WHAT A CLEVER SCARECROW!
AND HE IS WEARING GLASSES!
NOW THAT THE PEOPLE OF OZ ARE TAKEN CARE OF...
IF YOU'LL GRAB SOME OF THESE ROPES, I'LL SHOW YOU MY GREATEST TRICK!

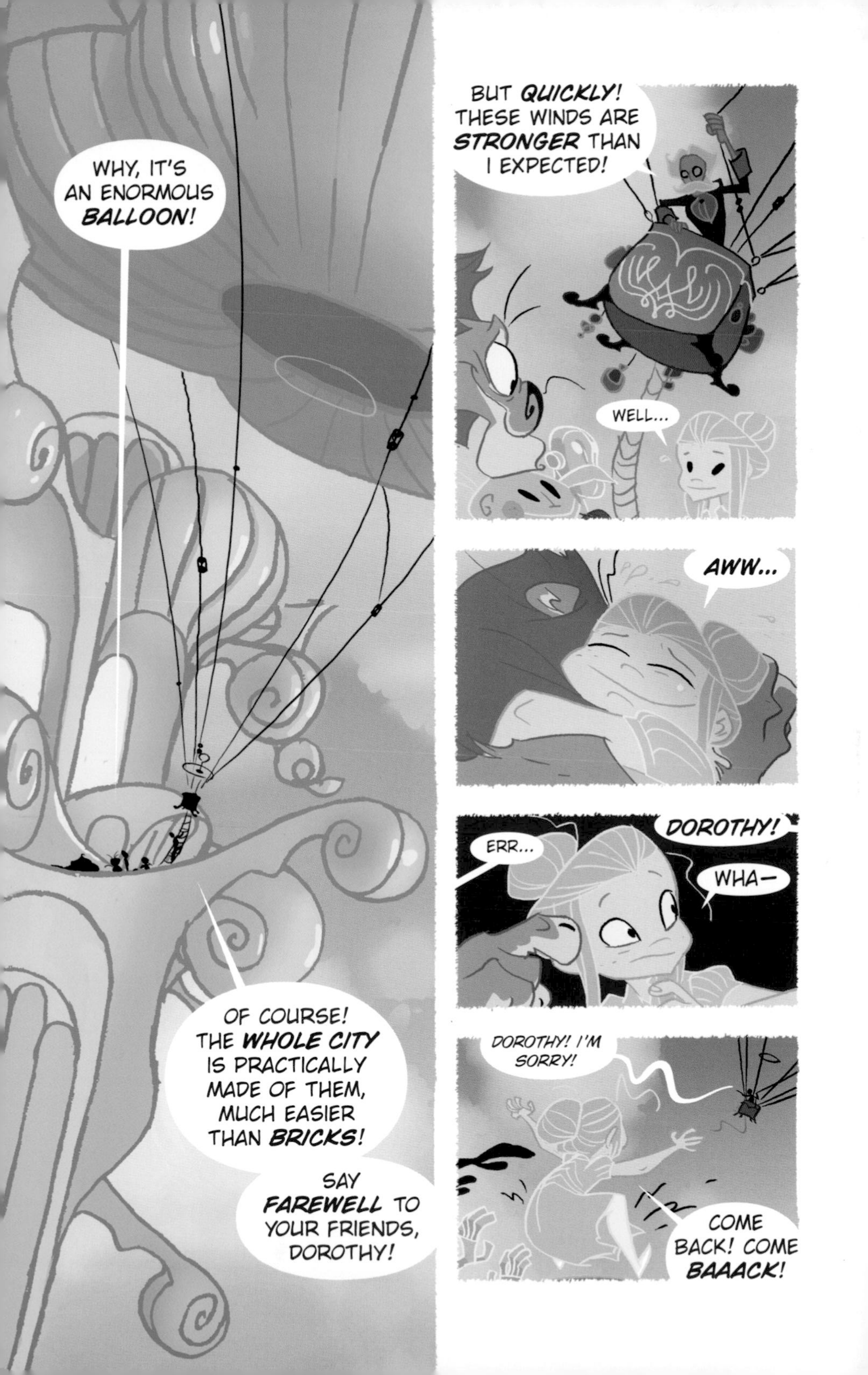
WHY, IT'S AN ENORMOUS BALLOON!
OF COURSE! THE WHOLE CITY IS PRACTICALLY MADE OF THEM, MUCH EASIER THAN BRICKS!
SAY FAREWELL TO YOUR FRIENDS, DOROTHY!
BUT QUICKLY! THESE WINDS ARE STRONGER THAN I EXPECTED!
WELL...
AWW...
DOROTHY!
ERR...
WHA—
DOROTHY! I'M SORRY!
COME BACK! COME BAAACK!

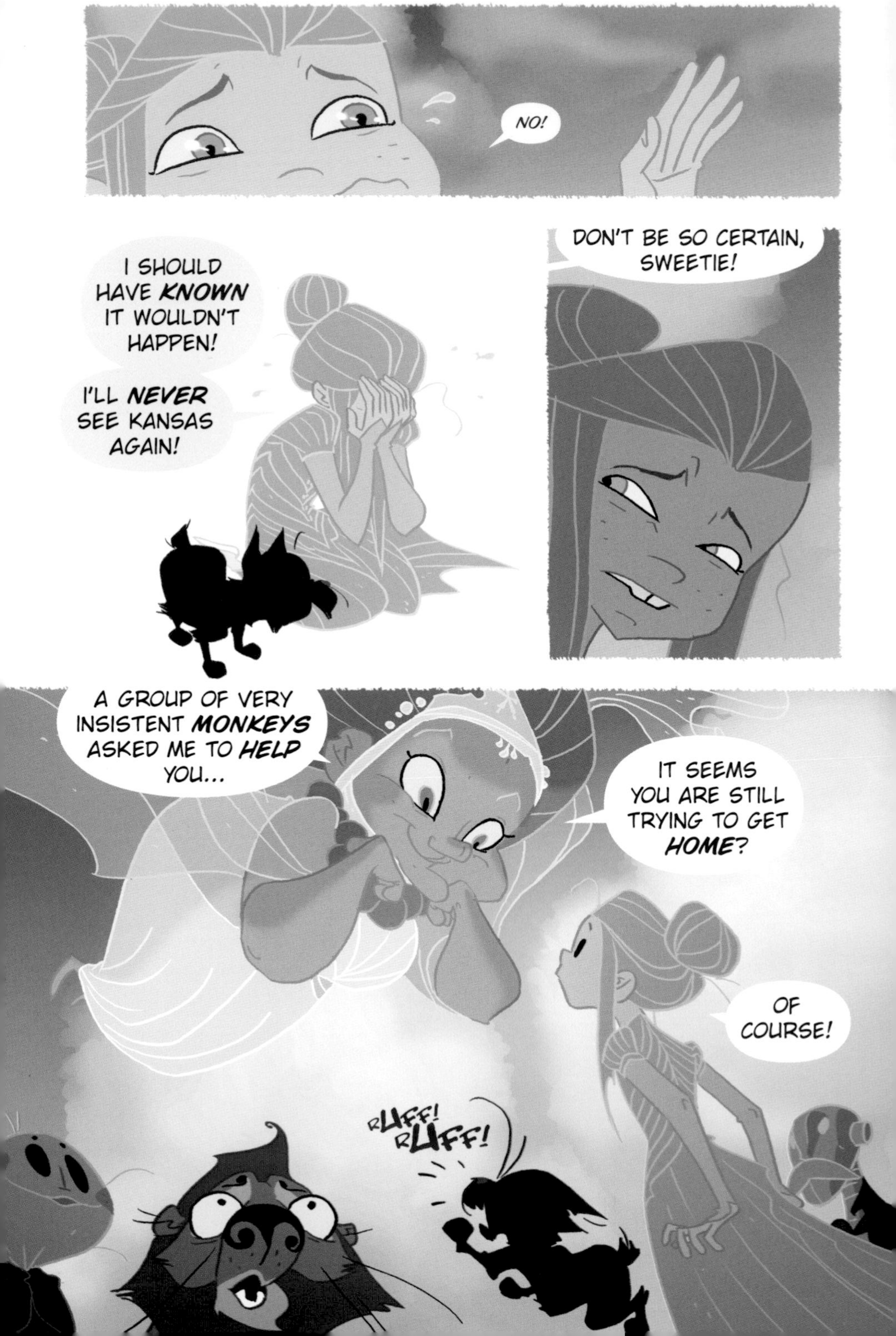
NO!
I SHOULD HAVE KNOWN IT WOULDN'T HAPPEN!
I'LL NEVER SEE KANSAS AGAIN!
DON'T BE SO CERTAIN, SWEETIE!
A GROUP OF VERY INSISTENT MONKEYS ASKED ME TO HELP YOU...
IT SEEMS YOU ARE STILL TRYING TO GET HOME?
OF COURSE!
RUFF! RUFF!

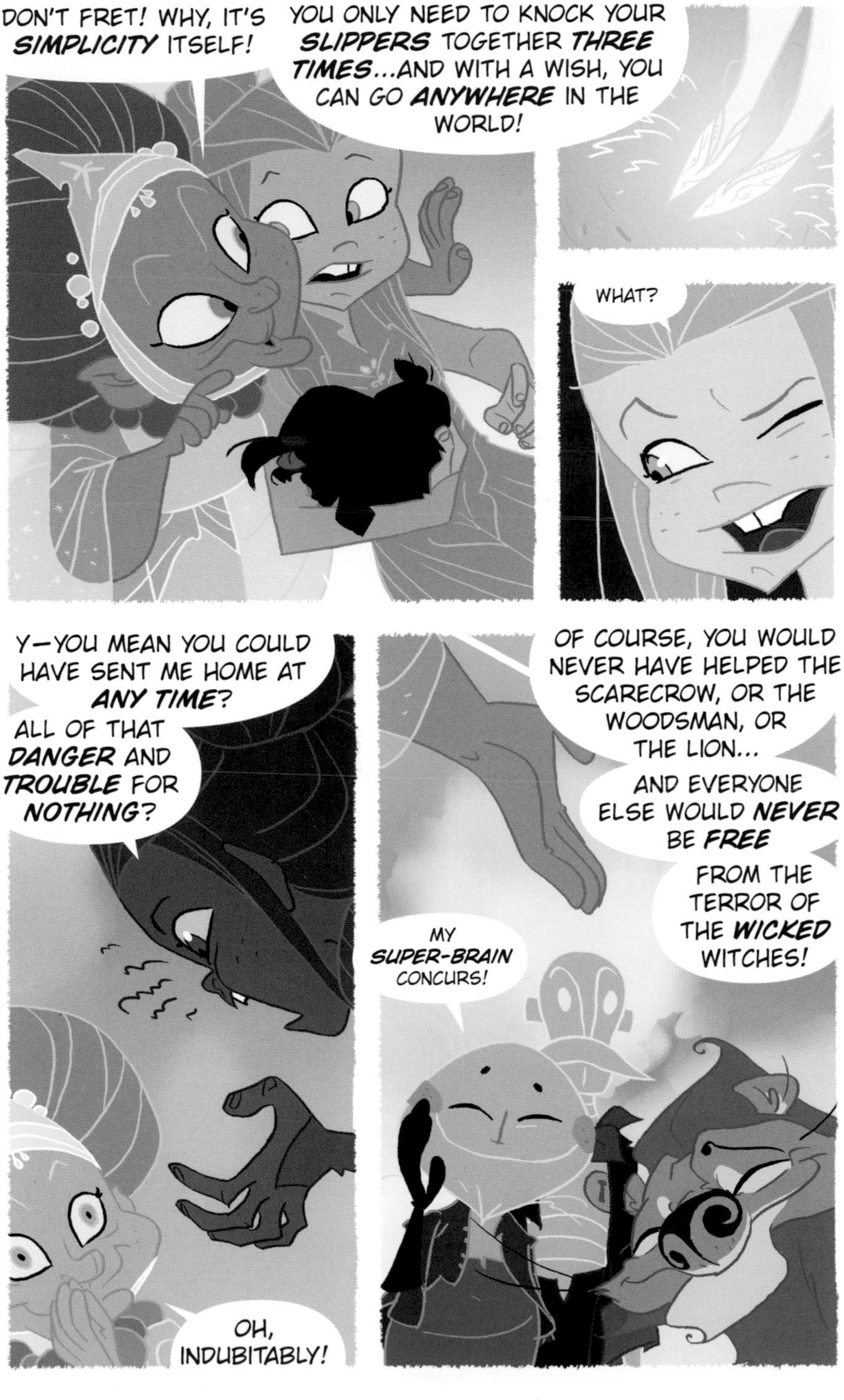
DON'T FRET! WHY, IT'S SIMPLICITY ITSELF!
YOU ONLY NEED TO KNOCK YOUR SLIPPERS TOGETHER THREE TIMES...AND WITH A WISH, YOU CAN GO ANYWHERE IN THE WORLD!
WHAT?
Y—YOU MEAN YOU COULD HAVE SENT ME HOME AT ANY TIME?
ALL OF THAT DANGER AND TROUBLE FOR NOTHING?
OH, INDUBITABLY!
OF COURSE, YOU WOULD NEVER HAVE HELPED THE SCARECROW, OR THE WOODSMAN, OR THE LION...
AND EVERYONE ELSE WOULD NEVER BE FREE
FROM THE TERROR OF THE WICKED WITCHES!
MY SUPER-BRAIN CONCURS!

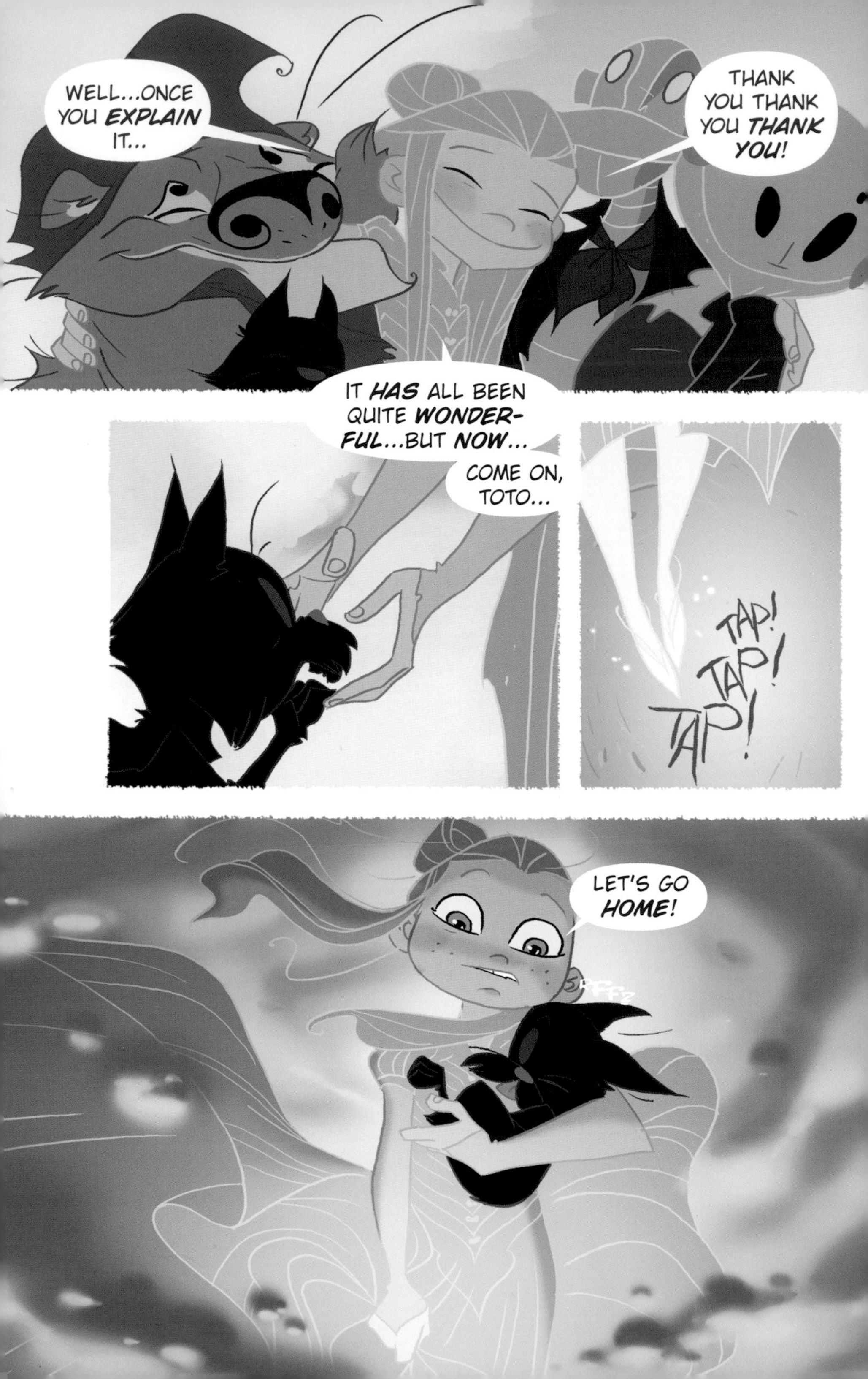
WELL...ONCE YOU EXPLAIN IT...
THANK YOU THANK YOU THANK YOU!
IT HAS ALL BEEN QUITE WONDERFUL...BUT NOW...
COME ON, TOTO...
TAP! TAP! TAP!
LET'S GO HOME!

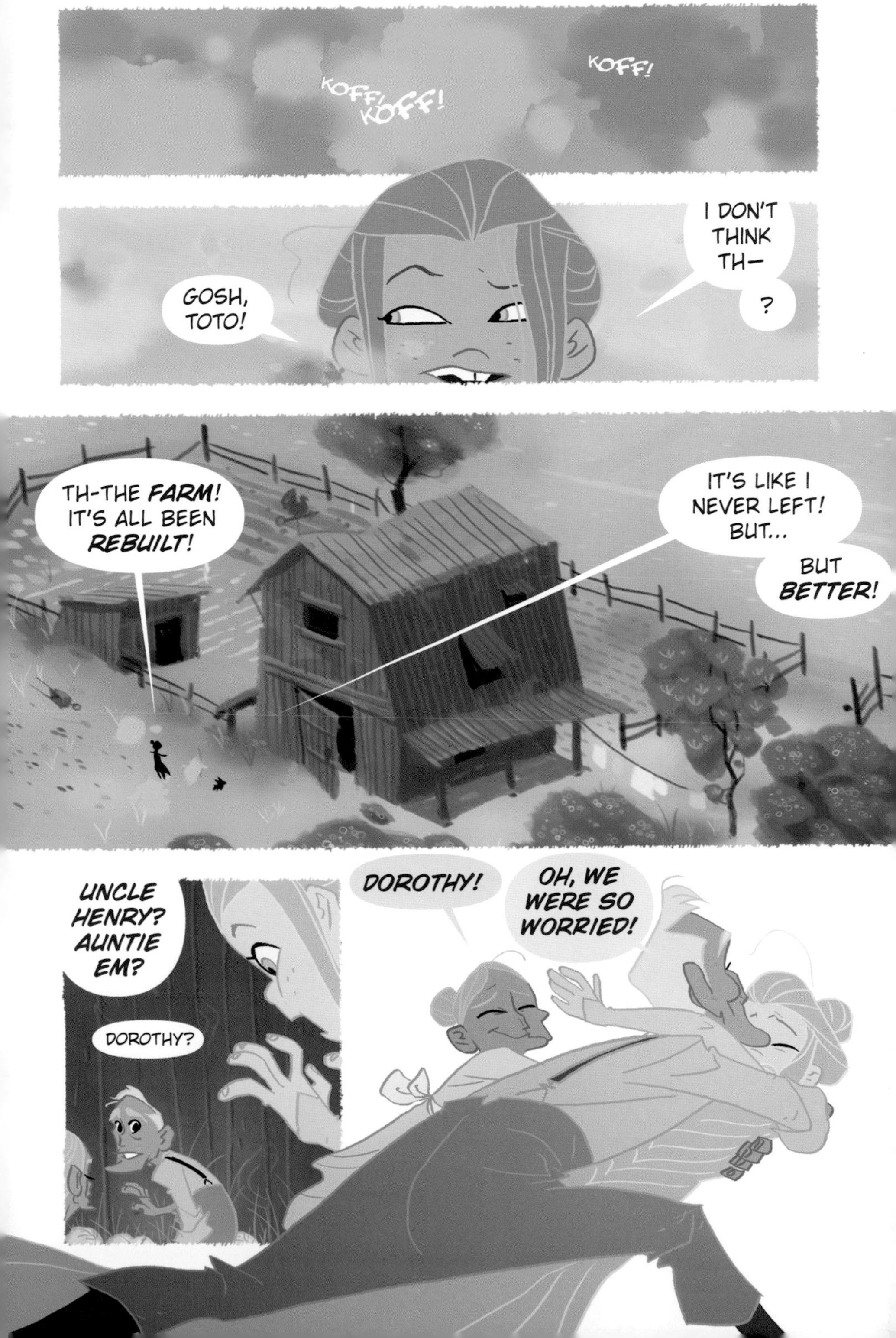
KOFF! KOFF!
KOFF!
GOSH, TOTO!
I DON'T THINK TH—
?
TH-THE *FARM*! IT'S ALL BEEN *REBUILT*!
IT'S LIKE I NEVER LEFT! BUT...
BUT *BETTER*!
UNCLE HENRY? AUNTIE EM?
DOROTHY?
DOROTHY!
OH, WE WERE SO WORRIED!

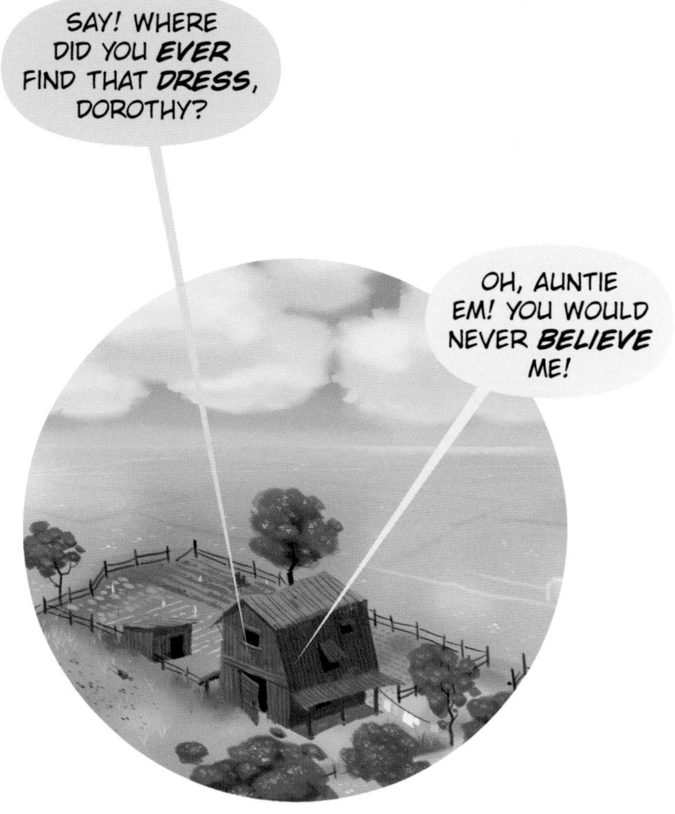
SAY! WHERE DID YOU EVER FIND THAT DRESS, DOROTHY?
OH, AUNTIE EM! YOU WOULD NEVER BELIEVE ME!

FOR **MORE** INFORMATION
ABOUT **"THE WIZARD OF OZ"**
AND **L. FRANK BAUM**, ALONG
WITH **BONUS ART** AND **NOTES**
FROM THIS STORY, VISIT

WWW. ACTIONCARTOONING .COM

I MEAN...
"WOOF"!

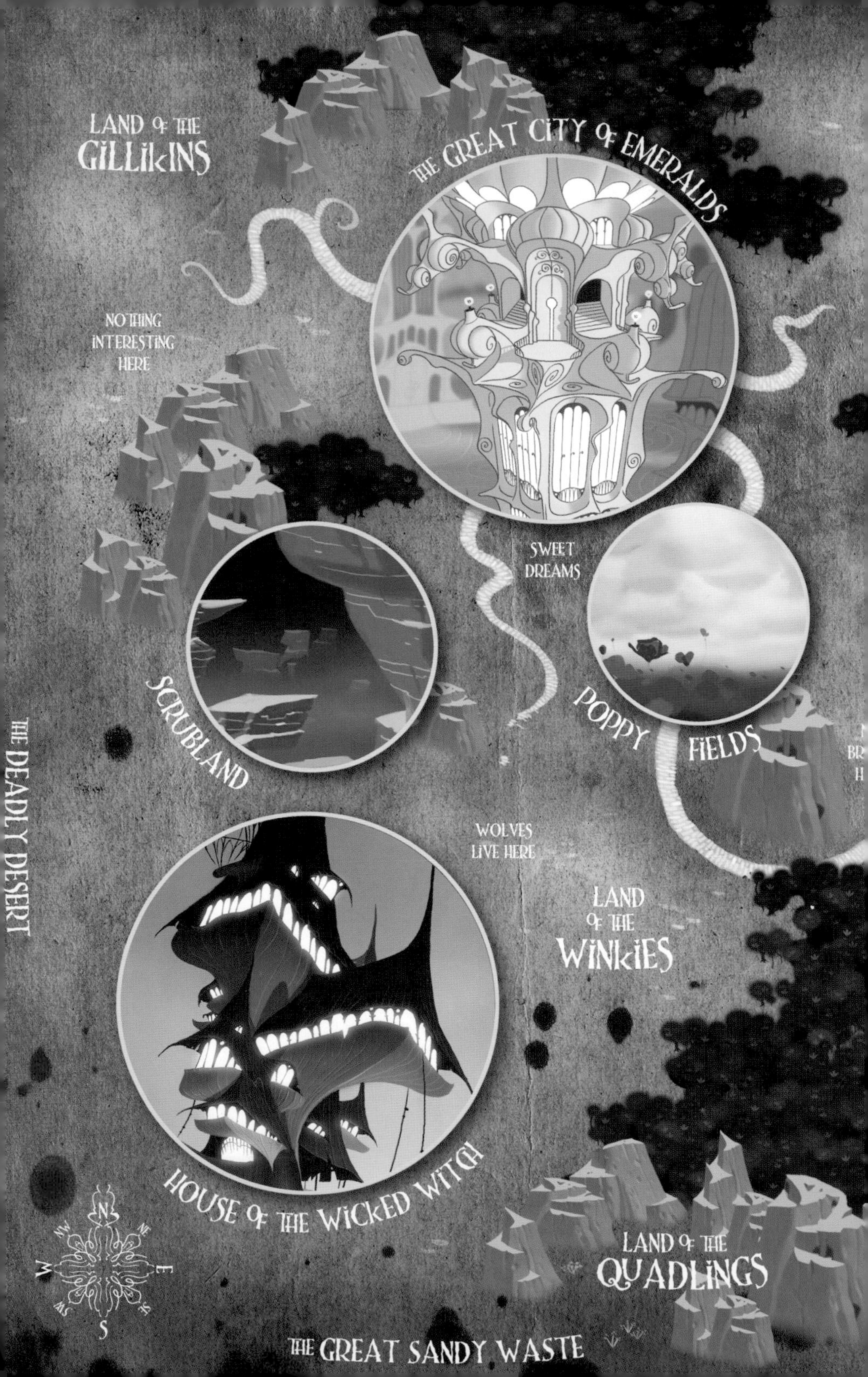
LAND OF THE GILLIKINS
THE GREAT CITY OF EMERALDS
NOTHING INTERESTING HERE
SWEET DREAMS
SCRUBLAND
POPPY FIELDS
THE DEADLY DESERT
WOLVES LIVE HERE
LAND OF THE WINKIES
HOUSE OF THE WICKED WITCH
LAND OF THE QUADLINGS
N
NE
E
SE
S
SW
W
NW
THE GREAT SANDY WASTE

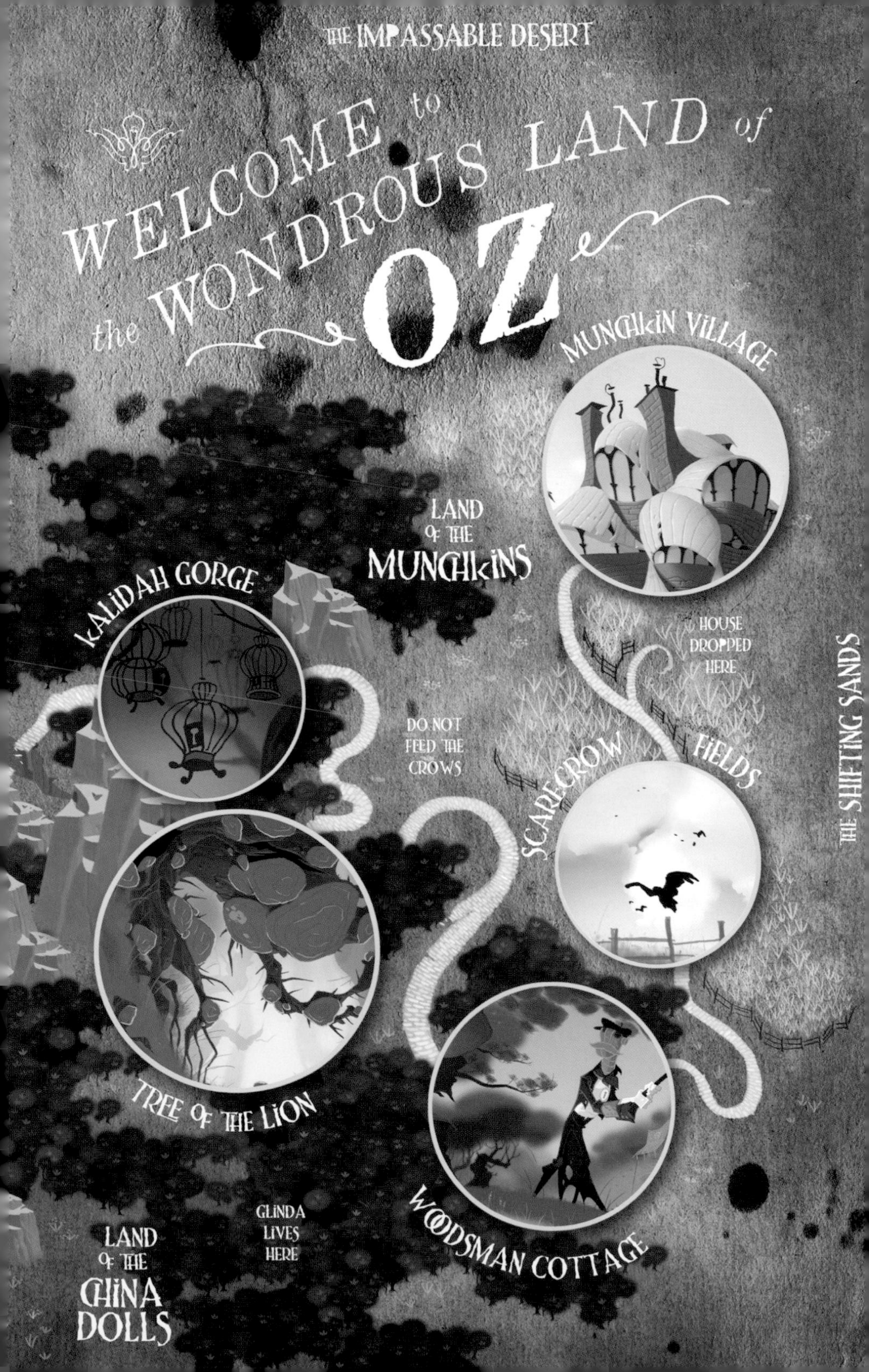
THE IMPASSABLE DESERT
WELCOME to the WONDROUS LAND of OZ
MUNCHKIN VILLAGE
LAND OF THE MUNCHKINS
KALIDAH GORGE
HOUSE DROPPED HERE
THE SHIFTING SANDS
DO NOT FEED THE CROWS
SCARECROW FIELDS
TREE OF THE LION
WOODSMAN COTTAGE
GLINDA LIVES HERE
LAND OF THE CHINA DOLLS

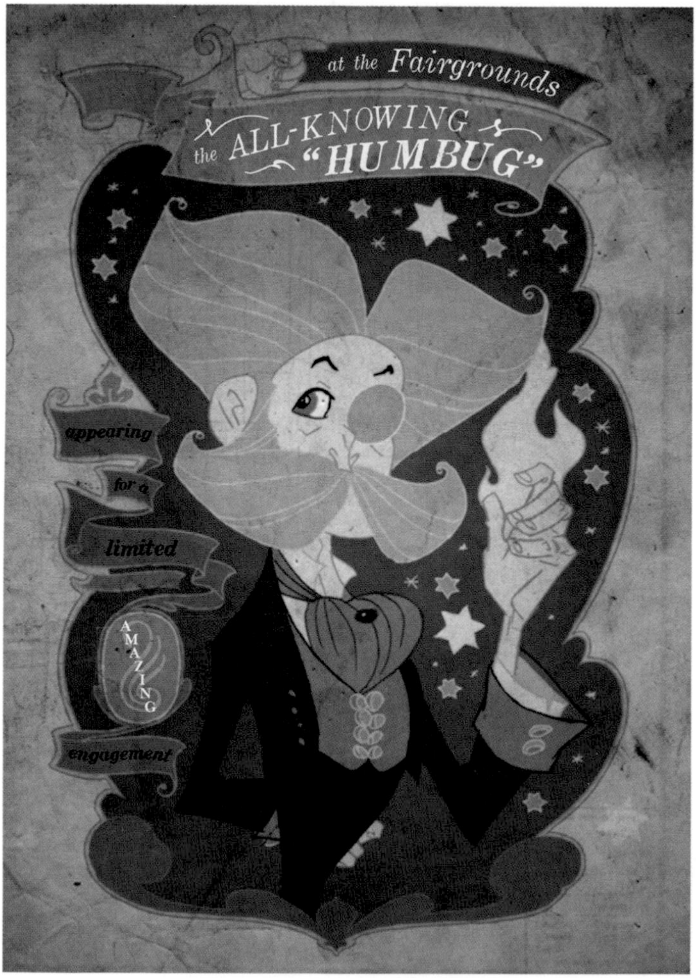
at the Fairgrounds
the ALL-KNOWING "HUMBUG"
appearing
for a
limited
AMAZING
engagement